Fools Walk In

• • •

So Wicked My Love

BRUNO FISCHER

INTRODUCTION BY NICHOLAS LITCHFIELD

Stark House Press • Eureka California

FOOLS WALK IN / SO WICKED MY LOVE

Published by Stark House Press
1315 H Street
Eureka, CA 95501, USA
griffinskye3@sbcglobal.net
www.starkhousepress.com

ISBN: 979-8-88601-124-1

Text design by Mark Shepard, shepgraphics.com
Cover design by Jeff Vorzimmer, ¡caliente!design, Austin, Texas
Proofreading by Bill Kelly
Cover art by Arthur Sarnoff

First Stark House Press Edition: January 2025

FOOLS WALK IN

What do you do when you're an English professor living with his needy sister and you pick up a young lady on the run who wants your company? You've played it safe all your life. You've let your sister call the shots, even when that means she chases other women away. Then one rainy night you stop for gas and spot a woman with a suitcase hiding in the bushes. As you start to get in your car, she asks for a ride. You drop her off but next day, she's at your front door. Your first inclination is to ask her to leave. But temptation beckons… how it beckons… and now you're living in a secluded cabin with a gang of thieves—and they think you're one of them!

SO WICKED MY LOVE

Ray Whitehead has just been dumped by his fiancé Florence. He's still carrying the diamond engagement ring when he runs into hometown girl, pretty little redheaded Cherry Drew. Feeling sorry for himself, he gives it to her, happy to be rid of the thing. How could he know that he had just opened a door to a world of gangsters, robbery and death? Because Cherry is on the run from some very tough customers she has double-crossed, and white knight Ray is suddenly just the man she's looking for. No matter that Florence soon changes her mind. Cherry has the ring, and before she's through, she's determined to have Ray all to herself—if he lives that long!

BRUNO FISCHER BIBLIOGRAPHY (1908-1992)

NOVELS
Ben Helm Series
The Dead Men Grin (1945)
More Deaths Than One (1947)
The Restless Hands (1949)
The Angels Fell (1950; reprinted as
   The Flesh Was Cold, 1951)
The Silent Dust (1950)
The Paper Circle (1951; reprinted
   as *Stripped for Murder*, 1953)

Rick Train Series
The Hornets' Nest (1944; aka
   Murder Wears a Skirt, 1944)
Kill to Fit (1946)

Unrelated Novels
So Much Blood (1939; reprinted as
   Stairway to Death, 1951)
Quoth the Raven (1944; reprinted
   in the UK as *Croaked the Raven*,
   1947; in U.S. as *The Fingered
   Man*, 1953)
The Pigskin Bag (1946)
The Spider Lily (1946)
The Bleeding Scissors (1948;
   reprinted in the UK as *The
   Scarlet Scissors*, 1950)

House of Flesh (1950)
The Lustful Ape (1950; originally
   pub as by Russell Gray; reprinted
   as by Fischer, 1959)
Fools Walk In (1951)
The Lady Kills (1951)
Run for Your Life (1953)
So Wicked My Love (1954)
Knee-deep in Death (1956)
Murder in the Raw (1957)
The Fast Buck (1958)
Second-Hand Nude (1959)
The Girl Between (1960)
The Evil Days (1973)

Collections
A Mate for Murder: And Other
   Tales from the Pulps (1992)
Hostesses in Hell and Other
   Stories (2011; as by Russell Gray)
My Touch Brings Death and Other
   Stories (2014; as by Russell Gray)
The Letter Death Wrote and Other
   Stories (2018)

As Jason F. Storm
Domination (1970; erotica)

Fischer's Foolish Teacher and the Wicked Redhead

by Nicholas Litchfield

German-born American author Bruno Fischer (1908 – 1992) was a successful novelist and a prolific writer of pulp yarns during the Forties and Fifties. His trove of stories, somewhere in the region of about five hundred (Gale Literature: Contemporary Authors 2001), appeared in eminent magazines like *Black Mask*, *Dime Detective*, *New Detective Magazine*, *Manhunt*, *Popular Detective*, and *Mike Shayne Mystery Magazine*. His twenty-five novels, translated into twelve languages, sold more than ten million copies, and his 1950 bestseller *House of Flesh* achieved sales in the region of 1.8 million (Lovisi 2015).

As with many writers, he began his career writing for newspapers. He was employed as a sports reporter and police reporter for the *Long Island Daily Press* while in his twenties, and later, he worked as a book reviewer, magazine editor for *Modern Monthly*, and contributor to weekly magazines of opinion, such as *Commonsense* and the *New Republic* (Fischer 1946). While editing the Socialist Party-sanctioned periodical *Socialist Call*, a writer friend persuaded him to try his hand at genre fiction, resulting in an immediate sale to *Dime Mystery* in November 1936 (Server 2002). He sold more stories under the pseudonyms Russell Gray and Harrison Storm, contributing to the graphic, spicy pulp subgenres weird-menace pulps (also known as "shudder pulps") and "defective detective" tales, in which the crime-solving protagonists were outlandishly handicapped. Fischer's tales featured "the deformed, crablike private eyes Calvin Kane and Ben Bryn" (Server 2002).

When those markets vanished, he became a highly productive writer of detective fiction, amassing several hundred stories and gracing the covers of top-selling magazines. His spine-tingling first novel, *So Much Blood*, published by Greystone Press in 1939 (later reprinted by Pyramid as *Stairway to Death*), was a critical success. It was "lush and lurid," according to *The American Weekly* magazine *The Saturday Review of Literature*, with *The New York Times* decreeing it had "plenty of mystery."

More novels followed in quick succession, including *Murder Wears a Skirt* (William Morrow, and reprinted by Dell as *The Hornets' Nest*) and *Quoth the Raven* (Doubleday imprint Crime Club, and reprinted as *The Fingered Man* by the Ace Double paperback line). Famed book critic Anthony Boucher became a strong advocate for Fischer's reliably good stories, recommending the latter book as a "solid 1944 suspense story" (Boucher 1953), while fellow critic Isaac Anderson applauded the rare fact that Fischer's protagonist, grocer Sam Tree, was "a detective who does not drink, smoke or chase women" (Anderson 1944).

With *The Dead Man Grin*, published by David McKay Publications in 1945, Fischer introduced NYC ex-cop turned private eye Ben Helm. As a member of the American Socialist Party who stood for the New York Senate in 1939 on behalf of the party, Fischer allegedly based his detective on Norman Thomas, the American socialist leader and three-time presidential candidate (Whale 2010). Likable and laid-back, his protagonist was sharp-eyed, erudite, and analytical, and he proved popular with readers. A *New York Times* book critic thought him "gratifyingly quiet and sensitive" (Bullock 1949). Boucher called him "one of the subtlest and most civilized of private eyes" (Boucher 1951), and vintage book blogger August West referred to him as "an updated American Sherlock Holmes," valued by the local police who "study his published articles and books on criminology and eagerly accept his help" (West 2008). Anthony Award-winning author Bill Crider considered him an atypical 1950's sleuth, "more intellectual than physical" and "one of the few successfully characterized married private eyes in fiction." (Crider 2006)

Helm would feature in six books during a six-year period, with each story garnering critical acclaim: *The Saturday Review of Literature* commended the series opener as "well-worked-out and suspenseful," critic Jack Glick praised the "innovative" way Fischer skewed the narrative in *More Deaths Than One* to contrive "seven different and contradictory views of this homicidal enigma" (Glick 1947), and regarding *The Silent Dust*, reviewer Hillis Mills extolled the virtues of Fischer's storytelling, declaring that "his yarns have a certain depth because he writes of crime with a sense of sadness and views his shoddy sinners with compassion" (Mills 1950). It was an assessment Boucher concurred with, maintaining that even though *The Angels Fell* had an unoriginal plot, the author's "warm understanding of human relationships" resulted in an exceptional novel, highlighting that "there's nothing inferior about Bruno Fischer" (Boucher 1950). Even Dorothy B. Hughes, who wasn't enamored with the plotting in *The Paper Circle*, appreciated "the sincerity of detective Ben Helm" (Hughes 1951).

The great mystery behind the Ben Helm series concerns why the author didn't persist with more of them. Helm's last full-length case was in August 1951, although his final appearance is the short story "The Quiet Woman," published in *Dell Mystery Novels Magazine* in 1955. Likely, Fischer didn't have the time or passion for more, as he was embroiled in numerous projects during the Fifties. For years, he produced one, sometimes two novels a year, and when iconic writer John D. MacDonald recommended him to the editor at Fawcett Publications' new paperback imprint Gold Medal Books (Server 2002), it proved a lucrative markct for the author. Ten of his novels were Gold Medal originals, starting with the big seller *House of Flesh* in October 1950. Following *The Lady Kills*, released in March 1951, *Fools Walk In* hit the newsstands in December 1951, its cover featuring a rather sumptuous woman in a red dress with tousled, dirty blonde hair and royal blue eyes that could pierce the soul. There is an earthy sincerity to her striking good looks, and the tagline on the front poses this intriguing question: "Good girl or bad girl, was she worth the professor's life and reputation?"

This is a story that ranks as one of Fischer's best. The fluent, expressive, character-focused prose accenting mood and morality, captures the period and the prudish narrator's regard for class and propriety, and through delicate plotting, Fischer propels his staid, cultured, imprudent protagonist into a seedy, disordered, fearsome underworld full of escalating danger.

Primarily set in New Hampshire, this absorbing drama begins with a simple setup: a young, attractive woman at a gas station is desperate for a ride. The fact that she's lurking in the bushes, afraid to be seen, and that she'll go absolutely anywhere, just so long as it's far away from her present whereabouts, are the first red flags. However, her knight in shining armor, the well-mannered high school teacher appropriately named Lawrence B. Knight—Larry to those outside of his classroom—is so intrigued by her that he can't resist her, even though he senses she's trouble. By his own admission, he's "a somewhat prissy bachelor, rooted in dullness," and besides, "a man had a right for once in his life to be a damn fool."

Larry, a trim, handsome thirty-four-year-old bachelor, lives with his matronly sister and would never dream of fraternizing with his students, and yet, the uncouth, promiscuous Jeanie King uses her womanly guiles to seduce and manipulate him. It's a union that's detrimental to his reputation on many levels. Despite her claims to be twenty, Jeanie is no older than the pupils he teaches, and she's physically immature: "leggy and slim-hipped" with a "naïve, almost childlike" mouth and an "adolescent's body." Personality-wise, she is incompatible: coarse, uneducated (a high-school dropout), licentious, deceitful, and outside of the law. Nevertheless, he wants to be with her, in spite of her flaws, to the extent that he leaves behind his inadequate, lackluster way of life and shacks up with Jeanie and her crooked associates.

At times, *Fools Walk In* feels like a novel Lionel White might have written, but Fischer perverts the familiar scenario, presenting the naked blemishes in his righteous hero as the repressed, snobbish educator descends into the shadowy underworld, faking it with felons and gangster's molls and coming off the greater evil. Arguably, he's a disloyal charlatan living off a woman he has little respect for, while Jeanie, though cunning and vindictive, is affectionate, loyal, and generous.

The others, holed up in a remote house in the woods, are an odd band of outlaws who are likewise ill-suited to each other. There's the aging homeowner, Hank, tough guy Tom "Fatso" Evergreen, and the wild and unstable Ronnie. Then there's the beautiful Elsa and her spouse, gang leader Stan Crocker, a man who "lives by violence and reacts with violence." It's an environment where the air is thick with envy and distrust and where treachery and disaster loom.

The novel shares similarities with *So Wicked, My Love*, the second story in this collection. Right down to the femme fatale with a bag of stolen money who desperately needs a ride out of town. This time, the woman is Cherry Drew, a beautiful, sly, resourceful woman in her mid-twenties whose beau has been murdered by the gang members she has double-crossed. In contrast to *Fools Walk In*, the narrator, Ray Whitehead, a truck driver who operates a small business with his father, is an average Joe who's just been dumped by Florence, his fiancée, in favor of a handsome doctor. Ray is at the beach at Coney Island, trying to take his mind off Florence, when he spots Cherry, a woman from his hometown of Hessian Valley, between the Hudson River and Connecticut, whom he hasn't seen for seven years. Appropriately enough, she kicks sand in Ray's face, but he still makes the mistake of calling out her name.

The accidental meeting, convincingly described by Fischer, is a monumental moment in each of their lives and one that will forever haunt the sympathetic narrator. Cherry is a dangerous temptress, materializing on the beach like a siren from Greek mythology. She's attractive and desirable, but her "pretty, childish face" and "button nose and upturned little chin" remind one of Jeanie's immature features. Likewise, she's from the wrong side of the tracks and nothing but trouble, mixed up with hoodlums and criminal enterprises and wanted by the police. Quite simply, she's utterly lethal, a toxic brew for anyone who gets involved with her.

While initially feeling like a slight variation on the same story, *So Wicked, My Love* quickly veers in a very different direction and turns out to be an exceptionally well-crafted page-turner that coils like a dying snake. The physically tough principal character, a man who has seen combat during WW2, is no callous snob but a regular, decent guy, a "boy scout" type, whose poor choices land him in a new combat zone. The woman he rescues becomes an albatross around his neck, a recurring nightmare he cannot escape, and their association makes him equally toxic.

Moving, thrilling, and increasingly unpredictable, this is one of those intelligently plotted, character-focused crime dramas that merit a place on anyone's bookshelf. *The Morning Telegraph*, a New York City broadsheet, described it as "Fischer at his terrifying best." It's a fair assessment.

Interestingly, the story's first appearance in print was as a novelette in the November 1953 issue of *Manhunt* under the title "Coney Island Incident." That story is a fully-rounded piece—the first eight chapters of *So Wicked, My Love*, almost word for word, but with a very different, morally responsible conclusion. Whether Fischer expanded his story or whether it was an abridged version, I can't quite tell. Fawcett would publish the story in October 1954 as *So Wicked, My Love*, and as with *Fools Walk In*, American painter Barye Phillips (1924-1969), a prolific illustrator of pulp magazines and paperbacks, was responsible for the appealing artwork. Told in five parts, spanning an eventful calendar year, the constantly fascinating fuller version is much more effective and powerful. It's a novel that holds the attention with an iron grip, and when it ends, it leaves a mark.

—March 2024
Rochester, NY

Nicholas Litchfield is the founder of the literary magazine *Lowestoft Chronicle* and editor of twelve literary anthologies. His stories, essays, and book reviews appear in various magazines and newspapers, including *BULL*, *Colorado Review*, *Daily Press*, *Pennsylvania Literary Journal*, *Shotgun Honey*, *The Adroit Journal*, *The MacGuffin*, *The Virginian-Pilot*, and *Washington Square Review*. He has written introductions to numerous books, including twenty-one Stark House Press reprints of long-forgotten noir and mystery novels. Formerly a book critic for the *Lancashire Post*, syndicated to twenty-five newspapers across the U.K., he now writes for *Publishers Weekly*. You can find him online at NicholasLitchfield.com or Twitter: @NLitchfield.

Works Cited

Anderson, Isaac. 1944. "The Crime Corner." *The New York Times*, October 29: BR18.

Boucher, Anthony. 1953. "Criminals at Large." *The New York Times*, November 22: BR48.

—. 1951. "Criminals At Large: WHEN DORINDA DANCES." *The New York Times*, October 7: 231.

—. 1950. "Reports on Criminals at Large: Journey Into Crime Spinster Sleuth Fake an Alibi." *The New York Times*, April 2: 190.

Bullock, Elizabeth. 1949. "Criminals at Large: Hunt for a Killer." *The New York Times*, September 4: 138.

Crider, Bill. 2006. "A 1001 MIDNIGHTS Review: BRUNO FISCHER - The Silent Dust." *Mystery*File*. United States, April 27. https://mysteryfile.com/blog/?p=39733.

Fischer, Bruno. 1946. *The Pigskin Bag*. First edition. Chicago, IL: Ziff Davis Publishing Company.

Gale Literature: Contemporary Authors. 2001. "Bruno Fischer." *Gale Literature: Contemporary Authors*. Farmington Hills: Gale, Nov. 1.

Glick, Jack. 1947. "Missing People Plus Some Mayhem." *The New York Times*, July 27: BR19.

Hughes, Dorothy B. 1951. "Fall mystery season marked by flood of fine whodunits." *Daily News*, October 20: 8.

Lovisi, Gary. 2015. "Rediscovering Bruno Fischer." In *The Bleeding Scissors / The Evil Days*, by Bruno Fischer, 7-10. Eureka, CA: Stark House Press.

Mills, Hillis. 1950. "Criminals At Large: Two-Story Archdeacon Murder Came Too." *The New York Times*, October 1: 225.

Server, Lee. 2002. "Fischer, Bruno." In *Encyclopedia of Pulp Fiction Writers*, by Lee Server, 96-98. New York, NY: Facts On File, Inc.

West, August. 2008. "The Quiet Woman by Bruno Fischer." *Vintage Hardboiled Reads*. United States, August 4. https://vinpulp.blogspot.com/2008/08/quiet-woman-by-bruno-fischer.html.

Whale, Mick. 2010. "More on noir…." *Socialism Today*. Vol. 135. London, February. https://socialismtoday.org/archive/135/noir.html.

Fools Walk In
BRUNO FISCHER

Chapter One

In the late afternoon it started to rain, a pinpoint drizzle that broke the July humidity. By then I was well into Virginia, rolling east down the mountains on a secondary road my brother George had recommended as a shortcut. The gas gauge needle hovered close to empty. I saw pumps ahead and slowed and swung off the road.

The filling station looked very lonely in the rain. A low wooden shack that hadn't been painted in a generation sagged behind a pair of ancient pumps. Nobody was in sight. The only other car was a twenty-year-old Model A Ford resting off its rear tireless wheels on two milk boxes.

My horn brought no stirring inside the shack or out. I felt remote and isolated sitting there. I got out to stretch my legs, and the rain was like heavy mist on my face and hair.

I was moving to the shack when I noticed the woman watching me.

She stood among the trees and brush that formed a backdrop to the filling station, and she was so still that she would have blended with the dark foliage if her dress hadn't been bright yellow. Her face was obscured by an overhanging bough; all I could distinguish of it was that it was turned to me.

"Is there anybody here to sell gas?" I called to her.

She didn't answer. The yellow dress drew back deeper among the trees, disappearing.

A wizened old man with one suspender indifferently holding up droopy pants came out of the shack. He contemplated my New York license plate as if dubious that any car to which it belonged could mean business for him. The few outstate cars that took this road would breeze by to tank up at the snappy, efficient layouts in the towns.

"Ten," I said, handing him the key.

The pump handle creaked as he laboriously turned it.

Again I saw the yellow dress—a piece of it, a patch from hip to hem, like a splash of sunlight in the rain. She had resumed watching me without letting herself be wholly seen.

I wondered where she could have come from. There was no house on either side of the road and no parked car but the disabled Ford. If she belonged to the shack, she wouldn't make it a point to keep away from a customer. She was acting like a shy little backwoods girl spying on a stranger, but what I could observe of her figure was adult, and that was a pretty good city dress she was ruining in the wet brush. So here was a random mystery that would likely never be solved for me because in another minute I would be gone.

"Is there a town nearby?" I asked the old man.

"Darson. Three miles that way."

"I came from there and passed nothing. Darson's a fair-sized city, isn't it?"

"It's off the road a piece. Crossroads a mile back. You shoulda turned right."

"I don't want Darson. I'm merely curious."

He took another look at the license plate. "Bound back to New York?"

"Yes."

"Well, mister, you follow this road to U.S. One and that'll take you to Richmond and all the way to New York."

"I know," I said.

He hung up and fished change for a five out of his sagging pants and shuffled back into the shack.

As I was about to get into my car I looked back. The girl in the yellow dress had come out of the woods.

Wind fluttered her shoulder-length hair across her face, glistening with rain. She was carrying a large tan valise. Both her hands gripped the handle and the weight pulled down her right shoulder. She was leggy and slim-bodied and quite young.

I went up to her. "Let me give you a hand."

"That's okay." Panting a little, she clung to the valise. "I can use a lift to Richmond."

She didn't ask me if I were going there. She already knew, because she had heard me tell the old man, and it occurred to me that perhaps that was why she had come out of hiding.

"Of course," I said, and reached for the valise.

She twisted away, swinging the valise with her as if to prevent me from snatching it. The straw handbag she wore slung from her shoulder slapped her hip as she lugged the valise to the car. About all I could do to be a gentleman was to hurry ahead and open the right door. She pushed the valise in behind the seat and pulled the seat down and settled herself into it. I closed the door and walked around the car and slipped behind the wheel.

"I suppose you got caught in the rain," I said to make conversation as we drove.

"Somebody was supposed to meet me and didn't show up."

I didn't ask her if that were the reason she had been lurking in the woods. I said, "Do you come from Darson?"

"No, I don't."

She fluffed out her hair as if to dry it that way. Her yellow pique dress clung damply to a tight figure. If she had been older, I might have become more subjective about her, but she was too close in age to the girls in my English classes to take personally or seriously. To me they were all children to be regarded with tolerance and amusement, which may have been a protective attitude assumed by a bachelor who during his working hours was surrounded by too much blatant young femininity.

I kept glancing sidelong at her. Eighteen? Her eyes, a shade lighter brown than her hair, had a limpid innocence, and her small mouth was naïve, though all of it—mouth, eyes, cheeks—was too overpainted for my taste. At the moment she was occupied in renewing the paint. She had her straw handbag open on her lap and had taken out compact, lipstick, rouge.

I said, "Do you mean that somebody abandoned you on that empty road in the rain?"

"Well, not exactly."

Evidently she didn't care to explain and I had no right to persist. We were, after all, strangers who after a very few hours would never again see each other.

The cosmetics were back in her bag. Her mouth had become redder, larger, more sensuous, but it was still an adolescent mouth.

Older than eighteen, I thought. Possibly as much as twenty-two, which would make her a woman to think of as a woman. A man, at any rate, could play around with notions.

She bent to finger her shoes. "They're sopping," she declared, and proceeded to remove them. Mud covered the heels and grass stains stippled the natural-colored linen.

She sat up and reached under her skirt and unfastened a stocking and began to peel it off.

In the close confines of the car that act had a kind of intimacy.

"I'll stop the car so you can get dry things out of your valise," I offered.

"Don't bother."

"It will take only a minute."

"I'm okay," she said sharply, irritably.

She was unfastening the second stocking. I glanced down at a long, rounded thigh and then quickly looked away. Normally I didn't embarrass easily, and it was foolish to be embarrassed by a smooth, bare thigh, but there it was.

I felt her stir and took my gaze off the road. She had pulled up her bare legs under her, sitting on them, and her knees almost touched me. The hem of the dress negligently remained a good six inches above the knees.

"You got a cigarette?" she said. "I ran out."

When I handed her my pack, she asked if I wanted her to light one for me. I said yes. She stuck two between her lips and applied the dashboard lighter to each in turn and gave me one. I tasted the flavored stickiness of her lipstick on the cigarette. It was like the lingering residue of a kiss.

The rain gathered volume. As I peered through the whirl of it in front of the windshield, I thought of how she had been hiding in the woods and how she had refused to let the valise out of her hand for an instant and how she had turned short-tempered when I had suggested that she get dry stockings and shoes out of it.

On impulse I said, "What's so valuable in your valise?"

Her eyes went wide and startled under the severely plucked eyebrows.

"What're you getting at?" she demanded.

"I didn't intend to frighten you."

"I ain't scared. Maybe just a bit upset because I had to wait in the rain." She touched my arm; I felt her knees against my right hip. "Sorry I snapped at you. You're a sweet guy."

I was flustered at her words, at her closeness, at her bare legs. And I regretted that she withdrew her hand, that she shifted along the seat to the other end, where she lounged against the door.

Miles passed in silence. A direction signpost at a crossroad said thirty-four miles to Richmond. She looked back at it and then at me.

"Mind if I stick with you all the way to New York?" she said.

"I intend to stop overnight pretty soon."

"That's okay by me. But I bet we can make New York by morning if we take turns driving all night."

I glanced at her. "Are you running away from somebody or

something?”

“What an idea!” Her laugh was a brief explosion of breath. “I figured on taking the train from Richmond and hitting New York by morning, but I’d just as soon stick with you.” She exhaled smoke through her nostrils. “But maybe you don’t want my company.”

“I’m delighted,” I said. “If we’re going to spend that much time together, let’s introduce each other. My name is Larry Knight.”

“Hello, Larry, I’m Jeanie. Go oh, say it: Jeanie with the light-brown hair. Everybody does. That’s why I’m think of dying my hair.”

“You must have more name than just Jeanie.”

She hesitated. “Jeanie King.”

I wondered if so far she had told me the truth about anything.

She stretched her legs, pushing her bare feet against the floor board. Her toenails were painted, though not as deeply red as her fingernails. She put her head against the seat and for a long time studied me.

“Are you married” she asked presently.

“Why ask?”

“You look like a guy who’d have a nice little wife and a couple of cute kids.”

She sounded like my sister-in-law insisting that I was the type that required a real home complete with wife and children.

“So far I haven’t even got started,” I said.

And as a man will when he finds himself alone with a pretty girl, I spoke about myself. I told her that I was returning from a visit to my brother George and his family in Kentucky, that I lived with my sister in the borough of Queens in New York City, that I taught high school English.

“You a schoolteacher!” Jeanie exclaimed. “I never would’ve guessed.”

“It’s a job.”

“A good-looking guy like you teaching English!” The idea, for a reason completely beyond my understanding, amused her. “I left after the first year of high school,” she said. “If they’d had teachers as good-looking as you, I bet I would’ve hung on.”

“Where did you attend school?”

That killed the topic. “Oh, out West,” she replied vaguely, and lit another cigarette and was silent.

When we entered Richmond, I suggested stopping to eat.

Jeanie stared at the business street through which we were rolling. “I’m not hungry yet. Let’s wait till we reach Washington.”

"I prefer to stop for the night before Washington."

"Well, I'm not hungry."

The storm had faded off; the rain-washed streets of Richmond and the fields that followed smelled wetly fresh. We drove without words. Jeanie smoked one cigarette after another. When she had exhausted the pack, I told her there was another in the glove compartment and she started on that. And all the time she was watching me, as if weighing me in some sort of balance of her own.

Twilight spread over the open highway. I turned on the headlights. The panel light didn't reach her. Her figure dimmed, receded, and for the next half hour it would have been like driving alone if I hadn't been so acutely conscious of her femininity in that clinging dress.

We approached a motor court that had a roadside lunchroom as part of a row of wooden cabins.

"How about this?" I said. "We can eat here as well as sleep."

"It looks clean." She slipped her feet into her shoes and picked up her stockings.

I pulled up in front of the lunchroom. A roly-poly boy came out. My side of the car was away from him, and when Jeanie opened her door he went over to her. "Have you a cabin for two?" she said.

I opened my mouth and closed it without saying anything.

The back of her head remained toward me, her hair fluffy to the neck of the yellow dress. She was listening to the fat boy saying that Cabin 3 had a double bed with an innerspring mattress and would cost three and a half dollars. And she said brightly, "My husband and I will take it."

I waited for her to face me, but she didn't.

The boy spoke to me past her. "You sign the register inside."

I ran suddenly sweaty hands around the curve of the wheel and then got out of the car and followed the fat boy. At the lunchroom entrance I looked back. She had closed the car door, with herself inside.

A couple of men were being served at the lunchroom counter by a weary-looking middle-aged woman. The boy went behind the counter and spread open a register and thrust a fountain pen at me. I stared down at the blur of names. The last was a scrawl that looked like John something from Boston.

"You gonna sign it?" the boy said impatiently.

I was aware of the rules. When a respectable, right-thinking, right-living citizen like myself hired a bed for the night with a girl who wasn't his wife, convention required a false name. I wrote the date, then hesitated. I could sense the boy's boredom; he wasn't concerned with my morals, which he probably suspected, but with three and a half dollars.

Suddenly I grinned. With a flourish I wrote: "Mr. and Mrs. Lawrence B. Knight, New York, N.Y."

I wasn't sure who or what I was defying by signing my real name. Maybe a school system that hemmed in its underpaid servants with inhibitions; maybe my sister Marjorie; maybe simply myself. The fact remained that I felt daring and exhilarated, as if with a stroke of the pen I had severed a chain.

The boy accepted my money and muttered, "Cabin Three, key's in the door, towels and soap in the bathroom," and wandered off.

When I got outside, my car wasn't there.

I stood in the emptiness between me and the road, and for a long moment I felt ridiculous. She hadn't wanted me or even needed me. She had been after my car and she had gone through that act to get me out of it so that she could steal it.

I took a few steps from the squat lunchroom building and looked about. In the glare of the floodlights I saw my coupé parked alongside one of the cabins. My breath came out slowly.

I walked to the car. Through the slats of a Venetian blind I saw light in the cabin and movement inside. I opened the car door to take her valise to her. She had beaten me to it; it wasn't there.

Had she gone ahead to make sure I wouldn't as much as touch that valise?

I removed the ignition key and got my Gladstone bag from the car trunk and went into the cabin. Jeanie was standing beside the double bed and unbuttoning her dress.

Chapter Two

Five large pearl buttons ran from the collar to the waist of the yellow pique dress. She was opening the last of them. I shut the door and stood against it.

"Did you register?" Jeanie asked.

I nodded. Most of her brassiere was visible. It was pink mesh, holding her breasts high and snug. She was completely unabashed, completely casual, as if we were lovers of long standing who took each other's undressing in stride instead of strangers whose only physical contact had been for a brief moment in the car when she had put her hand on my arm.

She pulled the open parts of the dress away from skin that was the color and texture of cream. "It's still damp," she said, but didn't take it off. She turned to the mirror above the pine chest of drawers. Her hands went up under the light-brown hair, fluffed it, let it fall back to her shoulders.

"You going to hold that bag all night, honey?" she said.

I hadn't realized that I was still hanging onto it. Her own valise had been pushed in between the chest of drawers and the wooden armchair. I set my bag down at the foot of the bed, which occupied half the room.

That bed was the essential reason for the room. Her grass-stained linen slippers stood neatly beside it and her nylon stockings were draped over the footboard. No setting could have been more intimate, and there we were. But it wasn't that simple.

"How old are you, Jeanie?"

She turned her head. Her mouth, for all its redness, remained naïve, almost childish, and her slender, partly exposed body was an adolescent's body.

"Twenty." Then she added mockingly, "I'm plenty old enough, if that's what's eating you."

"That's only part of it," I said. "You don't have to pay me for this cabin."

She swung away from the chest of drawers. The way her dress fell away from her scarcely covered breasts made her look particularly wanton. Her eyes blazed, and for the first time I noticed the yellow flecks in them.

"What the hell d'you think I am?" Her voice was shrill with outrage.

"I only said—"

"Listen! I can buy this whole damn cabin if I want to. I bet I got more dough on me than you. Who're you to talk so snooty? A crumby schoolteacher!"

"I merely wanted to make it clear that you owed me nothing," I said stiffly.

"I never owed no man nothing and never will. How d'you like that?"

What was I doing here with a vulgar, semiliterate girl? I said, "I'll ask for separate cabins."

"Don't be such a stuffed shirt, honey." She was looking me over with an amused smile now, and then she laughed. She had a fine laugh, low and musical. "You're a funny guy. Different. I guess that's why I like you. Can't a girl just like a guy?"

I was willing as she to make peace. "I'm sorry, Jeanie, if I said anything out of line."

"Forget it."

"Put on dry clothes and we'll go out for a bite."

"I don't feel like eating. But you're hungry, so you go. I'll wait here."

"All right."

I was turning the doorknob when she said, "Don't you like me?" and she was coming to me barefooted with the top of her dress open and her slim hips undulating. She put her hands flat on my chest and threw her head back. I kissed her. My lips shifted from her mouth to her throat.

She broke it up then, laughing gaily. "We got all night, honey. I'll wash up while you go eat."

"All right."

"Hurry back." A quick kiss dismissed me. When I reached for her, she squirmed away and pattered into the bathroom.

I crossed the floodlighted area to the lunchroom. Two boys and two girls at the counter filled the place with raucous and vapid chatter. The girls were not much older than my students and about the same age as Jeanie, with whom I was about to go to bed. As I waited for the weary-looking woman to fry up a couple of hamburgers for me, I felt like a middle-aged roué sniffing after very young girls.

But I wasn't old. Only thirty-four. And Jeanie, whatever her real age, had in her a harder adult core than any woman I had ever known. So that part was all right, but the rest wasn't. Because there had to be more. There had to be something that was deeply troubling her; something that explained her actions from the moment I had spotted her half hiding in the woods to her refusal to leave the car or the cabin for food; something that likely included preparing for a night together with me.

The hell with it. For once I would stop looking all around whatever it was I wanted; I would stop turning it inside out and examining and debating. For this time at least I would stop being the lonely and increasingly prissy teacher of adolescents. Jeanie, we're going to have fun tonight.

The hamburger sandwiches were dried out and the coffee was

anemic, but I ate and drank heartily. I bought a couple of packs of cigarettes and paid up and sauntered out like a man who knew where he was going and was pleased with what was waiting for him.

The fat boy and a uniformed policeman were standing near the rear bumper of my car beside Cabin 3.

"That's the gentleman," the boy said, pointing to me.

My stride broke. I recovered instantly and went on. The cop had the law's usual imposing bulk, running to flesh in all three dimensions.

"This your car?" he demanded.

"Yes."

"Where's your wife?"

"Inside."

"You sure she's your wife?"

"Don't get insulting," I snapped, working at being an indignant citizen.

"Well, I'd like to see her."

"What's this about, Officer?"

"We're looking for a girl wore a yella dress and was carrying a big luggage bag. She got a lift near Darson from a black Chevy coop with a New York license. We don't know the license number, but the man who saw it says it was a fifty Chevy coop." His jaw indicated my car. "Fits your coop perfect."

"There must be thousands like it on the road."

"Where you coming from?"

"Kentucky."

"So you could've passed Darson around four this afternoon?"

"I may have, but I wasn't aware it was against the law."

"Don't you be smart with me. Man at a gas station near Darson says the driver told him he was bound for New York, then he saw this girl come out of the woods and get a lift in the Chevy."

"I can assure you my wife and I gave nobody a lift."

The cop's chin shifted toward the fat boy. "This fella says your wife wore a yella dress. I aim to talk to her."

"I bet your wife has a yellow dress, too," I said.

"I'm checking, that's all."

There was no help for it. Together we went to the cabin door. I knocked.

"Come in," Jeanie called drowsily.

I pushed in the door. She was in bed, but had left the light on. The cop was right behind me.

Abruptly she sat up. The blanket fell down to her hips. She had gone to bed without nightgown or pajamas or anything else on. She gaped at the cop, startled, then threw her arms over her breasts.

"I thought you were alone, dear," she gasped.

The cop mumbled an embarrassed apology as he got out of there in a hurry.

When we were alone, Jeanie dropped her arms to yank the blanket up to her chin. She huddled against the headboard.

"What's he after?" she asked thinly.

The yellow dress wasn't in sight and neither was the valise.

I didn't have to answer her. She would know a lot more about it than I did. She would know why she had been afraid to show herself in public by leaving the car or the cabin to eat. I stepped outside and closed the door. A short distance off the cop waited for me. He couldn't look me in the eye. The fat boy was again with him.

"I ought to report you, Officer," I said, assuming the offensive.

"Jees, sir, she said to come in."

"She said it to me. She was half asleep and didn't realize I wasn't alone. We've been driving since dawn."

"I got orders to check everybody in black Chevy coops. Tell her to put something on."

"She's tired and too embarrassed to face you. I see no reason why she has to be annoyed further. Check with me. You might have asked me to identify myself before barging in on my wife. I'll have you know we're highly respectable people." I dug out my wallet. "Here, look at these."

He examined my driver's license and my Teachers' Guild card. "Lawrence B. Knight," he read aloud, and asked the fat boy if that was the name I had signed in the register. The boy said it sounded like it, but he couldn't say for sure.

"There's an easy way to make sure," I said, pressing my advantage.

We walked to the lunchroom. The fat boy got out the register, in which I had written "Mr. and Mrs. Lawrence B. Knight." Nothing could have looked more innocent. The cop compared that signature with the ones on my license and union card, but he was simply going through an expected routine to show that he was on his toes. He had already been sold. A solid citizen, member in good standing of a reputable profession, might very well bed down for a night with a girl he'd picked up a few hours ago, but he wouldn't be so foolish as to use his real name.

I accompanied him out to his car.

"This woman you're looking for," I said. "What did she do?"

"She was mixed up in a shooting this afternoon in Darson."

I watched him get into his car. Then I said, "Did she kill anybody?"

"All I know, sir, there's a three-state alarm out for her. A guy with her got plugged and a Darson cop got wounded. She's wanted real bad." He threw in the gear; having no more use for me, he was impatient to get going. "You tell Mrs. Knight I'm right sorry."

"Yes," I muttered. "I certainly will."

I returned to the cabin.

Chapter Three

She was still in bed. She lay flat on her back under a sheet and a single blanket, and she looked at me over the footboard with a wide-eyed artlessness that came close to making me shudder. I turned the key in the door and dropped into the chair.

"He's gone," I said.

Only her eyes moved, sliding in their sockets to watch me sitting at the side of the bed. "Yeah, I saw him go."

Her yellow dress was under the bed. From where I sat I could see a piece of it crumpled against the wall like a discarded rag, and her valise was under there too.

"You spent a lot of time at the window before and after I came in with the cop," I said. "You must have heard him earlier when the fat boy brought him to look my car over and they were talking outside this open window. You knew that pretty soon he'd come in here. You tore off your clothes and—"

"I was undressed. I was waiting for you in bed."

"How touching. But you didn't hide your yellow dress until you heard him tell me the girl he was after was wearing one. Then you crawled into bed to dramatize the theme that we were husband and wife. To help it along, you planned to shock the cop. You did, all right. The sight of you naked set him back on his heels. After that he was ashamed to face you."

"What did he say when he saw the register?"

"You needn't worry. I signed it Mr. and Mrs. Lawrence B. Knight. Lawrence for Larry—my name. That was the clincher; he's convinced.

Why did I do it when I registered with a strange woman? I'm not sure. Perhaps I prefer to go through front doors. Can you understand what I'm talking about?"

Jeanie King, or whatever her real name was, uttered a small sigh of relaxation. "But what did the cop want?"

"You, of course. You've been running from the police since this afternoon and made sure you weren't seen outside of my car. But you made two mistakes. The first was not changing your dress right away. The second was letting the old man at the filling station see you. You were careful enough until you were sure I was going far enough in the right direction, but you had to come out before I drove off, and from the shack he saw you get into my car. Even so, it's not working out badly for you. I'm serving my purpose. I'm supplying you with protective coloration until you reach New York."

"My God, how you jabber away!"

"Does this bore you? I'm telling you nothing new. But where do I stand? Somebody got killed and somebody got wounded. The cop didn't know the details, or more likely he didn't care to give them to me. Did you do any of the actual shooting?"

"Honey, you don't think I had anything to do with it?"

"I'm not thinking," I said. "I stopped thinking when I registered you as my wife. There's no reason why I shouldn't have told the cop the truth, but I didn't and I won't. I'm sentimental. Even gallant. I take seriously the stories I read in my youth—that when a lady in distress asks a man for help, he helps her, even when she's no lady. You're safe enough, as far as I'm concerned."

Languidly she stretched. The blanket molded her body. I tried not to recall the thrust of her breasts when she had sat up in bed a few minutes ago. Her cheek had turned against the pillow, burying one eye and her cute little upturned nose and half her mouth. The visible eye and the visible half of her mouth smiled.

"You're a sweet man, honey. I knew it the minute I got into the car with you."

"A sweet man meaning sucker in your lexicon," I said.

"My what?"

"Never mind. I'm in it and I'll stay in it until we reach New York. Pleasant dreams."

She twisted on her side. The blanket slipped, not much, but enough to show those creamy shoulders and remind me that she was naked under it.

"Come to bed, honey."

"I told you earlier that you don't have to pay me. I can be your protective coloration just as well as by spending the night in this chair."

"I want you."

I rose and took off my jacket and draped it over a wire coat hanger on a wall hook. Her eyes never left me as I removed my necktie and shoes. That was as far as I proposed to go to make myself comfortable. I switched out the light and settled back in the chair.

After a while I could hear the gentle rhythm of her breathing. The police of three states were looking for her, but within a few minutes she had dropped off into the serene sleep of the unconcerned. She was quite a girl. She was the only female I had ever met who frightened me. My head slumped to my shoulder. I had driven close to five hundred miles that day, and even in that chair, even with my mind and emotions in tumult, I dozed off....

Voices outside the cabin roused me. I jerked awake, cramped and stiff, and for a moment didn't know where I was. Then I saw Jeanie standing at the front window with her back to me.

The cabin light remained out, but she had partly opened the blind, and the outside floodlights covered her with a mellow glow. She must have jumped out of bed and gone directly to the window, for she wore nothing. Or almost nothing. Only panties, which she must have had on all along in bed—pink mesh like her brassiere had been, fitting as snugly as her skin.

"... here around an hour ago." The voice was close to the cabin and sounded like the fat boy's. "He spoke to the gentleman who owns it."

Jeanie had a gun. I saw it when she shifted her body a little. She held it along her bare right leg and her finger was curled around the trigger.

"... a black Chevy coop," a second voice was saying outside. "Like this. Who'd you say checked?"

"The cop they call Willie," the fat boy said. "Why don't you cops get together?"

"Well, he spoke to the gentleman and his wife and looked at licenses and things and at the register and then he went away."

"Then I guess I don't have to waste my time."

The voices receded, faded. Jeanie turned from the window and saw me staring at her.

The diffused light covered her as gently as moonlight. Her panties might as well not have been on her and her breasts were saucily uptilted like her nose. The corners of her mouth lifted in a small smile; she was no more abashed by the gun in her hand than by her nakedness. The gun was polished nickel and quite small. It seemed hardly more than a toy, but it could spurt death.

"Is that the gun with which you did the shooting in Darson?" I said.

"I didn't shoot nobody." She pouted. "You don't have to believe me."

"You couldn't have intended to shoot it out with the cop if he came in here and then run for it the way you are. So it was for me, to make sure I wouldn't yell out to the cop if I woke."

She moved then, coming slowly toward me along the foot of the bed into the dimmer part of the room, and her sweet, tight body had the muted tones of a nude photographed through a filter. Her bare feet stepped over my outstretched legs. At the chest of drawers she replaced the little gun in her straw handbag.

"You see, honey, I trust you."

"I'm flattered," I said.

She bent over the chair and kissed me. A breast pressed against my shoulder. It wasn't easy to keep from touching her, to force my mouth to be unresponsive under hers.

She lifted her head. "What's the matter with you?"

"Go back to bed."

"Without you?"

"Look," I said. "I thought I made it clear that you can rely on me without that or without a gun either."

She put her hands on her hips and drew her shoulders back, tantalizingly.

I made myself remain in the chair.

"I can spend the rest of the night outside in my car," I said, "but the fat boy might see me there and get ideas and call the cops."

She said sullenly, "Nuts to you!" and climbed into the bed. She pulled the cover to her chin and turned her back to me, curling up.

I sat with my hands gripping the arms of the chair. I was afraid. For all my moralizing to myself, what I was actually doing was playing it safe. I was already pretty deeply in whatever she had done to make the police hunt her; if I got into bed with her, I would be in over my head. I would be committing myself to see her through all the way.

I was not a man who cared to take any step that would disturb the even and uneventful tenor of his life.

My bones protested against the unyielding chair. Jeanie was using only one blanket; two others were folded at the foot of the bed. When I pulled them off the bed, she turned her torso around to watch what I was doing. I spread one blanket on the floor and stretched out on it and covered myself with the other. Looking up, I saw the pale blob of her face hovering over the side of the bed as she peered down at me.

"Of all the crazy dopes!" she said.

The bedsprings creaked as her face withdrew. Then there was silence. This time I had trouble falling asleep, but eventually I did.

I woke to the morning sounds of the motor court—voices calling, doors slamming, cars departing. The floor was no place for drowsy lingering. I rose, and Jeanie wasn't in bed.

She wasn't in the bathroom, either, because the door was open and I could see all the way into it. And her shoes weren't beside the bed and her stockings weren't over the footboard. I looked under the bed. Her yellow dress and valise were not there, which made it definite.

Sometime during the night she had dressed and slipped away. She no longer needed me. In fact, with the police searching for her in a 1950 black Chevrolet coupé with New York license plates, my car and I were a danger to her.

I was well rid of her.

All the same, I was saddened by a sense of loss. I couldn't understand it. She could have meant nothing good for me, but there it was.

I showered and shaved and dressed and stepped into the bright, fresh morning. I started toward the lunchroom for breakfast; halfway across the clearing I turned back. The fat boy would find it curious that my wife wasn't eating with me. After the goings on last night, he might be alert enough to take a look in the cabin and, finding her gone, get in touch with the police. I hurried to my car.

My keys weren't in the left pocket of my trousers where I always kept them. As I searched for them, I discovered that my wallet was missing from my left hip pocket. So she was a crook. I might have expected that. A girl who would sleep with any man who picked her up. A girl who carried a gun in her handbag and was involved in shootings with the police. A tart and a crook.

A moment later I came across both key case and wallet. They were in one of my jacket pockets. I counted the money—fifty-odd dollars, exactly what there should have been. The money mattered only a little; I was glad chiefly because she hadn't stooped quite so low.

When I unlocked the car trunk to put my Gladstone bag into it, I found her tan valise.

That explained the keys not having been in the proper pocket, and the wallet too. Without awakening me, she had managed to lift them from my trousers, in which I had been sleeping. She had returned them more conveniently by simply dropping them into my jacket pocket. It appeared that I still had a purpose to serve. She didn't care to be burdened with luggage as she made her way to New York. It was up to me to transport it for her. The wallet she had needed to learn my home address.

So after all I wasn't yet clear of her. And I wasn't quite sorry.

I stuck my bag beside hers and locked the trunk and drove off.

Eight o'clock. I snapped on the radio for news. A Richmond station came on. War in Korea and the threat of war everywhere else. Then suddenly there was a name in the air.

Jean. Jean for Jeanie.

Not Jean King, as she had told me. Jean Tropp. She had given me, at any rate, a half-truth.

That was my Jeanie, all right. The radio voice said that she had just been identified, though little was known about her except her real name and that she had been living with Bertie Bride when he had been shot and killed yesterday afternoon in Darson. But by now it was stale news, except for the continuing search for Jean Tropp, and there were few details.

Half an hour later I stopped off for breakfast at a lunch wagon in a small northern Virginia town. Next door was a drugstore that sold newspapers. I bought a Richmond and a Washington morning paper and read them at the lunchroom counter. The Washington paper had only a couple of paragraphs, but the Richmond paper gave it a play on page three.

The story went back to last Friday, when four armed, masked men had staged a payroll holdup in Knoxville, Tennessee, and had gotten away with more than twenty thousand dollars. Yesterday, Monday, the Virginia state police had got a tip that one of the holdup men was a well-known criminal named Bertie Bride, who was holing up with a woman in a boardinghouse in Darson, where they were using the names of Mr. and Mrs. Baxter. Bride was leaving the house when state and local police arrived. He pulled out a gun and began to shoot. He wounded one cop before he was mowed down. During the gun fight the girl who was known as Mrs. Baxter, and later identified as Jean Tropp, slipped out of the house. The landlady saw her leave, wearing a yellow dress and carrying a large tan valise.

Several hours later Jean Tropp was observed getting a lift in a New York car and there followed a description of my coupé and a safely vague description of myself.

According to the news story, the police were particularly anxious to get their hands on the girl because her valise might contain part or all of the holdup loot.

"What's yours?" the plump blonde behind the counter asked.

My stomach felt as if it couldn't take anything solid. "Just orange juice and coffee."

There was a two-column photo of Bertie Bride. I stared at it. A youthful, handsome face with a sleek mustache and startled eyes. He didn't look like a crook and a killer. I supposed that the real ones seldom did.

And what was a gunman's mistress supposed to look like? I knew. Naïve and adolescent, leggy and slim-hipped, with light-brown hair and saucy breasts.

I drank orange juice and coffee and paid and got out, leaving the two newspapers on the counter. I drove until I reached an uninhabited stretch of highway and pulled my car off on the grass and unlocked the trunk door. Her valise had no lock to it. Leaning into the trunk, I opened the valise.

Her yellow dress and stained linen shoes were on top. My hands dug in. Dresses, skirts, blouses, hose, underwear, nightgowns—whatever a girl would need in the way of, clothing on a trip. And nothing else.

I closed the valise and locked the trunk door and stood at the side of the highway watching the cars shoot by. After a while I got back into my car and continued to drive north toward home.

Chapter Four

The square block of house consisted of what were called garden apartments, which meant that the entrance of each of the six units was from a courtyard where a patchy lawn and a few shrubs had been planted. From the fourth-floor apartment that Marjorie and I shared, you looked down at four newly transplanted trees in a freshly paved street, and on a clear day you could see the mast of the Empire State Building and the sparkling spire of the Chrysler Building across the East River.

When I returned home that evening, I found my sister Marjorie in her usual position in the wing chair and engaged in her usual activity of watching the television screen across the room. I put down both bags—two because I had also brought Jeanie's up from the car—and kissed Marjorie.

"You said you'd be gone only a few days." She greeted me with an inevitable complaint.

"Only five," I apologized. "They wanted me to stay at least a week."

"Leaving me all alone! I haven't been feeling well. My stomach."

Her lips quivered. But she didn't break into tears. She sniffled, and suddenly I was more disgusted than contrite.

"Don't you ever stop feeling sorry for yourself?" I said.

She looked at me, startled that I would deliberately say something to hurt her. "Why, Larry, what a way to talk to your poor sister!"

"I'm sorry."

And I was sorry. Poor sister, poor Marjorie. It wasn't any fun to be an unattractive, forty-year-old virgin who spent most of her days and evenings watching television as her big frame kept adding fat and her legs swelled and she nursed real and imagined ailments. My mother used to say—though never, of course, within Marjorie's hearing—that it was a pity her only daughter couldn't have shared some of the good looks of her two younger brothers.

"Why didn't you let me know when you were coming home?" Marjorie was saying. "I've no supper prepared for you and nothing in the house."

"That's all right. I had a big meal on the road a couple of hours ago."

I carried both bags in to my room.

I wondered what to do with Jeanie's. With the police all over the East hunting her, she wouldn't be concerned over losing some clothing. Chances were she would never bother to pick the valise up. Well, I couldn't leave it here in my room. Marjorie would be sure to have a look inside when she cleaned up, and I'd have a devil of a time explaining. I should have left it in the car trunk. Later I'd take it down again.

I started to shed my clothes in preparation for a shower. When I was down to my underwear, I paused to look at myself at the mirror. I was a big man. We all ran to size in my family, but while Marjorie had always been heavy and had kept expanding through the years, and while George was beginning to acquire jowls and a potbelly, most of my bulk was in height and shoulders and chest. In an outburst of vanity I thumped my hard belly. Put it down to handball and tennis and clean living.

Maybe too damn much clean living.

The point was, why wouldn't she have wanted me for no other reason than that I was a palatable male animal? Meaning Jeanie. There needn't have been any strings attached. A simple meeting of the sexes, if I hadn't been such a . . .

Cut it out. Wipe her from your mind. Forget the way her breasts tilted; forget the clean sweep of her flanks; forget the briefly experienced taste of her mouth. All that was left of her was her valise, and that you could easily get rid of.

More easily than to get rid of the memory.

I didn't continue undressing. Tired from two days of driving and restless hours on the cabin floor, I flopped down on my bed.

So you sidestepped that, too, I thought, unable to let go of myself. Last night you moved a little way toward adventure, to actually stepping out into the vital, living world, and then you stopped to examine and moralize and let the chance pass. You're safe, you're secure, but what did you get out of it? What you always got—back to this lonely bed in an apartment that was never a home with a nagging, imposing sister.

Sunday night my sister-in-law, Alice, of whom I was very fond, had bawled me out. The children had been put to bed and Alice and George and I had sat in the living room of their neat little house in the small Kentucky city where George had moved a dozen years ago and had set up a moderately successful lumber business. And I had broached the subject that had been the real reason for my visit.

"Look," I had said. "Marjorie has been living with me since Ma died. You've been good about it, George; you send her money for her clothes and extras. But I've done more than my share. You've got plenty of room here, and—well . . ."

"No!" Alice had burst out. "She's not going to ruin my home the way she's ruining your life."

George had looked at his cigar and said nothing.

"We don't have to be nasty about Marjorie," I had protested. "She's very devoted to me."

"But you want to get rid of her," Alice had said.

"I merely suggest that we ought to take turns boarding her."

"She's never been devoted to anybody but herself," Alice had said. "If she cared a hoot for you, would she be so selfish?"

"That's not fair. Marjorie would do anything for me."

"Like keeping you a bachelor, for instance," Alice had said.

"What?" I had said. "What are you talking about?"

"He doesn't even suspect." She had looked at George and had thrown up her hands in a hopeless gesture. "Larry, how many women have thrown themselves at your feet?"

"Oh, come."

"Don't be modest. You're a big, charming, handsome man. You have a good job."

"Not these days," I had mumbled. "Remember, I'm the lowliest of the low—a schoolteacher."

"What do you earn?"

"Fifty-four hundred."

"That's still money. Good money. And you have more security than anybody I know. I'll introduce you to a dozen lovely girls right in this town who'd be delighted—"

"Spare me your matchmaking, please."

My sister-in-law had become pugnacious while my brother had remained silent and uneasy, occupied with his cigar.

"You ought to appeal to Marjorie to spare you her unmatchmaking," she had flared up. "Last time I was in New York you introduced me to a fine girl you were going out with. Sally Ewing. You see, I even remember her name. When we left, I told George it was all arranged, there would be a wedding soon. I could see it. But what happened?"

"It didn't work out."

"Why not."

"Just one of those things."

"Just Marjorie, you mean," Alice had said. "I know what she did. Marjorie spoke to me about Sally Ewing. She found fault with her background—as if the Knights are such hoity-toity people. She didn't approve of her clothes and manners. She tore her down the way only one woman can tear down another. Perhaps you don't know what happened, Larry, but I know. Marjorie drove her away from you and drove you away from her. The way she's done with every woman you ever knew since she lived with you. Don't imagine she's interested in your welfare. She cares about her home, such as it is—the home you make for her. She knows that no wife of yours would tolerate her sniffling and nagging and complaining for a day."

"What this long speech means, in short, is that you don't want Marjorie here," I had said.

George had spoken for the first time. "Now, Larry, why can't Marjorie get a small apartment of her own somewhere in New York? You and I will each contribute half to her support."

"I can't do that to her," I said. "I can't drive her out and make her live alone."

"But it's all right for her to make you live alone," Alice had said. "In heaven's name, Larry, use your head. She can get along all right. There's nothing really wrong with her. She can go out and get a job. Other women work for a living. Don't you understand what you're letting her do to you? You're the domestic type. You deserve a decent, normal, healthy life, with a wife and children."

"Forget I brought up the subject," I had said stiffly, "Marjorie will stay with me."

"Which is exactly what she wants," Alice had said. "To keep you tied to her."

"Then let her," I had said. "She gets little enough out of life."

"And what do you get out of life?" Alice had said.

I had shrugged. That had been no answer, but it had been the only one I could give.

The phone rang. I sat up on the bed, then slumped back when I heard Marjorie answer it. I could have spent last night in a bed— spent it with considerable pleasure.

Aw, stop it. Does a man have to keep apologizing to himself for having done the sensible and proper thing?

He does, sometimes.

Marjorie knocked on the door. "Can I come in?"

"What is it?"

"That was Katy on the phone. She wants me to come over to help her with some sewing. Will you drive me?"

"I'll be ready in a minute."

I was back in my clothes in less time than that, after which I had to wait another twenty minutes for Marjorie. She took as much time primping as an attractive woman, but somehow she always did the wrong things to herself. She wore something black and flowing that added to her bulk, and she had got into shoes that made it almost impossible for her to walk on legs already overburdened by what they had to carry.

Waddling, she clung to my arm on the way to the elevator and complained that she was finding it harder and harder to get about.

"You could watch your diet, the way a dozen doctors advise," I said.

"What do doctors know?"

"Nothing, I suppose, because they all insist that the only thing wrong with you is that you eat too damn much."

Her puffy lips quivered. If the elevator hadn't arrived at that moment and if people hadn't been in it, she might well have gone into one of her weeping acts.

She was grimly silent during the mile drive. When I stopped the car, she whined, "Larry, what's come over you? You've snapped at me ever since you came back. Did anything happen at George's?"

"No."

"Then why are you like this?"

"Let me alone." I got out and opened the door for her and helped her out of the car and up the porch steps.

"I'll phone you when I'm ready to leave," she said.

"All right." I started off the porch.

"Larry, you haven't said goodbye to me."

I returned to her and kissed her.

When I entered my apartment several minutes later, I found I had a visitor. Jeanie was coming out of my room carrying her tan valise.

Chapter Five

At that moment she could have passed as one of the quieter seventeen-year-old girls in my senior classes. Her face had a wholesome, scrubbed look achieved by the simple method of leaving off all make-up except a subdued pale red on the small mouth; and a cotton blouse and striped skirt and bobby socks and low-heeled shoes, completed the teenage effect. She couldn't have found a better disguise from the police who were hunting a gangster's girlfriend.

"I got the address out of your wallet last night," Jeanie said brightly. "The door was unlocked, so I came right in."

"I see you found your valise."

"That's what I came for." She set the valise down. "Who's the fat dame who's living with you? Your mother?"

"My sister. Did you see us leave?"

"No, but I had a look in her closet while I was waiting for you. Her dresses could be used for tents."

"Why were you waiting?" I said. "You've reached New York and now you have your valise. What further use can I be?"

"I can't dope you out, honey. You stick your neck out to help me, but you keep acting like you don't like me at all."

I wished that she would take her valise and get out my life, and I wished that she wouldn't. I stood facing her in my living room and said nothing, because I didn't have any clear thoughts to put into words.

She shrugged. "Okay, I'll be on my way. But I been traveling all day and I'll be doing lots more. I'd like to get cleaned up. Can I take a shower?"

"You'll find the bathroom down the hall." I tried to sound casual, indifferent, but I didn't feel that way. Every act of hers had something of intimacy in it. As now. Standing beside her valise, she started to unbutton her blouse.

This was like last night all, over again. But not quite like it, either, because this time I knew who and what she was.

"You can get undressed in the bathroom," I said harshly.

She laughed derisively. "I won't embarrass the great big shy schoolteacher." And with an impudent shake of her hips she left the room.

I lit a cigarette and sat down on the sofa. I heard water running. I remembered that the entrance door was unlocked and went to lock it. I returned to the living room and stubbed out the cigarette and lit another.

A gangster's girl, I thought. His mistress until yesterday, when he had been killed by the police. So what? She was not, never, at any time my kind of girl, but so what for an hour or two?

In the bathroom the water stopped running.

"Honey," she sang out, "I have no towel."

The people in the adjoining apartments could hear through the walls every raised voice. Marjorie didn't call me honey and they would certainly recognize that that lilting young voice wasn't hers. I wondered if anybody had seen Jeanie come in here.

The hell with them!

The bathroom door was open a crack. Through it I said, "There are towels on the bar."

"Hand towels. Haven't you got a big one?"

I fetched a bath towel from the hall linen closet. The bathroom door opened several more inches and a bare arm appeared.

"Hand it to me," she said.

For a long moment I did nothing. Then I said, "I'm coming in to dry you."

Her arm withdrew. I pushed the door in, and there she stood on the bath mat. Her creamy skin glistened wetly. She faced me with eyes curiously tight at the corners, and she waited.

I spread out the towel and dried her. I dried her from neck to feet, not touching her except through the towel, and she didn't stir. I could sense her all wound up inside the way I was.

I dropped the towel and rose to my feet and placed my hands on her hips. Yellow flecks swam in eyes which were wide with intensity. Her face seemed to have thinned, tightened, the skin stretched taut over the cheekbones. I was not aware of either of us moving, but suddenly we were together, her mouth under mine.

"My God, how you torture a girl!" she whispered.

I swung partly away from her, and with my arms about her snug waist I moved with her out of the bathroom and down the hall to my room. I yanked off the bedspread and pulled down the blanket, but she waited, standing, for me to undress, and then she seized me and our hands groped, sought, found each other.

And afterward I felt fine. Night had fallen and the darkness was snug and warm and intimate as she lay against me with her head on my shoulder. Her hair tickled my nose. I turned my face away and her hand came affectionately up to my neck, and I kissed her tenderly and sank back into the delightful lethargy we shared now as our bodies had shared passion.

I must have dozed off, because her voice startled me before I recalled that I wasn't alone in my bed.

"You know what, honey?" she was saying. "I was beginning to think there was something wrong with you. Sick or something."

"That wasn't what kept me from you last night."

"Well, I sure found out it wasn't." Her soft hand moved over me. "My, you're strong. Some chest."

"I can go into raptures over yours."

"You say the nicest things when you want to. You're the man for me, honey."

I said, "Was Bertie Bride the man for you too?"

She lay very still against me. "Why should we talk about him?"

"All right, let's not."

"I didn't like Bertie much."

"Do you generally sleep with men you don't like much?"

"Don't be like that. I liked him all right for a while, then I didn't. He was mean to me."

"But you continued to live with him?"

"Well, not so much in the end. It was only . . ."

Her mouth turned against my shoulder. I didn't ask her what she had been about to say. I didn't want to know about Bertie Bride or about a holdup in Knoxville or a shooting in Darson or anything else about her. She was a girl to make love to rather than to love, to hold for another few minutes in the drowsy aftermath of fulfillment before she left. And I would never see her again, and that would be all right.

The phone rang.

Jeanie's leg was flung across my body. It held me pinned down as I started to move. "Don't answer."

The radium dial of my alarm clock said a quarter after ten. Normally too early for Marjorie to call. The ringing ceased, then started again, urgently. "I might as well," I muttered, untangling myself. I put on the bedside lamp and got my robe from the closet and padded out.

Marjorie's voice said, "Larry, pick me up."

"This early?"

"I'm finished. I'd like to get home."

"Can't you hang around till eleven?"

"What are you doing?"

"Something!" I snapped.

"Larry, what's come over you tonight?"

"All right, I'll be there in half an hour."

"You must make it sooner. Katy wants to go to bed."

"I'll try," I said, and hung up.

Jeanie had blandly kicked the cover down to the foot of the bed. In the glow of the bedside lamp, she lay outstretched with the indolence of a kitten in front of a fire. She pouted when I told her she would have to leave right away.

"What's the rush, honey?"

"I have to pick up my sister."

Yawning, she looked down the length of her body and wiggled her painted toes. "Honey, why don't you come with me? I'm going to New Hampshire. Drive me there tonight."

"More protective coloration?" I said wryly.

"You make me tired. I got friends here in New York who'd be glad to drive me, or I can take a train. But I want you."

"Tonight?"

"We can start out tonight. Say we drive a few hours and sleep somewhere and get there tomorrow. And you can stay as long as you want to."

I sat down on the edge of the bed. "Where in New Hampshire?"

"A place called Stoker Hill nobody ever heard of. A fella named Hank has a fine place near there in the mountains."

"Another boyfriend of yours?"

"What'd you take me for? I got only one, and you're it. Anyway, Hank's an old geezer. Being you're a teacher, you don't work in the summer, do you?"

"Most take summer jobs if they want to make a decent living, but I'm innately lazy."

"So we can spend the whole summer there. You and me together, honey. What's to stop you?"

Nothing and everything.

I said, "What is it, a hideout?"

"Well, I'll be safe there."

"A gangster's hideout?" I persisted.

"There'll be nice people. Honest, you'll like 'em. We'll have a swell time, honey."

Her evasion of my question was an answer. And it was odd that I should be tempted, that I should even consider the notion.

"It's impossible," I said.

"Why is it?"

"I don't belong in a gangster's hideout. I don't belong with you, either. I'm a stuffed shirt, a funny guy. You said so yourself."

"You don't have to get sore." Her hand was on my thigh. "Lay down here."

Her uncovered loveliness was like a pain in my throat. "For just a minute," I murmured.

A great deal more than a minute passed.

I jumped out of bed. It was a wonder Marjorie hadn't phoned again about being kept waiting.

"Let's get a move on," I said, leaning over to slap her playfully where it resounded most.

Jeanie turned flat on her back to protect herself. "You'll come with me, honey?"

"Don't be silly."

"What's so silly about—"

"I haven't time to argue," I said irritably. "Get dressed."

"You had plenty of time for other things with me."

I said, "I'll bring your clothes from the bathroom."

"I don't want you to do a single damn thing for me," she said crossly. Her legs swung off the bed. "You don't catch me chasing after no guy, much less a crummy schoolteacher."

I was fascinated by her indignant wiggle as she stalked out of the room.

A few minutes later I was pulling on my pants when I heard a key turn in the entrance door. I remained bent over, listening to the door open and close and then to Marjorie wheeze in the hall.

"Larry, are you home?"

"Yes."

It could have been a lot worse; she could have arrived when we had been in bed. As I buckled the belt, I heard her heavy tread move into the living room. I would introduce Jeanie as a girl who had dropped in to visit me; and after Jeanie had left I could imagine Marjorie saying, "That mere child, and so uneducated. I'm surprised at you." And I would grin rather sheepishly and say that she didn't mean anything to me, which would be more or less true.

"Larry!" Marjorie's voice was shrill with a kind of horror. "What does this mean?" she demanded on a lower key.

"You Larry's sister?" I heard Jeanie ask placidly.

"I am. And who may you be?"

"Take it easy, lady," Jeanie said, "or you'll bust a blood vessel."

"How dare you! And in my house practically naked!"

By that time I had reached them.

Before she had finished dressing, Jeanie had gone from the bathroom to the living room, probably to hunt for a cigarette, which she had found and was now lighting. Standing there in scant brassiere and panties, only one stocking on and that crumpled below the knee, the cigarette slanting from a corner of her mouth, she looked piquantly wanton, like a girl in one of the milder French photos. And she was completely unabashed.

"Look, Marjorie," I said.

My sister stared at me with stricken eyes. "You—you have the nerve to bring a—a creature like that into my home!"

"Say, don't you go calling me names," Jeanie said.

"Get her out of here!" Marjorie screamed at me.

And the hysterics came. I watched her flesh shake, but I was too angry to be contrite, as I always had been before at her tears. She took her plump hands from her face and saw me silent and bitter, and she turned ponderously and hurried out of the room. She came closer to running than I had ever before seen her. Her bedroom door slammed.

Jeanie said, "What's eating her? She's only your sister. My God, you'd think she was your wife or something."

Sick anger churned in my stomach, flowed up and through me.

I started out of the room and stopped. "Don't leave yet, Jeanie." I moved on to Marjorie's room.

My sister sat in her rocking chair beside the window. Her huge shoulders heaved. When I closed the door behind me, she removed the handkerchief from her face.

"That's why you refused to call for me," she wailed. "I waited and waited and Katy wanted to go to bed and drove me home. And I found you with a naked tart in my home."

"My home too," I said, "though it's never been much of one. And it was in my bed that we made love."

"Do you have to talk as well as act obscene?"

"I'm a big boy now, Marjorie. I'm entitled to at least a bit of life. You don't give a hang who or what the girl is. You don't give a hang for my happiness either. You care only for this apartment and me in it to keep it up. You're afraid of any woman who can tempt me to set up housekeeping with her instead."

"Larry, please don't be cruel to me."

I clung to the doorknob. It wasn't so much Marjorie, I thought. Alice hadn't been quite right. It was mostly myself. Lawrence B. Knight, the somewhat prissy bachelor, rooted in dullness.

All at once I knew what I had to do. I must tear myself out by the roots violently.

"I'm going away with her," I said.

She gawked at me. "With that young tart!"

"Is everybody who cares for me a tart? All right, probably she is one. I don't know her very well yet. I'm going to tell you something else about her. She's a gangster's moll."

"A what?"

"You see them every day in your television plays. A girlfriend of gangsters. Only she's the real thing."

"Larry, you're joking."

"All right, I'm joking," I said tiredly. "But I'm going off with her."

"For—for good?"

Now there was nothing left in her but the terror of loneliness. And I was able again to feel pity for her. "I'll be back, I suppose, before the summer is over. Perhaps much sooner. I'll leave a check for you. You'll get along. If you need anything, get in touch with George. He's your brother too."

I stepped out to the hall.

"Larry, wait!"

I closed the door.

In the living room I found Jeanie fully dressed. I told her that I would be with her as soon as I repacked my bag.

Chapter Six

At midnight we left Merritt Parkway west of Bridgeport to search for a bed. We found one in the converted attic of a private tourist house. For the second night in a row I signed a register "Mr. and Mrs. Lawrence B, Knight"—this time without hesitation.

Wearily we flopped into the big poster bed and fell asleep after only a few goodnight kisses. But in the morning we lingered long, like a honeymooning couple, in delightful dalliance.

"Honey, honey, honey," Jeanie whispered. "My own wonderful lover boy. God, how I love you!"

There was a silence then, a void I was expected to fill with words similar to hers. I said lamely, "You're very beautiful." Which was true, but still an evasion, and she knew it.

"But you don't love me," she said sullenly.

"I do."

"Then say it."

"I love you."

And that was not quite a lie at that moment, when she was ardent and demanding in my arms.

Presently we put on our clothes and resumed our journey.

Our destination was Stoker Hill in central New Hampshire. Jeanie knew the way. She told me she had spent a week there in June.

"With Bertie Bride?" I asked.

"Sure." She gave me a sidelong glance. "You're not jealous of Bertie?" The idea seemed to give her satisfaction.

"Jealous of a dead man?" I said.

"I know all about men. They always want to be the first one."

I shrugged. "Will you have trouble explaining a new boyfriend to the people who knew him?"

"They ain't so particular. Anyway, it's none of their business."

"But will they accept me? I mean I'm not—well, I assume I'm not their kind."

She didn't answer at once. It was early evening; we were passing through Concord and were less than an hour from Stoker Hill according to the map. "Turn right next corner," she said. She lit a cigarette and smoked it down in silence.

When we were again on the open road, I said, "So it does bother you?"

"I been thinking all day, honey. Stan won't let you stay if he knows who you are."

"Who's Stan?"

"He's staying at Hank's with his wife, and there are some fellas too. Stan's their boss."

"Are these the men who were involved in the Knoxville holdup with Bertie Bride?"

"Well . . ."

"And they won't trust an honest and upright citizen, is that it?"

Jeanie shifted closer to me and hugged my right arm. "Honey, the cops are looking for me and Hank's is a safe place and real nice and I want you to be there with me."

"But it doesn't appear that they will tolerate me."

"You ever hear of Prof Glow?" she said.

"No."

"He's a big shot on the West Coast. I know for a fact Stan and the other fellas never saw him. We were talking about Prof Glow one night the time we were all in Hank's place in June. Bertie used to work for Prof Glow and I met him last winter when Bertie took me out to California. Anyway, like I said, Bertie and me were the only ones knew him, and Bertie's dead. You look a lot like Prof."

I drew in my breath. "No doubt this Prof Glow is in the rackets."

"A real big shot. Gambling, but mostly girls. If they think you're him, they'll be real pleased to have you stay."

"By girls, I suppose you mean prostitution?"

"Prof's got half the houses on the West Coast lined up," she said in a tone of respect for a successful captain of industry.

"Fine," I said. "They'll have no trouble taking me for the type."

"I'm not kidding, honey."

"Neither am I. But if he's famous, there might be pictures of him around."

"I'm not saying you can pass for him with anybody who's seen him. You're bigger and handsomer and younger. But like I told you, they don't know what he looks like. And you don't have to worry about pictures. He's not famous like a movie star. He's a quiet guy; keeps out of the limelight. I never once seen his picture anyplace. You can get away with it easy."

I didn't ask what would happen to me if I didn't get away with it.

I said, "What do I do to act like him—talk out of the side of my mouth?"

"Prof Glow is even better educated than you, I bet. That's how he got his name. Prof is short for Professor. Maybe he was once a teacher like you. Nobody knows much about him. I been thinking and thinking how to pass you off at Hank's. I almost made up my mind we'd say you were a con man. Then all of a sudden it hit me how much you're like Prof Glow. You don't have to act at all. Just talk and act natural and you'll be just like him."

"I'm disappointed. Here I was hoping to cash in on my knowledge of criminal literature and have a chance to play tough guy."

"He's tough, all right. He speaks nice and educated and has good manners, but inside he's tough as they come."

"They'll ask questions about my enterprises and cronies."

"Prof Glow just isn't a talkative guy. Me and Bertie spent a whole evening with him last winter. He sat smiling and listening and saying yes and no, but not a word about himself. That's how he is."

"No name but Prof?"

"Oh, yes. I should've told you right off. It's Chester. Chester Glow. But Prof's the only thing I ever heard anybody call him. People wouldn't know who you meant if you said Chester Glow."

"Has he a family?"

"None I ever heard of. Never got married."

"No girlfriend or friends?"

"Sure. Me, beginning right now." She took my hand off the wheel and held it against her breast. "I'm Prof Glow's girl and you're Prof Glow. Okay, honey?"

"Okay," I replied gaily.

Chapter Seven

Stoker Hill consisted mainly of a service station that also sold groceries. As we rolled by, Jeanie said, "There's Fatso. He's one of the fellas staying at Hank's."

I glanced back at a brilliant plaid shirt coming out of the store. "Should we pick him up?"

"He'd have a car—Stan's Kaiser or Hank's jeep. It's a far walk and Fatso don't like to walk. Look for a dirt road on your left."

Alone I would have missed it completely, and Jeanie almost did. She yelled late, and by the time I stopped the car we were fifty feet past. I backed up. Trees and shrubs obscured the entrance. There was no marker of any kind.

"Is this Hank's private road?" I asked.

"I guess not, but nobody else lives on it. He's at the end, about three miles."

The road wound and climbed and dipped. If you drove all the way in second gear, you could manage to keep your teeth from being rattled loose. On the left was a steep wooded slope and on the right a deep ditch; between there was hardly room for one car. What worried me was what would happen if another car came from the opposite direction.

Suddenly, halfway around a particularly nasty curve, there was a car facing us.

Luckily it wasn't in motion. I honked my horn. Nobody was in the car; the woods around remained unresponsive.

"What a place to park," I grumbled.

"That looks like Stan's Kaiser," she said. "Better see if something's wrong."

I got out to investigate. The left front wheel was over on its side in the very deep ditch. Evidently the driver had come too fast around the curve and the wheel had hit the ditch with an impact that had knocked it askew on its axle. I explained to Jeanie that there would be no way to get through until the Kaiser was hauled out of the way. "Fatso must be in Stoker Hill to get a towing car," she said.

"Then we'll have to wait."

"You don't know the service around here. Nobody's in a hurry. It might take hours, and it'll be dark very soon."

"Let's walk."

"There's no sense both of us walking," she said. "It's a good couple of miles and I'm dead. I'll wait here in the car. You come back with Hank in his jeep and pick me up. You can't miss it. Walk till you get there."

"All right."

"Honey, you haven't kissed me in hours."

This was like Marjorie reminding me when I forgot to kiss her hello or goodbye. But with the kiss itself the similarity ended. I kissed Jeanie and started out.

It was considerably more comfortable walking on that shaded road in the warm early evening than driving over it. Alone now for the first time since last night, away for a little while from the propinquity of her lovely body, I could be astonished at being here. I had no desire to get out of it. A man had a right for once in his life to be a damn fool.

The woods ended in a meadow rolling gently away from the low knoll on which I stood. Distantly the wavy crests of mountains were fringed with purple by the setting sun. The house was on my left, square and gray and close to the ground. Beside it stood a jeep.

At one of the uncurtained downstairs windows I glimpsed movement. Somebody was watching me. I was about to call out when I heard a rhythmic creaking sound. I went out.

A woman was pumping water from a well in front of the house. I stopped some hundred feet away and watched.

Her hair, piled on top of her head as if to get it out of the way, was like corn silk glinting in the slanting rays of the disappearing sun. Much of her body was exposed—a strong, tanned, richly smooth body. The legs of her shorts were rolled up as high as possible, baring her fine thighs, practically to the hipbones. The only other thing was a strip of flowered cloth knotted at the back, a scant halter that by no means covered all of her conspicuously full breasts as she stood bent over the pump handle.

"I'm not going to tell him, Ronnie," the woman was saying, "but don't ever try anything like that again."

She was speaking to somebody near her but out of my range of vision. I moved a few feet and all of the front of the house came into view. A young man sat tilted back in a canvas chair. He was naked to the waist.

"What's the matter with a little fun, Elsa?" he said.

She turned her back to him and resumed pumping water into a galvanized pail. His eyes absorbed her.

I started toward them. I had taken only a step when a voice behind me said, "You after somethin', mister?"

A man carrying a rifle approached me from the rear of the house. The week-old stubble on his pinched face was gray, and ragged gray hair protruded past a soiled, frayed Panama hat. At the open collar of a faded blue shirt more tufts of gray curled. He peered at me through thick, black-rimmed lenses.

"Are you Hank?" I asked.

"Yuh. This is my property and you're snoopin'."

"I came with Jeanie Tropp. We couldn't get through the road. She's waiting a couple of miles back in the car for you to pick her up."

The two in front of the house were looking at us. The woman named Elsa had straightened up at the pump and the man named Ronnie had risen from the chair.

"He claims he came with Jeanie," Hank called to them. "Says his car's stuck."

"Keep him covered and bring him over," Ronnie said.

I preceded Hank and his rifle. Now I could see the woman's face clearly. It was strong-looking, like her body the features prominent but finely molded. Her violet eyes lay flatly on me.

"Start talking," Ronnie ordered.

"A Kaiser sedan went into a ditch and broke a wheel and we couldn't get past it," I explained. "Jeanie says it's Stan's car."

The woman said, "Well, Stan and Fatso left right after supper. And Stan drives like a madman. Where are they?"

"Evidently they walked to Stoker Hill for a towing car. We glimpsed Fatso in the service station when we passed through."

"You know Stan and Fatso?" Ronnie demanded.

"No. Jeanie pointed Fatso out to me."

"Who the hell are you?"

I had a name to give them, but I preferred to hold off until Jeanie was present. They might ask questions that would require covering up, and she was the lass to do it. "A friend of Jeanie's," I told him.

Bleakly Ronnie studied me. He was young, in his early twenties, slim and flat-bellied, with a shock of disordered mouse-colored hair.

His face had two strikes against it—bulging eyes and not enough chin.

"And that crazy little dope brought you here?" he said.

"Why not?" I said. "I know the score, if that's what's worrying you."

"Maybe you know too much." Ronnie looked past me. "What's your idea, Hank?"

"Well, now." Casually but steadily Hank's rifle continued to cover me. "We ain't seen him with Jeanie. We don't know he's with Jeanie. He didn't come right up to the house. I caught 'im snoopin' and he don't give his name."

Ronnie nodded. "Last we heard, the cops were looking all over for Jeanie after they burned Bertie down. Could be they caught up with her and she talked her fool head off."

"Me a copper!" I uttered a laugh of sorts. "That's downright funny."

It was, as a matter of fact, as funny as that Lawrence B. Knight could be Prof Glow.

"Funny things happen." Ronnie stepped to me and ran his hands over my clothes. "He's clean." But his hands didn't leave me when they found no gun. He fingered my wallet through my buttoned hip pocket. "Let's have a look at that."

Our first blunder, mine and Jeanie's both. We had overlooked my identifications in my wallet.

I said harshly, "Get your filthy hands off me," and drove my shoulder against Ronnie's bare chest.

He staggered backward and almost lost his balance.

"Hank, take it easy," the woman said sharply. "We don't want shooting."

I turned my head. The rifle had tilted up in the crook of Hank's arm. But his pinched face didn't look menacing. Merely cautious. As for Ronnie, he stood rubbing his chest where my shoulder had struck, and for the moment at least contented himself with glowering.

"Look," I said. "I'm not a small-timer to let any punk maul me or any old geezer with a rifle scare me. It's true you haven't seen me with Jeanie, but that's easily fixed. I walked here to ask Hank to drive back with me in his jeep to pick her up. Let's do it first, and then you can throw your weight around if you still care to."

"That makes sense," the woman said. "Besides, Stan isn't here."

Evidently that was the important thing: Stan wasn't there. The way she said it left no doubt who was the boss.

"He don't get tough with me," Ronnie growled to make clear his own toughness. "You go see if Jeanie's there, Hank, but this character stays here. Leave your gun."

Hank handed his rifle to Ronnie and shambled to the jeep. Keeping me covered, Ronnie backed to the canvas chair and eased down into it.

I took out cigarettes and extended the pack to the woman. She said, "No, thanks," and bent to pick up the pail.

"Let me," I said, and reached down for it.

She didn't release the pail handle. Each of us gripped it. Bent over like that, we faced each other. My eyes shifted down from her corn-silk hair, drawn by her rather splendid breasts half spilling out of the halter in that position. She straightened up with the pail, saying briskly, "I can manage," and my hand slipped away from the handle

Ronnie was leaning forward in the chair, at that moment more intent on the woman than on keeping me covered with the rifle. His gaze followed her stunningly feminine figure as she carried the pail into the house, and there was blatant hunger in his eyes.

I lit a cigarette and for the first time I had a chance to look around. That gray, shingled, weather-beaten house went far back into the last century. It hugged the ground as if it were part of it, and from whatever angle you saw it, it would look two-dimensional, like the paintings of farmhouses in American primitives. White paint elaborated the window frames by arching them in the shape of pagodas.

On the right there was a breezeway connecting the house with the barn. During the rugged down-East winters you used to huddle with your livestock under the same roof, as it were. Now, of course, there was no livestock, because obviously for a long time this hadn't been a farm of any kind. Nothing was planted in the meadows sweeping toward the mountains, and the ruin into which the barn had been allowed to crumple was no place for domestic animals.

Another kind of animal was now inhabiting the farm—gangsters from cities. And here I was among them, and my task was to persuade them that I was one of them.

Chapter Eight

The woman came out of the house. She said to Ronnie, "I put up water to heat for the dishes."

"It's Fatso's turn. I washed the lunch dishes."

"Fatso helped me get dinner."

"Hell, why don't Stan do anything?"

"I do more than my share and Stan's share too."

Grunting, Ronnie returned part of his attention to me. The woman stood quiet and relaxed beside the door and looked out at the mountains that were fading with the coming of night.

"Are you Stan's wife?" I asked her.

She adjusted the halter a trifle higher over her breasts—an automatic, abstracted gesture intended more for comfort than for modesty. "Yes," she said. "Mrs. Crocker."

Stan's full name, then, was Stan Crocker. That rang no bell, any more than had the names of Bertie Bride and Prof Glow. I wasn't up on the criminal Who's Who, but give me time.

The jeep appeared from among the trees. Jeanie rode beside Hank. "Hi," she sang out brightly to all of us. Ronnie stood up, the rifle dipping. I strode over to where the jeep was rolling to a stop.

"Why didn't you tell me who you was?" Hank said as he climbed out. "Glad to know you, Prof."

He extended a leathery hand. After I had shaken it, he hurried over to the two who were now standing by the pump.

"The bags are in the back seat," Jeanie said.

As I pulled them out, I whispered, "They're suspicious."

"What do you expect if you just come barging in and refuse to give a name? Hank said Ronnie got mean. Don't let Ronnie throw you. He's naturally mean. You nervous, honey?"

"A little."

"There's nothing to worry about. Hank helped me back your car off the road on some grass so a towing car can get to Stan's car. Here's the keys."

I dropped the keys into my pocket and picked up the bags and Jeanie and I strolled over to join the others.

"Prof Glow hisself," Hank was telling them enthusiastically. "You know, from out West. That Prof Glow. Ain't no bigger shot out that way." He turned his head. "Ain't that who he is, Jeanie?"

"Of course," Jeanie said. "But don't blow it around. He's laying low."

"Ain't a better place," Hank said.

Ronnie shifted his feet uneasily. His finger was off the rifle trigger. "Jees, Prof, why didn't you say so? You can't blame a guy for being careful."

"I don't have to explain myself to every wise punk."

"Well, we gotta be careful here," Ronnie insisted.

If Prof Glow was a lad whose mere presence struck terror into the hearts of minor gangsters, I had to act the part. "But you don't have to be dumb," I said crisply. "And get rid of that gun."

The way he meekly obeyed gave me my first experience with the heady sensation of power. He leaned the rifle against the house.

Elsa Crocker spoke in that quiet tone of hers. "Have you got it, Jeanie?"

"Sure thing," Jeanie said. "How're you doing, Elsa? Slaving away again for these heels?"

They stood together, the ripe-bodied woman and the slender girl— Jeanie taller, prettier, and, by contrast with the other, now more than ever looking like an unworldly child.

"I don't mind cooking, and the boys help," Elsa said. "Is he staying?"

The question referred to me, but she asked it of Jeanie, as if I were incapable of answering.

I spoke up for myself. "Any objection?"

"I'm not sure how Stan will feel about it," she said exclusively to Jeanie.

"Who the hell's Stan?" Jeanie said. "Prof's got a slew of guys on his payroll ten times bigger than Stan. Anyway, Prof knows all about the Knoxville caper. He was wise already when I met him in New York last night."

"It didn't require great deduction." I was determined to say my own piece. "The papers carried the story Saturday, the day after the caper, and then yesterday I read that Bertie was burned down in Darson and that the girl who was with him had been identified as Jeanie Tropp. You don't expect me to yell copper, do you?"

Hank chuckled. "That's funny, Prof Glow yellin' copper. Only thing is, Prof, I ain't got no more rooms empty unless you double up with Ronnie or Fatso."

"Who's using the room I had last month?" Jeanie asked.

"Had it waitin' for you and Bertie," Hank said. "Your clothes are still in it. But that's the last empty room, and Prof here will have to double up with—"

Jeanie cut in, "He'll double up with me," and smiled her naive, small-mouthed smile and fluffed her light-brown hair.

Hank looked pleased; that solved the problem of enough rooms to go around. A shadow crossed Ronnie's face; possibly he had nurtured a hope of replacing the dead Bertie Bride in bed. And Elsa Crocker had a comment.

"You don't waste time, do you, Jeanie?" she said quietly.

"Is it your business?" Jeanie retorted.

"I suppose not."

"Then shut up," Jeanie said without sounding particularly disagreeable. She hugged my arm. "Let's go up and change our clothes, honey."

We went into the house.

Hank was right behind us. In the big center hall he said, "They pay in advance, Prof. No tellin' when one of you'll light out. A hundred bucks a week." He held out his hand palm up. "That'll be two hundred bucks for both."

"That's a lot more than last time," Jeanie protested.

"Last time there wasn't no heat on you folks. I'm takin' a big chance."

"What a racket!" Jeanie said. "No electricity and no running water and we got to do the cooking ourselves."

"I clean the house and pay for the food. Steak we had tonight. Meat twice today, and how them guys eat!"

The haggling was pointless. My wallet contained some thirty-five dollars, but I couldn't say so. Prof Glow wouldn't go anywhere without a fat bank roll. I looked at Jeanie.

She understood. "Honey, didn't you put your big bills in the bag?"

"Yes."

"You can wait till we unpack, Hank. You don't think Prof will do you out of a lousy two C's?"

"I get the dough tonight," Hank stated flatly. "A week in advance. Okay, Prof?"

"Okay," I said, because there wasn't anything else I could say in his presence.

Hank drifted off. He wasn't required to show us up to our room; Jeanie knew where it was. I tagged after her up the stairs.

It was a nice enough room, a large corner room with cross ventilation and a fine view of the mountains through uncurtained windows.

The dark-wood bed had an immense, ornately carved headboard and was covered by the usual patchwork quilt. A corner washstand held a chipped porcelain basin, and under it stood a galvanized pail. Two hundred dollars a week. Criminals were easily exploited.

I wiped my face with my pocket handkerchief. It seemed to me that for the last half hour I had been holding my breath.

Jeanie kicked off her shoes. "You didn't do so bad, honey, but don't push it. Prof Glow is a very refined guy. You talked too hard-boiled for him."

"That's what I get for watching gangsters in the movies."

"Prof is no mug. He's real class. Mingles in society. Just act yourself."

"If I acted myself," I said, "I would never have come here in the first place. And I don't see how I can stay. I've only enough money for both of us for one day. I can't cash a check here and I can't wire my brother for money because I can't use my real name."

She was pulling her dress over her head. She spoke through it. "I'm loaded, honey. I got plenty for both of us."

"No."

She flung the dress on the bed. "My God, are we going to have another argument?" She pressed herself against me. "If it'll make you feel better, let's call it a loan. You can pay me back when you can cash a check. Where's that kiss, honey?"

I held her against me.

"Um, good," she, said. "Ain't you glad we're here?"

"Yes."

"Light the lamp, honey."

Twilight was closing in fast. I released her.

As I removed the globe from the kerosene lamp, I said, "Is the holdup money in your valise?"

She was pulling out a drawer of the ponderous mahogany dresser, which could have been as old as the house. "Yeah. Half of it."

"Why only half?"

"Bertie and Stan split it right afterward so if one was caught it wouldn't be all lost."

"That would make it about ten thousand dollars, according to the papers."

"I guess so. I didn't count it."

"I assume the bag has a false bottom."

"So you looked inside?"

"Not thoroughly," I said. "I'm not very experienced at such things, though my education is progressing. You took a big chance leaving it in my car."

"It wouldn't have been a big chance lugging it around with me." Hands on hips, she appraised her body approvingly in the mirror. "Maybe the real reason was I wanted an excuse to see you again."

"That could've been a highly expensive excuse."

"Could be I figured you were worth it. What would you've done if you'd found the dough?"

"Probably turned it over to the police. But I don't know. I'm no longer sure of anything about myself, except that I know I wouldn't have transported the loot for you."

"Larry!" That was one of the few times she called me by name. I had the wick trimmed and the lamp lit; I replaced the globe and saw that her eyes were anxious. "You're not getting ideas?" she said.

"Isn't it too late for ideas? In effect, I've become an accessory to the holdup."

"You sure have. If you stepped out of line, the cops would jump on you anyway, and if they lct you go, the boys would kill you." Her features relaxed. "But you never would, would you, honey?"

"No. I remain a funny guy."

She carried her valise over to the dresser. I removed my jacket and went to hang it up in the closet. Besides several dresses, the closet held a man's blue serge suit and a pair of linen slacks. Bertie Bride's, no doubt. Because of a policeman's bullet, he was not now here in this room with Jeanie, who in fragile underthings was placidly getting settled by transferring clothes from the valise to the dresser.

I couldn't bring myself to hang up my jacket beside the dead man's clothes. I draped it over the back of a chair and sat down and watched the charming curve of her flanks as she crouched in front of a lower drawer.

Her valise was almost empty, but only of its unimportant contents. What was really valuable was out of sight beneath the false bottom.

I said, "I suppose the reason you all gathered up here in June was to plan the Knoxville holdup."

"They talked about it."

"Who was the leader—Bertie Bride or Stan Crocker?"

"You could say both. It was Bertie's idea. He cased the plant. Stan had the men. Ronnie and Fatso are Stan's boys."

"How did you participate?"

"Participate?" Jeanie frowned, then laughed. "Say, you don't think

I was in on the job?"

"You merely waited for Bertie in Darson, was that it?"

"Well, Bertie was a careful planner. Everything doped out in advance. We took a room in a Darson boarding house. Darson was far enough from Knoxville, but not so far he couldn't get there and back in one day. We called ourselves Mr. and Mrs. Baxter, and Bertie said he was a salesman and looking over the territory. That's what he was doing, all right. Friday Stan and his two boys met him in Knoxville and they pulled it. Bertie and Stan split the dough two ways, and Stan and Ronnie and Fatso went to Stoker Hill, and Bertie came back to our room in Darson."

"Was that the final split?"

"No. The idea was for me and Bertie to hang around for a while in Darson, then check out and come up here. The way they arranged it, Bertie and Stan would each get two shares to one apiece for Ronnie and Fatso."

I said, "It hasn't turned out so badly after all. You're here with the rest of the money and you have a man to share this room with you, even though it doesn't happen to be the same man whose clothes were waiting for him in that closet."

"Why, honey," she said happily, "don't tell me you're jealous of poor Bertie!"

"Let's say I'm squeamish."

"Sure, we'll get rid of the clothes." She dropped down on my lap, snuggling in that kittenish way of hers.

During a kiss I heard a car arrive. Outside the house a man said, "Keep the change," and the car drove off and the man said, "I had a little accident, baby," and Elsa's voice said, "Someday you'll break your neck, darling," and he said, "That lousy road," and the voices drifted off.

"That's Stan." Jeanie told me what I had already assumed. "He'll want to see me right away." She left my lap. "Bring up some water, honey, so I can wash?"

I pulled out the pail from under the washstand. It wasn't particularly clean, and neither was the basin.

On the way out to the pump I passed the living room, off the downstairs center hall. Ronnie was in there with the short, fat man I had seen outside the service station in Stoker Hill. I recognized him by his plaid shirt. Fatso, of course. I heard my name mentioned— that is, Prof—but I didn't pause to listen.

It was lighter outside the house than inside, but the mountains were gone. A breeze smelling of growing things had come up. I pumped and water gurgled in the well and gushed out.

Somewhere near me there were voices. I looked about in the gloaming and located two shapes sitting with their backs to me on a wooden bench some distance away. Elsa Crocker's blonde head leaned on a man's shoulder. His arm was about her waist.

I rinsed out the pail and for a minute did no pumping. In the silence I could distinguish words.

"I don't like it," the man said. "Why'd the crazy kid bring him?"

"That's Jeanie for you," Elsa said.

"She's going up in the world," he said. "From Bertie Bride to Prof Glow."

"I don't think that matters to Jeanie," she said. "She's too elemental. She lost her man and had to have another right away. This one isn't quite as handsome as Bertie, but certainly much nicer."

"How long did he say he's staying?"

"He didn't say, but probably as long as Jeanie."

Stan Crocker grunted. "I shouldn't kick. I been worried she'd get picked up or lam with the other half of the dough. Maybe it's a good thing there's somebody here to keep her happy while the cops are looking for her."

The creaking of the pump handle attracted their attention. They turned on the bench. I pretended to be unaware of them and filled the pail to the brim. On the way to the house water sloshed on my shoes.

Jeanie lay stretched out on the patchwork quilt in her underwear. She said, "Ain't it lovely here, honey?"

"Yes."

"Make yourself comfortable. At least take off that necktie. Did you bring any sports clothes?"

"Some, but there's no point changing tonight."

Outside the voices of Elsa Crocker and her husband approached the house. Stan would come up here or very soon we would have to go down to him. He would be the toughest hurdle.

I extracted from my wallet my driver's license and operator's license and union card. One at a time I burned them in an ash tray on the dresser.

Jeanie lifted her soapy face from the washbasin. "What're you doing?"

"Destroying my identity," I said.

Chapter Nine

Jeanie was getting into a summery white dress when somebody knocked. With my hand on the knob, I waited until she had straightened the shoulder straps before I opened the door. A thickset man stepped quickly into our room.

"Hi, Stan," Jeanie greeted him. "They tell me you read the news in the papers."

"I sure did. And I've been listening to it on my car radio." He turned his head to me. "So you're Prof Glow. I'm Stan Crocker."

We shook hands.

His shoulders were impressive. He hadn't more to them than I, but his made him look top-heavy because he was built considerably closer to the ground. What hair he had left was clipped close around the edges. Unlike the others, he wasn't one to discard city clothes simply because he was in the country. He wore a conservative pin-stripe suit and a white dress shirt and a subdued gray necktie. He could have been coming home from an office or from a classroom. I wasn't sure what I had expected a boss holdup man to look like, but his very ordinary face wasn't one that would make you unusually nervous if you met it in an alley. He was well into his forties.

"Staying long?" he asked me amiably.

"That depends on Jeanie."

"The heat's on her and she knows too much. If the cops pick her up, we're all in the soup."

Jeanie said petulantly, "You think I'd sing?"

"Dames!" he explained to me. "You see how it is, Prof. She has to stay here."

"Suits me," I said. "I came East so I wouldn't be seen around for a while."

Stan didn't care for that. "Somebody gunning for you? We got enough troubles of our own here."

I made myself smile patronizingly. "A businessman like me has more trouble dodging subpoenas than slugs. A state investigating committee wants to ask me questions. I prefer not to answer them just yet. Of course; if I'm not welcome . . ."

"Hell, Prof, I didn't mean that. Proud to have you. D'you play chess?"

"Not well."

"The only one here can give me a game is Ronnie, and he stinks."
He looked at Jeanie. "So you managed to bring it with you."

"In there." Negligently she nudged the valise with one of the brown-and-white play shoes into which she had changed.

"What happened?" he asked.

"All I know is Bertie went out around twelve o'clock for cigars. Monday morning that was. A minute after he left I heard shooting. I looked out the window. Bertie was laying on the sidewalk. He was so still I knew he was dead, but they were still blazing away at him. I grabbed this bag that had the dough in it and tore down the stairs and out the back door."

"You mean it was a raid and they didn't surround the house?"

"They must've got there just as Bertie was coming out," Jeanie said. "They were busy shooting it out with him and I had a chance to run across the backyard. I climbed over a fence and walked up a street and came to some woods. I hid behind the bushes for a few hours. The landlady must've seen me leave and described my dress. If I'd known, I would've changed it right there."

"Did you have time to take your clothes too?"

"Bertie had made a false bottom on this bag for the dough and put some of my clothes on top. Most of my stuff's still in the Darson boardinghouse or the cops got it. Anyway, after a while I walked through the woods and came out on a road and got a lift."

"I heard on the radio you were seen getting into a car just outside Darson."

"Well, I was lucky. I kept away from trains and I don't know how many lifts I got before I reached New York."

"Where did he come in?" Stan indicated me with a thumb.

"In New York. I would've got in touch with you if you had a phone here. My God, you'd think Hank never heard of modern inventions." She was completely composed, completely glib. "I was tired and figured on staying in New York for a day or two before I came on to Stoker Hill. I was walking along Seventh Avenue when who did I meet but Prof Glow. You remember last June Bertie told you I got to know Prof pretty good when we were on the West Coast."

Stan glanced at the bed. "I didn't get the idea you knew him this good."

Jeanie actually blushed, or made herself blush—a picture of youthful undefiled modesty. Shyly she said, "There was nothing between me and Prof till last night."

"Isn't this exclusively my concern and Jeanie's?" I put in. "I wasn't informed that a high moral standard was required of Hank's paying guests."

"Bertie was my pal," Stan said.

"But now he's dead," Jeanie pointed out with sweet reasonableness.

"Yeah, he's dead," Stan said dryly. "Go on, Jeanie."

"I met Prof on Seventh Avenue, like I said. He'd shaved off his mustache and he was a bit heavier but I recognized him right off. He'd read in the papers all about the Knoxville caper and how they'd shot Bertie and were after me. He bought me a dinner and we talked and I told him about Hank's place here, where I was bound for, and—well, here we are."

"Go on, Jeanie," Stan said.

"That's the whole story."

"You left out the important part. Bertie was the most careful guy I knew. How'd the cops catch up with him in Darson?"

"How should I know? Maybe somebody fingered him."

"Who?"

"My God, all I know is there was shooting and I looked out and there was poor Bertie dead on the sidewalk. Maybe he was recognized by somebody in Darson."

"Nobody knew he was on the Knoxville job except us here in Stoker Hill and you."

She threw her cigarette into an ash tray. "Say, listen! Maybe he was recognized leaving the plant."

"We were masked. It went off without a hitch."

"What do you want from me? The cops didn't take me into their confidence about how they found out. They damn near caught me too. Look what I went through to bring the dough here to you. I didn't have to, but I played square with you all the way, didn't I?"

"Sure you did, Jeanie." Stan's tone was placating. "But we got to know the answers to protect ourselves."

"Well, don't ask me. You ought to be grateful I got here with the dough. And you ought to thank Prof for helping me bring it from New York."

"Many thanks, Prof," Stan said.

I would have been happier without those words of appreciation. I waved a hand as if to say it was nothing, that people were all the time doing such little favors for each other, and the atmosphere in the room was quite friendly.

"Now that we have all the dough together," Stan said, "let's get the split over with."

Jeanie fluffed her hair. "I'm in no hurry."

"But the boys are. They're not going to be able to spend it for a while because they're not going anywhere, but they want their hands on it. Let's go downstairs."

He took over possession of the valise, carried it out.

I lingered to turn out the lamp. Jeanie came close to me and whispered, "Stan had me a bit worried, but we're in, honey." She squeezed my arm. "Glad you came?"

"Yes."

In darkness we made our way hand in hand out to the hall and down the stairs.

Light flowed from the living room, or what would more properly be called the parlor in a house with as many years behind it as this. Stan had placed the valise on a table under a hanging kerosene lamp; he was opening it as Ronnie, still bare-chested, looked on. The round little man in the plaid shirt had been about to close the door. He pulled it wide open to let us enter.

"Hi, Fatso," Jeanie said. "Meet Prof Glow."

He seemed somewhat awed of me and became flustered when Prof Glow, the big shot, shook his hand.

At the table Stan grunted, "Looks like all of it." He had lifted the false bottom out of the valise. Fatso and Jeanie and I joined Stan at the table.

Compactly that half of the payroll loot covered the real bottom of the valise. Each neat stack was bound by its original bank wrapper.

Ronnie said bitterly, "Fifty grand Bertie claimed it would be. Maybe sixty."

"Twenty ain't peanuts," Fatso said.

"It ain't fifty or sixty like Bertie claimed it would be." Ronnie looked at Stan. "A lousy twenty grand."

Stan said softly, "You wouldn't have an idea, Ronnie, there was more than twenty grand?"

Ronnie lowered his popeyes. "I'm not saying you and Bertie held out."

"I'm glad you're not." Stan smiled; I would have been mighty uneasy if he had smiled at me like that. "These are the breaks. So it isn't fifty. It's a little over twenty, We're lucky Jeanie got here. Otherwise it would be only ten. Any more complaints, Ronnie?"

"I wasn't complaining." Ronnie glanced about and found a change of subject. "How come Prof is in on it?"

"He's not." Stan transferred his smile to me, and this time it was wholly affable. "Mind leaving us for a while?"

I not only didn't mind; I very much preferred not be present. I said, "I'll go pick up my car."

"Hank will drive you," Stan offered.

"I'd rather walk, if somebody will lend me a flashlight."

Stan pulled one out of his hip pocket and accompanied me to the door. Jeanie, sitting cross-legged on a Mission oak chair, blew me a kiss. Stan closed the door after me.

A balmy breeze made the night fine for walking. As soon as I was in among the woods, I felt an easing of my nerves, my muscles, even my bones. I had been more on edge than I had admitted to myself. Now here I was going away from that house, and there was nothing to stop me from going on all the way home.

There was nothing to stop me and if I drove all night I would be back in my apartment in Queens by mid-morning. And I would find Marjorie doing the minimum of house cleaning to keep the apartment in some sort of order or reading the current best-seller or already watching television, and with a martyred smile she would lift her face to be kissed, and she would say, "I knew you wouldn't stay with that illiterate slut for any length of time, Larry, because you're really not the type," and I would make no answer because I would have no answer, and I would shower and take a nap and wake up to—what? I would wake up to Lawrence B. Knight, who, in the final analysis, hadn't run off with anybody or from anybody so much as he had run away from himself, and had hardly got started when he was back in meek confession of utter defeat.

I reached the car. It was possible, with enough effort, to turn the car around here and head it back to New York. I hesitated for perhaps five seconds, then drove back to that ancient gray house where three holdup men and a girl who was my bedmate were dividing up the loot from an armed robbery.

As the car reached the knoll on which the house stood, a shape moved across the outer fringe of the headlights. I glimpsed bare legs and blonde hair before the headlights swung away. I pulled my coupé up beside the jeep.

An argument was going on inside the house. There was a jumble of furious voices, each trying to override the others. Jeanie's was the shrill one, and another almost as high-pitched with anger said, "I'll be damned if I will!" and the voices tapered off to mutterings.

I got out of the car. Under a maple standing alone and magnificent where the ground started to slope away to the meadow, a tiny spot of light glowed, faded, glowed again. I snapped on the flashlight and walked to the cigarette smoker.

As protection from the evening coolness she had put on a thin cotton jacket. It hardly reached her thighs, which looked burnished in the flashlight beam. Because of the rolled-up shorts, she appeared to be wearing nothing but the jacket and open sandals on her bare feet. Leaning against the tree trunk, she watched me approach.

"Your light is in my eyes," Elsa Crocker said.

"Sorry."

I turned it off. Here under the tree starlight could not penetrate, but whenever she drew on the cigarette the lower part of her face was gouged dimly out of darkness.

She said conversationally, "Did you drive from the West Coast?"

Every question any of them asked was a possible trap. This one was obvious. She must have noticed the New York license plate.

"I came east by train," I told her. "Last night when Jeanie asked me to drive her here, I borrowed that Chevrolet from a friend in New York. He said I could use it as long as I wanted to."

"A man like you must have many people under obligation to him."

She dropped the cigarette and stepped on it. I could see nothing at all of her now, but the sense of her femininity so close to me had a physical impact.

"I had an idea Prof Glow was older," she said.

It occurred to me that she might be more dangerous than Stan or Ronnie.

"I'm not exactly a kid," I said. "Did we ever meet before? I'm sure I would have remembered you."

"No, we never met, but . . ." She didn't finish it.

The argument in the house again rose noisily. Jeanie's voice dominated the rest, then Stan roared, "Shut up, all of you!" and abruptly there was a silence as deep as that under this tree. Stan was very much the boss here,

I said, "They're sore, I suppose, because there isn't enough take after all that planning and risk and one of them getting killed."

Elsa uttered a short, bitter laugh. "There's never enough. Before I met Stan, he had served two years in the pen, and all he would have got out of the job was three hundred dollars. Were you ever in jail?"

"I've been lucky."

"Not lucky. Big. The big shots like you get it all and are never hurt."

"Must I apologize for being big?"

"Oh, that's not it," she said wearily. "But this was going to be the last time. Stan promised me. The big caper. Fifty thousand dollars at least. That was what Bertie Bride sold Stan. Just this one, Stan told me, and after it he would lay off for good. But now he'll have an excuse after a few months. It's never enough."

I had nothing to say. Silence merged with darkness.

"I'm going in," she said suddenly. "Good night."

"Good night."

Starlight touched her when she stepped out from under the tree, and she became a shadow drifting toward the house. I restrained the impulse to turn on the flashlight and watch her walk, watch her thighs ripple and her hips undulate.

After a while I went up to my room and lit the kerosene lamp and took off my shirt and shoes and sat waiting for Jeanie.

Ten minutes later she entered, carrying a paper bag. Petulantly she flung it on the dresser.

"Of all the nerve!" she burst out. "You know what Ronnie and Fatso had the nerve to say? They said I shouldn't get a cent. I lugged that dough all the way here from Darson, and they claim just because Bertie's dead I shouldn't get his two shares."

I didn't comment. I wished she would leave me completely out of this. "They couldn't pull anything like that on me," she went on. "I was right here when Bertie planned the caper with them and they agreed how they would split. Two shares for Bertie, two for Stan, one each for Ronnie and Fatso. Okay, it wasn't as much as Bertie said it would be, but it was still around thirty-five a share, and me getting Bertie's two shares would be seven grand for me. But the nerve of those guys, they said because Bertie's dead I'm not entitled to his. They said I wasn't his wife and got no right to his dough. I told them. I said, 'Didn't I level with you heels?' I said, 'I could've kept all the dough in my bag, the ten grand that was half the take, but like a dope I brought it here and I want Bertie's two shares.' That's what you get for being honest."

Jeanie removed her shoes.

"I imagine this was one of the more profitable capers," I said, "but so far I haven't been impressed by crime as one of the better-paying professions."

"Ask Prof Glow. He makes it pay."

"So Elsa said. The big shots always make out. The rest never do."

"You been talking to her?"

"Briefly."

"What d'you think of her?"

"I don't know. She's very quiet and seems to be lonely."

"She's a quiet one, but why lonely? She and Stan are nuts over each other. You're not lonely with a man you like." Jeanie yawned; her rage had melted away. "Stan's a pretty decent guy. He said we'd split five ways instead of the six they'd planned. Ronnie and Fatso didn't like it, but that's how it was. Stan got two shares and me and Ronnie and Fatso one apiece. It could've been worse. My cut is over four grand." She yawned some more. "I'm pooped, honey, all this traveling and everything. Let's hit the hay."

"All right."

I remained in the chair until she had finished dropping a pink nightgown over her head. She looked very sweet in it, quite girlish. As I changed into pajamas, she turned down the patchwork quilt and the two blankets. This was Wednesday night and we had met for the first time on Monday, and here we were going not so much to bed as to sleep, a man and a girl already in the routine of living together.

There was a knock on the door.

"Yes?" I said.

"Them two hundred bucks," Hank's voice said through the door. "You promised you'd pay tonight."

Jeanie whispered from the bed, "On the dresser, honey."

I dug out of the paper bag a bundle of twenty-dollar bills. I broke the wrapper and counted out ten bills and opened the door wide enough to thrust them out to Hank.

"Thanks, Prof."

I locked the door and finished buttoning my pajama jacket. All of a sudden I started to laugh.

"What's so funny?" Jeanie said.

"Probably not very funny. Up to now this was a kind of lark. A caper in the dictionary meaning of the word rather than the gangster meaning. But I didn't quite bargain on becoming a kept man, and on holdup loot at that. What's required is a sense of humor."

"Don't you ever stop talking silly?" she said testily. "Put out the light and come to bed."

I put out the light and went to bed.

Chapter Ten

The best view of all was from the outhouse. In front of it the ground fell away so sharply that when you left the door open you had an impression of being suspended in space above the sweep of rocky meadows undulating toward the distant, thickly wooded mountains.

An up-to-date note had been injected. Instead of the traditional Sears catalogue, there were *New Yorker* magazines and comic books.

I stepped out into the morning sun. In T-shirt and lightweight slacks and fresh from a cold-water shave in my room, I felt cool and presentable. I followed a footpath past the breezeway to a rear door and entered the kitchen.

Both Crockers were in the kitchen—Elsa washing clothes and Stan eating breakfast. We exchanged cheery good mornings.

This was the largest room in the house, as was sensible. Particularly in the winter, when the heavily embossed kitchen wood stove was the main source of heat, it became sitting room and sometimes bedroom as well as kitchen and dining room. The stove wasn't used in this weather except as a work table; water was boiling on a smoky kerosene range that stood beside it. The only modern touch was a wooden counter in which was set a two-basin sink, but there it ended, without even an indoor pump. Every drop of water used had to be lugged in from the well in front of the house.

"Would you like your eggs fried or scrambled?" Elsa asked me.

"Scrambled, please."

She scraped soapsuds from her arms and set fire to a second kerosene burner. This morning she was all in white, polo shirt and shorts and sneakers, and the contrast enriched the bronze of her bare legs and arms and throat.

The huge round table was covered with red-and-white checked oilcloth. No two chairs were alike, except that all were painted red. I pulled one out and sat down opposite Stan.

This morning he had discarded his jacket, and he had made one other concession to the season and place by leaving unbuttoned the starched collar of his shirt.

"Where's Jeanie?" he asked.

"She's still asleep."

Stan put down his coffee cup. "It's ten-thirty. What's she think she is, a grand lady?"

I said, "The poor kid's had a rough time these last few days. Besides, what's wrong with sleeping late in the country?"

"What's right about Elsa's getting up early and making breakfast without help from Jeanie?"

Elsa turned from the stove. "She'll make lunch, darling."

"Yeah, like the last time she was here," Stan growled. "She'll start making lunch and say she's stuck and call you to help her and you'll finish it. Nuts to that. You do too much work around here, baby."

"I'll be glad to pitch in," I offered. "Just give me orders. Can I start by doing the dishes?"

Elsa brought me a glass of juice. "It's Fatso's turn this morning. I'm sure Jeanie will cooperate. Do you care for tomato juice?"

"My favorite."

"I hate the stuff," Stan said. "Baby, tell Hank to buy some fresh oranges for a change." He drained his coffee and rose. "I'm driving to Stoker Hill in the jeep to see how bad my car was damaged yesterday."

As he passed his wife on the way out of the kitchen, he affectionately patted her hip.

And as soon as he was gone and we were alone together, there was tension in the kitchen. The way there had been last night under the maple tree. I couldn't quite explain it to myself. I sat back and looked at her scrambling eggs.

Through a window sunlight poured over her, brilliant on her piled-up corn-silk hair. Her white shorts were rolled up as high as her blue shorts had been last night. She had the thighs for it and you couldn't blame her for showing them off. My impression of her last evening had been that she was somewhat lush-bodied. But that wasn't it at all. She was firmly built, gracefully curved. Her ripeness was the firm ripeness of a peach picked at the right moment.

She was one of the few women I had ever seen, perhaps the only one, who looked every bit a woman.

She brought a plate of bacon and eggs to me, and her full breasts, molded by the rather thin polo shirt, stirred as she walked. Her eyes met mine as I stared at her. She flushed and placed the plate in front of me with her face averted and returned to the sink.

I said to her back as she resumed washing clothes, "Don't you find it dull here?"

"Not very, as long as Stan is with me."

She was telling me off, though, I hadn't meant it that way. I had a woman of my own, didn't I? I ate.

After a while I said, "You're not like the others here."

"Aren't I?"

"That's what I mean—that 'Aren't I?' While I don't approve of that rather affected contraction, only an educated person would use it. And you seem—well, refined."

"Refined!" she echoed, and uttered a brief laugh. Leaning against the kitchen sink, she faced me. "We've something in common, Prof. They say you once taught school."

And Larry Knight and Prof Glow had that in common too. To that extent I could remain in character.

"Did you teach?" I said.

"I never got that far. I quit teachers' college after a year." Her mouth went wry. "Somehow you sink lower when you start off being refined. Even as you, Prof. You and your houses."

"Houses?" I muttered before I remembered. Prof Glow's main source of income was from brothels. I said, "None of us is in a position to discuss morals."

"No, but I think there are limits. Stan is what he is, but he has standards. He respects women, and he very much respects me. Even if he stopped caring for me, he would die before he did to me what you did to Mary Creed."

A shrug could be my only comment. I would have to do a lot of shrugging here.

"Do you take coffee or milk?" she said.

"Coffee, please."

Elsa placed a cup and saucer before me and brought the coffeepot from the stove. She stood close to me as she poured, and if I had moved my hand an inch or two I would have touched her thigh.

"I knew Mary Creed well before she went west to try her luck in Hollywood," she told me. "She didn't make it and then got mixed up with you."

I reached for the milk bottle and the sugar bowl. I stirred the coffee.

She was back at the sink. "Mary used to write me. I know what you used to be to each other. And recently she wrote what you had done to her and how she had ended up in one of your houses. How could you do such a thing?"

I drank. She kept looking at me, and I wondered what Prof Glow would have replied, if anything, and if he would have cringed inwardly the way I did under her contempt.

"Then you don't deny it?" she said, refusing to let go of the subject in the face of my silence.

Another shrug, but even the taciturn Prof Glow would eventually have to open his mouth for more than drinking coffee. I drawled, "I'm not in the habit of discussing my personal affairs with everybody I meet."

That, at any rate, ended it.

I set down the empty cup. "Thanks for the breakfast, Elsa. Is there anything I can do around here? I wield a mean broom."

"Hank does all the cleaning," she said crisply.

She didn't care for Prof Glow. Along with his name, I had taken over his sins. I wandered out of the house.

"Morning, Prof."

Fatso sprawled on a reclining aluminum chair under the big sugar maple. His plaid shirt was open, showing flabby, hairless flesh. The comic book he was reading dipped. I sauntered over to him.

"Prof, I wanna ask you something. Did Hi Globeman ever speak to you about me?"

Another name. Jeanie had assured me that all I would have to do was remain smilingly uncommunicative, but it wasn't turning out to be easy.

"About you?" I muttered, sparring.

"Tom Evergreen's my real name. Or maybe he said Fatso Evergreen. I seen Hi last winter in Philly and he said maybe you'd have a job for me. Did he speak to you, huh, Prof?"

"I don't recall."

"I'd like to tie up with a big organization like yours. You don't have so many worries. I'll do anything, I'm a good man. Ask Hi."

At the south side of the house Hank was cutting wild grass with a scythe. That would be about the only graceful thing he did. I watched the clean, coordinated movements of his wiry old body.

"You got room for me?" Fatso persisted. "I bet there's hundreds of guys on your payroll."

"Don't rush me."

"Yeah, sure. But keep me in mind, huh, Prof?"

"We'll see," I said.

"How's Hi doing?"

I shrugged.

Elsa Crocker appeared around the rear corner of the house. On her hip she carried a small wicker basket.

"Fatso, you're to wash the dishes now," she called.

"In a minute."

Where Hank was scything, a clothesline was strung between two small trees. She set the basket down on the ground and started to hang up clothes. Dazzling sunlight glinted in her hair, laved her bronzed skin. As she lifted her arms to the clothesline, her breasts lifted also, tightly against the polo shirt.

"Man, is she stacked!" Fatso had sat up. "I'll tell you about Stan. He don't look at another dame. Why should he? Where would he find anything else as good as that?"

Hank was leaning on his scythe and speaking to her. And beyond them Ronnie had appeared. His palm rolled with steady rhythm on his bare chest, but the rest of him was as motionless as the outhouse against which he stood.

It was as if her coming out to hang clothes had drawn every man in the place but her husband.

"Does she do the washing too?" I asked Fatso.

"Naw. Hank takes our laundry in to Concord. Anyway, we don't wear so much around here. She don't either. Them's her own things." Fatso cackled. "Lookit, a brassiere. I would've bet she didn't wear 'em."

Elsa picked up the basket. "Fatso, the dishes!" she called.

He pushed himself up from the chair. "Orders from the big boss herself," he told me with a sheepish grin.

Elsa had returned into the house. Ronnie, having nothing left to watch, moved off. Only Hank and I remained outside.

I walked over to Hank, who was honing his scythe "It's going to be another scorcher today," I said.

"Lucky you ain't in New York. Them sidewalks is like fryin' pans." He pushed his frayed Panama hat back over his wispy gray hair and scowled. "Trouble's comin'."

"About what?"

"That woman. Elsa. I'm gettin' old and you got yourself a nice piece of your own. But them two boys, Ronnie and Fatso. Young bucks. Nothin' for them to do and no woman around for them. And there's Elsa paradin' around half naked all the time. It ain't healthy. Bound to be trouble."

"They would be afraid of Stan."

"He'll tear the heart out of anybody puts a finger on her. But young men. Sap runnin' high. Especially that Ronnie. I ain't worried so much about Fatso. No harm in him. But that Ronnie. All the time lookin' at her with his popeyes like he wants to eat her up." Hank shook his head. "I don't hanker for no trouble. It'll be bad for me on account this is my place."

I recalled the first words I had heard Elsa utter last evening when I had come upon her and Ronnie in front of the house. Something like "I'm not going to tell him but don't do that again." Evidently Ronnie was ridden by an emotion stronger than fear of Stan.

"Why don't you ask Stan to send Ronnie away?" I suggested.

"He don't want Ronnie runnin' around loose while the heat's on 'em so strong. Anyway, I'd be losin' Ronnie's board." Hank mopped his brow with a blue bandanna "I gotta get this patch cleared."

I said, "Is there anywhere to go swimming around here?"

"There's a crik down that hollow behind them trees. But you won't do no swimmin'. Not deep enough."

"Is it deep enough for a bath?"

"Some of 'em do it."

Doubtless he himself never had.

I followed a footpath down from the knoll. Through a copse of young trees the creek ran shaded and clear. At this spot it was some twenty feet across and fairly free of rocks. The trees formed a protective screen all around, particularly from the house. I would, at any rate, be able to get wet.

I shed my clothes and stepped in. Icy water stabbed my legs. I hesitated, then heroically waded forward. At the deepest, water reached my knees and certainly didn't get any warmer. Clenching my teeth, I sat down like an old woman dunking herself at the beach. After I'd caught my breath, I ducked my head under. That was as much of that bath as I could endure. I fled.

A flat rock jutted partly out into the creek from the bank. I stretched out on it and soon stopped shivering. The sun felt fine on my wet body. I was at peace.

Somebody approached humming "Loch Lomond" considerably off-key. Startled out of a half doze, I sat up. There was probably not enough time to leap for my clothes or, closer at hand, a tree. I twisted my torso away from the path and looked over my shoulder. Jeanie appeared in a strapless sun dress. She had brought along two Turkish towels and a cake of soap.

"Hank told me you were down here," she said. "Were you in already?"

"Brrr!" I said.

"It's not so bad when you get used to it."

I propped myself up on an elbow and watched her shrug out of the sun dress and kick off her slippers. Those two items had been all her attire. Soap in hand, she nonchalantly stepped into the creek. I laughed aloud at her expression of shock. She cowered in water halfway up to her knees, and at that moment she was a dead ringer for September Morn—tight and slender and cream-skinned and so young. After a moment she let herself fall in full-length, an act of sheer courage. She came up sputtering and serenely proceeded to soap herself.

Under the circumstances, I couldn't remain craven. I joined her in the creek and took over use of the soap. After we had both ducked under to wash off the soap, we scrambled onto the big rock and let the sun dry us.

"Ain't this lovely, honey?" she said.

"Um. This and you both."

"Why did you run out on me this morning?"

"You were sleeping peacefully."

"Don't ever do that to me again. I was so disappointed when I woke up and you weren't there."

"I forgot that a kept man has to keep himself on tap."

Pouting, she put an inch or two of space between "Do you always have to spoil it by talking that way?"

"It's true, isn't it?"

"No, it ain't. I told you if you feel like that about money you can pay it back sometime."

I slid an arm under her shoulders. "Look, Jeanie. Why do we have to stay here?"

"You know why."

"I've been thinking that you'd be as safe if we went off and rented a bungalow in some remote place."

"This is remote. Besides, Stan wouldn't let me go. The cops have pictures of me. I told Stan last night. Bertie was a camera bug and he had loads of snapshots of me in his bag that the cops got hold of in Darson. Stan says those pictures are already in every police station and maybe in the papers too. He don't care what happens to me so much, but he's scared I'll sing if I'm picked up. He's watching out for himself and his boys, and I can't blame him." She snuggled. "Anyway, what's wrong with this?"

I said, "Did you ever hear of Hi Globeman and Mary Creed?"

"Who're they?"

"Hi Globeman works for Prof Glow. Fatso knows him and asked about him."

"Lots of guys work for Prof. I never knew but a few in his organization. What'd you tell Fatso?"

"I brushed him off. Mary Creed's name was brought up by Elsa. It appears that they were friends and that Mary Creed was once Prof Glow's mistress or something like that."

"I don't know nothing about his girlfriends. Like I told you, don't say yes or no. You don't talk about your affairs. If they get too nosy, tell 'em off. But friendly and refined. Not tough."

"I'm learning how to act refined," I said.

There was no breeze. The sun was as hot as the water had been cold. We were dry now without having had to use the towels.

I said, "We'd better put some clothes on. Somebody might come down."

She stirred against me. Her skin felt very warm to the touch.

"This is heaven," she murmured.

"Uh-huh."

"Love me, honey?"

"Uh-huh. But our privacy might be invaded at any moment."

"We'll hear anybody coming."

"I doubt that we'll be listening."

"I don't care. You ran out on me this morning. You can't again. You can't now, honey."

The sun blazed down on us.

Chapter Eleven

Thursday the heat wave broke. Friday evening it started to rain, and for two dreary nights and days it didn't let up.

Saturday afternoon dampness invaded the house, mingling with a chillness that additional clothing couldn't banish from our bones. It was more like September than July. Elsa suggested building a fire in either the kitchen stove or the parlor Franklin stove, but Hank had driven off to shop for food, and nobody else roused himself.

I sat on a Mission oak chair at a parlor window with a pile of popular magazines Elsa had given me permission to bring down from her room. I leafed through one after another and couldn't maintain interest and looked out at the gray rain swirling over the fields. Behind me Stan and Ronnie played chess. Fatso, his lips moving soundlessly, struggled with the harder words in his comic book and occasionally asked me to define one. In the kitchen Jeanie and Elsa were baking pies. A household like any others, its members bored by the need to keep out of the rain.

Suddenly Ronnie exclaimed, "Aw, nuts!" He pushed his chair back from the table. "No radio, no television, no nothing. At least we should go to the movies."

Stan picked up a white bishop and held it. "You'd get movies in the pen. Once every week if they pick out good one for you."

"Hell, you let us go to the store in Stoker Hill. What's so different with Concord?"

"Concord has cops," Stan said.

Fatso looked up from his comic book. "It'd be a twenty-year rap, Ronnie. Life for you, maybe, on account of you're a three-time loser. We got plenty to eat here and soft beds. I never had it so good."

"You!" Ronnie sneered. "You got it good when they let you sit on your tail all day." He spoke to Stan. "We're a thousand miles from Knoxville, and a guy's gotta do some living."

"You don't want a movie. You'd head straight for a bar and then for a dame." Stan set down the bishop, endangering the black queen. "You'd get stinkin' drunk. You'd go on a tear. Maybe your tongue would waggle."

"You ain't my nursemaid," Ronnie grumbled. "You don't tell me when I should wipe my nose."

Stan said softly, "It's your move."

Ronnie placed his hands flat on the table. Over the chessmen his protruding eyes rested bleakly on Stan. A killer's eyes, I thought, the first time I had ever seen anything like them. And that was, after all, what he was by trade, and Stan too and Fatso—men who worked with guns in their hands and masks on their faces and lived always in violence and fear and resentment.

Stan didn't trouble to look up from the board.

"Prof, you got a big organization." Fatso was anxiously appealing to me. "You know all the ropes. How long d'you think we should sit here tight?"

I very much didn't want any part of this.

Stan turned to Fatso. "I'm running this show, not Prof or anybody else."

"That's right," I said, perhaps too eagerly. "I run my business and you men run yours."

Stan said, "Your move, Ronnie."

Slowly Ronnie pulled his hands off the table. He moistened his lips. You could see how he hated to knuckle under to his boss and how he dared not to. Then he lifted his queen and the tension was over. Fatso returned to the derring-do of comic book criminals and I left the parlor.

I wandered through the breezeway and into the barn. The roof was in better condition than the walls; rain trickled through in only a few spots. In a dry corner I found cordwood and kindling. This would give me something to do. I carried a load of wood into the kitchen.

Jeanie was trimming the edges of an unbaked pie and Elsa was sticking one into a portable tin oven on top of the kerosene range. Both were in slacks and sweaters. Jeanie's outfit made her look boyish, but nothing could detract from Elsa's intrinsic womanliness.

"Oh, good," Jeanie said when I entered with the wood. "Now we'll be able to bake the rest of the pies in a real oven."

Elsa watched me put in paper and kindling as if she'd never seen it done before.

I lit the paper. "Anything wrong with the way I build a fire?"

"I'm not used to men who stir themselves without being nagged," Elsa said dryly.

Jeanie put an arm about me. "Isn't he sweet, Elsa? I told you." And she kissed my cheek and with playful sensuality rolled her hips against me.

I wished she wouldn't exhibit such possessiveness in public. There was plenty of time and opportunity up in our room. Perhaps too much. I was especially annoyed by her doing it in front of Elsa. I eased away from her and raised the stove lid and added another log.

Pie and coffee brought the other men into the kitchen, and the warm stove kept them there. Somebody suggested poker. Fatso dug up cards and we seated ourselves around the big kitchen table. Everybody joined in, including the women. When Hank returned from Concord, it became a seven-handed game.

We played fifty-cent stud, terrifically steep for me, who was used to five-and-ten. But here I was Prof Glow, a professional gambler among other things, and indicated polite tolerance of such small stakes. In my wallet were thirty-six dollars.

I won a bit and lost a bit. By the time we knocked off for supper, I had fourteen dollars left.

After we had eaten and the dishes had been stacked in the sink, we resumed with a dollar limit. On my first hand I pulled two pairs, but was completely wiped out by Stan's three jacks.

I didn't know what to do then. Prof Glow couldn't confess himself broke, and he couldn't say he wanted no more poker when he had just sat down to the resumption of the game.

Jeanie excused herself and left the room. She was aware of my predicament; I had an idea where she was going. Elsa dealt. I caught kings back-to-back, but I had to fold because I hadn't a dollar to open. The hand wasn't quite finished when Jeanie returned. She leaned against my back and kissed my ear. "For luck, honey," she said, and I felt her hand slip into my jacket pocket and leave something there. It turned out to be a stake of several hundred dollars.

By the time we knocked off at four in the morning, I had lost most of that roll.

Next day, Sunday, nobody came down until noon. The rain was unrelenting. Still poker weather. At two o'clock we were at it again, and again the stakes were doubled. Two-dollar stud was madness for anybody like me, but I was beginning to absorb the point of view of the others, that money came hard and went easily.

Jeanie slipped another roll of bills into my pocket. I continued to lose.

"You big-shot gamblers!" Fatso chuckled. "You get in a small game like this, Prof, and you can't buy the time of day. I heard you once bet Giggy fifty grand on a card and won. That true, Prof?"

I gave him an enigmatic smile.

"Chip or fold," Ronnie growled at Fatso.

Ronnie was a normally sullen player. The fact that he was an even heavier loser than I didn't improve his disposition.

"Up two bucks," Hank said. He put his grizzled face close to the table to peep at his hole card. He seemed to play mostly by prayer and hunch. Perhaps that was what was required in a poker game, for with irritating consistency he won.

I turned down my cards and considered the other players. Stan stuck strictly to mathematics. When the odds were against him, he couldn't be lured in; when they were on his side, he squeezed every possible cent out of the pot. That was how he and Bertie Bride must have planned the Knoxville caper. Jeanie's play varied between reckless and cautious spurts, according to mood; it was never possible to figure out her hand from the way she chipped. Fatso chattered continually, gloating over good luck, agonizing long and loud over bad. Elsa played the way she did everything else, quietly and competently, and appeared to be in the game only because everybody else was.

It's been said that poker is a good indication of character. Perhaps. But what about me? I was an angle player. I couldn't check myself, even at these stakes. In the modest games I played once a month or so with friends in Queens, I was known as a speculator, a taker of chances. I who had seldom taken a chance in anything else until the last few days. Had my poker playing been all along an expression of the repressed inner man?

We didn't break up until an hour after sunrise.

The rain had ceased some time before, and a visible sun was rising through dispersing clouds. The orgy was over. We were cramped from too much sitting, logy from lack of sleep, stupefied from the overheated, smoke-filled kitchen. I sensed that winner and loser alike were now merely bored.

In our room I counted out thirty-six dollars and tucked the bills into my wallet. That was my own money, my original stake; I had to hold onto it as a small measure, very small, of financial independence. At least I would be able to buy cigarettes without asking Jeanie. Of the seven hundred dollars she had slipped to me during the two days, about a hundred remained. I had lost some six hundred dollars, a fortune to a schoolteacher.

Jeanie was already in bed. When she was sleepy, she got under the covers without dawdling. I told her how I had made out in the game.

"Drop it on the dresser," she said indifferently. "I won a couple of hundred, so together we're only four hundred behind."

"Let's not start that again," I said. "I owe you six hundred, plus two hundred for board. That's eight hundred. By Wednesday, when we pay another week's board, it will be an even thousand."

I went to the window and breathed in the moist early-morning air. Stan came out with a pail, which he filled at the pump. Moments later I heard him ascend the stairs and enter the room across the hall. I thought of Elsa and Stan together in the intimacy of that room, as Jeanie and I were together in here; and I thought of how every moment during those two days of poker I had been acutely aware of Elsa sitting at the table with me. There had been moments, I remembered now, when, amid the smoke and chatter and suspense of falling cards, nobody else had seemed to be there, only the two of us, Elsa and I.

I didn't want to face up to what was happening to me.

"How are you fixed for dough, honey?" Jeanie asked from the bed.

I laid what money of hers I had on the dresser and started to unbutton my shirt. "I've a few thousand saved, and a teacher's credit is good. You'll get your money."

"Someday I'll smack you across the mouth for talking like that," she said. "If you figure you have to pay me back the board dough, it's a hundred a week for your share. I'll pay my own."

"No. At least let me salvage that much pride."

"What's pride got to do with it?"

"Did you pay your own way with Bertie?"

"I didn't have no dough of my own when I was with Bertie. Now I have and you haven't. Honey, you make too much fuss over money."

At such moments I could respect her. I had known too many respectable, virtuous women who determined a man's eligibility as a bedmate by his financial rating.

In a burst of affection, I leaned over the bed and kissed her brow. Her arms pulled me down to her.

But that wasn't what I was after. There was no longer edge to desire, no longer driving hunger. I put her off.

"Tired, honey?" she said, and I said that I was.

But that wasn't it either. I was beginning to understand what it was.

Chapter Twelve

At one o'clock Monday afternoon I was up and dressed. Considering when we had gone to bed, that was an early rising. Jeanie slept on. As far as I could hear and see, so did everybody else.

In the kitchen I found a full pot of freshly made coffee on the kerosene range. That meant that Elsa had already been at work. I sliced a couple of peaches into a bowl of cereal and ate while the coffee heated. I was drinking my second cup of coffee when Elsa entered the kitchen.

"I see you've helped yourself," she said.

"I was properly brought up."

She gave me a curious sidelong glance. Evidently I had said the wrong thing.

"Would you care for scrambled eggs?" she said.

"I've had enough, thanks. Elsa, how would this household get along without you?"

She stooped to the sink cabinet and brought out a pot. "I'm going berry picking," she said, making it a flat and impersonal announcement.

Now that the storm was over and the temperature again up, she had returned to scant attire. Today she wore something more dashing above the rolled-up shorts than a halter or a polo shirt—a very much off-the-shoulders cotton jersey cut so wide and low as to deliberately and remorselessly tantalize the eye.

Holding the pot against her knee by the handle, she looked steadily at me. Our gazes locked, and it seemed to me that there was some sort of communication between us. I found it a little harder to breathe.

"May I go with you?" I said.

"If you wish."

She couldn't have sounded more indifferent, though that didn't change my belief that she had waited for me to ask her. She pulled another pot out of the cabinet and handed it to me.

We descended the west slope of the knoll. I commented on how lush the vegetation was after the long rain. She had nothing to say to that or to anything else. I stopped speaking. Silently we walked side by side.

We reached the edge of a two-acre field of scattered high blueberry bushes. I sidestepped a rock and swerved against her, and our shoulders and hips touched. It was nothing at all, the briefest of inadvertent contacts, but she made it into something big. With a kind of violence she swung away from me.

"Am I that repulsive?" I said banteringly.

She strode to the nearest bush and started to pick blueberries. When I joined her, she moved on to the next bush.

"I can't imagine what I've done," I said.

"If you came to pick berries," she said tartly, "you'd better start."

So her quietness was all on the surface, I thought, a protective mantle that was slipping from her.

I picked. I discovered how little space blueberries covered at the bottom of a pot. After a while I took time off to light a cigarette.

Elsa was some fifty feet away. Her skin seemed to glow with an inner light, as if the sunlight were inside her shining out. I picked up my pot and went to her.

"Is this your private bush," I said, "or may two use it?" Her head remained dipped as her fingers plucked berries low on the bush. The jersey didn't cover and couldn't restrain the rich upper slopes of her breasts.

I said, "Does anything about me in particular annoy you?"

"Yes." Her head lifted. "Who are you, really?"

We stood on opposite sides of the bush, and the sun focused us in its full glare.

"I don't understand," I hedged.

"You're not Prof Glow. You're not a cop either, or you would have made your move the night the money was divided. Who are you?"

"I believe we've been introduced."

"I felt almost at once that you and Jeanie lied."

"Woman's intuition," I taunted.

"Perhaps. And there was your attitude, like offering to wash dishes and be helpful around the house. That's out of character for one of them."

"Them?"

"The other men here. The tough guys outside the law. Housework is demeaning; it's for women. And you have a woman. It's her duty to fetch and carry for you the way I do for Stan." She put a hand up to her brow, brushed back a strand of hair that had come loose from the tight bunch of it piled up on her head. "I'm not complaining about Stan. I like keeping house for him. What I'm trying to say is that Prof Glow would have the same attitudes, only more so. Because he's one of the biggest and richest in the rackets. He's used to giving orders and having them obeyed promptly. Everybody is eager to get on the right side of him. It wouldn't occur to him to pour his own glass of water."

"I'm on vacation. I hanker to be just one of the boys."

"You never could be. You're soft. Soft in a good way, and the bigger you are in the rackets, the harder you have to be."

"That's your evidence?"

"No." On the other side of the bush from me Elsa shook up the berries in her pot. "But Mary Creed is. You remember I spoke to you about her the day after you arrived. I asked you how you could have let her end up in one of your houses after what she'd been to you."

"I see. Since then you heard from Mary Creed."

She said tiredly, "There is no Mary Creed. I made her up. I was sure you weren't Prof Glow when you didn't deny knowing her."

"In short, her name was a trap."

"Yes." And Elsa demanded again, "Who are you?"

So I had been right when, the first night in darkness under the maple tree, I had told myself that she was the one to fear most. But now I didn't fear her.

"I'm nobody at all," I told her. "One of the anonymous masses. An unmarried, underpaid schoolteacher whose only brush with the law was when I received a parking ticket last year."

She refused to compromise with my attempt at flippancy. She said sternly, "How did you meet Jeanie?"

"I was the one who gave her the lift outside of Darson last Monday afternoon."

"What happened then?"

"Does it matter? The fact is I'm here and harming nobody."

"It matters a lot if you told anybody who Jeanie was and where you were going with her."

It was ridiculous to maintain that blueberry bush between us like a barrier. I stepped around it, and Elsa turned to me and stood in hot sunlight with her weight on one hip and her violet eyes troubled as she listened. I told her how Jeanie and I had spent the first night in a northern Virginia cabin and how in the morning I had found her gone and how in the evening she had turned up in my apartment for the valise.

When I finished, she burst out, "And then she endangered everybody by bringing you along. How typical of Jeanie! How irresponsible!"

"She knows she can trust me."

"In this rotten racket you can't trust any outsider. Often not an insider either." Elsa drew in her breath and spoke more quietly. "Oh, I suppose I can understand her taking the chance. She fell for you and wanted you with her while she hid out. She loves you very much, you know."

"Well . . ."

"There's no need to be modest," she said irritably. "I wouldn't be surprised if you're the only really lovable man she ever knew." She made that sound like an accusation. "Especially after a heel like Bertie."

"She stuck to him."

"I suppose he had a certain amount of animal charm. But we're not talking about Bertie." She paused and then asked sharply, as if I were being cross-examined in some kind of court, "Do you love Jeanie?"

"She's a good kid."

"That means you don't love her." The quietness I had associated with her was completely gone. Her strong face was mobile with emotion. "Then why in the world did you come with her? Didn't you realize the risk?"

"Uh-huh."

"And you don't even have the justification of being in love with her." Her mouth twisted scornfully. "You don't strike me as a man who has to go to such lengths to sleep with a pretty girl."

It was terribly important that she understand.

"It wasn't Jeanie," I said. "I mean it was, partly, but not primarily."

"I can't think of any reason except that you're out of your mind."

"That's possible."

I took out cigarettes. She shook her head when I extended the pack, then said, "All right," and extracted one. We stood close as I held a light for her. As she leaned to the match, her bunched-up hair almost brushed my face. I had never in my life wanted to do anything so much as I wanted to touch her.

I stepped back.

"Call this my private caper," I said.

She stared at me with the cigarette lax in her mouth. "Caper? You can't mean you're after the money?" She inhaled smoke. "No, of course not. You wouldn't have hung around so long. You would have made your try sooner and beat it."

"I'm not using 'caper' in the gangster idiom, meaning an organized robbery."

"Don't sneer at us!"

It struck me that at that moment she hated me.

"I'm sorry," I said. "I didn't intend to sound supercilious. Maybe I'm naturally a stuffed shirt. That's it. I want to get out of myself. This is my caper in the accepted sense of the word."

"You mean like a frolic?" She looked as if she could have slapped me. "I see. You're slumming. You're having a fling at the seamy side of life. Then you'll go home and tell your friends how much fun you had in the underworld."

"Please, Elsa. I'm trying to explain. It's not simple. I'm not clear about it myself. One definition of a caper is an irresponsible escapade. At least once in his life a man needs to be irresponsible."

"How dare you play games with our freedom?"

Abruptly she turned away. I glimpsed her bosom heaving before her back was to me. She strode to a bush a short distance away and tore furiously at berries.

I remained where I was to give her a chance to calm down. Presently I put down my pot and went to her.

She stopped picking berries when I stood behind her, but she didn't turn. I couldn't get in front of her because she was close to the bush. I said, "Elsa."

"Let us alone!" she said harshly without looking around at me. "You and your capers! Do you know what it can mean to Stan and the others? Twenty years in jail. Go away. Let us alone."

I said to the back of her head, "Look. It's been days since you tricked me with that Mary Creed trap. But you haven't told Stan. Why not?"

"I don't want your blood on his hands. Do you imagine that he and Fatso and Ronnie could afford to take the risk that you wouldn't turn them in for the reward?"

"I had no idea there was a reward."

"There generally is. Go away from here. Go back to your home, wherever it is."

"If I leave, how would you know I wouldn't head straight for the police and claim the reward?"

"I have to take that chance."

"Does my safety mean more to you than theirs? Than Stan's?"

Her back remained to me. She said nothing.

I said, "Days ago you knew I was an impostor, but you didn't tell me until a few minutes ago. You didn't tell Jeanie to get me away from here. You didn't urge me to leave. Not until now, when it had to come out. You wanted me around, didn't you?"

She made no answer by word or gesture or movement. I looked up at the knoll. Bushes and trees blocked us from the house. This for a very small time was a world of our own. And she stood silent and motionless with her back to me, and her bare shoulders were like honey.

I kissed one of those shoulders. I pressed my mouth against its sun-warmed, intoxicating smoothness.

"No," she said. "Please."

But when I put my hands on her, she turned. The berry pot was between us, digging into me and her hair was in my face.

"Elsa," I said.

Her head tilted back. Her violet eyes swam under mine. The pot fell, slid down my leg, and landed on my shoe. I kissed her mouth.

Her fists clenched against my chest and her mouth was hard under mine. Standing beside the bush under the blazing sun, I held her, and suddenly her lips quivered and parted, and I could feel her uncoil, let herself go. She uttered a moan and brought her hands up to my cheeks, and there was the clinging of breasts and hips and thighs, he blending of desire and more than desire.

Abruptly she was fighting me, gasping, "Let me go!"

"Elsa, listen."

Panic possessed her. She tore at my arms to get them away from her. I released her.

"Let's face it," I said. "There's no doubt how we feel about each other."

She pulled erect her sagging body. "This is another reason why you must leave at once."

"No."

"Do you change your women every week?" she flung at me.

"Elsa, this is the real thing. The way you kissed me. Elsa, look at me."

She didn't look at me. She stooped for the pot, which lay on its side. Few berries had spilled out. She straightened up with her back to me and headed for fresh bushes, as if after a brief diversion it was urgent to return to berry picking.

I followed her. "We've got a lot to talk over."

"Can't you get it into your head that no good can come of this?"

"Nothing better ever happened to me."

She swung around to face me. "Your caper! Your irresponsible escapade! Well, I'm not going to be part of it."

Her contempt was like a physical assault. In a way I deserved it. But contempt was only on the surface, a shell under which she was fighting herself as well as me.

"Elsa!" I put my hands on her.

"No!" She thrust herself away. "Don't touch me."

And she moved on to still another bush, fleeing from me, fleeing from herself.

I let her alone. Both of us needed time to orient ourselves. I returned to where I had left my pot and stood watching her pick berries. No good could come of it, she had said. Probably she was right, but that couldn't change anything. For the first time in my life I understood how a woman could mean everything that had meaning to a man.

I resumed berry picking. We remained apart, but there she was in the same field, the womanliness of her in sunlight, close and at the same time far, within and beyond reach.

"I guess we have enough," she called out.

She was at the side of the field nearest the knoll. She waited there for me to come to her.

Tonelessly she said, "Tell Jeanie you have to be gone for a few days on business and then don't come back."

"I'm not leaving."

"Because of Jeanie, I suppose." The sneer didn't come off at all; her heart wasn't in it.

"Because of you," I said.

She strode off ahead of me.

At the foot of the knoll she stopped. "Don't get it into your head to get Stan out of the way by having him arrested."

"You don't flatter me."

"I want you to know that if you do, I'll never forgive you."

She started up the knoll. When we reached the top, we saw Stan outside the house.

"Where've you been, baby?" he said. "I haven't had breakfast yet. I'm starved."

She waved her pot. "Prof and I picked blueberries. How would you like them—with cream?"

"Swell."

She took my pot from me and said, "Thanks a million, Prof," and moved on to Stan.

He peered into one of the pots—as it happened, mine—and scooped out some berries and shoved them into his mouth. "Delicious," he said. "I'm a sucker for blueberries." He slipped his arm about her waist and together they continued on to the house.

I watched the husband's hand spread intimately and affectionately on his wife's hip.

Chapter Thirteen

Next morning at breakfast, which for the first time we all ate together, Stan announced that he was driving to New York.

"Time I got off my tail," he said. "Reason I couldn't go before, my car wasn't fixed till late yesterday. I'll be back tomorrow night or Thursday."

"How about me coming along?" Ronnie asked without hope.

"How about you having a brain in your head?" Stan said. "Think I'd show myself if I didn't have to? The cops got a line on Bertie and Jeanie; could be they also got a line on the rest of us. Somebody has to find out how much they know."

"What you gonna do, ask 'em?" Fatso said.

"I know who to ask, wise guy. I got connections in New York—guys who can make phone calls to the right people anywhere in the East and maybe learn a thing or two."

Ronnie indicated me with his negligible chin. "Prof's got more connections than anybody. Could be he'll be willing to scare up some inside dope for us."

The four men looked at me. The two women carefully didn't look at me.

I gave one of my shrugs. "I'm always glad to do pals a favor. But around here I'm way out of my territory. I have to ask favors myself, and for a while I'd like not to come out of cover." I smiled affably. "But of course, Stan, if it's absolutely necessary . . ."

"Thanks, Prof, but I can manage in my own small way. Anything I can do for you while I'm in the big town?"

"One thing," I said. "Don't mention to anybody I'm here. You know how it is."

"Sure thing, Prof," Stan said.

An hour later from a parlor window I watched Elsa accompany him to his car. They walked slowly arm in arm. At the car she said, "Be careful," and he said, "Don't worry, baby, I know my way around." At the car he gathered her to him and kissed her for a long time. I turned from the window.

That house oppressed me. I had to get away from it. Perhaps permanently, if it was not too late to untangle myself. I had been up half the night trying to think it through, but I hadn't got even a start at organizing my thoughts with Jeanie sleeping beside me and the bitter awareness of Elsa in bed with her husband in the room across the hall. What was required was to get off completely, by myself.

"Honey, where are you going?"

That was Jeanie before I was fifty feet from the house—Jeanie, who blandly assumed that I was irrevocably bound to her for twenty-four hours each day. Resentment was like sandpaper on my nerves as I waited for her to come up to me.

"Do I owe you an explanation for every step I take?" I said.

"You don't have to get sore."

"I'm going on a hike."

"Where to?"

"Wherever my feet take me. I'm the outdoor type. I used to be a Boy Scout."

"You're still a Boy Scout," she said tolerantly. "Will you be back for lunch?"

"I doubt it."

"I'll fix you some sandwiches."

"Look," I said testily. "I'll buy food on the way, if I can, or I'll skip a meal. All I yearn to do is get off my tail for a few hours, as Stan would put it."

I couldn't get away without kissing her goodbye. She complained that the kiss was too brief and I had to try again. Then at last I was walking away from there and from her and from Elsa too.

Beyond the meadows rolling away from the knoll I came to a dirt road and followed it. I was angling toward the mountains, but after two hours of hiking they looked no closer. They seemed to be always the same distance away, like the fulfillment of desire. They were there, but somehow out of reach.

Like Elsa?

Like Elsa if I was sensible. But hadn't I, a week ago, abandoned common sense?

Now and then I passed an isolated, rocky farm. At one I stopped off for a handout of well water from a suspicious woman who kept a snarling hound close to her side as I drank from a dipper. She told me that Stoker Hill was six miles away.

That gave me a destination. At any rate, a destination for my feet.

In midafternoon I reached Stoker Hill. I bought a container of milk and a box of doughnuts in the general store. I ate and drank on a bench outside. I walked a short distance up the highway and turned into the narrow, wooded road that led to Hank's house. I came to the spot where last Wednesday evening Stan's car had blocked the road and I had left Jeanie in my car and had walked on alone to the house where I had paused to watch a woman pump water.

Now it was Tuesday and I was again approaching the house and the woman would be there. In the intervening days, whatever I had been looking for, groping after, I had found. But having found it didn't mean that I had it.

In my hike I had made a complete circle of some sixteen miles. A man walking in circles.

The house was very quiet. Nobody was outside or in the downstairs rooms. Where could they all have gone? In the upstairs hall I heard snoring. That accounted for one person, and possibly others were also taking naps.

Jeanie wasn't in our room. I took a fresh towel from the dresser and the cake of soap from the basin and set out for the creek to wash off the dust of the country roads.

When I neared the trees that fringed the creek, I saw a man. He was off to the left of the bathing area, but turned to it, standing motionless against a tree. His floppy straw hat and scrawny build identified him.

A woman out of sight giggled. I couldn't be sure whether it was Jeanie or Elsa.

Hank was so intent on what he was watching that he didn't hear me until I was a step or two from him. His head spun, and through his thick-lensed glasses his eyes looked startled.

A narrow lane through the trees afforded a view of the bathing hole. Elsa was on the bank and Jeanie was kneeling in the water. Neither wore a stitch of clothing.

Evidently they had come down together to wash their hair. Jeanie's was white with shampoo; Elsa was pulling pins out of hers. "Here goes," Jeanie giggled, and pushed her head down under the water. Her back arched over the surface; even at that distance I could distinguish the submerged part of her shimmering like cream in the clear, sunlit water. She came up sputtering, stood knee-deep shivering. Elsa's hair was now a silky blonde cascade over her bronzed shoulders. With languid grace she stepped to the edge of the water and tested it with her toes.

Hank whispered, "Ain't a prettier sight than pretty women bathin' naked."

For a long moment I had almost forgotten him. He was grinning widely at me with an old man's blatant shamelessness.

I could agree with him. No prettier sight—no more completely charming scene. Jeanie's slim, pert figure was no less delightful because of my familiarity with it. And the woman—the overwhelming, blood-tingling femininity of her!

"Jeanie, where did you put the shampoo?" Elsa said.

I roused myself, remembered the need for outrage, and gripped Hank's arm. "We're getting away from here," I whispered harshly.

Meekly Hank moved away with me. When we were halfway up the knoll, I released his arm.

"You're lucky it wasn't Stan who caught you," I said.

"You got me wrong, Prof. I was gonna warn 'em Ronnie's on the other side of the crik."

"Is he still there?"

"Guess so. I seen them girls do down the crik with towels and they wasn't carryin' bathing suits. Couple minutes later I seen Ronnie sneakin' off that there way where you can cross the crik and get around the trees on the other side. I ain't no dummy. If he's lookin' at 'em all the time they got clothes on, he'll look ten times as hard when they're naked. I think maybe he'll jump out at 'em or somethin' and Stan will find out and there'll be hell to pay. So I went down to warn 'em."

"You weren't doing any warning when I saw you."

"What harm's a look for an old man? But that Ronnie! No tellin' what he'd do." Hank peered anxiously at me. "Don't start nothin' with him, Prof. I don't want no trouble."

Trouble was the one thing I definitely couldn't afford. I raised my voice. "Hey, Ronnie, I want to see you."

He didn't answer, of course. But Elsa did. "Don't come to the creek."

"I won't. This is Prof. I'm looking for Ronnie."

"I hope he isn't around," Jeanie called. "We'll be dressed in five minutes, honey."

I said to Hank, "That ought to flush him out without embarrassing the girls."

"You ain't gonna make trouble, Prof?"

"No."

Dolefully Hank shook his head. "It ain't healthy, them young bucks with nothin' to do." He went up the hill.

I sat down on the ground. In a minute or two Ronnie appeared at the creek a couple of hundred feet south of the bathing hole. There the creek wound and narrowed and came out of the trees; the bathers weren't in his view, or he in their view, as he crossed by jumping over stones. He saw me and walked uphill to me.

"You call me, Prof?"

I waited until he reached me. "I won't make anything of it this time, but don't try it again."

"What're you talking about? All I did was take a walk."

"Well, don't walk in that direction."

His popeyes didn't meet my gaze. He muttered sullenly under his breath and continued up to the house.

The five minutes turned out to be fifteen before Elsa and Jeanie came out of the woods, the strong-bodied woman and the long-limbed girl, the corn-silk hair and the light-brown hair both shiny and heavy with wetness. I rose to my feet.

"How was the hike, honey?" Jeanie said.

"All right. I need a bath."

I hoped she wouldn't greet me with a kiss. She did and clung while Elsa strolled on ahead. I cut the kiss as short as I could without actually thrusting Jeanie away.

These days I had to act out two false roles—that of an ardent lover as well as a gangster.

"Um, good," Jeanie commented on the kiss. "I have to run along, honey. It's my turn to cook dinner."

At last I got to the creek. The icy water was good for my body. I splashed around for some time before drying and dressing. Outside I felt clean and cool, but inside I felt neither.

I found Elsa picking daisies and black-eyed Susans on the hillside.

I said, "Do I dare hope that this is an excuse to speak to me alone?"

She straightened up. "Was Ronnie spying on us?"

"Not only Ronnie and Hank, I too. What can you expect? I admit I had trouble tearing my eyes away from you."

She didn't blush. She said with an edge to her voice, "Of course you're used to Jeanie's body."

"I hope that means you're as jealous of her as I am of Stan."

Stooping, Elsa plucked out a cluster of daisies and included them with the rest of the bouquet. "What decision did you reach on your hike?"

"You're clever."

"I went through the same thing, except that I spent most of the day in my room."

"Well?"

"There's only one answer."

"I know mine," I said. "I love you."

"You must go away."

"With you."

"No."

"Then I'm staying."

"You can't," she said.

Up on top of the knoll Fatso, his nap in his room finished, was reclining in a canvas chair. He could see us but not hear us if we kept our voices low.

I said, "I can't leave without you, and I can't keep on living with Jeanie. How do you feel when Stan makes love to you?"

"How you chatter!" She moved downhill, picking flowers on the way.

I tagged after her. "You see, you do love me."

"I didn't say so."

"You don't deny it."

We strayed over the hillside as she picked flowers.

She said angrily, "If you expect me to go off in the woods with you while I'm living with Stan, you don't know me."

"I'd think less of you if you did. And remember I'm living with Jeanie. There's an old-fashioned virtue called honesty."

"Then go home."

"I'm not that virtuous." I wished that we were unobserved so that I could touch her. "Elsa, if you make me hang around, I'll have to tell Jeanie something."

"You mustn't." She sounded frightened. "Jeanie will never forgive me."

"Neither Jeanie nor I promised each other a permanent arrangement."

"She lives from week to week. Right now she loves you very much. She could hate you just as much."

"And tell Stan who I really am, I suppose."

"Yes. And he'd have to kill you because you know too much about him."

"If I walked out on her now," I said, "wouldn't that be enough to make her hate me and tell Stan?"

The innate strength flowed out of her face. "Oh, you and your caper!

Now you realize the mess you've got yourself into."

"I realize I've found you."

"Stop acting the fool. A lot of good I'll do you if you're dead."

"There must be a way."

"There isn't. And I don't want to look for it."

She started up the knoll. I didn't follow. When she passed Fatso, he raised his head and looked after her until she disappeared into the house.

I tore a black-eyed Susan to shreds.

Chapter Fourteen

A thump half woke me shortly after I had drifted off to sleep. Then Jeanie was shaking me.

"Something's going on in Elsa's room," she said.

In another part of the house I heard a voice speaking with a panting, incoherent quality, and whatever was being said was punctuated by odd, scraping movements. I roused completely, opening my eyes into darkness only lightly diffused by moonlight.

"It's in Elsa's room," Jeanie was saying, "but it can't be Stan with her. He couldn't drive to New York and back in one day. And there was a chair or something just knocked over. Sounds like Elsa's in trouble. You better go see, honey."

I was groping beside the bed for the flashlight when Elsa cried out. It was more like a loud gasp than a scream, like a frantic call for help stifled before it could come all the way out.

My hand located the flashlight. I snapped it on and tumbled out of bed. My pajamas were modest enough. I dashed across the hall and pushed open Elsa's door.

The glow of the kerosene lamp revealed Elsa writhing under Ronnie. His weight pinned her down on the bed. One hand was at her outrageously disordered nightgown; his other hand was clamped over her mouth.

I dropped the flashlight and seized his shoulders and yanked. He turned on his side and glared up at me with a madman's eyes. He kicked out; his shoe caught my hip glancingly. I fell on him, my hands going for his throat and finding it. He strove to sit up. I forced him back and my thumbs convulsed, digging into his windpipe and driving the breath from his throat.

He clawed at my chest. Under me he thrashed the way Elsa had thrashed under him. I was bigger, stronger. He was helpless.

I couldn't let go. His normally protruding eyes stuck out like marbles. I knew I was going to kill him and I couldn't stop myself.

Somebody tugged at me from behind. "Let up, you hear? Let up!" And all about me there were voices shrill with agitation.

They were all in the bedroom. Fatso, wearing only pants, and Hank, still fully dressed, were on either side of me like restraining guards. Elsa was off the bed, cowering at the other side of it, her hair wild and her arms crossed over her heaving bosom. Just inside the door Jeanie stood in her rose-colored robe.

"You was trying to kill him, Prof," Fatso said in awe.

"I seen trouble comin'," Hank grumbled. "I said so all along. Now Stan . . ."

Attention shifted back to Ronnie as he climbed off the bed. His face was slack, the features falling apart; the demented eyes were now merely shifty with fear. He rubbed his neck and said nothing.

My flashlight was still on the floor. I picked it up and turned it off.

Elsa spoke. "Nobody is to tell Stan. Is that understood?" She had yanked a blanket off the bed and wrapped it around herself like a toga.

"Sure we don't tell Stan," Hank agreed anxiously. "You, Ronnie, git out of my house and stay out. Nothin' but trouble from you."

"No," Elsa said. "Stan will want to know why. Let him stay, Hank. He's learned his lesson."

Hank nodded. "Guess you're right. But he makes any more trouble, I tell Stan. You hear, Ronnie?"

Ronnie said in a constricted tone, "Hell, all I—" He drew in his breath and discarded what small measure of defiance he had been calling up. You could see his anger at his fear of Stan, and perhaps now fear of me too. "I figured you wrong, Elsa," he said. "I'm sorry."

He walked out of the room.

At the door Jeanie stepped aside to let him pass. For the first time I noticed the gun in her hand.

Elsa pulled the blanket tighter about herself. "I was reading in bed when Ronnie came in. For a while he simply spoke to me and wouldn't leave when I ordered him out. Then he—well, I thought I could handle him without help, but I couldn't."

Spying on her and Jeanie bathing this afternoon had been as much as the brute maleness in him had been able to take, I thought—that and Stan's being away overnight and Elsa alone in her room, building up in him to a frenzy stronger than fear. And my act, my frantic, blind attempt to strangle him, could be explained in the same way—love or lust or whatever else you wanted to call it to explain the driving desire to possess utterly a particular woman.

Jeanie said crisply, "Okay, you guys, beat it out of here." She put a hand on my arm, the hand that wasn't holding the gun. "Go on back to bed, honey, I'll be right with you."

She remained behind with Elsa. I followed the other two men out and went to my room and lit the lamp.

My pajamas were soaked with sweat. I extended my hands and stared at them. Strong hands, but smooth and inclined to softness, hands experienced at holding a pencil to mark English compositions; but they had clung to a man's throat and would have continued to cling if Fatso and Hank hadn't interceded.

What was happening to me here? I had shocked even these men who lived by violence.

Jeanie came in. She looked curiously at me. "What came over you, honey?"

"I was trying to pull him off Elsa."

"He wasn't near her anymore when you were still choking him."

I shrugged. "I was too excited to take stock of everything that was happening."

She opened a dresser drawer and shoved her gun in under some clothes. It was the small automatic pistol I had seen before, that first night I had spent with her when she stood at the tourist cabin window listening to the policeman outside. All along she had continued to keep it close at hand.

She stretched and yawned. "Good thing she's not going to tell Stan. The worst thing is bad blood in a hideout. Stan would kill anybody that went near Elsa."

Hank and I were digesting our lunch on the bench under the maple, the coolest spot anywhere in or out of the house. Fatso was washing dishes in the kitchen. Ronnie had missed breakfast entirely and had shown himself briefly for lunch, sulking through the meal, disappearing again the instant he had gulped down his coffee.

"Actin' like what happened last night was everybody's fault but his," Hank commented. "But you gave him a lesson, Prof. You scared 'im good."

"I hope so," I said.

Elsa and Jeanie came out of the house together, walking slowly.

For the first time in the week since my arrival I saw Elsa in a dress and shoes and heels. Obviously she was going somewhere.

"Size twelve," Jeanie was telling her. "I like bright colors. Like yellow."

"Let me add it to my list." Elsa took paper and pencil from her handbag and jotted down a note. Then she left Jeanie and moved toward us.

That dress of hers was gingham with huge blue and green and purple checks. It was tight at the waist and flaring at the skirt. The neckline was square and deep in both front and back. I was afraid my quivering, gnawing desire might show in my eyes; I looked down at her approaching black raffia shoes.

"Hank, I'm going shopping," she said. "May I use your jeep?"

"Well, now," Hank said unhappily. "Women drivers don't . . ."

That was my opening and I jumped into it. "I've been thinking of getting a haircut. How about both of us going in my car?"

"Why, thanks, Prof," Elsa said.

"I'll be ready as soon as I change my shirt." I started toward the house and there was Jeanie at the entrance, looking at me with that half-puzzled expression I had noticed on her face last night after the rumpus with Ronnie.

"You don't need no haircut," she stated.

"How about letting me decide?"

"Sure, honey, go ahead." Her manner of generously granting permission irritated me no end. "Do you need money?"

"I've enough for haircuts, thanks," I snapped, and swept by her.

On the way up the stairs I felt suddenly contrite. Without stint she gave me everything she possessed, her body, her devotion, her money. I had never asked her to, but I had accepted. At the least, I could spare her my bad temper, which I knew was induced by an uneasy conscience. But I didn't go back and say to her the easy, meaningless words that would bring an affectionate smile to her lips. That would be too much. In our room I changed into my last fresh shirt.

Elsa was waiting for me in my car. We drove in silence until we were halfway up the dirt road.

"Well, we're alone together," I said. "That's what you wanted."

"Did I?"

"The normal thing would have been to ask Hank if you could

borrow the jeep before you got dressed up. There was a good chance he would refuse. But you knew I would snatch at the chance to go with you. You worked it the same way Monday afternoon to get me to go berry picking with you. I'm not complaining, of course. I'm glad you feel that way."

She said, "This can't go on. Last night . . ."

"Don't worry about Ronnie."

"I'm worried about you. You men! You all frighten me. I thought you were so different from these—these others, but last night you were ready to kill another man because he wanted me."

"I love you."

"I know what love means. Like Ronnie last night. That's all you want."

"You don't believe that, Elsa."

"Does it matter what I believe? Stan will be back tonight or tomorrow. Suppose he finds out in New York that you can't be Prof Glow?"

We had reached the highway. I stared at it stretching out before us.

"We don't have to stop at Concord," I said. "We can keep going."

"You mean keep running."

"Isn't that what you've been urging me to do?"

"Alone you'll have a chance," she said. "Perhaps I'll be able to keep him from going after you. If we go together, nothing will stop him."

She turned her face away to look at the skimming countryside. Her hair was a corn-silk sphere, pulled back in a charming loop over the nape of her neck and caught with a broad velvet ribbon. My yearning for her was like a sickness.

The head of the dirt road along which I had hiked yesterday appeared. I slowed the car and swung it off the highway.

"Where are you going?" she demanded.

"You'll see."

She sat against the door, seeming to cower there as we drove through flat, unpopulated country. Yesterday I had learned that this road was seldom used. Presently I rolled the car in among trees some fifty feet off the road. She uttered a small sound, a kind of wordless plea. I pulled up the hand brake and cut the engine.

Elsa was half turned to me, her torso rigid, her cheeks taut, as if waiting an attack against which there was no defense. I put my hand on her arm below the elbow-length sleeve.

"No," she said thinly. "Please don't make me."

I shifted along the seat and slipped my right arm around her and my left hand lifted her face. Her eyes closed. She trembled when I kissed her. It was as if resistance trembled out of her, and suddenly her body lost its stiffness and her mouth opened.

"Now I'm sure," I said. "You love me."

"Oh, God, I can't help it."

She brought her mouth back to mine.

After a while she moaned, "Darling, I can't stop you. But not now. Please don't make me here and now."

She was right—not here and now. Not here, snatching crudely at passion in a parked car like high school neckers. Not yet, when tonight we would both have to return to beds that we shared but not with each other. The beginning had to be clean and honest in time, and complete and dignified in place.

So we just held each other, and gradually our passion turned tender and somewhat sad. A pickup farm truck approached. She stirred uneasily, then subsided again when it passed.

"I don't even know your real name," she said.

"Larry Knight."

"Larry," she repeated, and then said, "My darling Larry," and then, "Is that short for Lawrence?"

"Lawrence Bennett, to give you the works. I don't quite know how to go about asking a married woman to become Mrs. Lawrence Bennett Knight, but that's what I'm doing."

"You're not serious."

"I've never been more serious in my life. A divorce is possible."

I felt Elsa withdraw into herself.

"Nothing is possible for us," she said woodenly.

"Love . . ." I said, and her laugh interrupted me. Her laughter was like weeping. She was at the edge of hysteria. I ran my lips over her face. She sagged in my embrace, listless with the overriding sense of defeat. I lit cigarettes for both of us. We smoked holding hands.

"We'd better get on to Concord," she said.

I drove back to the highway. My right hand reached for her to regain the feel of her.

"Perhaps you underestimate Stan as a human being," I argued. "He may be civilized. If you tell him you no longer love him and ask for a divorce . . ."

She said tiredly, "It's your right to know this. Stan and I aren't married."

"What?" I took my eyes off the road; her profile was static. "Then that part is no problem."

"It changes nothing."

"But he has no claim on you."

"He'd go after us and find us." Elsa twisted her torso around to me. "Can't I make you understand? Stan is not like you, like your kind of people. He lives by violence and reacts with violence. And Jeanie will tell him who you really are and where you live. She cares as much for you as he cares for me, and she's his kind. She'd no more forgive us than he would. But that's not all. You know too much. You'd be a menace to him and Jeanie and the others. For that alone he'd have to go after us. How long do you imagine we'd be together?"

"This is a big country."

"He'll find us. What kind of life will it be for us, trembling at every shadow?"

"Then I'll fight back. I could—" I gulped back the rest.

"What were you going to say?"

"Nothing."

"You were going to say that you'd turn him in to the police. I told you the other day that if you did I'd never forgive you. Stan has been good to me. He loves me and trusts me. Could you turn in Jeanie?"

"Never." My hands tightened on the wheel. "All right, I'll talk to him man to man."

"Don't be an idiot."

"You're worth any risk."

"I want you alive, not dead."

"The way you raise obstacles, we'll never have each other."

"I don't raise them. They're there. I said nothing is possible for us." She clutched my arm. "Please, Larry, for my sake as well as yours, go away."

I stared at the road. "You know," I said, "I've never been a stubborn guy. But I've never loved like this. I'm not particularly brave either, I suppose. I'm scared of Stan, but not as scared as I am of losing you."

"Be reasonable."

"You be reasonable," I said. "Think it all the way through. You keep telling me how much Jeanie would hate me if I walked out on her."

"I meant if we walked out together."

"How would it be different in the end if I went off alone? Would she let me walk out on her and not tell Stan? You answer that. In many ways you know her better than I do."

"You may be right," she said miserably.

"A woman scorned," I said. "And Jeanie scorned would be a vindictive fury. I have a notion about her. I think she was—" I broke off.

"She was what?"

"Never mind. What I'm getting at is this: I won't be any safer without you than with you."

"Why didn't you stay home where you belong?" she said bitterly. "Then we wouldn't have got into this trap."

"And we would never have met."

There was a long silence. I took my gaze off the road and saw that her violet eyes were filled with tears.

I patted her knee and both her hands closed over my right hand. "I love you," she said, the first time she had put it into words. "No good can come of it, but I love you so terribly."

The rest of the way I drove with only one hand on the wheel.

When we reached Concord, Elsa said it would require an hour to shop for herself and Jeanie. I had my hair cut and was back at the car in half the time.

Aimlessly I strolled along the street. A haberdashery lured me. Yesterday Jeanie had made up a bundle of our personal laundry to take to town, but it wouldn't be back until the end of the week, and almost the last of my available clothes were on my body. I considered the few dollars in my wallet and decided I could afford three pairs of socks and a pair of underwear shorts. Once inside, I fell for the salesman's spiel; in addition to socks and shorts, I came out with a pair of washable slacks and a sports shirt. I left another four dollars in a drugstore for a carton of cigarettes and eight paperbacked novels.

There were packages in the car. Elsa had dropped them off and had gone to accumulate more. I waited on the sidewalk.

Presently she was coming down the street, picking her way through the afternoon crowd, and she wore her femininity like an aura. Always it was as if I were seeing her for the first time—a recurring experience of surprise and yearning that was almost more than I could bear. I stepped on my cigarette and went forward to relieve her of her packages.

"I'm dying of thirst," she said when I had deposited the packages in the car.

"How about beer?"

"Beer sounds wonderful."

We sat at a cool table. She took out her paper and pencil and did elementary arithmetic.

"How much did you spend on Jeanie's things?" I asked.

"Just a moment." She added a column of figures. "Seventeen dollars and three cents."

The beer arrived. I drank half of it and said, "I ought to pay it, but I have less than fourteen dollars left. I can't cash a check and I can't send for money without using my real name."

She curled both hands around her glass and lifted it to her mouth.

"Jeanie is paying my board as well as her own," I went on. "She covered my poker losses. This morning she slipped another two hundred dollars to give Hank for the coming week. That's a thousand dollars I've already taken from her. What kind of man does that make me?"

"You can pay her back sometime."

"That's what I keep telling myself and her, but it doesn't change much. The thing is, I'm living on her and with her, and on top of that I love another woman." I scowled into my beer. "Like a male prostitute."

"I know." Elsa looked away and her voice was very low. "Monday night when we went to bed I told Stan I had a headache. Yesterday I was glad when he said he would be away overnight. Probably he'll be back tonight. If not tonight, tomorrow night. I can't keep telling him I have a headache."

"This can't go on."

"I've been telling you it can't," she said.

"Then we mustn't go back to Hank's."

"I must, and you've convinced me that you must too. I didn't know about the thousand dollars. Jeanie's generous, but now she believes she's bought and paid for you and is entitled to her money's worth. We're in the same boat, darling. It's leaking, but if we try to get out we're sure to drown."

"Then what do we do?"

"I don't know," she said.

We finished our beers and returned to the car.

When we were out of the city, I said, "Elsa, tell me about yourself."

"I'm living in sin with a gangster," she replied wryly. "That's practically my whole story."

"It can't be. You're educated."

"In other words, you want to know how I fell so low."

"Don't put words into my mouth."

"I haven't risen from anything," she said. "The men in my family were no better than the men at Hank's, and in some ways worse. We lived in Jersey City, in the slums, and our slums can match any. My father was a drunk who couldn't hold a job and my two brothers were hoodlums before they were fourteen. I was the youngest, the only girl. I remember my mother as a tragic, worn woman, but I remember her dimly, as in a dream dreamed long ago, because she worked too hard to have time for me. She died when I was nine, just a few months before my eldest brother was sent to reform school. My other brother was smarter; he kept out of jail till he was nineteen. So you see, I haven't changed my environment."

"But the year at college . . ."

"Oh, I tried," she said. "Perhaps not hard enough later, but when I was young I tried. I was good at school and a great reader. My father was unhappy because I insisted on going through high school. I was old enough to work. I did work, after school in a five-and-dime store and all-day Saturdays and during vacations. We were always desperately poor. My brothers were gone; they never contributed to the house anyway. Just my father and I in that rotten, dirty little flat, and he drank up what little he earned and it was up to me to keep us going—to go to school and work and keep house and never have time or strength for fun."

She paused, and I thought of my own youth—the neat frame house, kind and loving parents, the carefree existence of George and Marjorie and I. And I said compassionately, "No youth."

"Almost none. I remember I was always dead tired when I went to bed. But I had to become a schoolteacher. That was the height of respectability to me. I got through high school with high marks in spite of everything, and then I was at teacher's college, living away from home at last, for the first time in a clean, decent room I shared with two other girls. It was a state school, so there was little tuition to pay, but I had to work every minute I could to pay for my room and board. Besides supporting myself, every now and then I had to send my father money to keep him from going completely to pot. Then a month after the second year of school started, I had an appendicitis attack and had to have an operation. Sickness is the worst thing that can happen to the very poor. It destroys them. I was a charity patient, but even so it took what little money I had. I left the hospital too weak to work and I was missing school and I had hardly enough money for food and nobody to turn to and terribly alone. And I married a man named John Reynolds."

A horn honked. I was in no hurry to end the drive; I dawdled along at thirty an hour. I pulled over to let a ten-wheel truck pass.

"We were married two days after we met," Elsa said. "John was quite handsome and had a lot of charm. I don't think I loved him, really, even at the very beginning. I liked him, and for the first time in my life somebody wanted to shelter and protect me. He was an appliance salesman. We agreed that I would go back to school, but it didn't work out. A week after we were married John told me he had quit his job because he was offered a better one in a Pittsburgh department store as a buyer. We moved to Pittsburgh. He got the job, but it turned out to be only as a clerk. Soon he had a fight with the department head and was fired. He said he was glad because a friend in Cleveland had a better job waiting for him. So we moved to Cleveland. There was no friend or job. For the next three years we were constantly on the move. John couldn't keep a job any more than my father could, but for a different reason. He couldn't get along with any kind of boss. But he got along too well with women. I began to find out that wherever we moved there was sure to be some other woman."

"I don't believe it," I said. "How could any man want another woman while he had you?"

She smiled wanly. "Thank you for the compliment. John was restless; he always had to have something new, and that included women. Perhaps sooner or later I would have left him anyway. When I learned he wasn't even loyal to me, that was too much. We were living in New York at the time. I rented a furnished room uptown and got an office job. I was very much alone until I met Stan Crocker."

"How long ago was that?"

"Five years ago last April. I was having dinner in a cafeteria and was trying to make up my mind whether to take in a movie or go right home to read. Stan sat down at my table. We started to talk, and after a while he said he had two tickets to a show and asked me to go with him. He seemed rather old for me, but very pleasant, and I was lonely and I said yes. He took me to a nightclub after the show. I had a lovely time. I told him I was married, but not living with my husband. He merely nodded. When he took me home, he didn't try to paw me. After that we went out together once or twice a week. I think he was the first and only man who was ever really kind to me.

Always considerate, a gentleman. I suppose you can't understand how a man like Stan . . ."

"I understand, all right," I said. "For a week now I've seen you and Stan together. There are two Stans—one the minor gang leader and the other the man who loves you. You insist he's kind to you, but you fear him. You're convinced that if you go away with me, Stan, the gentle lover, will give way to the other Stan."

"Yes." After a pause she said, "When I first met Stan, he told me he was retired and looking around for a business. He had plenty of money. Probably I wouldn't have gone out with him if I'd known the truth then; I'd had enough professional criminals in my own family. He seemed so respectable. In June he asked me to divorce John and marry him. I said I would, and that was the first time he as much as kissed me. He had a nice furnished apartment in Morningside Heights, near Columbia University, and I moved in with him. I called myself Mrs. Crocker. And Stan actually looked for John; he was very anxious to make it legal. But John had disappeared. I didn't care so much. I had a good home of my own at last. I felt secure. And when I found out the truth about Stan, I wasn't so shocked."

On our right was the Stoker Hill store. I thought of passing the road to Hank's place and driving aimlessly for another hour, but it wouldn't do for us to be away together too long.

"After all, criminals in my family were nothing new," she was saying. "I wouldn't have started going with one, but now he was my man and I was happy with him. Or as happy as I had ever been. So I went on and on with Stan, year after year, through crimes and capers and hideouts, and here I am."

"What about your husband? Did you find him and divorce him?"

"Stan found him. He has friends everywhere and had them search for John. Last year he learned John was living in Tampa, Florida. Stan flew down there and found John married to a rich widow. Stan must have frightened him. John showed him papers to prove that he had never been legally married to me. It turned out he'd already had a wife when he'd married me and had never taken the trouble to divorce her, or to divorce me when he'd married a third time."

"No wonder you thought Stan pretty wonderful after John."

We were on the dirt road. I took it very slowly.

Elsa said, "Stan flew back from Florida and wanted us to be married right away. I put him off. I said there was no hurry. I said a legal document wouldn't make any difference. You see, when I was actually faced with marriage to Stan, I couldn't go through with it. Because this wasn't the life I wanted and Stan wasn't the man I loved. I'd never really loved any man until . . ."

"Until me," I said.

She covered my hand with hers. "I love you so much I can give you up if it means your safety. Except for one thing. Stan mustn't be hurt."

"He'd be hurt by losing you."

"I know. But I can't let you have him put in jail. I can't let you do that to him."

"You have my word."

We were now close to the house. She released my hand and shifted away from me. Sedately apart, we approached the house.

Chapter Fifteen

Jeanie whispered, "Honey, are you asleep?"

"No."

"The way you toss, you keep waking me."

"I'm sorry. If you stay on your side of the bed . . ."

"Your side is my side. What time is it?"

"I don't know. Around two or three."

"Well, I'm wide awake now." In the darkness her breathing quickened. "Oh, honey!"

"You're shoving me off the bed."

Giggling, she shifted to the middle of the bed. I remained at the edge, my arm dangling over the side.

"What's the matter?" she complained.

"Nothing."

"You been acting funny lately. Like I'm poison."

"Look, Jeanie. It's the middle of the night and I'm trying to fall asleep."

"That's all I get from you. At night you're tired. In the morning you're still tired. What happened to you all of a sudden?"

"Maybe you overestimated my capacity. If you expected a stud bull, you've thrown away your money on me."

There was only the darkness then, no stirring, no audible breathing, no contact, but I could sense her stretched out taut as a bowstring inches from me.

Presently I said, "I didn't mean it, Jeanie."

"That's the nastiest thing anybody ever said to me. Bertie never hurt me so much, even when he smacked me."

"Did he beat you up?"

"I don't want to talk about him."

"Would you prefer me to beat you?"

"You wouldn't. I figured you as a real sweet man. You'd never hit a girl. But you do say things that hurt worse."

"So Bertie used to hit you," I said.

"Well, he was quick with his hands."

"And you stood for it?"

"He had a bad temper that went off like a shot. He'd give me a slap and then be sorry right away. Like you are when you say mean things to me. The only time he really socked me hard—"

She stopped speaking.

"What happened?"

"There was a party in New York last June."

"That must have been just before or after you and Bertie came up here to plan the Knoxville caper."

"Just before. There was a guy at the party. All I did was let him kiss me and Bertie saw it. When we got home, he worked me over. I was black and blue."

"And you let him get away with it?"

"I let you get away with the way you speak to me. Men are men. You got to take them like they are."

"You once told me that you stopped caring for Bertie because he was mean to you. Was that what you meant, that beating?"

"Yeah, I guess so." She was again all over me, and again I was being half forced off the bed. "Honey, that's why I fell for you so hard. You were so different. A sweet, good-looking man. But now you act like you don't care for me no more."

"What I tried to say is that I'm no superman."

"It's been days, honey. Turn around to me." Her voice became triumphant. "You see!"

The trap, I thought. While I remained in this house, I had to share her bed; while I shared her bed, I had to make love to her. But this was not love or even the hearty lust it had been at the beginning, only the mechanics of love; and afterward I lay back dull and listless, thinking emptily of the woman in the room across the hall as Jeanie lay contented on my shoulder.

A car pulled up to the house. Both Jeanie and I roused.

"Stan's back," she said nervously.

The people he had spoken to in New York might know Prof Glow.

She slipped out of the other side of the bed. Her bare feet made no sound on the floor. At the window moonlight touched her creamy slenderness.

"Stan," she whispered to me, and moved from the window, losing substance and shape.

Downstairs the entrance door opened and closed. I heard Jeanie fumble in darkness. The flashlight went on and I saw her putting on her robe. The stairs creaked under Stan's ascent. Jeanie went out into the hall, leaving the door open, and I lay listening to their muted conversation.

Most of what they said was incoherent. Once Stan raised his voice as if in anger. "Nobody has any idea. If I get my hands on the rat who fingered Bertie . . ." The voice lowered.

Jeanie returned. Just before she closed the door, I saw Stan behind a flashlight enter the bedroom across the hall where Elsa waited for him.

Jeanie dropped off her robe and crawled in beside me. "It's okay, honey. Stan kept his promise. He didn't mention to anybody that Prof Glow is hiding out here."

"Did he learn anything?"

"Far as he could find out, the only one the cops tied in with the caper was Bertie. But he ain't sure; Stan got no guarantee that was straight dope. Of course, they're still looking for me."

"Evidently he didn't learn who fingered Bertie."

"No." She snuggled. "You should be able to sleep good now."

I lay wondering if Elsa would again tell Stan that she had a headache.

They came out of the storm. Abruptly, above the driving fury of the rain, fists pounded on the front door.

The downpour was the culmination of a hot, sticky day. It had taken most of the afternoon to gather, bringing dusk and then night early, and still there had been a pause, an hour-long hush interspersed by distant rumbling before the sky had opened up with everything it had.

We were all in the parlor. I was reading one of the novels I had bought yesterday; at the opposite end of the room Elsa, her legs curled under her on the sofa, read another. Between us Stan and Ronnie huddled contemplatively over the chessboard on a small table, while on the Mission oak table, directly under the hanging kerosene lamp, Jeanie and Fatso played five-hundred rummy. Hank sat on the floor growling at the ancient wall clock he had taken apart and was trying to reassemble.

A cozy scene, seven people snugly sheltered from a storm raging and crashing against the solid old house; and for this little while, at least, the lusts and fevers and terrors of living had loosened their hold on us. Until fists battered on the door, and suddenly the room was filled with gagging tension.

Thunder growled, faded. There was a moment of silence. Every head was raised; every pair of eyes mirrored taut nerves. The pounding resumed, and a man's voice cried, "Hey, open up!"

This was the way they would expect it, I thought, this their waking and sleeping nightmare: fists on a door accompanied by the voice of the law commanding, "Open up!" This, I could fully understand for the first time, was what it meant to be a criminal.

And Fatso put it into a single word. "Cops!" he whispered.

The door flew open. It hadn't been locked; only the turning of the knob had been required.

"Anybody in?" a woman called.

There was suddenly sound in the room, a kind of collective sigh of relief. Stan and Hank stood up.

"Hello, there," the woman said.

The parlor light had drawn her from the dark center hall. She stood in the doorway, small and frail, dripping wet. Behind her, in shadow, loomed a man.

"Yes?" Stan said.

"Isn't this Hank Armstrong's place?" she said. "I believe that's the name. They told us it must be at the end of this road."

Her accent was so painfully Bostonian as to be almost comic to a native New Yorker.

"So what?" Stan said.

"Then it is the right place." Uncertainly she looked around at the intently watching people in the room. "They told us at the gas station—you know, on the highway—they told us you take tourists."

Evidently that was the word Hank had passed around Stoker Hill to explain his visitors. Now he was stuck with it. Hank looked at Stan to handle the situation.

"We're filled up," Stan said.

"Oh, dear. We have to sleep somewhere. And this terrible storm . . ."

"Sorry, no room," Stan said.

She turned her head to the shadow behind her. "What are we going to do, Fletch?"

The shadow uttered incoherent sound and swayed. A hand appeared over her head and clutched the doorjamb.

"I'm afraid he's practically out on his feet," the woman informed us gravely, and stepped into the room. She was small, precisely and delicately formed, somewhere in her thirties. Her round little face might have been pretty, but she had lost partial control of her facial muscles and her pale eyes were bleary and her hair straggled wetly down one cheek. Her drenched blouse clung like skin and her skirt dripped water to the floor.

"What's the matter with the guy?" Hank asked.

"Blotto," she said. "High as a kite."

She wasn't anywhere near sober herself.

"This isn't the only tourist place," Stan told her.

"But they're full and we can't look any farther. We got a flat tire on this road and I drove on it and cut it to pieces."

"You have a spare, haven't you?"

"But I detest driving at night and there's this terrible storm and Fletch can't possibly drive in his condition. I told him we should limit ourselves strictly to that thermos of Martinis. He shouldn't have bought that bottle of rye. And on top of that drinking in the roadhouse." Her lips quivered; her bleary eyes filled with tears. "Please! I don't care where you put us up."

Stan gnawed his lower lip. I doubted that she had roused his sympathy, but she had presented him with a dilemma. They might remember faces, particularly Jeanie's, whose picture was being broadcast. But it might be as risky to cause talk, even suspicion, in the neighborhood if word got around that two people, both soaked to the skin and one of them practically out on his feet, were turned away at night in a violent storm.

"Suppose we change your tire for you?" Stan suggested on a note of desperation.

"Even so . . ." She made a hopeless gesture. "We can't go looking any longer tonight. We simply can't. I'll die if I have to drive another inch. And Fletch—"

As if this last mention of his name were a signal, the man lurched through the doorway and into the light. He was a head taller than the woman and a good twenty years older. His bald pate glistened wetly. His flamboyant loafer jacket and white flannels hung soggily from a tall frame that had most of its weight around the middle.

He hunched, clutching his stomach, and said something that rattled in his throat.

"What is it, dear?" the woman said.

He got it out thickly. "Th' john. Wha's th' john?"

Hank told him, "It's outside, back of the—" Then he saw how green the man's face was turning and yelped, "Hey, not on my floor! Git outside!"

The man floundered into the hall. Nervously Hank hurried after him. We heard him throw open the door and a moment later close it. We heard the man retch.

"That should make him feel better," the woman said. She sank into a chair and passed her hand across her mouth and looked as if she would also need the outdoors. She recovered and turned her gaze pleadingly to Stan. "You see, you can't possibly put us out."

Stan gave in. He had no alternative. "Where can they sleep?" he asked Hank, who had returned to the parlor.

"I got an army cot I can put in here, and the woman's so little she can fit on the sofa."

"Oh, I'm grateful," the woman said. "Truly I am." She spread a smile around. "I haven't introduced myself, have I? We're Mr. and Mrs. Darrow. And now will somebody introduce you kind people?"

Nobody cared to name our names. Elsa diverted Mrs. Darrow's interest in the social amenities by saying, "Don't you think you ought to get your husband indoors?"

"Oh, he's wet anyway." She tittered. "Will somebody please let me have a cigarette?"

Ronnie sprang forward. As he held the light, he stared popeyed down at her trim little figure with the unabashed predatory expression he had for an attractive woman.

Stan had Jeanie by the arm and was taking her out to the hall. I followed with a flashlight.

"They haven't had a good look at you yet," he whispered. "Stay in your room till they're gone."

"Just because a couple drunks—"

"Do like I say!"

"All right, all right." By the light from the parlor she saw me. "Come with me, honey."

I was lighting the lamp in our room when I heard commotion downstairs. I said, "I'll see what's up," and left. If possible, I didn't propose to return until she was fast asleep.

Ronnie and Fatso were carrying Fletch into the house. Hank held a lantern high. Elsa and Mrs. Darrow hovered in the parlor doorway and Stan stood at the foot of the stairs.

"Hank found him passed out cold outside," Stan told me disgustedly. "My God, what a pain!"

Elsa said, "Bring him in here," and Ronnie and Fatso bore the limp man into the parlor.

"Put 'im on the floor!" Hank yelled. "He'll git my sofa all wet."

They eased him down on the floor, beside the table. He lay on his back, breathing raggedly through his open mouth. He was not a pretty sight.

"This is the best thing that could have happened to him," his wife said placidly. "He'll sleep it off."

Elsa was considerably more concerned. "We can't leave him here soaked to the skin. Have you dry clothes in the car?"

"There is a weekend bag in the trunk. I should like to change." Mrs. Darrow looked speculatively at the men in the room. Her smile lighted on Ronnie. "Would it be too much to ask you to bring our bag?"

"Sure thing," Ronnie said with unusual amiability.

I picked up the novel I had been reading and went with it into the kitchen.

Somewhere in the house there was whispering. Sitting at the big, round kitchen table, I looked up from the book and listened. The whispering seemed to come from everywhere, like the voices of conscience.

I rubbed my tired eyes. They were good eyes; they could read endlessly without glasses, but they weren't used to kerosene light. I turned the wick up higher and the lamp started to smoke. I turned it down a bit.

Whispers in an old New England house at midnight. People or ghosts or rats. People, in this case—no doubt the two drunken refugees from the storm in the parlor. The man named Fletch must have awakened, and those would be his and his wife's voices.

All the rest of the household was asleep by now—or anyway, up in their rooms. And in the kitchen I read on and on in a trivial so-called historical novel that didn't particularly interest me, reading to delay going up to the bed where Jeanie slept, reading because it fogged my brain against remembering too acutely how Stan had possessively slipped an arm about Elsa as they had gone upstairs together an hour ago.

The whispering died. The storm had passed by. I sat alone in utter silence. I pushed the book aside and propped my elbows on the table and rested my head in my hands. In that position I dozed off.

"Hello."

I looked up. Fletch stood in the kitchen, tall and pot-bellied and bald, his face lax and pasty. He had put on pants over his pajamas and he hadn't taken the trouble to lace his shoes.

"How do you feel?" I said.

"Rotten." His voice was fuzzy. Sleep had done him good, but he had a great deal to sleep off. He asked, "Are you a guest?"

"Yes."

"What happened to me?"

"You passed out. One of the men helped your wife undress you and put you in bed on the cot."

"Where's she sleeping?"

"I suppose you missed her in the darkness. Her bed was made on the sofa in the same room."

"A light was left on. She's not in the room." His dead-white hands closed over the back of a kitchen chair. "But I just woke up," he said in a rather odd note of eagerness. "She must've stepped out for a minute. Where's the john?"

"The best we can offer is an outhouse. You go through that door and follow the path a short distance to the right."

"I guess that's where she is. Thanks."

He started across the kitchen to the back door. He wobbled.

"You'll need a flashlight," I said. "Here's mine."

"Thanks." He accepted it from me. He took a few more unsteady steps and stopped. "But she would have had to come through this kitchen, and you say she didn't."

Anxiously he waited for me to reassure him.

I did the best I could. "She must have gone by way of the front door and around the house."

"Did you hear her?"

I saw no reason to tell him about the whispering voices. I said, "I was absorbed in my book."

"Yes. Well . . ." He seemed reluctant to leave, as if afraid he wouldn't find her outside either. "Thanks," he said for the third time, and shambled out in unlaced shoes.

My mouth was dry and my eyes were pasty. I went out to the pump. The sky was clearing and moonlight came through. With my left hand I pumped water into my right hand and washed my face. I filled the dipper and drank. There was no better water anywhere.

Somebody tittered. The barn showed no light through the doorless entrance, but I knew they were in there, whispering and tittering like children on a lark. They were the ones I had heard a short time ago, their whispers entering the kitchen through the breezeway. Probably they had whisky with them, which would be why they weren't quieter, but whisky would by no means be the only reason they were in the barn.

I returned to the house and looked into the parlor. A small lamp was on, turned down low. Nobody was in the room, of course. The table had been pushed against the wall to make space for the canvas cot. The sheets and pillow were rumpled; the blankets were on the floor, where Fletch had dragged them along with him when he had groggily arisen. The improvised bed on the sofa was as neat and undisturbed as when Hank had made it up.

She must already have spent quite a while in the barn. And now her husband was outside looking for her. He knew his wife, poor man.

I told myself that it was not up to me to do anything about it or to stop whatever might happen. Let the drunk watch over his drunken wife. And who was I to pass judgment on anybody who surreptitiously made love?

Then the shouting started. For a long moment it was just noise, loud and bitter recrimination. Suddenly the woman shrieked, shrill and pulsating, her voice breaking off as if for breath and rising again to a single keening note.

Upstairs a door slammed open. A flashlight beam knifed down the stairs, covering me as I stood in the hall.

"What's up, Prof?" Stan said.

"They're in the barn."

"That dame?"

"Who else? I think her husband found her with somebody."

By then he was down the stairs, his light wavering as he tied the cord of his dressing gown. It was silk, neat and conservative like everything he wore, tailored to his broad shoulders. Together we hurried to the barn through the breezeway.

Stan's flashlight swept around and found Fletch lying flat on his back. His eyes were wide open, not quite glassy. One hand flapped on the floor like the tail of a feeble fish out of water. A thin stream of blood trickled down his chin.

The light moved a little and focused on Ronnie. I hadn't been able to imagine anybody else. Stripped to the waist, he stood moodily sucking the knuckles of his right hand. Evidently he had cracked them against the man's jaw.

Mrs. Darrow crouched on a blanket. Ronnie must have brought it from his room and spread it out on the barn floor. Its purpose was obvious. She had changed into a dry summery dress that was awry on her small frame and had buttons open. Our arrival had lowered her shrieks and moans. She swayed, holding her temple, and blood seeped through her fingers.

And the reek of whisky pervaded the barn, not so much from the collective breaths of those three—though that helped—as from the bottle that had been knocked over, its contents soaking into the blanket.

Fletch had broken up quite a party. He had gone for his wife instead of the man, probably using as a club the flashlight I had lent him. After he had struck her with it, Ronnie knocked him down.

Ronnie said, "This here heel—"

"Shut up!" Stan said, and looked behind him.

The others were coming through the breezeway—Elsa first, then Hank and Fatso. It was like two nights ago, when Ronnie also had been the cause of bringing us tumbling out of our beds. But that other time Stan hadn't been here.

Stan gave crisp orders. "Baby, take the dame in the house and fix up her head. Hank and Fatso, carry the guy to his bed."

Fletch started to his feet. "I—I—" he sobbed, and fell against Fatso, who caught him. Fatso supported him as Hank led the way with a kerosene lantern. After them went Elsa with an arm about the moaning, unsteady woman. And nobody said a word, and in the receding and uncertain light it was like a procession of the wounded down the breezeway.

Then we were alone in the barn, Stan and Ronnie and I. Stan's light remained remorselessly on Ronnie, who continued to suck his knuckles.

"Leave us alone, Prof," Stan said.

I entered the breezeway and stopped and turned.

Ronnie said hoarsely, "Listen, Stan, all I did—"

"All you did was maybe bring the cops down on us. Suppose he's hurt bad, or the dame's hurt. Suppose he makes a complaint anyway and the cops investigate. You stuck all our necks out."

"She wanted it. I didn't have to drag her in here. Hell, I ain't a monk or something. It's all right for you. You got s woman in your—"

"Shut up!"

Stan transferred his flashlight to his left hand and with his right fist hit Ronnie in the face. Ronnie took a stumbling, cowering step backward and put up his hands. Stan hit him low, deliberately driving his fist considerably below the belt. Ronnie screamed and Stan hit him again in the face, always with his right fist.

Ronnie didn't attempt to fight back. He didn't dare. This was his gang leader ruthlessly keeping one of his men in line. And when Ronnie, whimpering and writhing, sank to the floor, Stan started to kick him with cold and methodical ferocity.

Sick to my stomach, I passed through the breezeway. Through the kitchen door I saw Mrs. Darrow seated at the round table with the side of her head on her arms as Elsa bandaged her head.

Elsa, the housekeeper, the mother, the ministering angel. I moved on to the hall. Jeanie's voice came down from the darkness at the head of the stairs.

"Who's down there? For God's sake, will somebody tell me what's going on?"

Dutifully she was remaining out of sight of the Darrows. I went up the stairs to her and told her.

"That all?" Jeanie's hands went to me. "When I heard all that yelling and running, I was scared something happened to you because you weren't in the room."

I said, "I'm going down again in case I'm needed."

"You'll be right up, honey?"

"Soon," I told her, because I couldn't tell her anything else.

In the parlor Fletch sat huddled on the cot, and he was sobbing. Fatso and Hank stood awkwardly, listening to him in embarrassment and contempt.

"It happens like clockwork," he was saying brokenly. "Every few months. I give her everything she wants. But every few months a man. Like clockwork." He wrung his hands, womanlike. "I never struck her before. I don't know what came over me tonight. I heard voices and went in there and I saw . . . I saw . . ." His body shook.

"Can't blame her," Fatso whispered to me with a leer. "An old buzzard like him." Abruptly his face sobered. "But Ronnie should've had more sense. Suppose this guy yells copper?"

Stan entered, cool and unruffled. There were flecks of blood on his right knuckles where they had split, but unlike Ronnie, he disdained to suck them.

Fletch made the effort to lift his head. "How is she?"

"A skin wound." Stan planted his feet apart. "You got a nerve. We take you in out of the storm, and what do you do? The two of you cause a scene, get me and my guests up in the middle of the night. I ought to call the police."

"You mustn't!" Fletch said frantically. "It will get in the papers. The Boston papers. Our friends will read it."

"Then take her the hell out of here. The storm's over. We'll change your tire while you get dressed."

"But—but where will we sleep?"

"I don't give a damn," Stan said. "You have ten minutes. Say fifteen. If you're not out of here by then, I'll call the police and say a wild man's here who tried to beat his wife's brains out because he caught her rolling in the barn with one of the guests."

"We'll go at once," Fletch stood up, wobbling.

"Swell," Stan said. "We'll all agree to keep quiet about what happened."

"Thank you," Fletch said with humble gratitude.

Stan turned his head to me and gave me a wink. Somehow that wink made me shudder.

Chapter Sixteen

During the night Ronnie disappeared.

Elsa was the only one who had gone near him after the beating. When she had finished bandaging Mrs. Darrow's temple, she had been drawn to the barn by his groans. Blood running from his nose had made him look in worse shape than he probably was. Though this was the man who two nights ago had tried to assault her, she had brought him a basin of water. He had cursed her and knocked over the basin.

"Don't bother with him," Stan had told her. "He's lucky I let him off so easy."

In the morning, as soon as Ronnie's absence was discovered, Stan jumped into his car and drove to the highway on the chance that Ronnie was walking along the dirt road. He wasn't.

When Stan returned, he and Fatso and Hank took Ronnie's room apart. Jeanie and Elsa and I watched from the hall. His bed hadn't been slept in, but there were droplets of blood on the stairs and on the floor of his room, evidence that, with his nose still bleeding, he had dragged himself up here after the Darrows had departed and we were all asleep. As far as could be determined, he had taken no clothes except perhaps a shirt. But his money was gone and so was his gun.

"With all that cash in his pocket, he'll head for liquor and dames," Stan said. "That means a city. Concord or Manchester or all the way to Boston. Could be even New York. Depends on where the first lift he got on the highway dropped him off."

"Good riddance," Hank commented. But he sounded dubious. If he was rid of a troublemaker, he had also lost a boarder who was worth a hundred dollars a week.

Stan said, "The trouble is, it isn't good riddance. I wish it was. I've known too many guys were sent up because they had somebody in their outfit who was a blabbermouth."

"It don't make sense for Ronnie to talk," Fatso argued. "He's a three-time loser. He'd get maybe life himself."

"A mug full of booze doesn't know he's not making sense," Stan said. "I don't say he'll go to the cops. He'll drink like crazy, and in a gin mill or with a dame his tongue will loosen up why he's sore as hell at me. Some stoolie will hear him and find out enough to go after the reward. It happens all the time. Maybe there's not a chance in a hundred we can catch up to him, but we'll do what we can near home. Fatso and Hank, you cover every gin mill in Manchester. I'll take Concord."

"Do we bring gats?" Fatso asked.

"Take one in your car, but don't carry it. If you find him, show it to make him come back. But watch him. He's got his and he'll be mean drunk."

I wasn't asked to participate in the search and I didn't offer my services. The three men drove off, Stan in the Kaiser and Hank and Fatso in the jeep.

Jeanie and I were the only ones who ate breakfast that morning. Elsa went back to her room. Her sanctuary, I thought.

"Stan's losing his grip," Jeanie complained as we ate. "What did he gain by beating Ronnie up last night? These men just like to use their hands every chance they get. If he knew Ronnie was so unreliable, why did he ring him in on the caper in the first place? Bertie didn't want Ronnie. He argued with Stan. Stan said Ronnie was the best man he knew for that kind of job, so Bertie gave in. But he told me he was worried about Ronnie. Bertie was always very careful. Looked at all the angles. Better than being sorry later, like Stan."

I said, "There must have been one angle Bertie overlooked. The one that killed him."

"Well, those are the breaks."

After breakfast I suggested to Jeanie that perhaps Ronnie hadn't had the strength to go more than a short distance and was lying near the house in pain or unconscious. I said I would go and see. I was like a small boy who couldn't leave the house without subterfuge. I wandered a quarter of a mile into the woods and sat down on a tree stump and lit a cigarette.

I wondered if Elsa, closed in her room, lying open-eyed on her bed or sitting in the armchair, was thinking the same thing as I—that if Ronnie in some way or another brought the police down on this house, our problem would be solved. Stan, the one person in the world between us, would then be out of the way in jail.

That must be occurring to her. And she must be wanting it and at the same time not wanting it because Stan was the first and only man who had ever been good to her.

I hadn't yet had a chance to be good to her, and perhaps in the long run I would be bad for her. It was becoming clearer and clearer that the best thing I could do for her was to go away from her.

I couldn't.

Let the police come. Elsa herself wouldn't be arrested. I wasn't a lawyer and I knew nothing about how the police mentality functioned, but I doubted that they would press an accessory charge against her. And probably not against Jeanie either, though she was in deeper trouble because she had run away from a shooting with the loot. Their interest would be in Stan and Fatso and Ronnie, the actual bandits, and in Hank, the paid keeper of the hideout. Why should I care if they paid for their crimes?

I wouldn't care. I could desire it, but not bring it about through any act of mine. I had given Elsa my word, and what would I gain if she hated me for breaking it? All I could do was sit on a tree stump and smoke cigarettes.

At noon I heard a car return. The dirt road was not far from where I sat; through trees I glimpsed the jeep. I remained where I was. Half an hour later I saw Stan's car. I started back to the house.

They were all in the kitchen, famished and edgy. Elsa was bringing a huge bowl of spaghetti and meat balls to the table and Jeanie was mixing dressing into a salad.

"No luck?" I asked, though the answer was obvious.

"Like lookin' for a needle in a haystack," Hank grunted.

I sat down. We ate.

Fatso said, "You know what I think? I think he'll go on a bat and buy himself a dame and wake up tomorrow and come back. He ain't no dummy. He knows there's no percentage for him anyplace else."

"Could be." Stan rolled spaghetti on his fork. "But we move out of here if he's not back by tomorrow."

Ronnie said, "I'm back now."

He stepped into the kitchen, and he held chest-high a black, hideous gun.

I had been pouring myself a glass of milk. The glass filled and overflowed before I managed to right the bottle.

For a long moment there was complete lack of sound in that room. Then Stan said, "Put it down, Ronnie."

Ronnie laughed. He was drunk, of course. He couldn't have gone far from the house, probably only to the nearest place where he could buy whisky and brood, and now he was back with his gun covering all of us at the round table and his popeyes as demented as they had been the other night when I had pulled him off Elsa.

"You don't give me no more orders," he said.

He had trouble speaking because one side of his mouth was swollen. All the blood hadn't been washed off his upper lip; flakes of it adhered like rust.

My hand remained fixed around the neck of the milk bottle as if glued there. I sat nearest to where Ronnie stood. Twisted around in my chair, I couldn't see the others. But I could hear their breathing, the sucking of air into lungs as constricted as mine.

"Nobody slaps me around," Ronnie went on. "Don't do this and don't do that. Don't drink and don't touch dames." The gun quivered with the violence of his emotion. "Who the hell are you, Stan? That dame last night, she was willing. But you—you got a hot-looking dame all the time in your bed. I have a party with one who wants it and you slap me around like I was a kid."

Stan said matter-of-factly, "If I wasn't around to wipe your nose, you'd be in stir or dead like Bertie. Put away the gat and sit down and eat."

"You want it standing or sitting?" Ronnie said. "You want the slug to smash in your face or tear up your guts? It's all the same to me."

The gun moved out from his chest.

I glanced over my shoulder. Stan sat broad-shouldered and rigid, his hands spread flat on the table. He and Fatso had taken guns with them on the futile search, but they wouldn't have brought them to the table. There was no room for guns in the light clothing they wore. Only Ronnie had one now, and it made him the master of life and death.

"What'll it get you?" Stan said. Not pleading, not arguing, an overtone of contempt in his voice.

A woman whimpered. Whether Jeanie or Elsa I didn't know. My gaze was on Stan. Everybody else at the table was a blur, and Stan had only courage and contempt to bring against Ronnie.

"You worry about what it will get you," Ronnie flung at him. He seemed enraged by Stan's failure to squirm and beg for mercy. "A slug for you," he said, "and then one for Prof."

There were enough bullets in that gun to satisfy all his hates. I was slated to be one of his victims because I had nearly strangled him.

But that couldn't be all of it. That, like the beating by Stan, was the surface impetus. His urge to murder went deeper, all the way to the roots of his lust for Elsa. He wanted Stan to die because Stan was the man who slept with her. He would include me because I had dragged him off her. And while he was shooting, while he was filling the room with death, would there also be a bullet for Elsa? Possibly.

"Ronnie, use your head." Fatso had found his voice. "Anybody burns a big man like Prof, he can't find a hole big enough to hide in."

Ronnie didn't hear him. He was transported to a world of death with himself as the avenging angel. His teeth drew over his swollen lip.

I had not released the milk bottle.

"You first, Stan," Ronnie said.

I threw the milk bottle at Ronnie's face.

Instinctively his hand holding the gun jerked up to protect his face. The bottle struck his elbow, splattering milk.

It fell on me because I had left my chair in a dive for his legs. I hit him above the knees and he crashed against the wall.

He would have been able to kill me, shooting down at me, if Stan hadn't been on him an instant later. Stan hit him and he sagged and then Fatso was all over him too. Somebody stepped on my hand.

"Okay, Prof, I got his rod," Stan panted.

I climbed up to my feet. Ronnie sat on the floor. I couldn't see his face because Fatso was in the way. "You sure done it, Prof," Hank chortled.

Elsa's face was buried in her hands. Jeanie chewed her fingers.

Suddenly Ronnie screamed. I whirled around to see Stan shoot Ronnie in the head.

They waited until darkness to bury him. From a parlor window I watched them bring the dead man out of the barn, where he had lain all afternoon and evening behind the woodpile. He was now tied in a blanket.

I wondered if it were the same blanket he had spread out for Mrs. Darrow and himself last night.

Stan led the way with a battery lantern. Hank and Fatso followed. The long, narrow burden dimly visible between them in the moonlight swayed from side to side. The three living men and the dead man disappeared over the crest of the knoll.

During the day Hank and Fatso had gone off with pick and shovel to dig the grave. Where they were burying him I did not know, and they preferred not to have me know. I had done my share, for which Stan had expressed gratitude. I had saved his life along with my own. I had disarmed a man and set him up for cold-blooded execution.

Jeanie was with me in the parlor. Of everybody in that household, she had been the least disturbed during the interminable hours after the killing. I turned from the window. She sat on the sofa with her feet tucked girlishly under her, and her small, naive mouth formed a circle through which she blew cigarette smoke.

"You're not thinking of doing anything foolish, honey?" she said.

"I no longer know what's foolish and what isn't."

"You're an accessory all the way. You're an accessory to the caper because you brought the dough here, and you're an accessory to the killing. The law won't make any difference between you and the others."

"I realize that."

Jeanie smiled. "Just so you know the score, honey."

Sometime later Elsa appeared. Tonelessly she asked for a cigarette, and it struck me that those were the only words I had heard her utter all day. In fact, I had seen her only twice that day, briefly, when we had searched the house for Ronnie in the morning and during that lunch which had abruptly ended with death. Immediately after the shooting she had gone up to her room, and she hadn't come down for the dinner that Jeanie had haphazardly thrown together.

I handed Elsa cigarettes and a match book. She lit up and sat and joined us in our silence. She was as indrawn, as alone with herself as if she had remained in her room, that quietness of her wrapped about her like a mantle.

The impossible situation had become still more impossible. I told myself that soon now something would have to snap.

We heard the men return, speaking in the properly muted tones of those who had just come from a funeral. Stan entered the house alone. Hank and Fatso were probably going on to the barn to put away the shovels.

Stan entered the parlor and stood broad and squat in checked worsted pants and the inevitable white dress shirt, without necktie but with sleeves buttoned. "So that's over," he said. He moved on to Elsa's chair. "You feeling all right now, baby?" he asked, patting her shoulder.

Elsa shrank away from him.

Stan's jaw muscles ridged. "What's eating you?"

"Don't touch me!" she burst out.

She leaped to her feet and ran out of the room. Stan started to follow, then halted and stood listening to her dash up the stairs.

When the sounds of her flight died, he turned back to the room with a very small smile. "She's upset," he explained as if apologizing for her. "Sensitive. She'll get over it." He looked at me. "You haven't said a word since it happened, Prof. You been sitting in here most of the time."

"Any objections?" I said.

"You look kind of upset. Like Elsa."

"I can't afford to have my name mixed up in this kind of thing."

"Prof," Stan said with that half-smile, "I'm not a big shot like you, but right here I'm top man. I didn't invite you. You asked to stay. Okay. I have to protect myself and my people. You're only hiding out from a committee—a subpoena, you said. It would be little skin off your back to be caught. But we—" He opened his hand and closed it. "I couldn't let him live, could I? The guy was off his rocker. Maybe he'd get another and try again. Maybe he'd get so crazy sore he'd turn state's evidence. You never can tell when they're like that. I couldn't take a chance on it."

"All right," I said.

"Sure. I'm not worrying about you, Prof. You'll keep your lip buttoned. Your name will be mud in the rackets if you step out of line."

"All right," I said.

Stan nodded, the smile broadening, and turned to Jeanie. "Ronnie's dough was in his pants. We'll split it the same way we split the other dough. Two shares for me. Hank claims he should cut in for a share because it happened in his house and he helped cover up."

Jeanie bristled. "My God, ain't he getting enough in board? Don't give him a red cent extra."

I walked out of there.

Somebody with a flashlight was ascending the stairs ahead of me. The light reversed to guide me up, and behind the light Fatso said, "I been meaning to talk to you, Prof."

"Yes?"

"You remember I told you Hi Globeman said maybe you had a spot for me in your organization."

"I'd rather not discuss business now."

Fatso held my ann. "It'll take only a minute, Prof. This here ain't no life. Like what happened today. You got plenty of jobs to give out. What say, Prof?"

"I've been away from the West Coast. I don't know what's doing there."

"But if you did have a spot for me . . ."

"Yes, yes, I'll keep you in mind." His persistence rasped my raw nerves. "Good night," I said, dismissing him.

"Good night, Prof. You'll think it over, huh?"

I closed the door of my room and lit the lamp and lay down fully clothed on the bed.

Too soon Jeanie joined me. She yawned, looked at her wrist watch, said, "I didn't know it was so late," and shed all of her clothes. She turned the lamp up higher. Standing at the dresser, she began to comb her hair.

"Stop letting it bother you, honey," she said into the mirror.

"Doesn't it bother you?"

"Ronnie wasn't anybody I'd cry over, and he had it coming. Like Stan said, what else was there to do?"

"Tell me one thing. Before Stan shot Ronnie, did he know that Ronnie had attacked Elsa?"

"Stan still don't know. We didn't tell him right off, so everybody's scared to tell him now. He'd get sore at us for holding out."

"So he hadn't that justification for shooting Ronnie."

"He had enough."

"What would Stan do if he found out you hadn't spilled everything about Ronnie—beat you all up?"

"Oh, Stan's all right," she said, "if you play along with him."

And if you didn't, I thought, he beat you up or killed you.

Lying on the bed with my face turned toward her, I watched the rhythmic stroking of the brush. Jeanie with the light-brown hair, who had given me what there was to give of herself, and within days her youthful, slender, ardent nakedness had become hateful to me.

I said, "I'm leaving here, Jeanie."

Because remaining under this roof was intolerable. Perhaps Jeanie would understand that murder had made it so and would release me. And it wouldn't mean abandoning Elsa for good. In a few weeks or months the situation would change, or somehow be made to change, and Elsa would join me in New York.

Jeanie was facing me now, looking down at me on the bed. "You're staying," she stated flatly.

"Look. There's a limit to what you can expect me to take. Murder is too much."

"You don't care for me no more." It was an accusation. I hedged. "I didn't say that. But I don't belong here."

"You're staying. I have to stay and I want you with me."

"Is that an order?" I said.

"You know what Stan would do if he found out who you are. Knowing all about the caper was bad, but now you saw him knock off Ronnie."

"So it is an order," I said. "Blackmail."

"I don't care what you call it, honey. I got you and I'm going to keep you."

Placidly she resumed brushing her hair.

I was normally an early riser, and earlier still these last few days when I didn't care to linger in bed with Jeanie. But next morning, at considerably after ten o'clock, she was up and dressed while I was still under the blanket.

"What's the matter, honey? Don't you feel good?" she said.

That was an idea. "Not very."

She pressed her lips against my brow. "You got no fever. What hurts you?"

"Nothing in particular."

She nodded understandingly. "Nerves, that's all. A rest will do you good. Want me to bring up breakfast?"

"No."

She kissed me and went. I curled up.

I was in bed for the same reason that Elsa was increasingly confining herself to her room—feeble attempts to burrow ourselves away from crushing reality.

I dozed and woke and dozed. The second time I woke Jeanie was in the room saying, "How're you feeling now?"

"Rotten," I lied.

"It's after two. You want to come down to eat or should I bring you up something?"

"I'm not hungry," I said, and turned my back.

She hovered over me, worrying about me, the way my mother used to and more recently my sister Marjorie. "I'm fine as long as I'm let alone," I said testily, and buried my face in the pillow.

But after she was gone, bed was no longer a comfort and an escape. It was, after all, necessary to have food and drink; more than that, I was assaulted by restlessness. I lay listening to the movement and voices inside the house and out—somebody humming an unfamiliar tune, a car arriving, the creak of the pump handle, Fatso calling, "Hey, where's Stan?"

I rolled out of bed and soaked my face in the basin. I needed a shave, but I didn't shave. I put on the slacks and sport shirt I had bought in Concord, neither any longer clean, and I left the room.

Hank was passing through the downstairs hall. When he saw me descend the stairs, he shouted, "He's comin', Stan," and continued down the hall.

I turned into the parlor. The two other men and the two women were in there, all turned to the door, all watching me.

Elsa stood closest, and her eyes were stricken. All of her seemed to have crumpled, face and body, her bronzed body in black shorts and black strapless elastic halter no longer exuding that impression of indomitable strength, her semi-nakedness making her look pathetically defenseless.

Stan, resting the backs of his thighs against the table, had eyes of ice in a face of rugged rock.

I told myself that he had somehow found out about Elsa and me. Then I looked at Jeanie at the other end of the room and I knew it couldn't be that. She would have been enraged; instead she was terrified.

Was it the other thing, then?

A step sounded behind me. I glanced around. Hank had returned with his rifle.

"Come in," Stan ordered me crisply.

I moved past Elsa. Fatso stood against a window, and for the first time since I'd known him his face wasn't friendly.

Hank and his rifle followed me into the parlor.

Stan said, "Fatso, tell him."

"I just got back from Stoker Hill," Fatso said. "I put through a long-distance call to Hi Globeman in Frisco on the pay phone. Last night you said you didn't know if you had a spot open for me in your organization." He paused, dominated by bitterness. "That's when I thought you was Prof Glow. I figured Hi being there, he'd know if there was a spot for me; and if he said yes and I told you, I figured you'd say okay. I could have it. I spoke to Hi. He said I was nuts. He said Prof Glow's in Los Angeles. He said he saw Prof Glow night before last."

There was nothing I could say.

Elsa was gone. I hadn't noticed her leave while Fatso had been speaking. She must be upstairs now, having shut herself in her room, while whatever was to happen to me would happen.

She couldn't have helped me by staying, but the fact was that she had run out on me.

Jeanie said hoarsely, "I told you, Stan. He helped me get away from the cops. You don't have to worry about him. Honest."

Stan turned his head to her. "You crazy little idiot! He's a lot more dangerous to us than Ronnie ever was, and after what he witnessed yesterday . . ." He pushed himself away from the table. "I ought to bash your face in, Jeanie. I think I will—later."

But first he would take care of me. He had said that I was more dangerous than Ronnie—and he had shot Ronnie in the head. There were plenty of bullets here.

And guns to fit them, and suddenly Elsa was back with one of those guns.

I saw the frown start to grow on Stan's face an instant before I heard Elsa's voice say tautly, "Don't move, Hank, I have you covered." I turned, hearing Stan say, "What the hell's that for?" and there she was holding the muzzle of an automatic pistol two or three feet from the small of Hank's back.

Stan's gun, probably. She had gone up to their room to fetch it when she had realized there was no other hope. She had removed her shoes to descend the stairs and cross the hall in barefooted silence so that she could slip behind Hank without attracting attention.

Standing there, she reminded me a little of Ronnie yesterday in the kitchen doorway—except that she had come to bring life, not death. But she had to be ready to kill in order to preserve life. And she said from deep in her throat, "Hank, I'll shoot if you don't put that rifle down. I'll shoot!"

"What's the idea?" Stan demanded.

"You're going to let him go," she said.

Stan started toward her, slowly, saying woodenly, "Why should you care, baby?"

Elsa retreated two jerky, barefooted steps and checked herself, her bare shoulders hunched as if pulled down by the tremendous burden she was carrying. Her gun wasn't as big as Ronnie's had been, but it overflowed her brown hand.

"I'll shoot!" she warned shrilly. And as Stan came on, starting to detour around Hank, who hardly dared breathe, she had to say what would convince him. "Because I love him. I'll shoot you to have the man I love."

Stan's face went gray.

"It's not true," he whispered.

"It's true. I love him. I won't let you hurt him. And you know I can shoot straight. You taught me, Stan."

Stan stood looking at her. They all looked at her the way they had looked at Ronnie in the kitchen, as fearful now of a woman in love as yesterday they had been of a demented killer. Experimentally I put out a hand to Hank's rifle.

Hank's eyes swung away from her and to me, but I could see in them that he wasn't going to try to keep the rifle from me. Not when a woman in love was behind him with a pistol she knew how to use. So I got the rifle, and for a while at least Elsa and I were on top.

If Stan had doubts that Elsa would use her gun, he had none that I would use the rifle. You could actually watch him shrivel, though I didn't think our guns had as much to do with it as what Elsa had told him.

I said, "We're taking all of you as far as my car. Get moving."

Our guns herded them out of the house and toward the three parked cars. They moved morosely and without words. Elsa and I walked together behind them.

"You have to come with me now," I told her.

"I know."

"Go back for your clothes."

"It's too much risk," she said. "What about their cars?"

"Do you know what the distributor cap is?"

"Yes."

"Pull out the wires," I said.

We had reached the cars. I kept those four covered while Elsa lifted the hood of the Kaiser and then the jeep and messed up their distributor wires. They stood as if huddled together, silent, Fatso's and Hank's faces simply ciphers, Jeanie's sullen, Stan's gray and crumpled except for his eyes. Death for me and for Elsa too was in his eyes.

When Elsa finished, she covered them with the pistol while I started the engine of my car.

Jeanie found her voice then. "You lousy, stinking two-timer! You and that rotten bitch!"

Then Elsa was with me in my car and we were driving away from there.

Chapter Seventeen

We headed north into the White Mountains. We kept away from main roads.

Whenever a car was behind us, Elsa would take a good look at it through the rear window.

"You're conjuring up ghosts," I scolded her. "Even if they repaired the damage to their cars in ten minutes, they'd have no idea which direction we took and which roads. By now there've been so many crossroads that twenty cars couldn't find us, let alone two."

"I know," Elsa said, "but I can't help it."

Deep in the mountains, I pulled up at a filling station that was much like the one in Virginia at which I had stopped less than two weeks ago and had noticed a patch of yellow dress among trees. This station was also off by itself and had hand pumps and a tired wooden shack, but the man who came out to fill my tank was on the youngish side.

As he cranked, he kept glancing at Elsa in the car. Her arms were crossed over her bosom, covering the strapless halter, and from outside the car she looked as if she might be wearing nothing. He must have known it wasn't possible, but evidently he enjoyed the mental picture. She moved her arms and the strip of black cloth was revealed. All the same, he kept staring at her.

Every man would, I thought. I didn't mind. Let them look at her and envy me.

The gas took three dollars out of my wallet.

"We'll have to buy clothes for you," I told her when we were back on the road.

"I've been thinking of it, but I didn't want to stop till we were far enough away. Is there a town near here?"

"A speck on the map some dozen miles away. They'll have to be mighty inexpensive clothes. I have eleven dollars and change left. We'll have to hold onto enough for food and lodging. I've no idea what we'll use for money tomorrow."

"Oh, I took care of that." She lifted a corner of the floorboard mat and straightened up with several bills in her hand. "Five twenties," she said. "They should see us through for a while."

"When did you put them there?"

"After we came back from the shopping trip to Concord. You remember you told me you had very little money left."

"So even then you intended to go away with me?"

"I had no idea what might happen. The money was for an emergency. You can't run very far without money."

I took the five twenties from her because I had pockets and she didn't. I was still living on a woman, I thought—now another woman. But I didn't say it and I didn't feel bad about it. This time it was different, because Elsa was different. I didn't even have to assure myself that the money was merely a loan. From now on everything each of us had we would have and share together.

I said, "I could kiss you."

"Then why don't you, darling?"

I pulled the car off the road and took her in my arms. That kiss was the first we could give wholly, the first that was not snatched surreptitiously in bad conscience and fear.

She started to weep softly. I held her cheek to my chest and stroked her hair.

"It'll work out," I said.

"It can't. You'll never be able to go home. He'll learn your address from Jeanie. Then he'll have your house covered."

"Never is a long time."

"He won't give up."

My fingers trailed from her hair to her cheeks to her shoulder to her body, tenderly learning the marvelous feel of her.

I said, "Then we have no choice. We'll have to turn him in."

"How will that help?"

"He can't get at us from behind bars."

"But there will be time before he's arrested, if they ever do catch him. Don't you see, darling? We'll have to step out into the open to make a charge against him. He'll hear of it, read it in the papers. He'll learn where we are."

"The police will give us protection."

"But can they protect us day and night, always, every minute of our lives? And he'll try. It's no longer so much that you can be a witness against him. It's mostly now that we went off together. He'll take any risk."

"Once he's behind bars . . ."

"Do you really imagine a jail cell will stop him? You don't know how they operate. I do. Haven't you heard of hired killers? Stan can hire one as easily from inside prison as outside. Many an outside killing is arranged from prison." She gripped me with a kind of frenzy. "Hold me, darling. We'll have at least a little while together."

"You're exaggerating," I said. "He's worried chiefly over his own sweet neck, and at this moment he's frantically headed for a new hideout. Chances are he won't stop until he's clear across the country."

"Perhaps," she murmured, not believing it. She sat up and glanced around at the empty, hilly countryside as if expecting ghosts. "Let's go, darling."

We had parked too long. When we reached the village, it was after six o'clock and the small business section was closed down tight. I studied the map. Within the next hour we passed through two more communities that had stores, but only drugstores and eating places were open.

Our inability to buy any sort of garment for her presented us with two problems. The first was eating. I hadn't had a bite all day; I was famished. In certain free-wheeling resort areas she might have got away with going almost anywhere in her irreducible minimum of clothing, but we doubted that they were as broad-minded around here.

But that was minor. I bought sandwiches and soda pop in a lunchroom and brought them out to the car, where we made our meal.

The second problem was how to spend the night in a bed under a roof. It had no solution. We entertained ourselves somewhat wryly with the picture of our car pulling up to a tourist place and she stepping out in those two bits of black cloth, wearing not even shoes. If I were to give her my sport shirt, that would leave me stripped to the waist, and we would still make a highly unconventional pair. I suggested that we say our clothes had been stolen, but Elsa didn't want to run the probable chance of being refused lodging.

"Besides, it will make us more conspicuous," she said. "Stan will ask if anybody has seen two people in a New York car and the woman wearing only—"

"Look," I cut in. "There's not one chance in a thousand that he'll be anywhere near."

"I'd rather not take any more chance than we have to. And I don't want to scandalize people and be embarrassed."

"That's different. There I'm with you."

"We won't be the first people who've slept in a car." Her head moved in that haunted and by now almost instinctive gesture of looking for pursuers. "Keep driving at least till dark," she said.

At twilight we crossed the Connecticut River into northern Vermont. Soon after I wanted to stop for the night, but she said, "Not yet, please," and I humored her.

I wondered how a man she claimed had been so good to her could frighten her so thoroughly. But I knew the answer. I had seen him coldly shoot down a man who had been disarmed, and I had seen his eyes after she had told him she loved me.

When night was complete and we were in the middle of what appeared to be nowhere, I rolled the car off the road, inched forward a good hundred yards over rugged terrain, and swung to the other side of a solitary pine. I cut the engine and the lights and lost Elsa in total darkness.

"Where are the guns?" her voice asked.

"Under the seat. Elsa, stop worrying. Even if by chance he comes this way, he can't see us from the road."

"I know," she said, and suddenly she was against me, tight and hard.

I felt her cold flesh. "Here, take my shirt."

"Then you'll freeze."

"Believe it or not, I'm hardy. I'll shut this window. If it gets colder, I'll turn on the heater for a few minutes."

I helped her on with the shirt. When she settled back against me, I found her chin with my hand and tilted it toward me.

Her lips remained long against mine, and they tasted of sadness.

After a while she said, "Darling, we can't make love tonight."

"Oh," I said.

"It's not that. It's just—I love you so much, but I feel chilled and frightened all the way through."

"All right," I said. "Anyway, a car's still not the place."

"I wouldn't care, darling. I wouldn't care anywhere with you. If you want to very much here and now, I will."

"I want to when you want to."

"I will, darling. Oh, I will. But tonight I'm so—oh, I don't know."

"I understand," I said, and pulled my hand away.

"Oh, no. I need you to hold me."

I held her.

We slept in fits and starts, adjusting ourselves as best we could to the confines of the car seat and the intrusion of the steering wheel.

Whenever in sleep we shifted apart to ease our bones, we would half wake and reach for each other as if we needed constant reassurance that we were together.

Once my groping hands found nothing. Instantly I was wide awake, frantic beyond reason. Gray dawn covered the empty field.

"Elsa!"

"Good morning, darling."

She appeared around the pine tree behind which we had parked. My shirt dangled over her arm.

I devoured with my eyes the bronzed womanliness of her. Mine forever and the hell with Stan.

As I put on the shirt, I said, "The first thing we do is buy you a dress."

"Have you forgotten that today is Sunday?"

"So it is. Maybe somewhere somebody is trying to do business in clothes in spite of Sunday."

Nobody was, as far as we could find. If we had been in the market for antique furniture or maple sugar, we could have bought all we wanted on the road, and in the larger towns an occasionally open drugstore or newspaper store could have stocked us up on newspapers and bathing caps and alarm clocks. But nowhere was there anything for sale to put on a woman's back.

For another day Elsa would be confined to the car. "I really don't mind," she said. "We'd keep driving anyway, and I have you with me all the time, and eating in the car is like a picnic."

We drove clear across Vermont to Burlington. Our choice of direction at that point was limited. Before us was Lake Champlain and not far north was Canada. We had to turn south. At the tip of Lake Champlain we crossed into New York State over a toll bridge, where the man who collected the toll looked twice at Elsa's very bare shoulders and down through the car window at more revealed flesh. We drove down the west shore of Lake George. Everybody was out on that warm Sunday. We drifted along roads crowded with tourists, yet we were alone together among hordes, our car a kind of prison that we did not wholly resent.

We had made an early breakfast in the car of pound cake and cookies and a bottle of milk and a box of cherries. At the edge of the teeming resort town of Lake George, which appeared to consist almost wholly of elaborate tourist cabins, I stopped at a lunch wagon for a container of hot coffee and four hamburger sandwiches to take out. It didn't occur to me to have a real meal at the counter without her.

She was laughing when I approached the car—the first time I had seen her laugh in a long time.

"What's so funny?" I demanded.

"What a couple of tramps we look like! You needing a shave badly and your clothes soiled and crumpled and me half naked. Soon you'll be ashamed to leave the car too."

"Wait until you see me cleaned up tomorrow. You might even fall in love with me."

"Darling, I'd love you in rags and a beard to your knees."

We ate and drank as we drove. I shook off traffic by turning northeast into the magnificent mountain lake country of the Adirondacks. As we bore deeper into the state park, other cars virtually disappeared. A roadside food stand popped up at an isolated village, and there, standing at the outdoor counter, we at last ate outside the car. The evening we spent on the shore of a crescent-shaped lake, nameless to us, and watched boats far out on the water.

If we had had a blanket, we would have spent the night on the ground. With twilight a chilly breeze came up. We returned to the car. We sat together, hardly touching each other and wordless, but closer than we had ever been, together in that lost little world we had made for ourselves and that we desperately wished could last forever. We watched the sun drop over the lake and night gather, and I could no longer see her.

I said, "As soon as we're settled tomorrow, we'll get a marriage license."

"No."

"Are you turning me down?"

She didn't answer. I felt her shiver beside me.

"Take my shirt," I said. "If that's not enough, I'll turn on the car heater."

I removed my shirt, but she didn't take it when I handed it to her. Her arms went around me. She whispered, "Oh, my darling!" and I felt her breasts against my chest.

So that was our nuptial couch, that cramped car seat which after all had its own perfection after the many hours it had been our home. Here then was the blending, the absorbing, the culmination, the marriage.

And later I said, "Whether you like it or not, you're my wife already."

"Yes, that way."

"Then why not legally too?"

"Because it doesn't matter."

"It matters very much to me."

"Please," she said. "Let's not argue now."

I picked my shirt off the floor board and put it on her. The night grew colder. I started the engine and turned on the heater and within a few minutes we were steeped in coziness. I removed only one hand from her to kill the engine, then put the hand back. We slept.

Chapter Eighteen

In the morning we hunted up a numbered road and followed it into a neat little valley town named Honey Point. It had a bank and a post office and four filling stations and one of every kind of store except a dress store. Elsa suggested I try the variety store, which had its windows crammed with toys and tools and magazines. I was dubious, but inside I found a rack devoted to what the girl who waited on me called ladies' garments.

I bought a size-twelve chocolate-colored cotton dress with roses climbing all over it and the cheapest size-seven shoes in the place.

Elsa couldn't quite restrain a gasp when she unwrapped the package in the car. If she didn't care for my taste, she didn't say so. Sitting in the car, she wriggled on the dress over what she already wore and slipped her feet into the shoes. At last she was released from the car. We crossed the road to a restaurant and ate a thumping breakfast.

I stroked my four-day beard. "Now that you have clothes on you, I feel by contrast like a bum you brought in here for a handout. I noticed a barbershop down the road."

"If you'll let me have some money, I'll shop for odds and ends meanwhile."

I handed her one of her twenty-dollar bills. "Your hundred may have to last us quite a while."

"Don't worry. You won't find me an extravagant"—there was the least hesitation—"woman."

"The noun is wife. That's what you're going to be. My wife."

She folded the twenty-dollar bill into a small square and stood up. "I'll meet you at the car," she said.

I had my shave. On the way back to the car, I passed a log cabin that housed a real-estate agent. I went in. Ten minutes later I came out with a name and driving directions on a slip of paper.

Elsa hadn't lost time changing out of the dress I had bought her. She was waiting for me in a high-necked polo shirt and a flaring gingham skirt and different shoes.

I said, "After all, that was the first clothing I ever bought for a woman. To me you look delicious in anything."

"Thank you, darling. Where will we go now?"

"We stop going, I hope. I got a line on a comparatively inexpensive bungalow for rent some ten miles from here."

The name on the slip of paper was Steelman. We found it printed on an RFD mailbox. An elderly, weather-beaten man sat on the porch of a one-story white clapboard house. He didn't rise as we walked up to the porch from the car.

Rocking unceasingly in a creaking rocker, he said that the bungalow was a quarter of a mile from the road; that his son had built it for himself and wife, but had found it too cramped when the baby was born and had bought a house close to town; that he himself lived here all alone since his wife had died last winter; that seeing the summer was partly over we could have the bungalow for only three hundred dollars, in advance, till Labor Day.

"The agent told me two-fifty," I said.

Mr. Steelman looked us over. "It's got running water and everything's electric—hot water, stove, refrigerator. Three hundred dollars."

"Will you take a check?"

"Where's your bank?"

"New York City."

"Nope," he said. "Cash."

"Look. Will you take fifty in cash and the rest in check? You'll know in a few days if the check has cleared and you'll have your fifty, so you can't lose anything."

"Let's see your cash."

Elsa spoke up. "Don't you think we ought to look at the bungalow first?"

She had something there. The three of us drove the quarter mile in my car over what was the vaguest indication of road. Under two stately elms the bungalow stood alone and white and tiny. We followed Mr. Steelman in. The interior walls were unfinished, the studs bare. There was one room, pretty small, and part of it was given over to the compact kitchen and its definitely secondhand equipment. As for the bathroom, a man my size could just about expand his chest in it with the door closed. But it was all very clean.

Elsa nodded to me and I said we'd take it.

"You provide your own linen," Mr. Steelman said.

"But the agent told me it was completely furnished," I protested.

"It's furnished. What do you call this furniture? I'll tell you what I'll do. Being I like the looks of you young people, I'll throw in sheets and towels and blankets for the whole summer, and all it will cost you is fifty dollars more. Three-fifty for the season."

He reminded me of Hank. All landlords were the same, I thought.

"All right," I said.

Mr. Steelman crouched at an electric switch box close to the floor and rose saying that we could use the stove at once and would have hot water in an hour. We drove back to his house. I had no blank checks; I used one of his, writing in the name of my bank. While I wrote it out, Elsa haggled with him over the number of towels and blankets. She won; he had met his match. I realized that I would have saved a hundred dollars if I had let her handle the negotiations from the start.

But it didn't matter. We had a home, a dream come true. As we drove up to the bungalow for the second time, Elsa said, "I've never seen anything lovelier."

I knew exactly what she meant.

We dumped the linens and blankets on the mattress. As soon as our arms were free, we filled them with each other.

After a brief minute she disentangled herself from me. "I need a shower desperately. After that we'll go out to stock up on groceries."

"The water isn't hot yet."

"I've become hardened to cold water in Hank's creek." She kicked off her shoes and started for the bathroom.

"Modest, sweetheart?" I said. "Is it necessary to undress with a door between us?"

She turned with her hand on the doorknob and smiled. "Of course not." She pulled the polo shirt over her head and stepped out of her skirt. That still left her in what she had been wearing for two days. The halter came off. She drew in her breath and smiled at me again, pausing a long, taut moment before she stepped out of her black shorts.

I kept myself from going to her. I stood watching the lift of her splendid breasts as she raised her arms to undo her hair. Once before I had seen her with nothing on, but that had been a brief and guilty glimpse, and last night in the car it had been totally dark. I thought that I would never want to stop looking at her like that—at the smooth, ripe, strong womanliness of her. And then her hair was down, the corn-silk flowing against bronzed skin, and she was still facing me, letting me see her, desiring me to see her.

"Now may I take my shower?" she said, half tauntingly, but with a queer constriction in her voice.

"Do you want to—at once?"

"No," she said.

I gathered her to me. Presently I released her and started to pull off the bed the stuff we had dropped on it.

"Wait," she said. "This is our home. Let's have a properly made-up bed."

I could wait. It was sheer delight to watch her move about as she spread a sheet on the mattress and stuffed the two pillows into pillowcases. I came up behind her as she patted the pillows into place. I seized her and she let herself fall forward on the bed, pulling me along with her.

"My wife," I said later. "We'll have a proper marriage as well as a proper bed. We'll go get a license this afternoon."

"I'll be no good for you."

"What nonsense!"

"What will your family and friends think of me?"

"They'll be as proud of you as I am."

"Will they be proud of me when they find out I was a gangster's mistress?"

"I won't let you speak like that about yourself. You're as decent as any woman."

"How do you know?"

"I've got eyes and ears and, I hope, something in my head. You're going to be my wife."

"No."

Playfully I knelt astride her and pinned her arms down on the bed. "Say yes and I'll let you up."

She lay limp, her eyes somberly staring up at me, and suddenly I didn't feel at all playful.

"What's the use?" she said. "You can't take me back to your home because of Stan. You can't go back to your job."

"We have a good six weeks ahead of us here. By then something will have happened."

"I know. He'll have caught up to us."

"Here? How the devil can he?"

"He will."

I was again lying flat on my back beside her. "Assuming you're right—I don't for a moment say you are, but assuming it for a moment—that's no argument against us getting married."

"I have as much of you as I ever will have. I mustn't expect more."

"You haven't given your real reason."

"I'm only part of your caper."

"You know better."

She said listlessly, "There were two women in your caper. I'm the second."

"Don't dare compare Jeanie to you."

"You made love to her too."

"And you made love to Stan. That puts us even. I was a damn fool to get into it, but if I hadn't I would never have met you. I love you. Do you love me?"

"You know I do."

"Then that's all that counts."

"Is it?" she said, and slipped off the bed. "The water should be warm now."

She had her shower and then I had mine. When I came out, she was dressed, waiting for me. We had hardly a word to say to each other.

Halfway to Honey Point I stopped the car.

"Elsa, are you going to let Stan stay between us?" I said. "After all, that's what it all comes down to."

"Can we help it?" she said.

I put my arms about her and she clung to me. Her mouth tasted salty—like tears.

Chapter Nineteen

While Elsa shopped in the food market, I sweated in a phone booth trying to get through to my brother, George, in his office. I juggled the quarters in my hand, trying to recall what the toll was from New York City to Kentucky and adding a dollar because this was almost three hundred miles farther north.

Whatever the sum was, I couldn't afford it. After I had paid for our late lunch and had bought for myself no more than a pair of denim pants and a couple of T shirts and a razor, we had twenty-three dollars left. Elsa had taken eighteen of that into the food market, pointing out that it wouldn't go far because she had to stock our larder from scratch. I considered reversing the toll charge and decided that it wouldn't do to get off on the wrong foot with George.

His voice came on for an instant before the operator cut him off to demand payment. After the clanging of quarters died away, George said, "Hello, hello."

"This is Larry."

"Where the devil are you?" he said.

"Somewhere in the Adirondacks. How are Alice and the kids?"

"Fine. Larry, what have you been up to? Marjorie has phoned twice and in between has been sending incoherent letters. As far as I can dope out, she found you with a naked woman in the apartment."

"Not quite naked."

"Alice said she hoped it was true. You know how Alice talks. Marjorie says you went off with this woman and you haven't been in touch with her since."

"I haven't had a chance to write."

"What's she like? Are you with her now?"

"Well, not with her. I'm with somebody else."

"You dog," George said cheerfully. "Alice will love this. What are you doing, changing them for new models every few days?"

"It's no joke. We're going to be married sometime this week."

After an uneasy pause, George said, "Is she nice?"

"She's wonderful. We intend to spend the rest of the summer here. It so happens I ran completely out of cash, and I can't cash a check because nobody knows me here. I was going to open a bank account today, but we got into town a few minutes after the bank closed at two-thirty. I'll have to wait until tomorrow, and then it will take days, maybe a week, for the check I'll deposit to clear. Meanwhile I'm flat broke."

"I'll wire you money right away."

"That's the rub. There's no telegraph office around here. Besides, I've lost my wallet and can't identify myself. Why don't you send me cash by registered special-delivery airmail? I need a hundred. No, make it two hundred."

"All that cash by mail?"

"I'll risk it. Of course, I'll pay you back."

"I just sent the girl out to make a deposit, so there's little cash in the office, but I'll try to scrape up two hundred and drop it in the mail today."

"Swell. My address is care of Steelman, RFD One, Honey Point, New York."

"Let me write it down. I've got it. And, Larry, call Marjorie, will you? At least write her. She's worried sick about you."

"She's worried because I'm with a woman. She'll have to get used to it."

"That's true. But write her."

"All right."

The operator broke in to tell us that our time was up.

"You haven't told me her name," George said over the operator's voice.

"Elsa."

"Bring her to see us when—"

We were disconnected. I hung up and went next door to the food market, where Elsa was having her order checked out.

The tiny bungalow looked better, more homelike, every time we rolled up to it. We stacked away the groceries on the open shelves and in the refrigerator and I helped Elsa prepare a lavish dinner. I felt contentedly domestic. She washed the dishes while I dried. Everything we did we wanted to do together.

As she stood at the sink, I kissed the nape of her neck below her piled-up hair. "Happy?" I said.

"Very." Then abruptly her tone changed. "Darling, are the guns still in the car?"

"I haven't touched them."

"Don't you think we ought to keep one in the house?"

The cheeriness of the bright little kitchen vanished.

"If it will make you feel better," I said.

I went out and fetched the automatic pistol from under the car seat. The hard, deadly feel of it stretched my nerves. I laid it down on the table.

"Do you know how to use it?" she said.

"I'm not bad with a rifle, but I've never fired one of these."

"I'll show you how."

She unloaded it. There were seven cartridges in the chamber. She told me that the gun was a .38 caliber, that it wouldn't kick as badly as a .45—for example, the gun Ronnie had had—but the tendency would still be to hit the ceiling or even put the bullet into your own head if you weren't careful. She showed me how to thumb off the safety catch and how to squeeze the stock rather than simply pull the trigger.

As she reloaded the gun, I said, "I hope you don't expect me to go around with it in my hip pocket."

"I don't suppose it will be any use to us anyway, but as long as we have it . . ."

She stuck it into the top drawer of the dresser.

We had a lot of sleep to make up for those two fitful and cramped nights we had spent in the car. We went to bed early.

During the night she woke me. "Darling, did you lock the door?"

"I think so."

"Make sure."

I got out of bed and found the door locked.

"What about the windows?" she said.

"We can't sleep with them shut tight. But the screens are locked."

"Are you sure?"

I made the rounds of the windows. I put out the light and crawled back into bed.

"There's not a chance he can find us buried away here," I argued.

"He will," she said. "Somehow."

Wednesday morning the money arrived from George. Now that we were again solvent, I returned to my insistence on marriage.

This time she didn't fight me.

"If you wish," she said.

"The point is, what do you wish?"

"I want to do whatever makes you happy."

"Then let's go get the license," I said.

We put on our best clothes, our going-to-town clothes, our one change of clothes. She wore her high-necked polo shirt and flaring gingham skirt, I the slacks and sport shirt I had had on my back when we had fled Hank's place and which she had since washed and pressed. We looked presentable enough. We set out for the town clerk's office in Honey Point.

On the way I said, "This is a hell of a note. I propose to you and you finally accept, and you show as much enthusiasm as if we were going out to buy a pack of cigarettes."

"You can hardly expect me to be a blushing bride." Her hands were quietly folded on her lap. "The truth is, darling, I'm happier than I've ever been is my life."

"But haunted by Stan," I said.

"It's not only Stan. I'm afraid off my past. Perhaps in some way we can get away from Stan, but I can't get away from my past. Sooner or later it will come out. How will you feel about me being your wife when I'm in jail?"

"Chances are I'll be in jail with you. You forget I made myself an accessory after the fact. But I doubt that the police will bother to get very tough with either of us."

"Perhaps not, but it will be in the papers. Everybody you know and respect will read about how your wife had once lived with a gangster."

"So we're back to that?"

"Yes. Marriage isn't only love and kisses."

"But love and kisses will help us through anything." She was silent and then said, "Darling, you're really very naive."

"Just a boy at heart."

"You are," she said, "and I love you for it. I'll be proud and happy to be Mrs. Lawrence Knight."

The town clerk was not exactly dozing in his swivel chair, but I had to speak to him twice before he sat up. He wrote out forms, handed us his pen with which to sign here and there, gave us the address of a local doctor for our blood tests, told us we would have to wait seventy-two hours.

"Will your office be open Saturday?" I asked.

"Till twelve." He leered amiably at Elsa. "I'd be in a hurry myself if I was twenty years younger. Prettiest one we've had here all year."

Elsa blushed, very much like a bride now. I said we'd be seeing him in seventy-two hours, and we went to get our blood tests.

We spent the rest of that day shopping, mostly for the clothes we needed so badly. When George's two hundred dollars were down to fifty, we called a halt. The cashier of the Honey Point National Bank had assured me that by Monday I would be able to draw on my account.

We discovered a wooded lake with a public beach some dozen miles from our bungalow, and Thursday and Friday we swam and lay in the sun.

Saturday morning we dressed in brand-new clothes and drove to

Honey Point to be married. A girl from the town clerk's office and a man from one of the other offices were the witnesses. Elsa kissed the clerk and the male witness and I kissed only Elsa, and we were man and wife.

When we passed Mr. Steelman's house, he called out that he had a letter for me. I stopped the car and went up on his porch. Without breaking the rhythm of his rocking chair, he handed me a letter.

"Came for you this morning," he said.

My name and address were in Marjorie's stubby script. I stared at it so long that Mr. Steelman asked me if it was bad news.

"No," I said, and stuck the letter into my hip pocket.

"Who's it from?" Elsa asked when I reached the car.

"From my brother, George," I lied.

"Aren't you going to read it?"

"There's no rush. No doubt he wants me to send him a check for the two hundred."

I carried her over the threshold. She squealed a great deal. She was gayer than I had ever known her, even carefree. My mood had changed to exactly the opposite, but I tried not to show it.

Later I locked myself in the bathroom and read Marjorie's letter. There wasn't anything in it I couldn't have guessed beforehand. She wrote that Wednesday she had phoned George again. I hadn't dropped her even a card and she was awfully, awfully worried. George told her I was getting married and gave her my address. Who was the woman? Evidently I thought so little of my only sister that I didn't even bring the woman home to meet her first. She hoped it wasn't the tart she had found naked in the apartment. George said it wasn't, but after the insane way I had acted she wouldn't be surprised if it was that tart or another tart. She was very lonely. Why didn't I write her? It was becoming harder and harder for her to get around on her swollen legs and she was awfully, awfully alone. Who was the woman?

I tore the letter and envelope into bits and flushed them down the drain. I didn't want Elsa to know that I had received a letter addressed here to me from my sister.

While Elsa was preparing dinner, I had a peek in the top dresser drawer. The pistol was there. And the rifle was in the car.

How much could I do with either?

That night we made a ritual of going to bed.

"Let's pretend this is the first time for both of us," she said. "I'm the timid bride and you're the awkward groom."

Anything she wanted. I couldn't let her discover that this time I was the one who was distraught.

In the spirit of the game, she undressed in the bathroom. When I had my pajamas on, I called to her. She came out with a coy show of modesty in a nightgown she had bought that day—a coral nylon mist over the bronze lusciousness of her. And indeed it was like the first time, like the first discovery of her body. And in a way for me it was as if this would also be the last time, as if now and never again would I experience the miracle of our blending love.

Then she slept, awakening briefly to cuddle down against me, murmuring, "My husband!" and drifting back to sleep.

I lay wide-eyed, staring into the darkness, listening to the night sounds of insects. I was certain that I could keep awake all night because it would be impossible for me to fall asleep if I tried.

But it was out of sleep that Elsa roused me, whispering, "I thought I heard somebody," and instantly I was alert, straining to hear.

The overhead light went on, and there in the room were Stan and Jeanie.

Chapter Twenty

His gun was held loosely, almost carelessly. Stubby and broad in a conservatively cut brown worsted suit, he advanced to the foot of the bed.

Jeanie closed the door and stood with her back against it.

Before having gone to bed, I had made doubly sure that the door was locked, and I had closed and locked all the windows but one. I turned my head, and there was the hole low in the screen of the one open window. He had cut it out with a knife and reached a hand through and unhooked the screen; then he had climbed through the window and turned the key in the door to admit Jeanie. Elsa had heard him, but by the time she had awakened me it was too late.

"Stan!" Elsa was staring up at the terrible bleakness of his face at the foot of the bed. "Stan, listen," she whispered, and lost her voice.

"I'm listening," he said tonelessly.

He was in no great hurry. He could have shot us down as we slept, but that would have made it too easy for us, too simple for him. He wanted us to know it was coming, watch it come, live through a lifetime of hell before it came. And there was another reason he delayed. He was driven by self-preservation as well as hate, and he had to find out if we had done or said or written anything that would further increase the menace of the police.

Patiently he waited for Elsa to recover her voice.

I could feel her gather her breath as she lay beside me under the blanket. "Stan, we don't intend you any harm. It's been a whole week. If we were going to go to the police, wouldn't we have done so already? I swear we never will."

He said, "I don't give one single goddamn what you swear. Get out of that bed."

Slowly I was drawing my hand up under the cover.

"Stan, you can't!" Elsa pleaded. "After what we've been to each other. Stan, listen!"

"I listened," he said. "So you didn't blabber yet. I'm here to make sure you don't."

Elsa twisted on her side and threw her arms around me. She shouldn't have done that. In another second or two I might have got my hand under the pillow. Her weight pinned that arm down.

But she didn't know. She held onto me in frenzy. "You can't, Stan. Let's talk it over, Stan!"

"Get out of that bed."

Jeanie spoke for the first time. The voice that tore quivering with viciousness from her throat was a voice I had never before heard.

"What're you waiting for? Give it to 'em."

The gun in Stan's hand became less casual. Its muzzle definitely pointed.

Elsa rolled away from me. "I'll get out, Stan. Look, I'm getting out."

She tumbled off the bed, pulling the blanket along with her. She had gained nothing. He preferred us to die apart rather than in each other's arms, and now he had separated us.

I said desperately, "You're not going to kill her."

"No?" He seemed curious to know why I was so sure. He glanced at her cowering against the chair in her nylon nightgown—in that coral mist scarcely concealing the flesh he knew even better than I. "No?" he said again, returning his bleak gaze to me.

I lay uncovered, in pajamas, the blanket hanging half off the bed, and my right hand was wholly visible. I could only talk.

"You'll hate yourself," I said. "If you kill, her, you'll never be able to live with yourself."

Something came into his eyes, the shadow of a shadow, the smallest of doubts. Hope started to stir in me. Possibly, just barely possibly, that doubt might have grown if Elsa had let it alone.

"Stan, listen to me," she implored. "I didn't cheat on you. We couldn't help falling in love. It's not just an affair. We were married this morning. We—"

"Married?" The shadow of doubt froze to death in his eyes. "You wouldn't marry me. I turned the country upside down looking for the guy you thought was your husband so you could get a divorce. Four years I looked, and I found him, and it turned out you weren't married to him. This heel came along and right away you . . ."

His voice faded tiredly. Over the foot of the bed his face hovered, the grayness seeping into it, and now it was much older than it had been a week ago—the face of death.

She had said too much, though silence wouldn't have changed anything. The vague, unreal hope had been no hope at all, for there were too many circles within circles, too many separate reasons why it was essential for the man he was to destroy us.

"Do it!" Jeanie shrieked. She might have been a stranger standing against the door, tall in a long green dress and high-heeled shoes, those normally pretty, childlike features—the small mouth, the clear eyes, the smooth cheeks—twisted and broken by driving fury. "Why don't you do it?"

I saw it then. It seemed to me that for some time I had known, but I hadn't believed, or hadn't wanted to believe; but her expression and her words made me sure.

"Jeanie fingered Bertie Bride," I blurted.

For all I could tell, his hand had already started to squeeze the gun. But what I said checked him. This was something he absolutely had to hear.

"Huh?" he said.

I had brought my hands up as high as my shoulders. I lay under his gun as if crucified.

"Think about it," I said. "Why was Bertie Bride the only one of you the police connected with the caper? How did they find out where he was staying and under what name? Why did Jeanie have a bag packed and ready, with the money in it and several complete changes of clothes?"

"He's just saying any old thing that comes into his head," Jeanie countered.

"Maybe." Stan didn't take his eyes off me. "Go on."

At the side of the bed the pink mist that was Elsa shimmered and subsided. I could hear her breathe, and I could hear the beating of my own heart.

I said, "Jeanie came along with you to be in on the kill. Jeanie, who cared for me, who wouldn't let me leave her, who even blackmailed me into remaining her lover. Now she wants me dead because I'm with another woman. She's like you, Stan. Essentially a primitive. Love violently and hate violently and react to any disagreeable problem with violence."

"You were saying she fingered Bertie," he said.

"In June he beat her black and blue. From what she's told me, I gathered she started to dislike him before that, but stayed on with him from habit or for convenience or simply because he was a man. Another girl would have left him after that beating. Not Jeanie. That wasn't her way; she couldn't let him get off so easily. The caper was being planned. She could wait until after it was pulled off. If she worked it right, she could kill him as surely as if she held the gun herself, and nobody would know. Also—though I believe this was less important to her—she would get his share of the loot."

"All he ever does is talk, talk, talk," Jeanie said peevishly. "You going to listen to him all night, Stan?"

"It makes sense," he observed softly.

"That morning in Darson she phoned the police," I went on. "They arrived quicker than she expected. She was still in the room when the street shooting started, but she managed to get away." I dared hardly pause for breath. I made myself sneer. "I don't know if Bertie Bride was her first victim. I'm slated to be her second. And after me it will be you, Stan, because now she fears you. She knows the code as well as anybody. A squealer must die."

"He's lying!" she cried shrilly.

His gun was again held casually. But in an instant he could bring the muzzle back to bear on me, and he would.

"We'll see about you later," he said, speaking to Jeanie but looking at me.

I said, "Do you imagine she'll wait until later? She won't take the chance now that you know. She has a gun in her handbag. She always keeps it near her. She'll—"

Stan turned to her then. I looked completely defenseless lying on the bed with my arms outflung, and he had to see what she was doing behind him. He saw her standing near the door with her hands not touching her straw handbag, which hung over her shoulder.

I snatched the gun from under the pillow and shot him.

The gun bucked wildly against my palm. I gripped it with both hands and kept squeezing. It was a very short distance from where I sat on the bed, and he stood at the foot of it with his face turned from me. Seven bullets couldn't miss him. Some of them didn't.

Two women were screaming.

I glimpsed Elsa move and pass out of my line of vision. Directly ahead of me Stan had sunk out of sight below the footboard, and at the door Jeanie was clawing at her straw handbag.

The smallness of the room helped. I was off the bed and had reached Jeanie before she could get the little gun out. I grabbed her wrist and twisted, and the sound of her pain hurt my ears. The little gun fell to the floor.

Elsa crouched over Stan. She lifted her face. "He's dead," she said.

We stood in the bungalow doorway and watched Jeanie disappear into the night.

"I had to let her go," I said. "I couldn't turn her over to the police."

Elsa put a hand on my arm. "What will she do?"

"She'll get along. She won't have trouble finding another man."

In the distance we heard a car engine start. We followed its progress from first speed to second and then the sound of it died.

The night remained silent. Mr. Steelman was our only neighbor within a mile. Probably he wasn't home, if the shots and screams hadn't brought him.

I entered the bungalow and placed on the table the two guns—the big one with which I had shot and killed Stan and the little one I had taken away from Jeanie.

He lay at the foot of the bed, his body curled like a weary child's, his dead eyes staring under the bed. I looked away from him and saw Elsa beside me.

"You had the gun under the pillow," she said.

"I expected him. The letter was from my sister. I hadn't written her because I had to keep our address, even our postmark, from her. But George gave her the address. I should have thought of that possibility. So there was the letter and I knew what would happen. Stan would call on Marjorie and pretend he was a friend who urgently had to get in touch with me. I imagine he visited her earlier this week, before she had the address, but he kept in touch with her by phone.

And when she got it, she saw no reason for not letting him know."

"You didn't tell me about the letter."

"I didn't want to frighten you. And I knew you would insist we start running again, and I was damned if I would. It had to be settled here and now. I thought of having the police set a trap for him, but you'd convinced me he could get us even from prison. No, it was my job. I assumed he would make his play at night. And he did. He had only our RFD address; it took time for them to narrow down the search. They must have done that much during the day and then waited for the middle of the night. And I expected them—him, anyway. I stuck the gun under the mattress, and after you were asleep I put it under my pillow. I intended to be ready when he tried to get in, but I botched it." I felt my mouth twist. "I'm not much good at this kind of thing. I keep making mistakes."

She shifted her feet so that her back would be toward the dead man. "Was what you told him about Jeanie true?"

"Probably. I had to keep talking. He was very good with a gun and I was very bad. I had to divert his attention from me, and I did it by telling him why Jeanie had fingered Bertie." I ran my hand over my face. "I had to kill him. There was no alternative."

"I know," she muttered.

"Steelman has a phone," I said. "I'll call the police from there."

"Wait. Nobody has to know what happened here tonight."

I looked at her. "You mean bury his body the way Ronnie's body was buried and keep everything from the police?"

"We could."

"We couldn't and we mustn't," I said. "The caper is over for both of us. Whatever there will be to face, we'll face together."

"Yes," she said. "We'll face it."

We dressed and hand in hand we went out into the night.

THE END

So Wicked My Love
BRUNO FISCHER

Part One: The Redhead

1

I came out of the water and searched for enough space on the beach to lie down. It wasn't easy to find. The thermometer was pushing ninety-five on that Sunday afternoon in July, and the usual million people were at Coney Island. You couldn't see the sand for the bodies, all that half-naked flesh in every size and shape and color.

Near the jetty at the end of Bay 19 I found a spot unoccupied.

If I didn't mind my face near the feet of a fat woman sprawled on a blanket and being tripped over every now and then by whooping children, I could stretch out quite comfortably in the sun. I didn't like getting sand in my hair. A loose sheet of newspaper drifted by on a half-hearted breeze. I snatched it and shook out the sand.

It was the first and last pages of the *Courier*. I could tell at a glance it was yesterday's because of the three-column headline in the left-hand corner:

ARMORED CAR HELD UP
IN BROOKLYN; BANDITS
ESCAPE WITH $80,000

For a little while Friday the robbery had interested me because it had happened a couple of blocks from our trucking concern near Bush Terminal.

The armored car had been making payroll deliveries to some of the big industrial plants when, in broad daylight, half a dozen or so men had shot down one guard and disarmed the other and helped themselves to the cash. Within a few minutes the neighborhood had been crawling with cops, but not until the bandits had made a clean getaway. Two detectives had come to our office to question Mort Levy, one of our drivers, who claimed he'd seen a black Buick filled with tough-looking men driving up Fourth Avenue shortly after the holdup.

That was all there had been to it as far as I was concerned, and I hadn't been concerned personally. The story was now no more to me than print on a newspaper that I was going to use to keep the sand off my hair.

I stretched out on my back. The sky was misty blue and the sun was a ball of fire. A police helicopter, what they called an "eggbeater," flew no more than a hundred feet above the water, watching for swimmers or boaters in trouble. Somebody walked close by and kicked sand in my eyes.

When I growled, a girl muttered, "Sorry." I raised my head. She was picking her way past people and lunch baskets and deck chairs, and her head moved from side to side as she looked for somebody. Her bare legs were very nicely turned and her tight hips in yellow Lastex swung just enough.

From behind she was built something like Florence. All of a sudden I knew I shouldn't have come here. I had thought that among a million people a man could get away from himself. But it wasn't working out that way. There were too many girls, and every once in a while I was sure to see one who in some way or other reminded me of Florence. Like that girl in the tight yellow bathing suit.

I closed my eyes. I said to myself: Look, it's over, finished, done. She returned your ring last night. There are other girls, thousands of pretty ones along the beach who wouldn't mind getting acquainted. Forget Florence by having yourself some fun.

I stayed where I was.

By and by I opened my eyes, and I found myself looking past my toes at the girl in the yellow bathing suit. I lay close to the high tide line where the sand was packed hard, and nobody was between us except a couple of small boys building a castle. She was standing at the edge of the water, a bathing cap in one hand and a striped white-and-yellow beach jacket over her arm.

I was sure I'd seen her before, many times before, but couldn't remember where.

If she was familiar to me, I wasn't to her. Her eyes swept past me, swept slowly back and forth twice over those thousands between her and the boardwalk. This was one hell of a place to find anybody from whom you'd become separated for as much as half a minute. Her mouth twisted with annoyance, and she dropped her jacket and started to put on the cap over her flaming red hair.

Then I placed her. The red hair had put me off. Last time I'd seen her, a good seven years ago, it had been brown. She was as pretty as she'd ever been, with a button nose and a slightly turned-up chin.

I sat up. "Cherry Drew," I called.

Her bare shoulders jerked, as if somebody had said boo to her in a dark room. Then she stared at me and stood very still with both hands fixed at the cap she had been pushing over her hair. I had an impression she was scared stiff of me.

But that couldn't be, so it had to mean she was scared of somebody she had mistaken me for.

"Don't you remember me, Cherry?" I said. "I'm Ray Whitehead."

I had started to move toward her, but I didn't take more than a couple of steps. Without a word or smile or any kind of acknowledgment, she picked up her beach jacket and walked away along the edge of the water curling around her ankles.

I was plenty burned up. Who the devil was Cherry Drew to be snooty? Her father had been the Hessian Valley town drunk and her mother had scrubbed people's floors to support the family and Cherry herself had started running around with anything in pants almost as soon as she had what it took.

The hell with her. The hell with Florence. I watched a big ship from Manhattan rounding the bend in the horizon at Sea Gate.

All of a sudden there was Cherry Drew coming back, and this time she had a friendly smile for me.

"Hello, Ray," she said, putting out her hand. "For a minute I didn't recognize you."

Maybe not, but she'd known who I was when I'd told her my name, and I had an idea that hearing it was what had made her scoot away from me. To avoid me, or to avoid anybody who had ever known her. For some reason she had changed her mind.

Now here we were shaking hands and asking each other how we were.

"You've put on weight, Ray," she said. "You used to be a skinny kid. Now you're quite manly."

Lightly she touched my bare chest with her fingertips, and my skin tingled.

"You haven't changed," I commented.

Her figure had been fully matured at fifteen, and it wasn't any different now at twenty-five—lissome and firmly curved. And her small-featured face still could have passed for a teenager's, except for her eyes, which had a look of having crowded in a lot of living in a few years. We'd stopped talking. Her head was dipped and she was digging into the sand with her big toe. But it wasn't really in the sand. Her toe punctured the newspaper I had spread out for my head; it went right through the headline about the armored car holdup.

"Are you with anybody?" she asked as her toe kept ripping away at the paper.

"No. Are you?"

"All alone." She gave me a bright smile. "Lucky I ran into you. I was getting bored."

I wondered whom she'd been looking for on the beach and why she'd been so nervous when she'd heard her name called.

We sat down on the sand and told each other what we'd been doing the last seven years. She told me her father had died and her mother had moved in with a sister in New Rochelle and she was living alone in New York, where she worked as a salesgirl in a department store. I told her that my folks had moved to Borough Park here in Brooklyn while I'd been in the Army, and when I'd come out my father had taken me in as a partner in the small trucking business he'd established on the waterfront.

"A truck driver," she said, and looked at me speculatively. "I guess you have to be pretty tough to do waterfront trucking."

"What do you know about it?"

"I've read about rackets and killings on the docks."

"We keep clean," I said. "Anyway, I can take care of myself."

"I'm sure you can, Ray."

She put her hand on my biceps, which were in good shape. Again I tingled at her touch.

After that we hadn't much to say to each other. After all, we'd never known each other well. Though Hessian Valley was a small town upstate a way, between the Hudson and Connecticut, where everybody knew everybody else, we'd gone with different crowds. She'd left high school after one year and had already been running around with older boys and even men. We would say hello on the street or in juke joints, and once I'd taken her for a drive in my father's car and we'd parked and necked. But I'd been too young, too inexperienced for her, and probably that was why it had ended there before anything really had a chance to begin. When I'd asked her for another date, she had laughed and said she'd wait till I grew up.

Well, I was grown up, and sitting beside her among a million other people I remembered the way her mouth had tasted. She had kissed more intently, more expertly, than any other girl I had come to know and make love to. Not kissed as sweetly as Florence, of course....

Never mind Florence.

I jumped up. "How about a dip?"

We went in hand in hand and swam out to the ropes. As we clung to them, she said, "Did you come in a car?"

"It's in a parking lot. I'll be glad to drive you home when you're ready to leave."

Cherry pushed herself off the ropes and let a wave carry her. I couldn't have met her at a better time. A man could forget a lot with a girl like her. I swam after her.

We were wading out of the water when one of the police helicopters passed directly over our heads. It was so low that we could see the faces of the men looking down at us from the glass bubble. Cherry glanced up at them and suddenly cringed, throwing an arm across her face.

"Anything the matter?" I asked.

"That thing up there startled me."

I couldn't see how she could have been startled after she had looked up at it.

"Let's get dressed," she said when we returned to where she had left her beach jacket.

"What's your rush? There's plenty of the afternoon left."

"I'm tired of the beach. But please don't leave because of me."

She knew damn well I'd leave because of her, and I was pretty sure she wanted me to. I said, "My clothes are in a bathhouse. Where are yours?"

"I'm staying at a hotel a few blocks away."

"You know something?" I said. "You're the first person I've ever met who stayed at a hotel in Coney."

The thing about Coney Island was that you either lived there all year round, or rented a room or bungalow by the week or season, or came out for the day by subway or car. If you wanted to stay at a hotel in a resort town, you went to the mountains or to the New Jersey beaches.

"Well," Cherry snapped at me, "now you've met somebody who does."

"But you're checking out today, aren't you? I mean, you want me to drive you home."

"Did I say so?" All of a sudden she seemed to have become sore at me.

"You asked me if I had a car and I thought—"

"Don't think, Ray." She brought out a very nice smile and took my arm. "It's more fun not thinking."

She had something there, I had to admit.

"All right, we'll have fun not thinking together," I said. "Where do we meet when we're dressed?"

"That's easy. We're not going to separate. I'll go with you to your bathhouse and then you'll go with me to my hotel." Hugging my arm as we plodded through the sand, she added gaily, "You see, I'm not taking any chance you'll get away from me."

2

I left Cherry Drew at the entrance to the bathhouse. I dressed in the locker room and stopped off at the cashier's desk for the brown envelope in which I had checked my wallet and watch. As I signed for the receipt, I remembered the ring.

I was wearing the same tan slacks I'd had on last night when Florence had broken our engagement, and my hand flew to the fob pocket where I had angrily shoved the ring she had returned to me. It was there—twelve hundred dollars' worth of platinum and square diamond.

The ring meant Florence, and feeling it through the pocket brought back some of the sense of emptiness. Though it wasn't as bad as it had been.

Cherry was standing beside the bathhouse entrance. She had put on her striped beach jacket, and her hair was like flame in the hot sun. She didn't see me when I came out, and when I touched her she jumped. Then she drew in her breath and slipped her arm possessively through mine.

"You were a long time, Ray," she said.

I'd been in there less than five minutes.

On the boardwalk I bought us hot dogs. Munching them, we walked to Surf Avenue. She stopped in front of the Tunnel of Love and said, "Take me for a ride."

She would pick that one, I thought. Evidently she hadn't changed from her Hessian Valley days, and there was no reason why I should have wanted her to. This time I was no fumbling kid. As soon as we were settled in the boat I pulled her to me, and a moment after we were in the dark tunnel I kissed her. Her mouth opened under mine and she took my hand and hugged it to her.

That ride was surprisingly brief.

From there we went into a beer parlor. We sat at a rear table and I watched her renew her face from a tiny make-up kit she took out of a pocket of her beach jacket. The color of her mouth became as vivid as her hair, and she put on too much.

I didn't care much for that shade of red, and I wasn't sure I cared very much for her. She was what she had always been, a tramp. But that was all right. I was in the mood for an honest tramp after what a decent, respectable girl like Florence had done to me.

I acted on sheer impulse. I took out the diamond ring and put it down in front of Cherry.

"Here's a little gift for you," I said.

She examined the stone. "Why, it looks real!"

"It is."

"Are you so rich, Ray?"

"No. It took a big slice of my savings to pay for it."

She slipped the ring on her finger. "She refused to take it—is that it?"

"She took it, all right," I said. "We were engaged. Last night she gave it back to me."

"Another man?"

"Her family doctor. That makes him sound old and stuffy, but he isn't. Young and good-looking and not a bad guy. She's known him a lot longer than she's known me."

"Two-timing you, huh?"

"Not the way you mean. She's not that kind of girl."

Cherry snorted. "What does any man know about any woman?"

I scowled in my beer. Why was I telling her this? But now that I'd started, I had to talk it out, and she was somebody to talk to.

"I've known her only six weeks, and we've been engaged for three weeks. Then last night she told me she'd been in love with him and they'd had a fight and she'd become engaged to me on the rebound. She hadn't seen him since then—anyway, until a few days ago, when she took sick with the flu and her mother called him in."

"Humph! There were plenty of other doctors. If you ask me, she fixed it up so he'd come back to her."

I hadn't asked her and didn't want her opinion.

"No," I said. "Probably her mother did. Her mother preferred her to marry a doctor with a flourishing practice on Eastern Parkway rather than a mere trucker like me. It must have been her doing. Florence told me she had no idea he was coming, and I believe her. Then there he was at her bedside, and he came every day for three days, and on the third visit he asked her to marry him. And last night we had one of those heart-to-heart talks that tear the guts out of you, and all I was left with was this ring."

Now not even the ring. Cherry was turning her hand this way and that so the diamond would catch the light. Twelve hundred dollars it had cost me, but last night, after I had left Florence's apartment, I had come close to throwing it down a sewer. I had done something like that now by giving it to Cherry.

I drank my beer.

"Honey," Cherry said, leaning toward me across the table, "would you like to go off with me for a few days? It'll do you good, help you get over her."

"You don't have to pay for the ring," I growled.

"It's not because of the ring. You're a sweet man. I haven't known many like you. Take the ring back and I'll still want you. We'll pick up my bags at the hotel and stop off at your place for some of your clothes and we'll drive to Vermont or New Hampshire, somewhere up north, and we'll have one swell time."

"You mean leave today?"

"Why not? We'll drive till dark and stay in a tourist cabin and go on in the morning."

I shook my head. "I've got to be at work tomorrow morning."

"But you said the business is yours—yours and your father's. You can take off a few days if you're the boss."

I could, but I didn't want to admit it. I said, "We've tonight ahead of us, and after that we can keep seeing each other here in the city."

"Either we go today or it's nothing." Her hand dropped on mine; her overpainted lips were parted with promise. "Let's make a real thing of it. If we don't go now, I'm afraid we won't at all, and the city's so hot. We get in your car and go. Huh, Ray?"

"I can't get off," I lied.

She sat back, pouting. "That means you don't want to."

I wanted a little diversion with her, that was all. I had already done one damn-fool thing by giving her the ring; I had a feeling I would very much regret making a real affair of it with her. Maybe she scared me by moving so fast. Why so much so quickly? I might be in the dumps, but not so deep that I didn't retain a sense of proportion.

I muttered, "I'm sorry, Cherry," and finished what was left in my glass.

She stood up and strode out to the street.

So that was that. She was gone and the ring with her. I didn't mind about the ring. What was the difference which sewer I had thrown it down? I minded a little more her walking out on me, but I could pass her off with a shrug. Likely it was for the best. I paid the check and went out.

She was waiting for me at the edge of a crowd that was listening to a freak show barker.

3

Cherry had a smile for me as if nothing had happened. "You can drive me home, if you still want to."

I'd won my point; this was nothing more than a date again. I said, "What about having dinner here in Coney?"

"We'll see. But first I have to get dressed."

She took my arm and we walked.

Her hotel was on the other side of Mermaid Avenue. It was a square, two-story wooden structure, and like most small Coney Island hotels it looked as if nobody ever went in or out of it. The dusty little foyer was empty.

"Should I wait down here for you?" I asked.

"There's nobody around to stop you from coming up."

We walked up a flight of dim stairs and she unlocked a door and I followed her into a room that held a bed and a chair and a dresser and a bit of extra space.

"Don't lift your arms or you'll knock something over," she said cheerfully. "The bathroom's in the hall. I'll be back in a minute."

I sat down on the chair. A Sunday paper was scattered on the bed. I hadn't looked at a paper this morning because I'd been too upset by my experience with Florence last night to keep my mind on anything. Waiting for Cherry, I picked up the news section and found it folded to the story of the armored truck holdup.

Only half a column was devoted to it now, two days later, because the police hadn't got anywhere at all. There was one clue, if it could be called that. A witness at a window had seen one of the bandits, just before he'd jumped into the getaway car, stop to talk briefly to a woman parked nearby in a convertible. What made the police especially curious about her was that she and her car had disappeared almost at once. They were looking for her; they had practically nobody else to look for. About all the witness at the window had seen of her had been her hair, and that had been bright red. The convertible, a late-model Oldsmobile, according to the witness, had also been red— a combination easy to remember.

I turned the page. Cherry came back.

She was carrying her beach jacket, and here in the closeness of the bedroom her figure looked even more tempting in the yellow bathing suit than it had on the beach. I put down the paper. She closed the door and tossed her jacket on the bed and opened a zipper. I stayed where I was, watching her get out of the suit.

Or get partly out of it. With the top of the suit dangling from her waist, she stepped to the dresser, on which some clothes were piled. Her breasts were firm and high and as young-looking as her face. In the dresser mirror she gave me a vague kind of smile.

What was I waiting for? I reached for her.

She turned to me and grabbed my wrists and held me off. "Will you take me up north tonight, Ray?"

She hadn't given up. She had brought me to her room because here she could be more persuasive than in a beer joint.

"We'll discuss that later," I said. "Meanwhile . . ."

She twisted her mouth away from my kiss. "Damn you, Ray! Take me away or get the hell out! For God's sake, take me away!"

It was as if something had cracked in her, letting pent-up hysteria through. Her fingernails were dug into my arms and she was shaking me. Suddenly I saw her as a frightened and lonely girl who needed me the way nobody ever had before. A lot more than Florence ever had.

I pulled her to me and she felt small and helpless against my chest. "Take it easy, Cherry," I said, stroking her red hair.

She clung to me, muttering, "We can have such a time together. Just us two in a little bungalow up in the hills. I won't hold you to anything. You can leave me any time you feel like it. I'll be so good to you."

It was beginning to sound fine. "All right, Cherry," I said.

She sighed and let herself go in my arms.

But after a minute she pulled away from me. "We've got to hurry, honey."

"That's what I don't understand—why the rush?"

She was at the door of the clothes closet. She paused with her hand on the knob, and I knew that she was fishing for an answer that wouldn't be the truth but that would sound more or less reasonable.

The answer never came because, after all, she hadn't hurried enough. The other door started to open, the one from the hall.

It opened very quietly. A man stepped in with a gun in his hand.

He was squat and his blue automatic was squat and half his wide face consisted of a squashed nose. His left hand reached behind him and closed the door.

"Pardon me for barging in like this," he said, grinning.

Her husband or her lover, I thought, and he held that gun as if he meant to use it.

Cherry was staring at him over one shoulder. Her uncovered breasts stirred slightly—her only sign of emotion, of anything. She uttered no sound.

The silence built up to unendurable tension. I felt as if I were filling most of that small room, making too big a target. There would hardly be space for me to fall when he shot me.

I said, "Wait a minute. Let me explain."

The squat man looked me up and down. Then he looked at Cherry and said, "Who's the guy?"

"Nobody. A pickup." Her voice was husky and less controlled than her face.

"Then what's he want to explain?"

"I guess he thinks you're my boyfriend," she said, and only now was she pulling up the top of her bathing suit.

He chuckled. "As if I give a damn who you mess with. And you don't have to worry that Georgie will ever give a damn."

A shiver ran through her. "What did you do to him?"

"What d'you think? Walt's smart. When you didn't show pretty soon after we got there, Walt got leery. He had the boys keep an eye on Georgie and they nabbed him trying to sneak away." He grinned hideously. "The Barber got to work on him and made him talk. That's how come we knew you was here in Coney."

"So Georgie is dead," she whispered.

It wasn't a question and he didn't bother to answer it. In their world there was a certain cause and effect. Georgie had done something and had been tortured until he had revealed what they wanted to know and then he had been killed.

"Where is it?" the squat man demanded.

Cherry straightened her shoulders, and whatever she felt about the death of Georgie no longer showed. "It's in the car, Shorty."

"Where's it parked?"

"A few blocks away."

"Don't kid me. The papers say your red heap's hot. It was spotted by somebody, and your red hair too. You'd ditch the heap, that's what you'd do."

I got it all then. I blurted, "You two—in that armored truck holdup!"

That reminded Shorty I was in the room. He pointed his gun at me more than at her. "So this is just a punk, eh?"

"You talked too much, Shorty," she said. "The papers are full of it."

He shrugged. "Big difference! He stepped in over his head. Open that closet door, Cherry."

She didn't move. She said, "It doesn't have to be split so many ways."

"Huh! Think I want what Georgie got? Me, I want to keep on living."

"Shorty, listen!"

He patted the gun barrel. "I have the heater, so you do the listening. Open that door."

She obeyed. She pulled the closet door open and sidled against the wall and stood with her back against the dresser. She hadn't said a word to me, hadn't even looked at me. Neither had Shorty addressed me directly. I wasn't worth it. I was just a punk.

All of a sudden I was more angry than anything else.

Shorty glanced into the closet. He grunted. "Two bags. Guess it's in the bigger one." He waved the gun at me. "Punk, lug both them bags out and open 'em. I want to make sure."

He stepped aside to let me get by. Most of that small room was taken up by the furniture, so he couldn't put more than a couple of feet between us. I'd fought a war in Korea against a lot tougher killers than Shorty and had learned a few tricks. My left forearm slammed down on his gun wrist and with the same motion my torso twisted and my right fist smashed into his face.

I might be a punk, but when I hit the hard guys they felt it.

He would have gone all the way down if a corner of the dresser hadn't stopped him. He bounced off it and tottered toward the bed.

The gun was still in his hand, but he wasn't doing anything with it. I couldn't be sure I'd paralyzed the nerve. With both hands I grabbed the wrist, and he uttered a gushing sigh and toppled against me.

And behind him was Cherry and something was flashing in her hand.

She leaned forward toward him, and over his shoulder our eyes met. There was a fever in hers. She pulled back, drawing out the knife, and he kept sinking. Then he pitched forward. His head struck the bed and he flopped over on his side.

Cherry slumped against the dresser and stared at the red wetness on the blade of the long, slender knife in her hand. She had stabbed him twice.

4

Shorty was dead, all right. He had no pulse. Crouching over him, I could see the punctures ringed with red in the back of his white shirt. There had been little bleeding because death had come quickly. One of the thrusts must have hit a vulnerable spot; probably the tip of the blade had gone far enough into his back to touch his heart.

The silence held. There were not even street sounds; it was too hot and too early in the afternoon for people to have come back from the beach.

I looked up at Cherry. She was wiping the blade on handful of face tissues.

The most shocking thing of all was her calmness.

"Doesn't it even bother you?" I said.

"He would've killed us both. Didn't you know that?"

"I had him. He was half out on his feet and I was taking the gun from him."

"How could I tell? I was behind him. I figured in a moment he'd shoot you and then me."

There was a click and the blade snapped out of sight into the handle. It was a switchblade knife—a killer's weapon.

"Where did you have it?" I asked her.

"Under the blouse on the dresser. I grabbed it when you socked him." She skirted the legs of the dead man on the way to the foot of the bed and wrapped the bloody tissues in a sheet of newspaper. "You were right, Ray, when you said you could take care of yourself.

I don't know anybody who could have taken him better."

"Not even Georgie?"

A shadow crossed her face—almost a child's face with that button nose and that cute turned-up chin. Not the face of a girl who had just killed a man and then had calmly wiped the blood off the knife.

I started toward the door.

"Where are you going?" she said sharply.

"Out of here, of course."

"For the cops?"

"I don't know." Without taking my hand from the doorknob, I turned to her.

She had picked up Shorty's gun. She wasn't pointing it at me. She simply held it by the trigger guard.

"The law will say you had as much to do with killing him as I did," she told me. "You want us both to burn?"

"It was self-defense."

"You know what's in the closet. How'll you explain that?"

"I'll tell the truth."

She laughed mirthlessly. "Try to make the cops believe you and me weren't out to get away with the dough when Shorty walked in and tried to stop us. And I'll swear you were in it with me all along. By God, I will!"

"All right," I said, "I'll keep my mouth shut."

I turned the doorknob.

"Ray, you can't leave me flat like this. I need you. Everybody's after me—the cops and Shorty's pals."

I hesitated. "You think the gang has surrounded the hotel?"

"I wouldn't be standing here talking if I thought so. It's sure they didn't find out from Georgie where I was staying. He didn't know, because I didn't know myself till I got here Friday. He was supposed to meet me as soon as he could near the jetty on Bay Nineteen. I guess they headed straight there, but we'd already left. Then they scattered to look for me."

"How do you know all this?"

"It figures. Shorty spotted me with you and tailed us."

"Then he may have phoned the others."

"No. Let me tell you. I know how they operate. At this minute the rest of them are still looking for me. They have no headquarters in Coney Island except maybe a car parked in a certain place. No phone where he could call them. Because look—would Shorty have come in here alone if he didn't have to? He knew you were with me; he must've seen us together outside. Two men would've been better than one. But he was afraid if he left to get help we might be gone before he could come back. I think he listened at the door and heard me say we were leaving right away. So he had to make his move then and there."

I was hearing her with only half a mind, my thoughts jumping about, and suddenly the whole thing became ridiculous, me lingering at the door, listening to this girl in a bathing suit who was twirling a heavy gun on her finger and talking quietly and reasonably and objectively while the body of a man she had killed a very few minutes ago lay huddled behind her on the floor.

I said bitterly, "What did you need me for—to help you carry away the eighty thousand dollars?"

"Our eighty grand. Yours and mine."

I just stood there.

Cherry came over. She reached around me and snapped the door lock shut. "In case anybody tries to come in," she explained. "Should have done it before." Finished with that piece of business, she pressed herself against me.

"Georgie is dead, so I'll have to do," I said tonelessly.

"Don't always argue with me." Her lips stirred. "Eighty grand. All of it in small bills. They can never be traced. Vermont or New Hampshire, like I said. A bungalow in the hills. Later Europe if we want. We can live like kings."

I didn't say yes, but neither did I say no.

I don't know if I thought of the money, at least consciously, or if at that moment I was only very much aware of her body imposing itself on me. It was as if I were drifting without moving from the spot, letting whatever currents there were take me and not particularly caring where. It occurred to me that Florence had a lot to do with the way I was reacting.

But then, so did Cherry.

I said, "I suppose if they catch you they'll kill you."

"Like they killed Georgie. But it will be easier to get away from them if you drive me."

"And from the police," I muttered.

"You see, Ray, how I'm boxed in."

I ran my hand over my face. "Well," I said, "I can't let them kill you."

5

I had to straighten out the legs of the dead man before I could shove him under the bed. That was a job I hated, but it didn't seem to bother Cherry much. She gave me a hand at it without being asked.

When that was done, I said, "The police will get a description of you from the others in the hotel."

She was wriggling out of her yellow bathing suit. "Shorty won't be found till tomorrow when the chambermaid cleans the room. Of course I signed a phony name. We'll drive all night, so by then we'll be hundreds of miles away. I'll change the color of my hair as soon as I have a chance. And you don't have to worry about yourself. Nobody saw you come in with me or will remember what you look like."

She left the bathing suit on the floor and moved to the dresser.

Her body was very beautiful. I almost reached for her. What stopped me was the dead man under the bed. That would be too much. I sat tight on the chair and worked at not looking at her.

The closet was open. Only one dress hung there. On the floor were a cowhide suitcase and a plastic weekend bag. I had no idea how much space eighty thousand dollars in small bills would take up, but I guessed they were in the larger bag, the suitcase.

I said, "It was clever. You were parked in advance of the holdup, close to where it was to take place. As they ran by, they tossed the money into your convertible. You drove calmly away. A pretty girl in a snappy convertible wouldn't be stopped by the police, wouldn't be suspected. And if the men were picked up while they were trying to make their getaway, the evidence wouldn't be found on them."

Shrugging, she took underwear from the top drawer of the dresser.

"But you and Georgie had worked out plans to double-cross them," I said. "No honor among thieves."

Cherry swung around to me. "There were six of them besides me to split it. Walt was going to get the big share because he was the boss, and from what would be left I wasn't supposed to get even an equal share. Less than anybody else, because I was a woman and didn't handle a gun." Her mouth got a hard, ugly twist to it. "All my life I've been poor. How long do a few grand last? You buy some clothes, you live decently for maybe a year, then you're back where you were, grubbing for every cent. This was my big chance."

And she had persuaded Georgie, I thought. It would have been her idea from the start, and if he had hesitated she knew how to work on him with her body, and he had given in, and he was dead.

"But it went wrong," I said. "Georgie was supposed to meet you at the jetty next day—yesterday. Coney Island would be a good place on a weekend; you can get lost in the crowds. But he didn't show up, and this morning you read in the paper that the police are looking for a redheaded girl in a red Olds convertible. The roads are being watched; the car became a menace to you. You drove it as far from the hotel as you dared and abandoned it in the street. Then it was Sunday afternoon and still no sign of Georgie and you were getting more and more nervous. Am I right so far?"

She merely pulled on a stocking.

"When I called your name on the beach," I went on, "you nearly jumped out of your skin because I might have been either a cop or one of the gangsters. It turned out to be only me, a guy you'd known in your hometown, and for a minute you weren't interested in old acquaintances. Then it struck you that here was a sucker you could use to transport the money for you."

She had everything on but her dress. "The bag's not so heavy. I could have taken a train."

"But a car is more convenient."

"I care for you, Ray. Really I do." Hips swinging, she came to where I sat and stood against my knees. "Would I have let you in on it if I hadn't gone overboard for you? I don't like being alone. It's you and me together, honey. And we're rich."

I kept my hands from her. I said without looking up at her, "I'll drive you, but that's all. I don't want any part of the money. I'll drive you out of Coney Island and then I'll go home."

She didn't argue. She smiled a little, as if she knew better. She turned from me and took the print dress out of the closet and dropped it over her head.

"Bring your car around," she said. "But not too near. There's a back way to the outdoor showers and an alley to the other street. While you're gone I'll wipe our prints off everything."

"Mightn't it be safer to wait till dark?"

"I can't stand waiting." She glanced at the bed. "Especially with that thing in here with us."

She wasn't quite as tough as she pretended, though she was tough enough.

"All right," I said.

I unlocked the door and opened it a crack and listened. The hall was silent; the hotel retained that feeling of being deserted. I didn't see anybody until I was out the back door and then there were only a couple of small children squealing under an open shower in the yard. I went up the alley to the street.

As I walked to the parking lot, I kept seeing in my mind the way she had looked in the yellow bathing suit and with it half off her and with it all off her. I told myself that if I wanted anything it was her and not the money, but the money was there as part of the whole, tied up with her and for at least a while with me. She hadn't believed me when I'd told her that all I'd do was drive her to safety. I didn't know if I believed myself.

How much temptation could a man resist when it came right down to it?

I walked sweating in the blazing heat and got my car from the lot and drove to the other side of the block from the hotel and parked as close as I could to the alley.

Two middle-aged women were in the hotel lobby. I averted my face, but it wasn't necessary. They were so busy gabbing they didn't as much as glance at me as I passed.

I found Cherry wiping her fingerprints from the dresser mirror.

Everything all right?" she asked.

"What could go wrong at this point?"

"Nothing, I guess."

I pulled the cowhide suitcase out of the closet and took it down to my car and locked it in the trunk. Then I went back to her room.

Cherry was closing her little weekend bag.

"We don't want to be seen leaving together," she said. "You go ahead and I'll wait a few minutes and then go out the front way."

"Will you have to check out?"

"I paid in advance through today. This place is run more like a rooming house than a hotel." She took a large straw handbag from the dresser and hung it from her shoulder. "Park on Mermaid Avenue, toward Sea Gate and on this side of the street. I'll come walking by. What kind of car have you got?"

"A tan Plymouth. I'll keep my eyes peeled for you." From where I stood at the door I could see the sole of one of Shorty's shoes a little way under the bed. "What happened to his gun?"

She tapped her handbag. "In here. Why, do you want it?"

"No." I looked at her standing trim and pretty and young in that gay summery dress, and it was hard to believe that she had been in with a gang of holdup men and had a little while ago killed one of them. I said, "I suppose you realize I can drive off with the money without waiting for you."

"You could, but you wouldn't."

"Don't tell me you trust anybody."

"You're not anybody, honey." She held my face between hands and kissed me hard on the mouth.

The kiss was no good. It was the wrong time and place.

I said, "I'll be waiting in my car," and left.

6

For eight minutes by my watch I sat in my car on Mermaid Avenue around the corner from the hotel. Add to that the time it had taken me to leave the building and go up the alley and drive here and maneuver into this parking space, which I was lucky to find so close by, and close to fifteen minutes had passed since I had left her.

Had anything gone wrong?

There would be no point in her leaving more than five minutes after I had. But say she had waited ten minutes, she would need only two more at the most to walk this far. I sat twisted around on the seat, staring up the street.

The second hand of my watch swept around three more times and then I couldn't stand waiting. I drove around the block, approaching the hotel from the Neptune Avenue side.

The two women I had met jabbering away in the lobby a good half hour and more ago were still at it, though by now they had got as far as the sidewalk in front of the hotel. I stopped my car smack in the middle of the street and debated with myself about pulling over and going up to the room. I had hoped I had got away from the dead man for good.

Behind me a horn honked. I gave a taxi room to slip by and I rolled slowly on. She could be ahead of me, having reached Mermaid Avenue while I had been driving around the block.

She was ahead of me, all right, but she wasn't walking. Near the corner she stood against the window of an empty store, her small weekend bag held against her knees, and two men were with her.

One was burly and had jowls. The other was distinguished by his completely bald head. What made them stand out from almost everybody else on that hot afternoon in Coney Island were their clothes, their conservative business suits and dress shirts and neckties. They could be detectives.

My first impulse was to keep going. But at the moment I had no reason to fear the police; they couldn't know anything about me or what was in my car unless Cherry told them, and she wouldn't. I paused where I was, no more than thirty feet from them.

The burly man had her straw handbag and was looking in it. The bald man held her arm with his left hand and his right hand was in his pocket.

I knew then that they weren't cops, because the burly man didn't take Shorty's automatic out of her handbag. A cop would have done that the first thing. He kept rummaging around inside.

The one who was holding her by the arm would have his other hand on a gun in his pocket.

Cherry lifted her head and saw me. Within minutes her face had aged. Her lips moved soundlessly, spreading, forming the same unspoken word over and over:

"Go . . . go . . . go...."

I didn't know what to do. They were armed and I wasn't. The fact that all this was out in the street in broad daylight was no help. With a dead man in the room she had just left and the money in my car, I couldn't go looking for a cop or make any kind of fuss.

Suddenly Cherry spoke up loudly. "Walt," she said to the burly man, "you got a bum steer from Georgie."

She was letting me know who they were in case I hadn't guessed. Walt—that was what Shorty had called the leader of the gang.

The bald man squeezed her arm and whispered something to her between his teeth. Then he looked around. I dipped my head over the wheel and raced the engine, hoping he'd take me for a driver who was having trouble with his car. Nobody else happened to be near at the moment.

The other man, Walt, took a piece of paper out of her handbag and read it.

A horn reminded me that I was again blocking traffic. I rolled the car to a clear space before a fire hydrant across the street from Cherry and the gangsters. I pulled up the hand brake and looked to the left, and they were no longer in front of the store window.

They were walking up the street, Cherry between them. Her weekend bag swung gently along her leg. From my car I watched them enter the hotel.

Walt must have come across the hotel receipt in her handbag. They would take her up to the room and find Shorty's body under the bed. But they wouldn't find the money.

She had urged me to go. It was too late for her; there was nothing I could do for her. Go and save yourself, she had said in effect.

I drove around the corner.

The space on Mermaid Avenue where I had been parked until a couple of minutes ago hadn't yet been grabbed up. I drove a few feet past it and stepped on the brake and realized I couldn't run out on her just like that. At the least I needed time to think. I backed in against the curb and cut the engine and lit a cigarette.

There must have been method in their luck at coming up that street just after she had left the hotel. Walt was smart, Shorty had said. He would have to be to mastermind an armored truck holdup and pull it off without a hitch. The organizer type of criminal, planning each detail to the second. In the same way he would have organized the hunt for Cherry. He would have reasoned that she wouldn't be staying far from Bay 19, where he had learned she was to meet Georgie, and in this part of narrow Coney Island there were only two and a half blocks between Surf Avenue and the bay. So his limited manpower wouldn't have a great area to cover; he would divide it into sections and detail a man to patrol each section and report back every so often to a central place, probably a parked car. Shorty's failure to report back had been the sign for Walt to go to his section, and on the way he had picked up another man.

Something like that. How could you fight that kind of highly organized setup if you were one man alone and couldn't go anywhere for help because you had put yourself also on the wrong side of the law?

I couldn't abandon her to them. She was as bad as they, she had double-crossed them, she had killed one of them, I owed her nothing—but I couldn't let them torture her and then kill her as they had Georgie.

She would be better off in the hands of the police.

But then what about me? I'd go to jail along with her and the others because the money was in my car and I had let myself be made an accessory not only to a robbery but to a killing.

The money! I could buy Cherry's life with it.

I pulled out the ignition key and locked the car doors and started walking.

They were coming out of the hotel when I approached it. They turned up the street as one, like soldiers on parade, with one man on either side of her.

She no longer had her weekend bag. It had contained only a few clothes; she wouldn't have bothered with it after they had been in the room and found Shorty's body and the money gone and were taking her away somewhere with them.

She stopped when she saw me and they stopped. This time she didn't pretend not to know me. She pointed at me.

The bald man hurried forward with his right hand in his pocket.

"This is a rod," he said. He pressed against my side so I could feel the muzzle poke against the material. He had a bony face and mean eyes. "Get over to the wall. Act like nothing's wrong or I'll blast you."

I stepped over to the brick front of an apartment building. A woman passed wheeling a baby carriage. The afternoon was wearing on; across the street a group of people was coming home from the beach. There could be no help from anybody.

Walt and Cherry came up to us. His arm was through hers as if in intimacy; nobody seeing them would guess they weren't on the best of terms. He also had his right hand in his pocket, carelessly, even jauntily, but I knew his finger was curled around a trigger.

The bald man patted my clothes, feeling for a gun.

I said, "Listen—"

Walt cut me off. "Take us to your car."

I looked at Cherry. Why should I have expected her not to betray me? She dropped her eyes.

"It will have to be a deal," I said. "The money is all yours if you let both of us alone."

"Sure thing." Walt smiled ingratiatingly. He didn't look like anybody to be afraid of, but I knew better. "Like I told Cherry," he said, "the dough's all I'm after. You go ahead with him, Trig."

The bald man named Trig walked on my left, his pocketed gun inches from my ribs. I thought I might have a chance to take him, the way I had Shorty, but not with Walt and his gun following ten feet behind with Cherry.

We crossed the street and turned right on Mermaid Avenue. And suddenly I was sure that I was taking both myself and Cherry to our deaths.

They couldn't afford to work it any other way. Shorty would be found in the room she had occupied, and if she was picked up for the killing she would have to tell the police everything to make out a case for self-defense. And that went for me as well. They knew nothing about me except that I knew too much for their safety.

Three people had already died because of the holdup—the armored truck guard and Georgie and Shorty. Why not two more? When we reached my car and I gave them the keys, they would make us go along with them. And from wherever they took us we would never come back.

7

Evidently Cherry had kept from them that she knew the make and color of my car. The tan Plymouth looked particularly conspicuous at the curb—at least to me it did, but Trig let me lead him past it without question. Behind us Walt and Cherry passed it, too.

We walked another block before Trig growled, "She said your heap was right here on Mermaid."

"But she didn't say how far on Mermaid, did she? You have to take parking space where you can find it."

"Well, how far?"

Not much farther, because a cop was coming toward us. It has been said there never is one around when you need one most, but his blue uniform was the law of averages catching up. After all the rotten luck Cherry and I had been having, it was time we got a break.

"Don't try anything," Trig warned me.

I sure was going to. The cop was sauntering close to the building to keep in the shade. He had a potbelly and his red face looked bored. He would be anything but bored if he knew who three of us four were, but that was one thing I couldn't tell him, considering how deep I was in it myself.

When he was a few feet from us, I sang out, "Officer, can you tell me where the El station is?"

"You're going the wrong way," he replied. Which of course I knew.

I turned. Walt and Cherry had also stopped. "He says we're going the wrong way," I said.

"Is that so?" Cherry left Walt and joined us. She gave the cop a rather demure smile. "Oh, dear, and we walked all this way for nothing."

The cop said it wasn't so far to the station on Stillwell Avenue, and moved on. Cherry stuck to his side and I to her side, and she was gushing at him how this was her first visit to Coney Island and how exciting it was.

And Walt and Trig tagged after us at a short distance, two ordinary-looking men in business suits. I didn't kid myself that they would hesitate to shoot the cop down along with us, but there was no percentage in it, because that wouldn't get them the money.

I was banking on the cop's walking all the way with us to my car, but at the corner our luck ran out again. We lost him. He went into a drugstore to cool off or get a drink or snatch a smoke in the back room. And we had to let him go because we couldn't let him know of our danger.

As soon as he was out of sight, Walt and Trig came at us, not exactly running, but closing in fast.

We couldn't hope to reach my car and unlock a door and get inside and be on our way before they were on us. All that would accomplish would be to lead them directly to the money.

"This way!" I said, grabbing her hand.

On our right, across the street and a block away, was Surf Avenue with its rides and shows and eating places and crowds. There among the thousands we could lose ourselves.

A bus charged down on us when we were halfway across the street—a break, as it turned out, because we ducked in front of it, putting it between us and them. When we were on the opposite side, I glanced back. A stream of cars trailed the bus and the two gangsters were stopped for the moment. We ran toward Surf Avenue.

Three teenagers, a girl and two boys, filled most of the sidewalk walking arm in arm. We dropped hands and Cherry ran around one side of them and I around the other. One of the boys cracked, "Take it easy, you'll live longer." That was all he knew! To him and his companions, and whoever else saw us running, we were just a couple of people who were late for something.

"Are they coming?" Cherry gasped.

"I don't see them."

Which didn't mean they weren't behind us. They could be blocked out by the teenagers or others on the street or by parked cars. They wouldn't give up, not ever, with all they had at stake. We were again holding hands as we ran on and her shoulder bag slapped against her hip and I could hear her sobbing for breath.

Surf Avenue, when we reached it, was a disappointment. There were no fewer people than there had been earlier, but since then my sense of proportion had changed. We needed milling crowds, the kind that form toward evening when the beach empties. The strollers seemed to take up very little space on the broad sidewalk.

We had slowed down to a rapid walk. Cherry wobbled against me with exhaustion. At any moment they'd round the corner and see us. Five hundred feet or less away a cop was directing traffic in the middle of the very wide street, but we no more dared appeal directly to him for help than we had to that other cop on Mermaid Avenue,

We passed a shooting gallery that had no customers. A roller coaster next to it had no line waiting to get on, and a car that looked about to leave had a few empty seats. This could be our chance to get out of sight without running anymore.

I thrust a dollar bill at the ticket seller. "Two," I said.

I didn't have to take time to explain to Cherry. She understood at once and hurried on ahead to the take-off platform. I snatched the tickets from the woman. She called, "Your change, mister," as I was rounding the booth, but of course I kept going. A corner of the shooting gallery prevented me from seeing down the street, but it would also prevent them from seeing us. I couldn't know how close they were.

Cherry was already in the car, asking the attendant to please wait for her boyfriend. He was a young fellow basking in her deluxe smile. I leaped in and he gave the signal and wheels creaked. We sat low in the double seat, our faces turned away from the street, and we held onto each other.

"Oh, God, Ray," she whispered, "I couldn't help telling them. Walt said he'd let the Barber work on me. You don't know what he does to people. I had to point you out."

"Forget it."

We were crawling up the first incline. I looked down. The people below were just people—nobody that could be recognized. I braced my feet against the footboard.

She shrieked and clung frantically to me when we swooped down. The car hurtled around a curve and leveled off for a moment and she recovered her breath and moaned, "How I hate these things!"

I laughed brokenly and held her close and we went down another dip and swung sickeningly around a curve and her voice mingled with those of other half-hysterical women in the car.

They were there when we reached the end of the ride, the burly gangster and the bald man standing on the platform. Each had a hand in his pocket.

Cherry saw them first, when the car was rolling to a stop. She whispered tiredly, "They saw us getting on. They'll stay there till we get off, and pretty soon the others will join them."

"Then we'll stay on," I said.

The attendant was collecting fares from those who weren't getting off. I paid him and put my hand back around Cherry. She was twisting on her finger the ring I had given her.

"We can't ride here forever," she said.

I hadn't anything to say. Again we were crawling up that long, steep incline. It was quiet up there. I could clearly hear the barking of a rifle at the shooting gallery next door.

She screamed and dug into me and we followed our stomachs down.

After a minute, when it wasn't so bad, I said, "Suppose we refuse to take them to my car? What can they do out in the open?"

"Anything they think they have to. These are men who held up a payroll car and got away with it."

"How will shooting us get them the money?"

"My God, Ray, you're not thinking of yelling copper?"

We were whispering, but it wasn't necessary. The rumbling of the car made our voices inaudible.

"If we're damned either way," I said, "why not take the lesser evil?"

"How is it lesser? You think I want the chair or a long stretch in the pen?" She rubbed her cheek against my shoulder. "And there's all that money. Think, Ray. Some way we can shake them and get to your car."

The money, I thought bitterly. She had risked her life for it; she had killed for it; she wouldn't give up on it.

We were almost at the end of the ride. We could stay on, but that wouldn't get us anything. It was time to take one last desperate chance. I had it figured out. It didn't look too good, but not too bad, either. If the police nabbed me as a result, one more charge against me wouldn't make much difference.

"Listen," I said. "When we get off and I start shooting, run. Don't stop for anything."

She lifted her head from my shoulder to look widely at me. "But Walt took Shorty's gun from my bag. You haven't got one."

"Maybe I have," I said.

8

They came forward and escorted us off the roller coaster car when it stopped.

Walt said, "Got wise to yourself, eh?" and I said, "Yeah," and patted Cherry's arm reassuringly. She gave me a kind of smile, working at it to show she had confidence in whatever I intended to do, but I didn't think she really had much.

Holding my elbow, Trig steered me off the platform. As they had on Mermaid Avenue, Walt and Cherry brought up the rear. We passed the roller coaster ticket booth and a few feet ahead was the sign reading, "10 SHOTS FOR 25¢." The only customer was a kid in a T-shirt shooting with his left elbow on the counter.

I wasn't taken past the shooting gallery. At the corner of it Trig stopped me, out of the flow of strollers on the sidewalk and the people going to and from the roller coaster. Walt and Cherry came up to us.

"Let's have your license and car keys," Trig demanded.

Cherry stood listlessly beside Walt, as if she'd lost interest in what was going on. She knew and I knew that once they learned the plate number of my car and had the keys it would no longer be important to them that we stay alive.

I said, "Will our deal still hold? Will you let us go?"

"Sure, pal," Walt told me heartily.

He lied, of course.

"Come on," Trig snapped. "This time we don't horse around."

The kid at the shooting gallery sighted and his rifle barked. I had hoped to get closer.

"All right," I said, "here's my wallet."

I started to bring my hand around to my hip pocket and slammed my shoulder against Trig. He spun away from me and I lunged past him.

There were repeating rifles all along the counter of the shooting gallery, but I knew they weren't loaded. The kid in the T-shirt was holding his rifle loosely after having taken a shot. He had no idea what I was about, and when I snatched it from him it came away easily from his hands.

"What the hell!" he said.

The rifle was fastened to the counter by a thin chain, but there was enough play to let me swing around with it. Trig was dragging his gun out of his pocket. I sprayed him with .22-caliber slugs.

Trig went down. Nearby a woman screamed stridently and then shouts overlapped her voice. I was conscious of shapes moving beside me, but all I was watching was Walt.

Cherry was no longer at his side. I couldn't see her. I didn't look for her. I looked at Walt. I could have shot him too, and he knew it and didn't try to bring up the gun that was in his hand. He leaped to the middle of the sidewalk, among the children and women and men scampering in near panic.

That was all right. I didn't want to shoot anybody I didn't have to, even if I'd been able to without endangering others.

I dropped the rifle. Held by its chain, it thumped against the side of the counter. I spun around and ran. Nobody pointed a finger at me and yelled, "He's the one!" Things had happened too fast. Maybe no more than half a dozen seconds had passed since I had snatched the rifle and everybody was still occupied with getting out of the line of fire. I became one of many scooting away from there—anonymous in the anonymous crowd.

Or so I hoped.

The movement away from the shooting gallery slowed down. People ahead of me had halted, were staring back.

Trig was alone, lying there writhing on the sidewalk. The cop who had been directing traffic was sprinting toward him.

I eased over to a hot dog stand where the crowd seemed thickest. People were talking it up. Somebody said a madman had run amok and somebody else said Murder, Inc. was doing a job. Nobody looked at me twice. I stayed among them, not wanting to call attention to myself by moving now that almost everybody else nearby had stopped.

Traffic had piled up in the streets, and the people in the cars were gawking along with those on foot. And between the halted cars I saw Cherry Drew make her way across the street.

I had only a glimpse of her, but I recognized her by her red hair and her print dress. She was alone; she had got completely away from Walt. Then she stepped behind one of the cars, and that was the last I saw of her.

The crowd trickled into motion, this time back toward the shooting gallery. Now that the danger from flying bullets was definitely over, curiosity had replaced fear. Two more cops showed up, and then there was nothing to be seen from the hot dog stand but a semicircle of men and women and even some children spread wide in front of the shooting gallery.

I walked away.

There wasn't much time. Walt wouldn't give up. He had lost two of his men this afternoon, but he was as alive and deadly as ever, and he knew approximately where my car was on Mermaid Avenue. Right now he would be gathering what men he had left.

I was ahead of them. I piled into my car and turned one block north to Neptune Avenue and took it to Stillwell Avenue, from where I cut into Shore Parkway. Then I was skimming along the open road with eighty thousand dollars in the car trunk.

Part Two: The Blonde

1

A girl was sitting on the porch with Ma when I got home from Coney Island. From my car as I rolled up the street I had only a fleeting glimpse of the back of her head. Probably one of Lanny's dates, I thought. Ma encouraged us to bring our girlfriends to the house.

One girl I would never show off to my family was Cherry Drew.

We lived on a street in Borough Park that hadn't yet been imposed upon by apartment buildings. We had a frame house with a lawn in front and a yard and garage in back and there were shrubs and a couple of trees. It wasn't much compared to the five acres we'd had in Hessian Valley, but by Brooklyn standards it was practically countrified.

I swung into the driveway, and when I reached the side of the porch I saw that the girl with Ma was Florence. My heart and my car stopped at the same time.

She was sitting on the porch, and above the porch rail she looked at me. She said, "Hello, Ray," and her dark eyes were as grave as they had been last night when she had returned my ring. I nodded, and then my car was moving on. I must have given it gas unconsciously.

Pa's Mercury was outside the garage. I squeezed my Plymouth up beside it and made sure that the keys were transferred to my pocket, considering what was in the trunk.

The shortest way to the porch was along the side of the house, but I didn't take it. I needed a little time before I could face her. I entered the house through the back door.

Pa was watching the ball game on TV in the living room.

"Listen to this," he said. "It was the last of the ninth and, the score was tied and bases loaded and none out. What d'you think the Bums did?"

Pa had dutifully become a Dodger fan when he had moved to Brooklyn, but I stuck to the Giants through thick and thin, mostly thin. Our truck drivers and the girl in the office couldn't make up their minds if this was treason or merely eccentricity.

"They tried to pull a squeeze," Pa explained bitterly. "The bunt turned into a pop fly to the pitcher and the man coming down from third was doubled by a mile. Then a deep fly to center would've scored the winning run, but it was only the third out. Now the Cubs are up in the tenth."

One thing I couldn't get excited about today was baseball. I started up the stairs at the other end of the living room.

"Did you see Florence on the porch?" Pa called after me.

"Yes."

"She's been waiting for you an hour, at least. Did you know she was coming?"

"No," I said.

Upstairs I looked at myself in the bathroom mirror. After all that had happened this afternoon, my hair wasn't even mussed. I washed up and changed my shirt and went down to the porch.

Florence had her head tilted back against the rocker. Her mouth started to twitch in what would have been a shy, constrained smile. It never developed, probably because of what she saw in my face. I felt my cheek muscles stiff and unyielding.

"Where were you?" Ma asked me.

"Swimming."

"And you didn't take Florence?"

I hadn't told my family this morning that it was all over between us. There was nothing I had to say now either, especially in Florence's presence. I put one thigh up on the porch railing and lit a cigarette.

The hot air was very still and very breathless.

Ma looked at me and then at Florence and she caught on that something was wrong. She rose from the wicker settee, ponderously because she was a heavy woman and had varicose veins, and said, "I'll go in and make supper. You'll stay, Florence?"

"I don't think so, thank you."

"Of course you will," Ma told her. "We're having cold cuts."

She went into the house, leaving us alone together.

Florence was dressed all in white, from the ribbon loosely holding her black flowing hair to the sandals on her stockingless feet, and her dress was a white summery thing with broad shoulder straps and a flaring skirt, the only touch of color a gold cinch belt snug under her lovely bosom. White for virtue, for clean, tender romance, for a home and children. But since last night that was for Dr. Steven H. Oakes.

And what for me now? A baby-faced trollop and eighty thousand dollars and fear of police and killers.

"Ray," Florence said, "I don't know how to begin."

She was sitting forward on the rocker with her hands clasped.

I said harshly, "Wasn't everything settled last night?"

"I thought it was, but I was wrong. Ray, it's you I love."

I mashed my cigarette out against the rail and split the stub and scattered the tobacco over the side of the porch and rolled the paper into a tiny ball.

"Is this another rebound?" I said. "Did you have another fight with him?"

"I suppose I deserve that. But the only fight I had was with Mother. Earlier this afternoon." The rocker squeaked, rocking, with the stirring of her body. "This morning I told her I had broken our engagement, and the first thing she did was phone Steve's mother and at noon Steve came over. That was like Mother, arranging everything for me always. Steve took me for a drive to the country. I should have been happy, but I wasn't. Since you left last night I've felt lost. After a while I asked Steve to turn the car around and take me home. You see, I didn't want to be with him. I wanted to be with you."

In the house the phone rang.

Half sitting on the porch rail, I listened to that ringing coming loudly through the screen door. The phone was in Pa's name. If Cherry didn't remember from her Hessian Valley days that his first name was Mason, all she had to do was work her way down the

Whiteheads listed in the Brooklyn directory and ask each number for Ray until she hit the right one.

The ringing stopped and I heard Pa say hello, and all the while Florence was talking about the quarrel she'd had with her mother this afternoon when she'd returned home from that drive with Steve Oakes.

"My declaration of independence," she said. "I'm through letting her live my life for me. She picked Steve out for me when I was only eighteen and he was in medical school. She had her mind set on my becoming a doctor's wife. And Steve is nice. Very nice. That's why she almost had her way. But I had to lose you last night to find out how much I really love you."

Pa didn't call me to the phone. It wasn't for me. Not yet.

"Mother tried to talk me into thinking it over for a few days. I just looked at her, then I went to the phone and called you. You weren't in, but I came here anyway to wait for you. I ran to the bus in spite of the heat. Something was driving me. I had a feeling I had to hurry."

But she hadn't hurried enough, I thought dully. More time had passed than she could guess.

"I don't blame you for being angry." She was standing, watching me perched on the rail with my head bowed.

"I'm not angry," I muttered.

"But you don't say anything."

"It's been up to you to do the talking."

"I did. And I'm here. Don't you believe it's honestly and truly you I love?"

"I believe you."

She stepped over to me. "And you love me, don't you?"

"Yes."

"Then nothing has changed, has it?"

Nothing except that I had gone to Coney Island and had met a girl on the beach and had become an accessory to a robbery and a killing and had shot a man who might be dying or already dead and had eighty thousand dollars of stolen money in my car.

She touched my cheek. I raised my head and her loveliness, so close to me, clouded my rational mind, which had been urging me not to involve her in this mess of mine. Standing before me, she was everything I wanted. I put my hands on her hips and she bent her head and kissed me.

The phone rang.

The kiss went dead. I held her without feeling her any longer, and then from the house Pa was calling, "Ray, it's for you."

Florence drew back, looking flushed and happy, and in her eyes was that tender glow I had seen after other kisses. I said, "Be right out," and went into the house.

The phone was in the living room, at the side of the stairs. The ball game was still on and Pa was pacing in front of the TV, mumbling to himself. He had become a typical Dodger fan; that was the effect the team had on all of them. I picked up the phone and stood holding it, thinking of hanging up without answering.

But she would keep calling, and if that got her nowhere she would come here to the house. What was I to say to her? There weren't many choices.

"Hello," I said.

It was a man's voice on the wire—my friend Bob Stern, telling me he and his wife were having some people over for drinks this evening and wanted Florence and me to join them.

"Sorry, Bob," I said, "but we can't make it tonight."

"Well, some other time," he said.

When I returned to the porch, my kid brother, Lanny, was with Florence. He was giving her a monologue on his favorite topic—his girlfriends. He had a date tonight with a new one.

"Man, what a build!" he said. "Picked her up in an ice-cream parlor yesterday. Minute I saw her . . ."

I sat down beside Florence on the wicker settee. Lanny's voice, relating in tedious detail what he had said to the girl in the ice-cream parlor and what she had said to him, was part of the drone of the listless street. Florence entwined her fingers in mine and rubbed her cheek affectionately against my shoulder. Everything was again all right with her world.

"What's the chance of you lending me your car for my date tonight?" Lanny asked.

"I'll need it."

"Know if the folks are using the Mercury?"

"Ask them."

He went into the house to ask them.

Florence and I sat side by side, holding hands, shoulders and hips and thighs touching, and after a while she mentioned the engagement ring. Now that we had made up, she was expecting it back.

"I lost it," I said.

"Oh, no, darling! How could you?"

"All right, I didn't lose it," I said. "I threw it away."

She stared at me. "That lovely ring! And so expensive! Perhaps if you looked where you threw it . . ."

"It's down a sewer," I said. "Gone for good."

"Oh, darling, I must have hurt you very much last night."

"Yes."

"Then I've only myself to blame." She snuggled up closer. "But everything is all right now."

Was it?

Ma called us in for supper. Florence had, of course, changed her mind about not eating with us, now that she was again one of my family, or going to be soon; and during the meal she was her gay and talkative self, advising Lanny where to take his date, gloating with Pa over the result of the ball game, which the Dodgers had managed to pull out in the thirteenth, complimenting Ma on her potato salad, and all the time looking so pretty that my fingers tingled.

This was her world, and mine too—the world of clean love and conventional marriage, where you raised a family in a modest home on a steady income. It was where I belonged and wanted to be, and everything that had happened earlier today could be wiped out like a bad dream.

As simple as that, with any luck at all, the way I had it figured out. The money in my car was only money, but Florence was the girl I loved.

During the meal there was no phone call.

After Florence had helped Ma clear the table and wash the dishes, she joined me in the living room. Lanny had his date and the folks were going out to play bridge; ordinarily it would have been a break to have the house to ourselves. But I had already hung around too long, and I told her I had to take her right home.

"I thought we were going to spend the evening together," she protested.

"Sorry, but I have a business appointment."

"On Sunday?"

"This is one of these personal deals in a private home. About an investment."

"What kind of investment?"

"Look, Florence—I couldn't know when I made this appointment this morning I'd ever be seeing you again. You know that."

"You needn't bite my head off. I've admitted it's my fault, but it seems to me that this evening, of all evenings, after we've just made up—" Suddenly she threw her arms around me. "Darling, of course go. I'll have to learn that business comes first. Are you going to make a lot of money on your investment?"

"I doubt that I'll go through with it, but I've got to see the people anyway. Fact is, I'm late already."

It was late only while I was where I could be reached by phone or in person. After I dropped her off at her house, I had plenty of time. I needed darkness for what I had to do, and a good hour of daylight was left.

I drove to Canarsie, past mud flats and industrial plants and boat basins and housing developments. Presently I found what I was looking for—a barren field in which a crumpled shack stood a hundred feet in from an empty, rutted street. Nobody would come this way unless he had to, and nobody would have to on a Sunday night.

I didn't linger there. Twilight was only beginning to roll up from Jamaica Bay. I kept the car moving aimlessly through Canarsie.

Night, when it came, wasn't very dark. I was back at that field, and quite clearly I could make out the shack. No car or person was in sight. I took the suitcase out of the trunk of my car and carried it to the shack. I had a flashlight in my other hand, but I didn't put it on until I was inside. There was no door and the windows were completely shattered and part of the roof was gone, but even though it was wide open to the air it smelled of mold and decay. Something scurried past my feet.

I dropped the suitcase on the wrecked floor. By the light of the flashlight I carefully wiped it with my handkerchief, especially the handle, until I was sure all fingerprints were off. Then I doused the light and returned to my car and headed toward Pennsylvania Avenue.

In Brownsville I stopped off at one of those large, crowded drugstores. Nobody paid any attention to me as I moved along the center counter to the phone booths. I dialed the operator and asked for the police.

"I'm calling about the eighty thousand dollars stolen from the armored truck Friday," I said. "I know where it is."

The cop at the other end of the wire worked at sounding casual. "What's your name, please?"

"Never mind. The money is in a suitcase." I described exactly where the shack was.

"Where are you calling from?" he asked when I had finished.

I had heard that calls couldn't be traced on pay phones, but I wasn't positive. Anyway, I had no more to say.

I hung up and left the booth and walked up the length of the drugstore to the double glass doors. It was an effort to keep from hurrying. But when I was back in my car and driving home, I felt as if chains had been dropped off me.

Nobody was home. I sat in the living room with only one dim light on and waited. It wasn't long before the phone rang.

Her voice said, "Ray Whitehead? Is that you, Ray?"

"Yes."

"This is Cherry."

"I know."

"I guess you've been expecting me to call. I've been calling every few minutes for the last couple of hours, but nobody answered. I became afraid you didn't make it."

"I made it."

"You've still got it in your car, haven't you?"

"No."

"Where is it?"

"Read about it in tomorrow's papers," I said, and I hung up.

Seconds later the phone rang again. I took it off the hook and left it off.

2

Next day there were three news stories that vitally concerned me.

The big one, of course, was about the recovery of the loot. Before leaving for work in the morning I saw a film on TV of the shack in Canarsie where the police had gone last night in response to an anonymous phone call, and of the suitcase found there containing what a quick count indicated was all or practically all of the eighty thousand dollars taken from the armored truck. All of the four morning papers I picked up on the way to work with Pa had headlines.

And all asked why.

That was the mystery, the puzzler, the teaser that made a more sensational story than had the actual robbery.

Why did the bandits—anyway, one of them—a few days after having robbed and killed for the money, return intact those unmarked, low-denomination bills that could be spent anywhere without risk? And if it hadn't been one of the bandits, but an honest man who had somehow got hold of the suitcase—an honest-to-goodness honest man, if such there was—he had certainly known where the money had come from because he had said so when he had phoned the police, so why hadn't he brought it in himself and claimed the twenty thousand dollars reward offered by the insurance company?

Pa was driving and listening to the story on the radio while at his side I was reading the more complete accounts in the papers. When the newscaster turned to a duller subject like the threat of war, Pa commented, "What interests me most is the kind of man who would throw away that kind of money."

"Would you have kept it?" I asked.

"How can a man who's never been tempted answer that?" Pa was an unbeliever from 'way back—a cynic who had never done a bad thing in his life.

"There must have been a conflict of temptations," I said. "I mean, the temptation to get rid of it was stronger than to keep it."

"One thing is sure," Pa said. "He had his reason."

Our truck drivers and helpers and the mechanic were lounging in front of the garage, and like everybody else I was to see that day, they were kicking around theories. Ordinarily Pa would have pointed out that it was ten after eight and time to get the trucks rolling, but this morning he joined the gab fest. I went into the office with the newspapers.

Trig, the man I had shot on Surf Avenue yesterday afternoon, was expected to live. I was relieved. I didn't want any blood on my hands, not even that kind of blood.

The story was far inside the papers and there wasn't much to it in any of them, but there was enough to tell that the descriptions of me the police had got from the panicky bystanders were as contradictory and vague as I had hoped. The wounded man himself claimed he had never even had a look at me, that he had been strolling along, minding his own business, when he had been hit. But of course the police hadn't bought that for a minute, not when he had been found writhing on the sidewalk with an automatic pistol in his hand, and especially not when it was discovered that he was Henry Watson, alias Trig Wacko, with a long criminal record. An assistant district attorney was quoted as believing it was a gang shooting.

The third story, the one about a man having been stabbed to death in a Coney Island hotel room, had to wait for the afternoon papers, and the later editions, at that.

It hadn't been until nine in the morning that a chambermaid had come across the body under the bed while cleaning the room. His fingerprints told the police who he was—Silvester "Shorty" Pond, a one-time minor member of Brooklyn's own Murder, Inc. The medical examiner said he had been stabbed to death between two and six o'clock Sunday afternoon.

The police had a first-rate description of the girl who had occupied that room from Friday evening until, as far as was known, Silvester Pond's death. Particularly her flaming red hair was mentioned by everybody who had seen her in the hotel, which was perfect for an inside-page headline: "REDHEADED BEAUTY SOUGHT IN CONEY ISLAND SLAYING." The name she had signed in the register was Joan Busby. Though it didn't say so in any of the papers, I imagined the police guessed it was a phony name.

How much else would they guess?

Three separate events in Brooklyn on the same day, and it seemed impossible to me that the police wouldn't see how at least two and perhaps all three were linked together. They had been looking for a redheaded girl in connection with the armored truck holdup on Friday, and two days later and a few miles away a redheaded girl was suspected of the murder of a criminal, while within an hour or two before or after that murder and three or four blocks away another man with a criminal record had been shot and wounded, and that very evening the holdup loot had been recovered in still another part of the borough.

It seemed so obvious to me, so cut and dried, but then I knew and they didn't. If they came up with any ideas or hunches, they weren't saying so for publication.

On Tuesday there wasn't a line in any paper or a word on the air about either the shooting or the killing. Both were pretty small stuff by New York news standards. The mystery of who returned the loot and why held on a bit longer, but as nothing new developed, interest trickled off, until by Friday there was nothing left.

On Sunday Florence and I set the date for our wedding.

3

Florence's twenty-second birthday was in September, two weeks before our wedding. We celebrated by making an evening of it in midtown Manhattan. We started off with dinner in a high-priced French restaurant, took in a musical comedy, for which I'd bought tickets a week before from a scalper, ended up in a nightclub.

The nightclub was one of the more subdued spots. Very swanky, with astronomical prices and no nudity. The floor show consisted of a woman folk singer who wore more clothes than any other female in the room and a comedian who told hardly any dirty jokes. We felt quite aristocratic being there.

And this, of all places, was where I ran across Cherry Drew.

We were dancing, Florence and I and dozens of other couples, on a patch of floor the size of a boxing ring. Somebody stepped on my heel and as I stumbled a woman said, "Why, hello, Ray."

I couldn't spot anybody I knew in that crush of slowly moving bodies. We maneuvered around the floor once, and suddenly there within arm's length was Cherry. She had become a platinum blonde.

I nodded stiff-faced and she gave me a scarlet-mouthed smile. Her partner was a towering, meaty man well up in middle age. He held her as if trying to break her in two against his chest. Her strapless black evening gown fitted her as snugly as had the yellow bathing suit.

I whirled Florence away through a momentary opening between dancers.

"Who is she?" Florence asked.

"A girl I used to know in Hessian Valley."

A minute later we again passed Cherry and her partner. Her right hand was on his shoulder and I had a good view of the ring on her third finger.

The ring I had given her.

Florence, to whom I was engaged, had none. I had offered to buy her another, but she had said that now that our wedding was so close we would have more important uses for twelve hundred dollars.

The music stopped and we went back to our table on the balcony. From there I could look down at Cherry and her escort. They had a ringside table, which meant that he was somebody who received special consideration. Nobodies like us were put up on the balcony. Their chairs were close together and he couldn't keep his hands off her, even out there in the open. Every now and then he stopped pawing her to take a nibble at her bare shoulder, while she placidly sipped from a champagne glass.

After a while she lifted her head and saw me looking down at her. She waved to me. I didn't wave back.

Florence said, "Do you know her well?"

"We were brought up together in the same town, that's all."

"Obviously she wasn't a blonde then."

"No," I said, "she wasn't."

I called over a waiter and ordered another round of two-dollar ham sandwiches and one-dollar Scotch sours.

Below us Cherry said something to her escort and rose and made her way between the tables to the balcony stairs.

He watched her go and I watched her come. I hoped she wasn't bound for our table.

But of course she was.

She ascended the stairs and moved toward us in that sheath-like black gown that rippled as she walked. Jewelry flashed conspicuously around her throat and around her left wrist. In a very short time she had become a fine lady, though not quite convincingly. That baby face looked as if she had got into her big sister's cosmetics and tried some of everything. And her hair, which had been too red, was now too blonde.

Then she was at the table, beaming down at me, saying, "How've you been, Ray?"

I got up on my feet and muttered introductions. I could see how she had been—at any rate, how she had done in the couple of months since Coney Island. That choker around her throat consisted of matched pearls, and the heavy gold bracelet on her left wrist was studded with stones—diamonds and rubies and emeralds. If the stuff was genuine, it went a good way toward making up for eighty thousand dollars.

"Won't you sit down?" Florence said.

"Sure." Cherry took the third chair at the table. "I told Brad I'd only be a minute to say hello to an old friend."

Florence glanced down at the man at the ringside table who was staring up at us. "Is he your husband?"

"Never had one. He's just a friend."

He was a friend and she had called me a friend. Florence's eyelashes flickered. I wondered whether in her mind she was making anything of that.

I said a little desperately, "What do you hear from the hometown, Cherry?"

She said she hadn't heard anything recently, and I said I had passed through Hessian Valley last year and it hadn't changed at all, and she said she guessed it never would, which was why she wanted no part of it. We were just uttering words, making conversation, and all the time the two women eyed each other, appraising and measuring and estimating each other.

It was no contest. Florence was better-looking, very much more so in my eyes, but that wasn't the point. In her simple beige taffeta cocktail dress Florence was the better dressed of the two. Cherry had the finery and the jewels, but Florence had the poise and the taste and the maturity. It all added up to class, something Florence had always had and Cherry never would have; and Cherry must have known it and wanted to hurt her.

Up to then she had kept her right hand with the ring on it more or less out of sight, mostly under the table. Now she put out that hand as if reaching for something on the table that wasn't there. She dropped it flat on the cloth and left it there. And she said brightly, "Anyway, Ray, we had a lot of fun together in the old hometown."

Florence looked down at the ring, at that square diamond in its platinum setting. She didn't say anything.

Cherry's scarlet mouth curved. Negligently she pulled her hand back. "I must be going," she said, standing up.

I knew where I wanted her to go.

We mumbled goodbyes. When she was moving away from our table, I beckoned to the waiter and ordered another Scotch sour. Florence said she had had enough to drink for one evening. She was staring down at the main floor, which by now Cherry must have reached.

"I had only one date with her in Hessian Valley," I said. "Many years ago."

"Why apologize?" Florence said.

"I'm just telling you. She was never my type and I wasn't hers."

"What type is she?"

"You've seen her."

"She's rather glamorous."

"So that's the name for it?" I said.

The drink arrived. I poured it down my throat, and when I put the glass down she said what I'd been expecting.

"Her ring," she said. "It was very much like the one I had."

"Which one?"

"The engagement ring you gave me."

"I didn't notice."

"In fact, it was identical."

I met her eyes; they were merely puzzled, which was good. "There must be a lot of rings like it around," I said.

"I imagine so," she said. "Let's dance."

The band had started up a rumba. We went down and danced, and after the number we prepared to leave. While waiting for Florence to come out of the powder room, I had another drink at the bar.

"You look unhappy, Ray."

I turned my head and my cheek brushed against Cherry's blonde hair. There was plenty of room at the bar, but she didn't leave any between us. The bared upper slopes of her breasts were very white against the black gown.

I said, "Let me alone."

"Your girl is very pretty."

"Damn right!"

"So you kissed and made up? She's the girl had this ring first, isn't she?"

"You knew she was. That's why you shoved it under her eyes."

"I wasn't sure she was the same girl, but I thought she might be. I found out she was by the way she looked at the ring."

"What the hell is it your business who she is?"

She merely smiled. The bartender came over and asked her what she was having. She shook her head. "I've only a moment," she told me. "I sent Brad to get my coat when I saw you were about to leave. I've got to see you alone. Tonight at my place."

"I want no part of you," I said, and I had never meant anything more in my life.

"Would you want part of Walt instead?" she said.

I drank. The trouble with Scotch sours was that after half a dozen the sugar in them made you sick to your stomach.

"Is this a threat?" I said.

"Stop being a dope. I can't guess why on earth you did what you did, but don't expect Walt to forget. Or Trig, whom you—" She broke off because the bartender hovered near us. "Come tonight, say about two-thirty."

"No."

"Think about it," Cherry said, tight-lipped. "Think about what I'll do to save my neck if Walt closes in on me." She opened her handbag and took out a piece of paper. "Here, I've got my address written out." She pushed the paper into the pocket of my jacket.

I made a half turn away from her and in the arched doorway from the cloakroom I saw the meaty, middle-aged man named Brad. He wore a camel's hair topcoat over his tuxedo, and he held a gray Homburg in one hand and a fur coat over his other arm. His face had nothing in it.

I said to Cherry, "Your sucker is watching us."

She glanced at him over her shoulder. "It's got to be tonight," she whispered to me, and went to him, smiling too brightly.

He helped her into her coat. It was too early in the season for a fur coat, but the weather would have little to do with a woman's urge to display herself in mink.

4

Florence said reflectively, "It's odd how identical they were."

We were walking west from the nightclub to Tenth Avenue, where my car was parked. The night was bland and her hand was on my arm and we were very much in love.

"Who?" I asked.

"The rings."

"My God, I offered to buy you another one. Tomorrow I'll go out and buy—"

"I keep telling you I'll be perfectly content with just a wedding ring. If you have money to spare, I'd rather we bought the more expensive bedroom suite."

So during the rest of the walk we discussed the bedroom suite she had taken me to look at in a department store a few days ago, and during the drive home we definitely decided on a certain sofa that up to then I hadn't been sure we could afford. She didn't mention the diamond ring again.

At her door we lingered a long time saying good night, and we told each other how fine it would be in a couple of weeks when we wouldn't have to part at any door.

The first thing I did when I was alone and waiting for the elevator was to light a cigarette. The second thing I did was to tear up the paper Cherry Drew had shoved into my pocket.

I carried the pieces out to the street in my fist, but when I got there I didn't throw them away, as I had intended. "Think about it," she had said. I thought about it.

I couldn't see how, in a pinch, she could save her own neck by throwing me to either Walt or the police, but the fact remained that she was the only one who knew who I was and where I could be found. For that matter, I knew the same about her. We were in the same boat sharing the same danger, and if either of us rocked it too much we'd both go over.

She must have learned something and had to consult me about it. I had nothing to lose by listening to what she had to say.

I got into my car and snapped on the dome light and smoothed out the torn and crumpled pieces of paper on the seat and put them together. There was an address in the East Sixties and also an apartment number.

But when I straightened up behind the wheel, I again hesitated. Everything in me but cold reason was against going.

Reason won out. She had herself a rich sucker who bought her jewelry and mink; she wouldn't waste her time on me now that she could get nothing out of me. Why should I be afraid of her? Why, despising her and loving Florence, should I be afraid of myself?

It was twenty after two. I couldn't get there much before three, but I could be sure she would be waiting for me. I drove back to Manhattan.

5

She wore a robe. It was heavy quilted silk with padded shoulders and a voluminous skirt, and it covered a lot more of her than had the black evening gown she had worn in public. I would have expected her to go in for something diaphanous and provocative. Maybe she had a negligee like that, along with her mink and jewelry, but not for me.

I didn't think she could tempt me these days, but I was glad that apparently she didn't want to.

"A drink?" she asked me after she had tossed my hat into the closet.

"Scotch, if you have it."

"Brad brought me a bottle this afternoon, but there's no soda. How about water?"

"Just the Scotch will be fine."

Cherry went into the kitchenette. I looked around. It wasn't much of a love nest, only a bathroom and kitchenette besides this room I was in. The divan against the wall would serve as the bed, and of course it was wide enough for two.

Her pearl choker and her gem-studded bracelet were on a coffee table, where she must have dropped them when she had undressed. I picked up the bracelet.

"Like it, Ray?"

She had returned with a bottle and two pony glasses.

"Are these things real?" I asked.

"I'm nobody's sucker. I made sure they were. As real as your ring, only a lot more expensive. Both of them together are worth better than six grand."

She had put the glasses down on the coffee table and was pouring. Her right hand held the bottle, and the diamond ring was under my eyes.

I said, "Now that you have these, you wouldn't want my ring."

"It's mine. You gave it to me for keeps."

"I'd like it back."

"So you can give it to that girl? Not a chance!"

"I'll buy it from you."

"Honey, can't a girl have some sentiment?" She handed me a full glass and lifted hers. "To the craziest guy I ever knew."

That was a toast I could drink to, though it didn't mean the same thing to me as it did to her. We drank.

Cherry sat down and primly adjusted her robe over her knees. Then she said, "Why did you do it, Ray?"

"Maybe because I'm not a crook."

"God, the things that happen to me! Of all the guys I had to run into in Coney! Why did I have to fall for a screwball?"

"Don't give me that," I said. "You were interested in me because I had a car to transport you and the suitcase."

"Busses and subways were running. The suitcase wasn't so heavy I couldn't have managed it by myself."

"But being driven would have been a lot more comfortable."

"Well, sure. When I recognized you on the beach, I figured here was a guy I used to know who could give me a lift at least as far as Grand Central and maybe a lot farther. That was all I was after at first, just a long lift. But then I had to get ideas." She turned the ring on her finger. "You gave me this in the beer joint. Nobody had ever given me anything for nothing. I was touched; I really was. And you were a sweet boy. I thought how nice it would be, you and me together in the country. I hate being alone."

Before me her face was like a child's painted to look grown up. I poured myself another drink.

"Don't think I was going to let you in on the dough," she was saying. "My idea was to take out what I would need when I needed it, but you wouldn't know where it had come from. It would be all mine. Then Shorty barged in and had to be killed, and on top of that you'd heard enough to guess what was in the suitcase. Well, all right. I didn't care if you did come in on the dough as long as we were together. You and me and eighty grand. It seemed to me that could be the first real good thing had ever happened to me in my life." Her scarlet mouth twisted. "Me and my bright ideas!"

I was standing as I drank the second one, and I began to float. I found myself looking down at her from somewhere near the ceiling, and it was stiflingly hot up there. I loosened my necktie.

"Take off your jacket, why don't you?" she said. "Make yourself comfortable."

"I'm staying only a few minutes."

"Suit yourself. There's one thing I have to hand you, Ray—you had guts. You got us away from two of the toughest hoods you can find anywhere. We were in the clear, money and all. But then what did you have to go and do? You handed it over to the cops." Cherry's painted eyelids fluttered as if she were about to burst into tears at the thought of all that waste. "Why the hell did you, Ray?"

"I told you."

"Yeah, you're an honest man," she sneered. "Nobody just throws away eighty grand, I don't care who he is." She rolled her empty glass against her little chin. "You and your girl made up, huh?"

"You knew we had when you showed her the ring."

"Going to marry her?"

"Two weeks from this Saturday."

She nodded thoughtfully. "I get it. You figured you'd have me on your neck if you hung onto the money." Something happened to her face, aging it a bit. "You'd rather have her with nothing than me with eighty grand."

"That's right," I said.

"You think I give a damn?"

"I'm glad to hear you don't."

"You don't like me, do you?"

"No."

"Good! Because I hate you like poison. Only—" Cherry looked down at her feet; she had kicked off her slippers, and of course her toenails were painted scarlet. "Only after all I went through for it, couldn't you have let me have the suitcase? How would it have hurt you?"

"I'd done enough that was wrong. I had to get out of it as cleanly as I could."

"Get out of it?" She laughed nastily. "You're cracked if you think you'll ever be out of it. There are people who're never going to forget what you did to them."

My glass was empty. I looked at the bottle, but I didn't go for a refill. I'd had more than enough for one night. I took off my jacket and hung it over the back of a chair.

"So you're set to stay?" she said, smiling.

"You haven't yet told me anything about what I came up here to hear. What about Walt and his gang?"

"Walt's somewhere down South, though I don't know where. Trig's in jail. I guess you read they found him with a gun on him after you shot him. When he recovered from his wound in the hospital, they slapped ninety days on him. The rest of the gang is scattered—those who're still alive."

"Have you been in touch with any of them?"

"You think I'm out of my mind? They hate me even worse than they hate you. I've a girlfriend has a boyfriend who knows everything goes on. She asks him questions and gives me his answers."

"What about the police?"

"I know as much as you do—what was in the papers. My guess is the cops are nowhere." She stroked her platinum hair. "Let 'em keep looking for a redhead. They haven't got another thing. Pour me a drink, Ray."

I took her glass from her and refilled it. While I was at it, I refilled mine too.

"Isn't it dangerous for you to live out in the open here in New York?" I said.

"I've got me a good thing here." She looked at the jewelry on the coffee table. "It's worth taking a chance. I'm playing a hunch Walt won't show in these parts for a while yet. He'll keep away till he's sure there's no police heat and that Trig doesn't talk while he's in jail. But sooner or later he'll be looking for me. Looking for us. He'll have to show that nobody can get away with what we did to him."

I dropped down on the divan. I sat hunched over, holding the glass between my knees.

"A gangster's pride and a gangster's hate," I muttered.

"Don't forget to mention the gangster's neck. We know too much. He has to protect himself from us. Especially from you. A guy who would turn eighty grand over to the cops just like that might someday get it into his head to do some talking to them."

"I see," I said. "Walt and Trig aren't the only ones afraid of me."

"There's no telling what a screwball will do."

"You needn't worry about my conscience."

"I don't trust a Boy Scout, that's all."

I drank. When my glass was again empty, I said, "So you might consider it to your advantage to let Walt know where to find me."

"What do you take me for?" Her eyes blazed; nothing I had said to her at any time before had outraged her so much. "You gave me a rotten deal, but you saved my life. And I'm no stoolie. You're safe with me. But am I safe with you? That's why I had to talk to you tonight. Am I safe with you?"

"You know you are."

Cherry looked at me a long time and then nodded. "I heard tell a Boy Scout doesn't rat on a girl."

"Put it that way," I said, and I lay back on the divan.

Time for me to leave. Tomorrow was Friday; I had to be at work at eight. But that last Scotch had really hit me; I was afraid that if I moved, my head would get away from me. I lay there and a crack in the ceiling squirmed like a snake.

"You shouldn't hang around New York," I said after a while.

A match flared. She held it to a cigarette in her soft little mouth and blew it out and said, "Don't tell me you're worried what happens to me?"

"In a way it would be my fault."

"It sure would be." She struck another match, this time just to do something with her hands. "Brad's going to Europe next month. I'm trying to persuade him to take me."

She watched the flame coming close to her fingers. "I might even marry the guy."

"Has he asked you?"

"You think I'm not good enough for him?"

"I didn't say that."

"You don't have to, damn you!"

There was nothing more we had to discuss. I should get up and leave. Soon. When I stopped floating. Lying on the divan with my hands under my head, I was floating up toward that squirming crack in the ceiling without getting any closer.

I felt rather than saw motion on my left. Cherry had left the chair and was striding back and forth, talking. She was saying, "Brad could do a lot worse. After all, he's old enough to be my father. Fact is, he has a daughter older than me. He'll be getting the break."

Suddenly I thought of Cherry's father. I was drunk, and since childhood drunkenness had been associated in my mind with Matt Drew. He had been a handyman, working at odd jobs in the village when he was sober, which had not been often, and drinking up much of what he earned. Mrs. Drew used to scrub my mother's floors once a week and other floors on other days, and on Christmas and Easter you thought first of all of the Drews when food baskets were distributed. I remembered once, when a group of us kids had been walking home from school, Matt Drew had come staggering out of one of the two saloons in Hessian Valley; ragged and unshaven and half blind with drink, he had blundered among us and we had scurried out of his way in disgust. One of us had broken into a run and kept running, and that had been Cherry Drew, who a minute before had been as jolly as the rest of us. She must have been about thirteen, and I could remember how her bare legs had flashed in the sunlight as she had raced sobbing up the street, away from us and from her father and from her shame.

Lying on the divan in her apartment, I said, "So to take a father's place you got yourself a sugar daddy."

She stopped walking. The voluminous skirt of her robe settled about her legs. "You're funny as a crutch, you are."

I was sorry she took it that way. I wanted to tell her so, but all at once it was too much effort to carry on conversation. I closed my eyes.

"You falling asleep on me, Ray?"

I jerked awake. "Had a few too many tonight," I muttered, and I started to sit up.

She put her hand on my chest. "No, stay where you are while I make coffee. You have a long drive."

"I better go."

"Fact is, I feel woozy myself. I could use some coffee. Have a cup with me."

"All right." I sank back on the divan and felt her fumble at my shoe. "Hey, what're you doing?"

"Taking your shoes off. You're getting my spread dirty."

I let her. As long as I was going to hang around for coffee, I might as well be comfortable. It was pleasant having somebody do little things for you like removing your shoes and lifting your legs up on the divan so you could stretch out full length. I felt pretty good in a lightheaded way. I floated, and somewhere water ran and something rattled.

After what seemed a long time she was back, saying, "All right, Brad is no youngster. He's not the romantic type. What the hell do I care? A lot of good it ever did me to fall for handsome young guys!"

As through a fog I saw she had resumed pacing, and her voice was as restless and agitated as her movements.

"He worships the ground I walk on. Jealous if I even look at another man. Tonight on the way home he was sore at me because he saw me talking to you at the bar. That's how much he cares for me. He'll do anything for me, buy me anything. He wants me to move to another apartment—bigger and swankier. I will as soon as I find one, if I don't go to Europe with him." I felt her pass me, go away, pass me. "I give him as much as I get from him. More. His wife died last year and he was very lonely. That's how it started—both of us needed somebody. After you'd let me down so awfully, I was all alone and broke and scared."

"You don't have to justify yourself for taking up with him," I said.

"You think I give a hoot in hell what you think of me? Who're you, anyway? A son-of-a-bitch who did me dirt. I'm better off right now than I would've been with you and the eighty grand. I'm telling you, Brad's a big man. Plenty rich, but not only rich. A very important man in New York. Bradford Smith. You must've heard of him."

I murmured something that was supposed to mean I hadn't.

"He's a paint manufacturer, but what makes him real big is politics. I don't mean he holds office. He's behind the scenes. You know, the one who says who'll be mayor and congressman and judge. His name's in the papers all the time. I can get him to marry me if I try."

I said, "How about coffee?"

"The water has to boil. He'll take me with him to Europe. There I won't have to worry about Walt. I'll ask Brad to take me on a trip around the world. Sure! Clear around the world. He's been talking about retiring; he'll do it for me. We'll be gone a year. Walt won't be able to reach me. Who needed you and the eighty grand? I'll be the wife of a big man. A real lady. That'll be a lot better than anything . . ."

I was drifting away from her. Her voice receded from my consciousness, faded.

My brow was being stroked by a gentle hand. There was pressure against my side, the coziness of a snuggling body. My hand moved and felt cloth and through it curved flesh, and I woke all the way, and there was Cherry stretched out beside me on the divan.

"Listen!" I said.

She turned on her side and her arm under me pulled my head to her. The top of her robe was open and my face was in the deep, warm, perfumed flesh.

I pulled away. I said, "Is the coffee ready?"

She laughed. "Coffee he's thinking of!"

I laughed too. It was very funny. When you were lightheaded like this, everything was funny.

She kissed me. I said, "No!" but I said it to myself. I lay under her mouth, and there was no will in me to stop her or to stop myself.

"Honey, honey," she said. "You looked so sweet sleeping there."

I started to argue with myself, telling myself that I loved Florence and was going to be married to her in sixteen days, but my face was back in that delightful deepness of Cherry's flesh and my hands moved to her, and I was drifting again, but in a different way, floating in a luxurious sea of desire beyond thought, beyond anything but doing.

And then she was tearing herself away from me.

I hadn't heard the key turn in the lock or the door open. They were well inside the room before I knew they were there, the tall, fleshy man named Bradford Smith and another man I had never seen before.

6

Holding the robe together, Cherry jumped off the divan. She said, "Brad, what—" and wet her lips, having run out of words.

She turned her back and pulled up the zipper of her robe.

Bradford Smith didn't look at her, or at me either. He stood in camel's hair topcoat and gray Homburg, a portrait of the dignified middle-aged politician and industrialist, and his pale, anguished eyes shifted from my jacket hung over the chair to my shoes on the floor. The key was in his hand, held pinched between thumb and forefinger—the key he was entitled to because he paid the rent, among other things.

The stranger wore a grin on a broad, hard-jawed face. Whoever he was, he was the spectator, the fourth in the room, and so could be amused.

I had never felt so ridiculous. I swung my legs off the divan, and all at once I had become stone sober.

Bradford Smith spoke. "Have you seen enough, Coogan?"

"No question about it," the other replied cheerfully.

Cherry had moved to the coffee table for a cigarette.

This was a time for one, for the process of lighting it and casually blowing out smoke, for making a show of being undisturbed while her mind skipped about for an explanation her rich lover might accept.

"Then arrest her," Bradford Smith said.

She jerked erect. "Arrest me?" She cringed under the stranger's amused gaze. "Who're you?"

He flashed a badge. "Detective Coogan."

I was bent over, putting on my right shoe. My fingers froze on the lace. They had caught up with her for robbery and murder, I thought, and where, did that leave me?

"So you're a cop," she said in a controlled voice. "So what?"

"I'm from the vice squad. I'm taking you in, sister."

"For what?"

"Prostitution."

I resumed tying my shoelace.

Cherry drew on her cigarette and plucked a shred of tobacco from her scarlet lower lip and said, "You're kidding."

"I don't kid when I have evidence." Coogan grinned at me, sitting on the divan with one shoe on and one shoe off, with my shirt unbuttoned and my untied necktie dangling from my neck. "Get your clothes on, sister. You're coming with me."

"Don't give me that. There's no law against having a friend visit me. He wasn't paying me. Isn't that right, Ray?"

"Yes." I put on my other shoe.

"Tell it to the judge," Coogan said. "There's still time to make night court."

All this time Bradford Smith hadn't stirred.

Cherry swung around to face him. "Your judge, I suppose, like this is your cop. What are you trying to do to me, Brad?"

"You—" His voice got stuck in his throat. He coughed and took a step toward the jewelry on the coffee table. "I gave you everything you wanted. I was extremely fond of you. But even while I was getting your coat from the checkroom you were making this—this assignation with another man."

"Spying on me!" She pouted like a child who considered it unfair to have been caught misbehaving. "A sneaky, jealous spy, that's what you are!"

Woodenly he stared at her. "I am not an utter fool, Cherry. At least not that kind of fool. You would not let me come up with you tonight. You said you had a headache. For a long time I sat in my car outside this building. This man entered—the man you had been so friendly with at the bar. I went for Detective Coogan." His hand touched his brow. "You're going to prison, Cherry—to the workhouse, where women like you belong."

She threw her cigarette down into an ashtray. It bounced out to the floor, where it smoldered. She stooped for it and rose trembling.

"You're out to frame me! Railroad me to jail with your cops and judges!"

He said quietly, "I propose to punish you. Do your duty, Coogan."

I was on my feet now, buttoning my shirt, and my sick sense of shame was giving way to anger.

"Sister, I'm telling you again, get dressed," Coogan said.

"I won't!" She ran barefooted to me and grabbed my arm. "Ray, don't let them!"

Coogan jabbed a finger at me. "You're in trouble too, mister, don't forget it."

I wasn't forgetting it. I was thinking that if Florence found out about this, there would be no wedding.

"Don't let them scare you," I told Cherry, patting her hand on my arm. "I know enough law to know they've got to prove a woman was soliciting."

"You don't know how a crooked cop works. He'll swear to anything, say I propositioned him, and a crooked judge will take his word. Brad's got them all in his pocket."

"He hasn't got me in his pocket," I said.

Coogan glanced around for instructions. "Do I take this wise guy in too, Mr. Smith?"

"No. He may leave."

That was what a man was supposed to be glad to do in this kind of situation, slink away and not give a hoot what happened to the woman as long as his part in it was kept secret from the papers or from his wife or from the girl he was going to marry. Let the woman pay, and in a way it would be no better than Cherry deserved. But then, did I deserve nothing? Was I innocent, if there was a question of guilt or innocence here? And was Bradford Smith, who was old enough to be her father, allowed to get away with playing a vindictive god?

So I said, "You're a pretty noble stuffed shirt, aren't you? You can let me off, but not her. Or are you afraid I'd raise the kind of stink not even your political weight would be able to cover up?"

"The blame is entirely hers. I have nothing against you."

"But it doesn't go the other way around. I have plenty against you." I knew the cockier I sounded, the more effective I'd be. "You've got a nerve talking of punishing her. Who the hell are you, anyway?"

"I have nothing to discuss with you."

"Neither have I with you. I'm simply telling you I'm going to bat for her all the way. You can own all the judges and cops in town, but you don't own all the lawyers and all the newspapers. I'm hiring the best lawyer I can find for her. I'll take the witness stand and tell how she's being framed and by whom and why."

"Who're you?" Coogan demanded. "What's your name?"

"I'll tell it to the judge. If it ever gets that far. If the almighty Bradford Smith wants the newspapers to find out about his little love nest and how he's the kind of heel who'd use his political pull to railroad his mistress to jail because she did something that didn't please him."

And I turned to the mirror over the chest of drawers and tied my necktie, and the silence behind me told me I had won.

Cherry broke the silence by laughing triumphantly.

I didn't feel triumphant. I remembered what had almost happened on the divan a few minutes ago, what had started to happen, and I felt unclean under my skin. I pulled up the knot of my necktie and turned around to the room.

Bradford Smith was picking up the bracelet and the choker from the coffee table.

Cherry had stopped laughing. As she watched him, harsh lines appeared about her mouth and eyes. He dropped the jewelry into his topcoat pocket.

"Well, what do we do, Mr. Smith?" Coogan asked.

The flesh of Bradford Smith's face seemed to have become looser, the jowls more prominent. He said woodenly, "Forget it, Coogan," and started slowly toward the door, stooped a little, an elderly man now.

He must have been very much in love with her.

"Wait, Brad!" Cherry said. "You forgot something."

He took one more step and hesitated and looked back.

She had opened the closet door and was pulling the mink coat off a wooden hanger. Somehow the coat got stuck. In her fury she kept yanking, and when it didn't come free she started to sob. Then she had it out of the closet, and she spun and threw it at Bradford Smith. It fell short, landing at his feet.

"You want my dresses and nightgowns and the other things you paid for?" she shrieked. "You want this robe?" She fumbled at the zipper as if she meant to strip the robe off right there in front of all of us.

Deadpan, Bradford Smith picked up the mink coat and without a word continued to the door, taking it and the jewelry and a trip to Europe and a rich marriage out of her life.

"All right, I'll keep 'em!" she yelled after him. "You got plenty out of me. More than the things you're taking are worth. I hated every minute with you. You made me sick, you—you nasty old man."

His shoulders jerked, but he kept going.

Detective Coogan didn't leave with him. He arranged himself in the armchair and peeled the cellophane from a cigar.

"What's keeping you?" Cherry demanded.

His grin was back. "Me and Mr. Smith are two different people. I have my duty. I'm still taking you in, sister."

"Give him some money, Ray," she told me with a scornful snort.

Coogan offered no protest. She had at once understood what he was after; they were the same kind of people living in the same kind of jungle. He rolled his cigar on his lower lip, waiting for me to give him some money.

"Look here," I said. "I'll be damned if I'll let this—"

"Sure, sure," she cut me off wearily. "He can't make anything stick without Brad behind him, but he can make himself annoying. Let's get rid of the louse."

I pulled out my wallet. Twenty-three dollars were in it. I handed him ten.

Coogan didn't reach for the bill. "You got to do a lot better," he said.

I couldn't afford to grab him by the collar and throw him out. I had to add the thirteen dollars to the ten and say almost apologetically, "This is all I have," and show him the empty wallet to prove it, and all the time I was fighting myself to keep my sweating hands from hitting him.

Grudgingly, as if doing me an immense favor, he accepted the money. He stuffed it away and snapped the brim of his hat. "Have fun," he said affably, and left.

I met the nicest people whenever I was with Cherry.

7

She wept on the divan as I put on my jacket. She lay face down, one bare leg waving in the air and her platinum hair straggling over her cheek.

"I'm going, Cherry," I said.

The leg fell alongside the other; her face turned to me on her left forearm.

"Go and be damned! Every time I see you it's bad luck."

"Not only for you," I said.

"First you cost me eighty grand. Then you cost me my big chance to be safe and secure and respectable. He would've taken me to Europe. He would've married me If—if . . ."

Her voice went to pieces. She wept some more.

"Goodbye, Cherry," I said.

"No, wait. Ray!" She sounded strangely frightened. She sat up, wiping her eyes with the back of her hand. "We were going to have coffee. It's all ready. I just have to warm it."

That had been a very long time ago, as much as thirty or forty minutes ago.

I said, "Something else sobered me up," and took my hat out of the closet.

"Ray, wait!" She had jumped off the divan; she was hurrying across the room. "Honey, don't leave me alone," she wailed. "I can't stand being alone."

"You'll always find a man to keep you company."

"Don't pretend you don't care for me. You wanted to make love to me."

"I was drunk."

"You weren't drunk in my room in Coney Island."

"Cherry, we're no good for each other. You said as much a minute ago."

"We can be. If you'll just give me a chance to show you how good I can be to you. Deep down you like me more than you like that Florence."

"You couldn't be more ridiculous."

"I know what I know. You were willing to give her up for me a few minutes ago when you stopped Brad from framing me. If you'd raised a stink, like you said you would, she would've found out. And then she wouldn't have married you. You were doing that for me."

"I was bluffing and he fell for it."

"If he'd called your bluff, would you've let me go to jail?"

"I don't know."

"Well, I know. I know you. You would've saved me no matter what."

"That doesn't prove anything."

"It has to, honey. There's no other reason."

"You thought of one a while ago. I'm a Boy Scout." I ran my fingers around the sweatband of my hat. "But what's difference? We're never going to see each other again."

She stepped back, and her eyes suddenly hated me.

"Never will be too soon for me," she shrieked. "All the trouble you caused me! God, where I'd be now if it wasn't for you!" She pushed her platinum hair from her twisted face, and there on that hand was the diamond ring in its platinum setting, the only thing of any value she had left. "Go on, what are you waiting for? Beat it!"

"Goodbye, Cherry," I said.

She turned her back.

As I left the apartment and the building, I could be grateful for one thing, at least, and that was that Bradford Smith and the detective hadn't arrived five minutes later.

Part Three: The Killers

1

We spent the first night of our honeymoon in a Manhattan hotel and the second night on a ship bound for Bermuda. It was pretty wonderful. I suppose we were very much like the newlyweds in the stories; the cruising and the touring, the dancing and the swimming, the sunbaked streets and the moonwashed beaches were mostly interludes between being closed in with each other in our room on either water or land.

Two weeks later we were back in Brooklyn, where the apartment we had set up beforehand was waiting for us. We were home, in our own home, and that was the best thing that could happen to two people in love. We settled down to married life.

Our apartment had two bedrooms. The smaller one was scantily furnished as a spare room, but we had more elaborate plans for it. We hoped we wouldn't have to wait longer than a year before turning it into a nursery.

We lived in a garden development in Bay Ridge—low, walk-up buildings with plenty of air and greenery. It wasn't over a mile from the office and garage of Whitehead and Son, Trucking. Usually I left the car for Florence and either took a bus or walked, depending on the weather.

On that brisk Tuesday in November I walked home, and at ten minutes to six I entered the building with my cheeks tingling and a much warmer tingling inside of me. After six weeks of marriage, that excited anticipation of coming home to her was as strong as it had been the first time. I walked up to the second floor, thinking how Florence would rush out of the kitchen when she heard me, sweet and lovely in something trim and just right for her figure, plus a frilly little trick of an apron, and she would fling her arms about my neck and after a minute I would pull her down on my lap and she would protest that something in the kitchen would burn if I didn't let her up, but all the same she would hold me tight as I kissed her....

But it didn't happen on that Tuesday.

I opened the door and closed it, and I heard her say to somebody in the living room, "That's Ray now." Unbuttoning my coat, I crossed the foyer for a look at the visitor. It was Cherry Drew.

2

I hung up my coat in the foyer closet. I took my time about it, wondering angrily if she would ever let me alone again.

"Darling," Florence called, "there's somebody here to see you."

"I know." I moistened my lips and stepped into the living room. "Hello, Cherry," I said.

They were sitting at opposite ends of the tweed-covered sofa, each with fine legs crossed, two attractive young women in the relaxed attitudes of a casual social visit. Too relaxed. I sensed undercurrents, a kind of watchful waiting. Florence had had plenty of time for further study of the diamond ring on Cherry's right hand.

"Congratulations, Ray, on your marriage," Cherry said brightly.

"Thanks."

I could have slapped her for being here at all, but especially for flaunting the ring.

"I was telling your wife," she said, "you have a charming home."

"We like it," I said.

I pulled out my cigarettes, needing something to do instead of just standing there like an idiot. I offered the pack to Cherry. She took a cigarette and I took one and I flicked my lighter.

"May I have one?" Florence said in a curiously clipped tone.

I turned to her end of the sofa, murmuring, "Sorry," and held the pack out to her. Florence had turned pale. I didn't know how I could have made such a blunder. The situation had been bad enough without that.

I held the light to Florence's cigarette, then to Cherry's, then to mine. Standing between them, I asked Cherry how she knew where I lived, since my number and address were not yet in the telephone book.

"Your mother," she said. "I phoned your old number and she told me."

That had been obvious, but the purpose of my question was to make it clear to Florence that it wasn't I who had given her my address.

"Well, what can I do for you?" I said, trying to sound impersonal and businesslike.

Cherry uncrossed her legs and sat rather primly, fully upright and with her legs straight down. She was wearing a gray sweater and skirt and low-heeled shoes, and she might have been a schoolgirl shy and proper in the presence of her elders. Though she was close to my age and several years older than Florence, you had to look into her eyes to guess that, and then you saw it had been a long, long time since she had been young.

"It's about a job," she said, uneasily fingering a pleat in her skirt. "I need a good reference. If a solid businessman like you would recommend me . . ."

I didn't for a moment believe that was the reason for her visit.

"Glad to," I said, playing along. "Do you want me to make a phone call or write a letter?"

"A letter on your business stationery would be better." Cherry stood up. She looked across the living room into the dinette, where the table was set for two. "You folks want to eat. I'll be going."

She seemed to be hinting at an invitation to stay to dinner.

I didn't have to fear that Florence would invite her, and I certainly wasn't going to. Florence clasped her hands on her uppermost knee and said, "Aren't you going to tell Ray where to send the letter of recommendation?" Was there a taunting inflection in her voice, or did I imagine it?

"I was about to," Cherry said. "It's an importing firm—the V. and V. Corporation. I forgot to bring the address, but it's on Whitehall Street. You can look it up. Say I worked for you three years in your office. You have an office, haven't you?"

"Sort of. What were you supposed to have done?"

"Receptionist. Answering the phone and a little typing and saying hello to salesmen."

"We haven't got that kind of outfit."

"You can say you have, can't you? Write them you were paying me sixty a week."

She sounded pretty convincing, and I did my share by taking an old envelope out of my pocket and scribbling down notes. As a matter of fact, I was beginning to think she might be serious after all. If she hadn't yet got herself another boyfriend with money, she would need a paying job.

"It was a pleasure to get to know you better, Mrs. Whitehead," Cherry said.

"I'll get your hat and coat," Florence said crisply.

Cherry's artificial smile twisted into a grimace as Florence went to the foyer. She said something under her breath, and when Florence was out of sight in the foyer Cherry whispered to me, "I've got to talk to you for a few minutes."

"Are you out of your mind coming here?"

"Can it, Ray. You better come outside with me if you don't want me to do my talking in front of her."

I nodded. What else could I do?

Florence returned with a hat and coat. I took the coat from her and held it for Cherry. It wasn't anything like the mink she had thrown at Bradford Smith; it was black broadcloth with a velvet collar, and far from new. Evidently this wasn't a period of prosperity for her. She adjusted a little black velvet hat over her platinum hair and said, "Goodbye, Mrs. Whitehead."

Florence said crisply, "Goodbye, Miss Drew," and moved away toward the kitchen.

I accompanied Cherry to the door and kept going with her out to the hall and all the way to the head of the stairs. There we stopped.

"The bitch!" she said.

"Cut it out!"

"Who the hell's she, giving me a freeze-out? All right she doesn't invite me to dinner. But where does she come off—"

"What did you tell her about the ring?"

"Not a thing. We were just talking, what a nice apartment it was, that kind of thing. I tried to be friendly. You're all wrong if you think I want to make trouble."

"You've made it. I think mostly it was giving her another look at the ring. You could have taken it off before you came up."

"It's mine. I'll wear it anywhere I damn please. What's she got to complain about? She has everything else. She has a wedding ring. She has you and that lovely home."

Cherry pressed her handbag against her midriff. "Anyway, all I'm here for—"

She broke off as somebody came up the stairs. I moved to let Art Fromm, who lived in the apartment next to mine, get by. He said hello to me, looking Cherry over as he said it. He smirked.

"Are you really after a job?" I asked her when he was gone.

"You kidding? What can I do in an office? The best job I ever had was behind a counter in a five-and-ten." Cherry glanced away from me. "Walt's back in town," she said.

Sooner or later it had been bound to happen. I had nothing to say.

"I found out this morning," she went on. "Somebody told me he saw Walt on Broadway last night. I don't know how long he's been in town, but not long. Probably Trig's with him. I checked with friends and learned Trig got out of jail a few days ago. Maybe others of the gang are here too, but just those two are enough. I don't know what to do."

"Are you living in the same apartment?"

"Where else? Though I can't afford it. I'm a month behind in rent."

"If they haven't yet found out where you're staying, they will."

"Don't I know it? They'll find me anywhere in the city. I've got to get away. But I'm broke, Ray. I had a few dollars left over after Brad and then I hocked a few things. All I have to my name now is eighteen dollars." She turned the ring on her finger. "And this. For some reason I can't bring myself to sell it. I was in a pawnshop this afternoon, but at the last minute I walked out."

"I haven't much cash on me, but I can let you have a check for one or two hundred."

"My God, I figure on heading for Mexico. I've some friends there Walt doesn't know about and won't find out about. I must have a thousand."

"That's a lot of money."

"It's not as much as eighty thousand. You're getting off cheap."

I ran my forefinger over my mouth. "So that's why you came to my apartment instead of going to my office or phoning me to meet you somewhere. You can hold telling Florence over my head. In other words, blackmail."

"You have a nerve talking like that. Look at all you cost me, but did I ever ask you for a cent before this? I'll tell you why I came here. To see how you were living. To see what a nice cozy home you have, while I have to go find a hole to pull over myself."

"All right," I said. "I made this offer before. I'll buy the ring from you."

She shook her head, smiling a little. "I don't have to sell you anything for that dough. You'll give it to me just because you know I must have it. Am I right, honey?"

She was right.

I said, "I suppose it has to be in cash."

"Of course. Nobody will cash a check for me that big. In fact, any amount. Can you raise it tonight?"

"You'll have to wait till my bank opens tomorrow."

"But make it early, huh? I'm really scared. Where's the bank? I'll meet you there—say at nine-thirty."

I told her where my bank was.

She squeezed my arm. "You're one guy I can always count on. See you tomorrow morning."

I watched Cherry go down the stairs and turn at the landing. Then I went back to my apartment, where I would have to tell my wife a lot of direct and indirect lies.

Florence was in the kitchen. She stood at the worktable, cutting up vegetables for a salad. Chops sizzled in the infrared broiler. I kissed the back of her neck.

She didn't stir. She said to the salad bowl, "Today was the first time you didn't kiss me when you came home."

"I prefer to do my kissing in private."

"Is that why you went out to the hall with her?"

"Holy cats! I needed more details for that letter, so I went after her to ask her a few more questions."

"You didn't kiss me hello," she said. "You didn't even say hello. You were so wrapped up in her you hardly knew I was in the room. Like when you offered her a cigarette and completely forgot me."

I plucked a slice of raw carrot from the bowl and nibbled it. "What d'you know, I have a jealous wife! Just because a girl from my hometown drops in to ask a small favor of me ..."

"She has my engagement ring," Florence said dully, turning to the refrigerator.

I leaned against the sink and watched her replace the vegetable tray. For one moment I thought of telling her everything, to free myself from what had turned out to be the worst of all, the need to keep lying to her. But I didn't dare.

"It's my ring," she said again, facing me, and the paleness of her face made her solemn eyes very dark. "I wasn't sure the first time I saw her wearing it, and I was anxious not to be sure. It's my ring."

I decided there was more to be lost than gained by continuing to lie about that part of it, as long as she knew it was a lie.

"All right, it is," I admitted. "It happened the day after you returned it. You remember when I came home that Sunday afternoon and you were waiting for me on the porch, I said I'd been swimming. Well, I'd run into her in Coney Island. We hadn't seen each other in seven-eight years and had never been particularly friendly, but I was heartsick and lonely. I don't have to tell you why."

She nodded gravely.

"I asked her to have a beer with me," I said. "The ring was in my pocket. I'd been thinking of throwing it away. Suddenly I gave it to her as we sat drinking. Just like that. Impulse. I wanted nothing from, her. It was a way to get rid of it—rid of the memory, the heartbreak. When you and I made up a few hours later, I was afraid you'd get the wrong idea if I told you what I'd done with it."

"I think I understand." Something like relief eased her cheek muscles. "But . . ."

"That's all there was to it," I said. "If there had been anything else, we would have spent at least the evening together. I left her in the beer joint and drove home and found you on the porch. I saw her twice after that—when we ran across her in the nightclub and here today. And that's another thing. If there were anything between us, would she pay me a visit while you were home?"

Florence moved past me to take a look at the chops in the broiler. "Does she know the ring was mine?"

"All I told her in the beer joint was that I had no more use for it. From there your guess is as good as mine."

"I don't think I like her."

"That's fine with me. I don't either. Anyway, now you know why I was upset when I came in and found her wearing the ring. I was afraid you'd act this way." I put my hands on her. "Sweetheart, don't ever imagine I could want another woman."

She turned to me within my embrace. "So she really did want a letter of recommendation?"

"What else? She could be sure I wasn't going to pass out more rings."

"How silly I was, darling! That shows how much love you."

And it was all right after that. All right for Florence anyway. But it hurt when she asked me to forgive her for doubting me, and when we kissed conscience made the sweet ardor of her mouth bitter for me.

3

Cherry was seated on a bench in the bank when I got there at a quarter to ten next morning.

Her black coat was open and under it she wore the same gray sweater and skirt she had worn yesterday and on her feet were the same low-heeled shoes. We glanced at each other the way strangers might; without breaking my stride, I continued to the counter to write out the check. What with furnishing an apartment and going off on a honeymoon, my balance could barely stand it, though in a pinch I could have dug into my war bonds to cover the check.

She disappeared while I was waiting on line. I got the money in fifty twenty-dollar bills and returned to the counter and sealed them in a mail deposit envelope and left the bank. She was down the street a way, waiting in front of a shoe store.

"I started to get nervous when you didn't show up at nine-thirty," she said.

"I was delayed at the office."

"Oh, I knew you'd show up. But the plane I want to take leaves at noon from La Guardia Airport, and I still have to stop off to change my clothes and pack my bags."

"If they're really after you, isn't it dangerous to keep going in and out of your apartment?"

"What do you mean, really?"

"You could pick up an easy thousand dollars by saying Walt was back."

"Say, listen! Did I ever try to do you out of anything? Even this ring—did I ask you for it? If anybody did anybody out of anything, you were the one."

She had raised her voice there on the busy street in a neighborhood where some of the people passing by might know me. I would give her the money anyway, so why delay getting rid of her?

I said, "Here it is," thrusting the envelope at her angrily.

Cherry stuffed it into her handbag, but that didn't shut her up. "I could've asked for two grand and you would've come across. I only asked for what I absolutely have to have. I'm fed up with the way you're always talking like you're so goddamn much better than me. You'd think I wasn't saving your neck as well as mine by getting out of town."

A passing woman wheeling a baby carriage shot us an interested glance.

"All right, all right," I said.

"It's not all right. I'll tell you why I'm wearing these clothes and haven't packed yet. I was scared to go to my apartment last night. You slept in a nice comfortable bed with your wife and hadn't a thing on your mind, but I had to buy a flop in a lousy hotel and worry myself sick. I'll be scared till I get on the plane, and even when I'm there and pull the hole over my head I'll keep on being scared. And you call this an easy thousand bucks." She had a way of making me feel like a heel.

"I'm sorry," I said.

"That's your favorite expression. You're sorry!" Furiously she tucked the handbag under her arm. "Don't think I'm going to thank you for this dough," she said, and walked off.

I turned in the opposite direction.

I was passing the bank when I heard my name called, and I stopped and looked back and Cherry was running after me. Her little velvet hat was crooked on her blonde hair.

"Ray!" She grabbed my arm and paused to catch her breath. "I have to pick up my things at the apartment, but maybe there's already a stakeout."

"Is there anything so valuable you can't pass up?"

"I have clothes and other things. I meant to ask you to go with me to get them, but then you got me so mad at you. Come with me just to the apartment, huh, Ray?"

"What good will I do? Walt and Trig know me by sight. You'll have enough left over from the money I gave you to buy other clothes."

"It's not only clothes. Personal things."

I didn't think I was a coward. I could give myself that much; I had been tested in a war and I had been tested that afternoon at Coney Island. If I had to take the chance of facing Walt and Trig, I thought I probably would, but I didn't see the need. All she had to do was go straight to the airport and get on the plane, and I would be free from her. If I could be finished with her here and now in front of the bank, I would be buying very much of a bargain for a thousand dollars.

"I don't see where it's worth the risk," I said.

Cherry let go of my arm, and her anxious, tilted face turned away from me. "I guess you're right," she said wearily, and again she walked away from me without saying goodbye.

I hoped that was my last sight of her, that slim figure with a little too much hip movement walking slowly down the street and being lost in the crowd.

I went back to the office and got to work checking past-due customers' accounts. And after a while, as I was writing, "Please!" on the statements, I told myself that I should have accompanied her from the bank to the plane.

But why? She knew better than I how to avoid them. She knew more about gangsters and killers, how they thought and operated, from having lived with them and worked with them and double-crossed them. My obligation or responsibility or, most accurately, my conscience had to end somewhere. She was nothing but trouble, and I'd been smart not to stay with her even another hour.

Time passed, and then it was twelve o'clock and I told myself she was boarding the plane, and when I left for lunch at twelve-thirty I told myself she was well out of New York. She would get into other messes. A girl like Cherry always did, if not with gangsters, then with rich and vindictive lovers who caught her with other men. Well, her messes would no longer be any concern of mine.

But I suppose I didn't really believe that, because when the phone rang shortly after eleven o'clock that night I knew that here it was still with me.

"Who can it be this late?" Florence said.

We were undressing for bed. I had stopped pulling off my socks to watch her get out of her underwear, a sight I didn't think would pall on me no matter how long we were married. The phone kept ringing, and suddenly I had a vivid memory of sitting in a cramped hotel room watching a girl with flaming red hair wriggle out of a yellow bathing suit while a dead man lay under the bed.

"You answer it, dear," Florence said. "You have at least some clothes on."

I went into the living room. I picked up the phone and said, "Hello."

"Ray? Is that you, Ray?"

A woman's voice, but not one I recognized.

"That's right," I said. "Who's this?"

"Cherry. Cherry Drew. I'm—I'm— Something happened to me."

It was her voice after all, but weak and broken. "What is it?" I asked.

"I never took the plane. I met a guy. A friend. He said he was driving to Cleveland this morning. I figured I'd go with him. We got as—as far as—"

I could hear her breathe raggedly as she paused for strength to continue. And I thought: There would always be a guy. Wherever she was and whatever she did, she would have a guy with her.

"I told him I had a thousand dollars on me," she said. "He took it from me . . . threw me out of the car . . . beat me up . . . left me there. After a while I managed to crawl to a house. That's where I am now. Haven't a cent and I'm hurt bad. Ray, come for me. God, how I'm hurt!"

She broke into a fit of coughing. Listening to her, I thought: Damn it, why does everything have to happen to her and therefore to me?

"Dear, who is it?" Florence called from the bedroom.

I put my hand over the mouthpiece. "Nothing important." Then I said into the phone, "Where are you?"

Cherry raspingly cleared her throat. "New Jersey. In the sticks. Ray, please, please come for me."

"Can't you stay there till tomorrow?"

"I can't." Her weak voice dropped so low I had to strain to hear it. "The people here, they want to call the police—to go after the guy who beat me up. The cops will ask questions. They'll dig." Her panic quivered over the wire, the panic of the hunted. "I told these people you're my brother. They'll wait till you get here."

"What will I be able to do?"

"I won't be on your hands. Honest. I know a private hospital in the city where they don't ask questions. Take me there. That's all I ask. I'm so terribly hurt and I've nobody but you, Ray, you're the only person in all the world I can turn to. Please, Ray. Please."

And she wept.

I wanted to say, "Not this time," but how could I say it?

"Where are you exactly?" I asked.

"A place called Belmont, in New Jersey. Ever hear of it?"

As a trucker, I was more or less acquainted with every city and village and hamlet within a couple of hundred miles. "That's in the northwest, close to the New York state line."

"Yes, yes."

"But what were you doing there?" I said. "It's not on any of the best routes from New York to Cleveland."

"I wouldn't know. It's an awful lonely place. Guess he drove here so he could rob me and beat me up."

"What's the address of the house?"

"Wait a minute."

I heard voices mutter, and twice I heard her cough. Then she was back on the wire.

"There's no number. It's outside the town. You go—" Another voice muttered at her side, evidently somebody giving directions. Haltingly she relayed them to me, and she sounded weaker and weaker. "Drive up Main Street . . . to a railroad trestle. Go under the trestle and turn right, along the tracks . . . Jupiter Avenue . . . four and a half miles." She coughed, and I heard her sobbing breath over the wire, and she went on: "On the right there's a filling station . . . crumbling . . . two old-fashioned pumps broken . . . house behind it . . . on a hill. A light will be outside. Have you got it?"

"Yes."

"Ray, I don't know what I'll do if you don't come. You'll start right out?"

"It will take me about two hours. What's the name of the people who live there?"

The line went dead at her end. I clicked the bar and the operator came on and said the party had hung up.

Standing there beside the phone, I thought that now again I would have to tell a whole series of lies to FIorence. I considered some and rejected some and came up with a story that would explain why I would be away most or all of the night.

"Aren't you coming to bed?" Florence called.

I went into the bedroom. She was sitting up in bed, reading a book. One strap of her pale-green nightgown had slipped down and she looked deliciously wanton. I very much wanted to be under the covers with her.

"One of our trucks broke down in New jersey," I said. "I have to go out there."

"This late?"

"He needs a new wheel. We have one in the garage. I'll drive it out to him and help him put it on."

Pouting, she tossed aside the book, "It seems to me that can wait till morning."

About the same thing I had said to Cherry a few minutes ago. I had an answer for that, as Cherry had had an answer for me. And when I had asked Cherry the name of the people at whose house I was to pick her up, she had hung up.

"Well, can't it wait?" Florence persisted.

I was pulling on a sock. I roused myself. "The truck has a load and he'd have to stay out there all night guarding it. Besides, we operate on schedule. Too much time has already been lost."

Maybe Cherry had hung up at that point, I thought, because she hadn't heard the question, or because she had been too weak to keep up the conversation.

"It's a shame," Florence said, "dragging you out in the night."

"That's the business I'm in, sweetheart. Full of emergencies."

I was becoming a pretty glib liar. Nothing like practice.

Abruptly, as I was buckling my belt, it hit me. I wasn't the only liar. A trap was waiting for me in New Jersey, and Cherry was the bait.

4

My army pistol was in a small trunk in the spare room closet.

I dug it out from among the uniforms and boots and hats and medals and souvenirs and trinkets, the odds and ends accumulated during a war and sentimentally clung to. I had never expected to have any use for any of them, especially not for the heavy Colt automatic, which was illegal for a civilian without a permit, and not in the best of shape anyway. It needed cleaning and oil, but there wasn't any in the apartment.

Still, for this one night it could return to its function, if necessary, which was to kill or carry the threat of killing.

Because by now I had little doubt left of what I was getting into. The fact that Cherry had hung up without telling me the name I had asked for meant little by itself, but it had started a train of thought while I had been dressing; and now, as I tested the rather stiff action of the pistol, I kept going over it in my mind.

Something else made more sense than that somewhere between the bank in Brooklyn and La Guardia Airport in Queens she had "met a guy," and had restrained her frantic urge to get out of the city in a hurry, hanging around until evening so she could drive with him only as far as Cleveland, instead of by then being well on the way toward Mexico, and that she, who played everything close, had recklessly told him about the thousand dollars in her handbag, and that this friend, as she had called him, had not only robbed her and thrown her out of his car in the middle of nowhere, but had pointlessly beaten her up. All this was barely possible, knowing Cherry and the kind of friends she had, but what made a lot more sense under the circumstances, what was less complicated and more reasonable, was that after she had left me this morning she had, after all, taken the risk of sneaking into her apartment for her clothes and hadn't got away with it.

I'd never heard where the gang had gone to hide out after the armored truck holdup to wait for Cherry to bring the loot. But somewhere in northern New Jersey would be likely, close enough and yet far enough, in the sparsely settled section near the New York state line. It could be the same place, behind an abandoned filling station, a place to take her after they had picked her up at her apartment house, a place to torture her as they had tortured the unfortunate Georgie last summer, to make her lure me there, the man they knew only by sight but whom they wanted to get out there badly.

So it was a trap, and here I was about to take the bait instead of getting into bed with my wife.

After more rummaging in the trunk, I found the box of .45-caliber cartridges. There were nine. I stuck seven into the magazine, fully loading it.

This morning she had begged me to go back with her to her apartment. Probably that wouldn't have saved her; it would only have made it easier for them, giving them the chance to pick us both up together or finish it right off by shooting us down where they saw us. But the fact remained that I had let her go off alone. At the least I should have got my car and driven her straight to the airport and made sure she boarded the plane. But I'd been too busy and too anxious to be rid of her. Later I'd told myself that my responsibility had to end somewhere, but I knew now it hadn't ended. I could no more abandon her to them this time than I had been able to that Sunday afternoon in Coney Island.

But if my responsibility to Cherry hadn't ended, what about my greater responsibility to Florence?

That was too easy a way out, and it wasn't even a way out. If they had forced Cherry to make that phone call, they had learned all about me from her, including my name and address. I would be shot down in the street, coming or going to work, or entering or leaving this building, or they might come up here to this apartment for me while Florence was home and then she would be in it too, which was the most terrifying of all possibilities.

The only way to keep them away was to go to them.

"Have you left yet?" Florence called from the bedroom.

"No."

I went out to the hall and stuck the gun into the deep pocket of the fleece-lined jacket I wore when working on a truck. I would wear it tonight because it gave me more freedom of movement than my overcoat.

Florence had resumed reading in bed.

"Don't worry if I'm gone all night," I said to her. "Driving there and back will take four hours, and it might take a couple of hours to change the wheel."

If I wasn't back by morning, or at least didn't phone her, she would have plenty of reason to worry. Because then I would never come back.

She smiled up at me from the bed. "This will be the first night since our wedding we haven't slept together."

"Will you miss me?"

"Um."

I choked up. I knelt beside her and kissed her many times, her mouth and face and throat and shoulder.

"I wish," she said huskily, "you didn't have to go out."

I tore myself away from her. When I was in the hall I put on my jacket, and the heavy pistol slapped against my right hip.

5

It was a lonely drive, up Shore Parkway and under the mouth of the East River through the Battery Tunnel, up the tip of Manhattan and under the Hudson River through the Holland Tunnel, across the New Jersey flatlands and past massed industrial plants, then northwest on the open highway.

At twenty minutes past one I reached Belmont. All of it was dark except the street lamps on Main Street, and nobody was in sight except a cop sitting in his car at an intersection. Passing him, I felt weighed down by a sense of isolation.

The railroad trestle loomed ahead. I drove under it and on the right I saw the road I was supposed to take. Jupiter Avenue, she had said. I couldn't see a signpost, if there was one, but the railroad tracks ran parallel to it. Then the road swerved from the tracks and changed from blacktop to oil and the town dropped away.

Into the night my headlights bored a tunnel through which time rushed at me. I was close now. This was another H hour, the remembered stomach-tightening, mouth-drying prelude to action out of which you might not come alive. Those other H hours had been perhaps the worst part of war, the waiting for the relentless instant when you left a foxhole to rush into deadly fire or set out with a patrol behind enemy lines; but I had never been alone, and I was learning the difference that made.

I discovered the moon. A cloud drifted away and that crooked yellow blob sailed beyond the left window. In the city, if you noticed it at all, it was merely decoration. Here it showed me woods and fields and a distant hill, but no house anywhere.

Four miles from the trestle I slowed the car down to a crawl. The road dipped, curved, and suddenly ahead and to my right was a glow. Seconds later my headlights, aided by the moon, picked out what was left of a filling station.

Two old-time, hand-cranked gas pumps stood shattered and forlorn in a bare, hard-dirt area between the road and a wall of trees. There was nothing else; if there had been any kind of building as part of the filling station, it was gone. The glow came from farther back and higher up, through the leafless branches of trees. She had said an outside light would be on.

The driveway, or maybe it was a side road, started not many feet past the pumps, a cinder track angling toward the glow. I didn't dare stop to look up it, because a car pausing anywhere in the vicinity might alert them.

Most of the way from Belmont this road had curved like a snake in agony, and within a hundred yards there was still another curve. When I was around it, I cut the headlights before stopping; by moonlight I rolled the car off the road and part way in among some bushes. I took the flashlight from the glove compartment and got out quickly.

The night was raw, much colder than in Brooklyn. My fleece-lined jacket should have been plenty warm enough, but the weather wasn't the only thing chilling me. Pulling up the collar, I went into the woods. My plan was to skirt around to the side or rear of the house.

The trees were rather sparse, mostly scrub oak and birch. The scrawny, leafless branches let enough moonlight through so that I didn't have to use the flashlight; when I did, I kept the beam down to the ground and partly shielded by my hand. The ground sloped upward, but it wasn't a real hill, as she had said on the phone. A low knoll, at the most. As I neared the top, the glow kept brightening.

Without warning I was there. I topped a hump and found myself at the edge of a more or less flat clearing in which house sat. I doused my light and dropped to the ground.

The house didn't look like more than a summer bungalow—a small wooden one-story rectangle built some three feet from the ground on a cement-block foundation. The narrow side toward me had only two windows, both dark. From where I lay I could just about see half a dozen narrow steps running up to a roofed front door landing. The glow came from a naked bulb over the landing, not bright, but bright enough to spread out to the cinder driveway and reveal a car, an old-model Nash, parked where it ended.

Nothing stirred. No sound anywhere. Only that light waiting for me. Step into my parlor, said the spider to the fly.

The ground was too damn open. Where the light from the bulb didn't reach, moonlight did. I could have seen anybody between myself and the house, so anybody would be able to see me. And see me first.

I drew back over the hump and stuck my flashlight into my hip pocket and took out my gun. I reconnoitered, keeping to trees and bushes wherever I could. Behind the house stretched a flat, open field; there was no grass high enough at this time of the year for a cover. Anyway, there was nothing in the back wall of the house to take me there—no door, no lighted windows. I swung wide and crossed the field far from the house, crawling, and worked my way down the other side. When I again neared the house, I got into an apple orchard.

The gnarled trunks and crooked, leafless branches offered little protection from the moonlight. But they cast shadows, and I slipped from shadow to shadow. When I reached the last tree, I was no closer to the house than I had been on the other side, but the Nash parked at the end of the driveway was about halfway between me and the house. It could be a shield—better protection, in a pinch, than this narrow tree trunk, and within fifty feet of the two windows on this side, both of which showed light.

I got down on my belly. This was familiar, this crawling and wriggling with a gun in my hand, pausing to peer and listen and then inch on, this that I used to do many thousands of miles from here on patrol. I was back at war.

I rose halfway up beside the car and crouched there. Time passed.

Were they all in the house, confident that I had fallen for her story and would drive up to the front door and knock politely and step into their parlor? Having been outwitted by me some months ago in Coney Island, chances were they wouldn't underestimate me.

Most of war consisted of waiting.

Cold wind tore at me. I thought of the warmth of my bed with Florence in it, desirable and wonderfully cozy, while I was risking my life for another woman, a woman I didn't even like. Silently I cursed Cherry, but I had done that before, and here I was.

The brittle silence was cracked by the sound of an approaching car. From up here on the knoll a piece of the road in front of the gas pumps was visible. Headlights approached slowly. About where the driveway began they seemed almost to stop. Was the car coming up here?

I turned my head, and through the windows of the Nash I saw a man step out from behind the steps.

He wore a tan overcoat but no hat. I didn't have to see his face to recognize him. The outside light shone on his completely bald scalp. Henry Watson, alias Trig Wacko.

He peered down the driveway at the headlights still moving by. The driver was merely being especially cautious on that dark, winding road with the sharp curve directly ahead. But he had done me a favor; he had brought Trig out from behind the steps. A double-barreled shotgun rested hunter fashion on the crook of his arm—at close range a more effective weapon than a handgun.

Waiting in ambush out in the cold was as lonely and muscle-cramping work as crouching behind a car. He didn't return at once. He flexed his shoulders and took a few steps toward the car and then turned his back and looked some more down the driveway.

I reversed the pistol in my hand. Holding it by the barrel, I slipped around the car. Trig was starting back to the steps. I leaped.

This was another thing I had picked up in war, a bit of experience I had thought I'd never have to call on again. I knew where to strike and how, at the base of the skull, sharply. The fact that he was hatless helped. Without a sound he pitched forward and lay motionless.

Trig had no luck with me. He had met me twice, and the first time

I had put a .22 slug in him and the second time I had perhaps smashed his skull.

I snatched up his shotgun. The light exposed me fully, but nobody shot at me. I ran behind the car and went back into the crouch.

After a minute I decided that Trig had been the only one outside and that nobody had been looking out of the house when I had knocked him out. Was anyone besides Walt left? My next step was to find out who was inside. With the shotgun under my left arm and the pistol in my right hand, I made for the nearest of the two lighted windows. I huddled against the cement-block foundation, then rose on my toes. If I had been an inch or two shorter, my eyes wouldn't have been able to make it.

Cherry was in there with a man I had never seen before.

It was a living room of sorts, small and sparsely furnished with a sagging sofa and a narrow table and several plain wooden chairs. The only homey thing about it was a fire blazing merrily in the fieldstone fireplace, probably the only heat in the house.

She was lying on the sofa the way a sick child would lie, curled up with her knees against her chest. She hadn't changed out of the gray sweater and skirt, which meant they had picked her up before she had reached her apartment. Her platinum hair straggled over her cheek, but a discolored eye was visible. She was holding a handkerchief to her mouth and I could see blood on the cloth.

The man sat at the table, pouring whisky from a bottle into a water glass. He had a huge head on skimpy shoulders. When there were a couple of fingers of whisky in the water glass, he stopped pouring and spoke to her. I couldn't hear the words through the closed window. Cherry took the handkerchief from her mouth and moved swollen lips. He rose, his slight torso out of all proportion to his big head, and started to carry the glass to her. Where was Walt?

He might be in one of the other rooms, though I doubted it. Up until a little while ago, at least, the windows of this room were the only ones that showed light. If he wasn't inside, he was outside, not close enough to have seen me knock out Trig, but at any moment he might come along and he couldn't miss seeing Trig, lying near the steps, and I would be almost as conspicuous standing in this light flowing from the window.

I dropped down on my heels and turned toward the front of the house, and that was when he started to shoot at me.

I hit the dirt.

Walt stood at the edge of the light from the landing, burly in a shaggy overcoat, and between us on the ground was the dark splotch that was Trig. The gun in Walt's extended hand roared twice more.

In my time I'd been shot at by better men firing a lot heavier stuff. He might be a big shot gangster, a feared killer, but at a hundred feet he was no damn good. His style would be pushing a gun up against a man's body and blasting away.

He must have thought he'd got me, because he paused, peering at where I lay in shadow against the wall. I could afford to take another second or two. The shotgun might be more accurate at this range, but I'd lost it when I'd hit the dirt; it was somewhere behind me. The heavy automatic would do; when a .45 slug hit them, they went down. I moved as little as possible to draw a bead on him, but I did have to raise my arm from the ground.

We shot almost as one, the sounds of our guns overlapping. He almost got me this time, his bullet kicking up dirt inches from my chin. Maybe I wasn't a better shot, but I'd aimed instead of simply fired, and he'd remained upright in the light, offering a lot easier target than I. Evidently he'd never been a soldier.

Walt staggered two steps forward and went down on one knee. His gun waved as he fought his arm to steady it. Again I took my time, aiming, squeezing my automatic twice more. He flopped over the way I had seen many men fall, as if all his bones had abruptly turned soft.

That still left one, the little man with the big head in the house. I sprang up, pressing myself against the wall in case he came to either of the windows.

The stillness had returned. But only for a very little while. Then I heard Cherry's voice.

"Ray! Is that you, Ray?"

A door slammed. I heard feet running down the front steps.

"Ray!"

She appeared at the front corner of the house. Her head was turned away from me; she was staring at the two shapes on the ground.

"Cherry! Where's the other one?" I said.

She saw me against the wall. She ran to me, swaying, stumbling, her hair wild and her face battered. She might have fallen at my feet if I hadn't caught her in the circle of my left arm.

I said urgently, "Where's the other one?"

"He went through a window. A back window."

I let go of her and dashed along the wall to reach the back corner before he turned it and started shooting. When I got there, I saw I didn't have to worry about him. The little man with the big head didn't hanker to fight. He was running for all he was worth straight out across the open field behind the house. The moon was on him and I probably could have brought him down, but there was no point to shooting a fleeing man in the back. I went back to Cherry.

She had gone to the front of the house. Standing huddled with her arms crossed over her bosom, she stared down at Walt.

"Is he dead?" she asked me.

I bent over him. He was sprawled face down and I couldn't see where my bullets had struck him. All I was interested in was his pulse. He hadn't any.

"He's dead," I said, rising.

She smiled grotesquely with her swollen, lopsided mouth and turned her head to Trig. Blood half covered his naked scalp and ran down under the collar of his overcoat. We could hear him breathe as if he were sobbing.

I said, "He'll keep till after we're away from here. Can you walk?"

She went into a coughing fit that shook her from head to foot. Blood appeared on her mouth. I gave her my handkerchief and held her.

When she was able to talk, she said, "I'm freezing. My coat. It's in the house."

She moved with me as far as the steps and sat down on them and put her head on her arms. I entered the house. Her coat wasn't in the living room. Using my flashlight so as not to leave my fingerprints on light switches and doorknobs, I searched the other rooms. I found her coat neatly hung up in a bedroom closet and her little velvet hat on the shelf.

I was on the way out when I heard the slam of a gun.

As I ran to the front door, I yanked my pistol out of my pocket. On the landing I stopped.

Cherry had found the shotgun. Swaying, she held it in both hands as she stared down at Trig's head. Or what was left of Trig's head.

With her coat over my arm and her hat in my hand, I went slowly down the stairs. She looked at me out of her good eye, and she muttered dully, "He was getting up," and the shotgun fell from her hands and she crumpled in a dead faint.

6

Cherry revived while I was struggling to get the coat on her limp form. I pulled her up to her feet, and as she leaned against me I pushed her arm through the second sleeve and stuck her hat on her blonde head any which way. "Trig was getting up," she said in her broken voice. "I had to shoot. I figured he had a gun."

I had no comment to make.

Somebody might have heard all that shooting and might be on the way to investigate. I tried to rush her away from there, but her legs weren't up to it. With my arm under her shoulders, she wobbled step by slow step down the driveway and along the road. When we reached the beginning of the curve, she collapsed. I picked her up in my arms and carried her the rest of the way to my car, half hidden in the bushes.

Inside the car, she let her head flop back against the top of the seat and muttered, "A cigarette."

I lit two at once and stuck one into the corner of her puffy, blood-smeared mouth. The first puff brought on the coughing. Her cigarette fell to the floor. I picked it up and killed it in the dashboard ash tray and started the engine.

"Wait!" She fought for her voice. When the coughing stopped, she said, "My handbag. The cops will find it. A letter's in it from my mother with my name and address."

I should have thought of her handbag when I had been up there, but I wasn't yet as experienced as she was in covering up after killings.

"Where is it?" I asked.

"Somewhere in the house. Walt had it last, when he took the money out. That's another thing—the money you gave me."

"Is it in his pocket?"

"I guess so."

I hated to go back, but there was no help for it. I opened the car door.

She said, "Ray," and I paused with one leg out and one leg in. "Don't worry about the Barber being there. He's still running."

"Was that the Barber, the little guy in the house with you?"

"Yes. There were only those three. And the Barber is yellow."

"Wasn't he the one who tortured your boyfriend Georgie?"

"Sure, he's brave when he has somebody tied down and helpless. You saw him run. Don't sit talking. Go on. And don't forget the money."

As I moved from the car, I heard her cough.

The night remained quiet and empty until I was halfway up the cinder driveway. Suddenly a car engine raced on the knoll. I jumped off the driveway to a scrawny tree and got out my pistol and snicked off the safety. The Nash came hurtling down behind glaring light. As it swept by me, the dash light revealed that oversized head above the wheel. The Barber had returned for the car.

For a moment I was afraid he would turn right on the road and spot my car around the curve and find Cherry there alone and defenseless. But he turned in the opposite direction, toward Belmont. I went on up the driveway.

When I saw Walt's body, I guessed the Barber hadn't come back only for the car. Walt had been lying face down; now his sightless eyes stared widely up at the moon. I searched his pockets anyway, though of course the money wasn't there. The Barber had come out of this not only with his life; he was a thousand dollars richer. I walked by Trig's body without looking at the shambles where his head had been. I entered the house. The fire in the fireplace was dying.

Her handbag was behind a chair, where Walt must have tossed it after he'd taken the money out of it.

As I was leaving, I remembered how after Shorty had been killed Cherry had been careful to wipe away possible fingerprints from everything in the hotel room. I got a towel from the bathroom. There was no time to do a thorough job, but I did what I could in the living room, including the whisky bottle and the glasses, and had to hope she hadn't left prints in other parts of the house. I took the towel out with me to wipe the shotgun that both Cherry and I had handled. It lay on the ground closer to Trig's body than I liked. I turned my back and ran the towel over the barrels and stock and triggers and trigger guards, then I dropped the gun and the towel and walked away from the two dead men.

Four dead men because of Cherry, beginning with Georgie, whom I'd never seen and had had no part of; but I'd been in on the other three killings, Shorty last summer and tonight these two, and one of them I had killed with my own hands. None of them was any loss to society, but that wasn't the point. She was a destroyer of men, and in a way she destroyed the living, too, like Bradford Smith.

And me.

Because I hadn't escaped. The police hadn't got me and the gangsters hadn't got me and I was married to Florence, whom I loved with all my being, but I knew I had been blighted by Cherry. I would never be the same man I had been before that moment when she had passed me on the beach and kicked sand in my face.

I paused on the driveway to light a cigarette and tasted bitter smoke and walked on to Cherry, waiting for me in my car. And as soon as I opened the door she demanded, "Did you get the dough?"

I slipped behind the wheel and told her how the Barber had returned for both the car and the money.

"Oh, the bastard!" she said against my handkerchief at her mouth. "Why did you let him get away? You should've shot out a tire and stopped him."

"I didn't know he had the money. Even if I had known it . . ." I backed the car onto the road and said, "I'm not your personal killer."

"You were wonderful, honey. I didn't mean you weren't. When I phoned you, I knew you'd get me out some way."

The winding road opened up before my headlights.

"All you knew," I said, "was that you were luring me to my death."

"What could I do? You see what they did to my face. But that's nothing. Trig worked on my body. He hurt me inside. I've been coughing blood. Why didn't you come to my apartment with me when I asked you?"

"All right, it's my fault," I said, "because you had to risk your life and mine for a few clothes."

"I'm not blaming you for anything. I admit I pulled a boner." She paused, her throat rumbling, but her voice had become stronger. "I thought I could slip up to my apartment by way of the delivery door and the basement and get my things. But they were in my apartment, Trig and the Barber, and they had guns, and they made me go down with them to their car. Walt was in the car. They drove me out here, and in the house Walt asked me who you were and everything. I wouldn't tell him." She pushed herself close to me and put her hand on mine on the wheel. "I held out a long time for you, honey. Long as I could."

"I'm not blaming you."

"Trig worked me over something terrible."

"So it was Trig who beat you up," I said.

"Yes, Trig. Walt and the Barber sat drinking whisky and watching him work me over. He'd hit me and I'd go down and he'd yank me to my feet and hit me again. In the face, but mostly in the body. It was awful. I wouldn't tell anything about you. I held out for you, honey. I—"

She coughed. Her body shook against my side.

When the spasm subsided, she said, "Then Walt—"

"Don't talk."

"No, I've got to tell you." Her voice was a hoarse rasping, dragged up from the depths of her. "I passed out from the beating. When I came to, they didn't touch me for a while. Then Walt said next it would be the Barber's turn. He said they would strip me and tie me down to the table and the Barber would work on me with his knife. That was too much, Ray. You heard what happened to Georgie last summer. Georgie was a strong, tough man and he was nuts over me, but they tied him down to that same table right there in that room, Walt told me, and the Barber worked on him, and Georgie spilled where he was to meet me. So I had to phone you, Ray. Don't you see, I had to phone you!"

"All right," I said.

"It turned out for the best, didn't it? We don't have to worry about Walt and Trig. They're gone."

"Especially Trig is gone," I said. "You made sure of that, because he was the one that beat you up."

There was silence except for the swishing of the tires on the oiled road. Then she said, "I told you he was getting up."

"You could've called me. It took you longer to go get the shotgun than it would've taken me to come out of the house. But Trig had to pay for beating you."

"You sound like you wanted me to thank him."

"I think he was still unconscious when you shot him," I said.

The road turned to blacktop and on the left the railroad track appeared. We were entering Belmont.

"Let me tell you something," Cherry said, hoarse with the effort to keep her voice going. "Walt was dead, but if Trig walked away from there we'd be no better off than before. You'd be worse off, because he'd found out who you were and where you lived, and he held a special grudge against you."

"Don't tell me you did it for me?" I sneered.

"For both of us."

"Where does that leave us with the rest of the gang?"

"There's only one left besides the Barber—an old guy who's been a punk all his life, and punks don't go looking for trouble if there's nothing in it for them. The Barber's another punk; you saw that yourself. No, it was only Walt and Trig we ever had to be scared of. We're safe now."

"Uh-huh," I said. "Because you murdered Trig."

"Look who's talking! I suppose you didn't kill Walt?"

"In a fair fight," I said. "In self-defense."

"I don't see where that makes him any less dead than Trig," she said. And she laughed and coughed as she laughed.

She could make my skin crawl. Driving down deserted Main Street, I had no more words in me.

Since starting out, we hadn't met a car. It was unlikely that the police had gone to the house from the other direction, from the north, because that was so close to the state line; if anybody had heard the shooting and had phoned them, they would have come from Belmont and passed us on the road. Days could go by, even weeks, before the bodies would be found, and whatever clues there were, if any, would be cold.

Our luck held, that core of good luck in the middle of all the bad luck Cherry and I had brought to each other.

We were alive, speeding southeast on the open highway, back to New York. For me it was back to home and wife. But where for Cherry, huddled silently beside me and holding the handkerchief to her ruined mouth? What was I to do with her?

We hit a broken stretch of road and the car bounced and jittered before I could slow it down, and the shaking made her cry out and then groan with pain.

"Is it that bad?" I asked.

"Getting worse and worse. I think something's broken inside."

The road was smooth again. The tires hummed and the headlights gouged a tunnel out of the night through which we hurtled away from damnation or toward it. The dash light caught the diamond on her hand holding the handkerchief to her mouth. What was I to do with her?

After many minutes I said, "Is there anybody to take care of you at home?"

"Home?" Her cheek moved against the seat and her battered eye was a wound watching me. "What home?"

"Your apartment."

"That?" She seemed to become smaller beside me, sinking further into herself. "The way I'm hurt I can't stay alone."

"Haven't you a friend who'll take care of you?"

"Me? I haven't anybody but you."

"What about your mother?"

"She has a job in New Rochelle, where she lives. Anyway, she has her own troubles." Time passed and Cherry said again, "I have nobody but you."

She didn't have me. Not anymore. Not if I could help it.

I said, "You mentioned a private hospital in the city."

"I did?"

"Over the phone. But I guess that was part of your story to persuade me to come for you."

"Yeah," she murmured in a voice that had no more strength in it. She pulled her legs up on the seat and curled up with her knees against my thigh and her head against my ribs.

Silent miles went by. Then I said, "Cherry."

She didn't answer. I touched her shoulder and she moaned.

"Cherry, are you asleep?"

"I hurt too much to sleep. I feel worse and worse."

"We're coming to a fair-sized town. They probably have a hospital."

"All right."

"We have to get a story ready. We'll base it on the one you told me tonight over the phone. Of course, we'll have to leave out—"

"I know what to leave out."

"I'm sure. But let's agree on it. Something like this: Earlier tonight you met a man in New York. Say in a bar. A stranger; you'd never seen him before. Know nothing about him but his first name. You became chummy and he invited you to drive out with him to a party in New Jersey. You got nervous when he took too long getting there. You insisted he take you back. He stopped the car and grabbed you. You went into a panic and fought him. For a long time you lay beaten up and unconscious off the road. Then you managed to get up and flag a passing car."

"Your car?"

"Yes. This is where I come in. We'll give our real names, but we don't know each other. I'm simply somebody who was driving by and stopped when you waved. That's all I know about you or you know about me. Not another thing. Have you got all that straight?"

"Yeah. You dump me off at a hospital and the hell with me after that. You go home."

"That's right," I said. "That's where I belong—home."

"With that snooty—" She changed her mind about saying it, or maybe her voice gave out. She lay curled up beside me on the seat, and sometimes she moaned.

When we reached the edge of the town, I pulled over to the curb and took out my wallet. I had fifty-seven dollars. I left seven dollars for myself and stuck the rest into her handbag.

She raised her head and watched me with her good eye.

"A small stake for you when you get out," I told her. "They'll have to keep you in the hospital without charge."

"A goddamn charity patient in a goddamn ward," she said.

"It's better than being dead back in that house."

"All right, you're a goddamn hero," she said thickly, brokenly, and let her head sag.

I didn't expect to be able to do anything that would please her, including saving her life. She was on my hands and I wanted her off my hands, and she knew it and hated me for it. I drove into the town.

7

The cop took his own sweet time coming. I was in the small waiting room off the small lobby of the small red-brick hospital. Cherry had been taken up the hall by a nurse, but I wasn't through. Another nurse, the plump one at the desk, had phoned the police as soon as she had heard what we said had happened to Cherry, and the police had told her they wanted me to hang around.

I could have sneaked out. Nobody knew my name yet. But it might be wiser and safer to act out my role as the helpful passer-by, the good Samaritan, by showing I was eager to cooperate. So I sat in the waiting room and lit a cigarette and opened a picture magazine. When an inch was left of the cigarette, I realized that the magazine was on my knees without a page having been turned. I put it back on the table and just sat.

The cop, when he eventually arrived, had the customary heavy face on a heavy frame. He labored at writing down my name and address in a frayed notebook with a stub of a pencil. A small-city cop.

"From Brooklyn?" he said. "How's it look for the Dodgers next year?"

"Bad, I hope. I'm a Giants fan."

"And you from Brooklyn?" He shook his head incredulously and put the pencil to his mouth. "What happened to this girl?"

"She couldn't talk much. Told me she was attacked by a man."

"Rape?"

"She didn't go into detail."

"Where'd this happen?"

"You mean where I picked her up?"

"Didn't it happen where you picked her up?"

"Search me. I was driving along and there was a girl staggering and waving her arms, so I stopped. One look at her face told me she needed a hospital."

The cop put his pencil on the page, but didn't write. I hadn't told him anything worth the effort.

"What road?" he asked.

"The highway. A few miles west of here."

He wrote that down and scowled at it. "A few miles. Can't you tell me exactly?"

"Sorry, but I don't know this neighborhood." I made show of looking at my watch. "Can I go now, officer? My wife will be wondering what happened to me."

He studied the notebook as if the few marks he had made on it could tell him anything. Then he said, "Okay, mister, thanks," and left the waiting room.

I put on my fleece-lined jacket. The gun was under the seat in my car. As soon as I had a chance, I would dispose of it somewhere in deep water. The best thing to do would be to take a ferry back across the Hudson River instead of the tunnel.

When I went out to the lobby, the cop was moving up the hall toward where the nurse had taken Cherry, and that nurse, a trim little thing, was talking to the plump nurse behind the desk.

"How is she?" I asked the trim nurse.

"Dr. Kellerhouse is examining her now. She got hysterical when I was putting her to bed. She raved about somebody named Ray."

I could see the cop up the hall, waiting outside a door or the doctor to tell him it was all right to go in and question her.

The plump nurse said, "Can this Ray be the man who attacked her?"

"I don't see how," the trim nurse said. "She was raving about needing him. She was crying to break your heart and saying, 'Ray, don't leave me. Ray, I need you.' Over and over till I felt like crying with her."

The cop had my name in his notebook, Raymond Whitehead. Ray for Raymond. He wasn't any too bright, but he would make the connection if he heard about it.

"Has she quieted down?" I asked the trim nurse.

"Yes, but she was still crying when I went out a minute ago. That poor thing. Ray must be her boyfriend or husband, and after what that other man did to her—well, she needs somebody."

The plump nurse heaved a sigh. "Men!" she said venomously.

I said good night to the two nurses and went out.

On the way to the parking area beside the building, I felt the raw wind knifing through my jacket. I bent to the wind, shivering, and I thought of her weeping at last, now that it was over, weeping among the strangers with whom I had left her, weeping, "Ray, don't leave me. Ray, I need you," alone there, battered and disfigured, not only hurt physically, but hurt deeper than Trig's fists had been able to reach, hurt still and without letup the way she had been since childhood. In the end my feelings for her always came to the same thing, and that was compassion. And I paused beside my car there outside the hospital, but it was only to take a cigarette out of my pocket before getting in.

I drove home to my wife.

Part Four: The Brunette

1

Two days later, on Friday, I phoned the hospital from a booth. I was told that Miss Cherry Drew was improving, but not what was wrong with her. Evidently that was classified information, at least over the phone, and one thing I didn't propose to do was visit her.

It wasn't until Sunday that the bodies were found.

The story appeared in the Monday papers. Some boys tramping through the woods had come across them; the dead men were identified through their fingerprints as Walt Kirby and Henry "Trig"

Watson, two notorious hoodlums; there was plenty of visual evidence that they had been killed in a gun fight several days before. This in a very few lines in some New York newspapers and nothing in others. Belmont was small and remote and in another state.

Next day, Tuesday, I couldn't find any mention at all in print or on the air. So I went looking for news. I knocked off work an hour earlier than usual—one privilege of being a boss—and hopped the subway to Times Square, where I bought a copy of the *Belmont Bugle* at an out-of-town newsstand.

The local paper was having a time for itself—pictures of the house on the knoll, interviews with the three boys who had found the bodies, statements by every politician and police official in the area, all expressing outrage at big-city gangsters coming to their peaceful, God-fearing community to carry on their wars.

I had a comforting feeling that nobody around there would overwork himself looking for the slayers of a couple of criminals who hadn't even belonged to the neighborhood.

I dropped the newspaper into a wire basket and went into the Times Building. From a phone booth one flight down I called for the second time the hospital where I had left Cherry last Wednesday night. A woman's impatient voice told me Miss Drew had been discharged at two o'clock that afternoon.

When I came out, the lights had gone on on Seventh Avenue and on Broadway and on Forty-second Street, all that colored, moving, flickering, advertising, story-telling brightness, and right over my head the news events of the day ran in lights around the four sides of the Times Building. I stood against the wall, out of the way of the jostling, hurrying mob through with work and headed for the subways. Not far from here Cherry would by now be back in her apartment.

That was nothing to me. After five and a half days in the hospital, she had been discharged, meaning that she hadn't been very badly hurt, that at any rate she had recovered enough to be able to get around. I'd done what I'd had to; the menace of Walt and Trig were eliminated. So it was over, definitely and for all time, having ended in blood and horror and bad conscience, as it had begun. She would let me alone now because there was no longer anything I could give her. If I knew her, she would not be long in getting herself another man.

One thing I could wish her, and that was that her next man would be good to her and good for her.

I stepped into the crowd and drifted along with it to the subway and rode home, where Florence would have a kiss and dinner waiting for me.

That was a fine winter. I taught Florence how to ski, and Sundays we would go up to Bear Mountain or some weekends to New Hampshire, and in February I took a week off and we went to Lake Placid. She was something to see in a ski outfit, made for a sweater, the healthy color of her face heightened by the brisk weather, her dark eyes always glowing, and each time I looked at her it seemed to me she had become lovelier.

It was a fine winter, and increasingly many days would pass without memory of Cherry and the things I had done because of her.

Then it was March, and spring was around the corner, you could feel it and smell it, and Cherry Drew was lost in the past. Until one afternoon when I came into the office and found a kid in a leather jacket waiting for me.

2

That day Mort Levy, one of our drivers, was sick, so I took out his six-wheeler. His helper and I picked up crated electric stoves in East New York and uncrated blonde-oak buffets from a cabinetmaker in Flushing and made deliveries in the Bronx and Yonkers and all the way up to Ossining. We returned shortly before five. I hopped out on the sidewalk, leaving the truck to the helper to take into the garage, and entered the office from the street.

The office had a lot of space, but nothing much else—a couple of steel desks, a cluttered table, a row of filing cabinets, scattered chairs, a water cooler. Marcia, the blowzy office girl, had the desk close to the storefront window. The other desk, the one all the way at the back, was nominally mine; but if I left it for a minute, I would find Pa using it instead of his own in his little inner office or a driver or a helper or the mechanic perched on it while making a call on my phone.

At the moment the only one in there besides Marcia was a kid of around twenty, sitting stiffly against the wall.

I dropped Mort Levy's delivery book on Marcia's desk. She swiveled from her typewriter and said in a low voice, "That young man, he's been waiting for you since two-thirty. Do you know him?"

I looked down the length of the office at him. He was a husky lad in a leather jacket. His hand clutched a rolled-up cap as he studied a large wall calendar. In over two hours he must have learned every detail of it, though it wasn't sexy, merely a picture of a gleaming truck.

"Never saw him before," I said. "What's he want?"

"He won't tell me or your father. Just wants to see you. I said I didn't expect you back for hours, but he said he'd wait. Since two-thirty he's been sitting there like a bump on a log. Gives me the creeps."

"This is news," I said. "A good-looking young man giving you the creeps."

"Oh, you!" Marcia said, showing her dimple.

I stopped at the water cooler. Drinking, I turned around to the kid, and now he was staring at me. His eyes, rather deep-set under a beetling brow, were sullen. I crumpled the paper cup and tossed it into the wastebasket and went over to him.

"Yes?" I said.

Taking his time, he looked me over, from my denim work pants to the open collar of my heavy flannel shirt. Then he spoke. "You Ray Whitehead?"

"That's right."

He didn't get up from the chair. He glanced past me at Marcia. "Can I see you alone?"

"What's it about?"

"We ought to be alone."

I said testily, "Look, if you've any business with me—"

"Cherry sent me."

In the garage beyond the partition an electric drill whirred and behind me Marcia's typewriter clattered. And the kid sat, holding his cap with both hands, and his head was thrust back so he could stare up at me.

"Cherry Drew?" I said, though I didn't know any other Cherry.

"Yeah. Only it's Cherry Todder since she married me."

The door to Pa's inner office was open and I could see that nobody was in there. I said, "Come with me," and walked away from him.

At the door I turned to watch him tagging after me. He was below medium height, but powerful in the chest and shoulders and slim in the hips. His cheekbones were high and prominent in a square face and his brown hair had distinct waves. A handsome, virile-looking kid, but a kid. Even adding a couple of years to the twenty I figured him to be, he was still considerably younger than Cherry.

He stepped past me into the small office. "Sit there," I said, waving him to a chair. He sat there, clutching his cap. I pushed some papers aside and seated myself on top of Pa's desk, making it very informal, and looked at him some more.

His shoes were broken and his pants had been around quite some time and his leather jacket was frayed at the sleeves and collar and was cracked all over. He was no sugar daddy, nobody who would buy her mink or take her to Europe or even pay the rent for a halfway decent apartment. But this one, this ragged kid younger than herself, she had married, which was all wrong for a girl on the make. I had thought I'd had her all figured out, but apparently I hadn't.

"How's Cherry?" I asked him.

"She ain't feeling so good."

"What's the matter with her?"

He shrugged. "I don't know. She's got to stay in bed all the time and don't get better."

I wanted to ask him if it was still, four months later, because of the beating, but I couldn't know if she had told him about that or much of anything else.

"All right, we're alone," I said. "Say your piece."

"Cherry said you'll give me a job."

Only a job—the least and simplest request she had ever made of me. And I could grant it. One of our helpers was going into the Army soon.

"What did you say your name is?"

"Frank Todder. I can drive anything on wheels."

"Do you belong to the union?"

"I'll join. Cherry said I can make a hundred a week."

"Maybe as a driver, but you can't rate better than a helper to start."

He thought it over, scowling. "How much does a helper make?"

I didn't tell him. All of a sudden I realized it wouldn't be simple after all. What she represented and what we had done together had to be kept as far from me as possible. Having her husband working here would bring her and keep her at least a little closer to me, because you couldn't make a clear-cut distinction between a man and his wife, not even on a job.

I said, "Sorry, but we haven't anything."

The sullenness spread from his deep-set eyes all over his square face. "You sounded like you did."

"Well, there's nothing."

"But Cherry said—"

I snapped, "Cherry isn't running my business," and slipped off the desk.

Frank Todder remained seated, holding onto his cap as if afraid somebody would snatch it from him. "Then I have to ask you for the grand you owe her."

"I owe her what?"

"A thousand bucks. She said you promised it to her last fall, but she never got it."

I could have laughed out loud. No, she hadn't got it; the Barber had. Instead all she had got was her life.

From under his beetling brows, his sullen eyes rested watchfully on my face. How much had she told him about me? For that matter, about herself?

"Why was I supposed to have promised her money?" I asked him.

"I know all about you and her."

"You do?"

"She leveled with me. Told me she used to be your woman."

That was the one thing she had never been, not quite, but if she preferred to explain me to him in that way, I could let it ride.

I took out cigarettes and offered the pack to him. He pinched one out and lit it with one of his own matches dug out of his jacket pocket before I could snap my lighter. I lit my own and said, "You don't seem to mind."

"Hell, that was before I ever met her. I never figured she didn't know other guys before me." He gathered up what pride he had and glowered. "I'd cut your heart out if there was anything between you and her now."

"But how do you feel about coming to me for a job and then a handout on the basis of what you think your wife used to be to me?"

The way he lowered his head told me how he felt about it. I shouldn't have turned the knife in him; I had nothing against him, really. He hated every bit of it, but he had come. Because Cherry had sent him. Cherry talked and he jumped. And maybe that was why she had taken up with him, married him; maybe she needed somebody like that, if only a kid without a dime to his name.

His head snapped up. "You know what you can do with your lousy job! But the grand, that's coming to her. Cherry said last fall you split up with her because you were marrying another dame. You promised her dough, but you never gave it to her. She figured the hell with, you, but now she's sick and has to go to a sanitarium."

"Is that how she told you to work it—if I don't give you a job, to demand a thousand dollars?"

"It's coming to her. And she sure needs it. She's sick in bed all the time."

The door opened. Pa stuck his head in and looked at Frank Todder and withdrew. He left the door slightly open. I closed it and went behind the desk and sat down. "What's your address?"

He told it to me and I wrote it down. It was far over on the west side of Manhattan, in the Twenties.

"You going to send the dough by mail?" he asked.

"I don't know what I'll do."

"Cherry said—"

"I don't give a damn what Cherry said. I'll make up my own mind. Goodbye, Todder."

He stood up and looked as if he would tell me to go to the devil. I gave him credit for wanting to, but he didn't. He put on his cap with an angry yank at the peak and muttered a sulky goodbye and left.

I heard his footsteps in the outer office and I heard the street door slam. I sat behind the desk, and it was very quiet in here behind the partition, because it was past quitting time. She had a husband now, I thought; let him take care of her. Giving her the money wouldn't be an end, but another beginning. After that there would be something else, some other demand.

Pa came in for his topcoat, hanging on the coat tree in a corner. "Who was that boy?"

"He was referred to me for a job. I told him we had nothing."

"We'll need somebody when Ralph is drafted."

"I know, but he didn't impress me."

"He looked clean-cut and strong."

"Pa, I was the one interviewed him, and I turned him down."

"You don't have to yell at me."

"I'm sorry."

He buttoned his topcoat. "All the trucks are in. Are you leaving?"

"I've something to take care of."

"Be sure to lock up. Good night, Ray."

"Good night, Pa."

And I sat alone in the silence and the seeping twilight, and I knew that telling myself she was now her husband's responsibility was no good. He couldn't pay her medical bills and I could, and it wasn't because of him that she needed treatment, but because of me. She had endured that beating because she had resisted as long as she could before giving me away to the killers. I had dumped her into a hospital as a charity patient and scooted off without having made sure that she would receive the care she needed to recover.

So I would foot the medical bills. But I would not send her money—no definite sum, no handout. Whatever she got out of me would be for that one purpose only, and I would make sure by having the bills sent directly to me and the limit of my commitment would be to pay them.

It had turned so dark in the little office that I could hardly see the paper on which I had written the address. I folded it twice and stuck it into my wallet.

3

One building was like any other on that block west of Ninth Avenue. They all had four stories and a stoop. They had the broken, nameless mailboxes in tiny vestibules, the dim, narrow halls, and the dim, narrow stairs, the smells of old dirt and new cooking and abiding mustiness; and as I climbed up to the third floor I had a feeling of the decay of people as well as of things. I knocked on a door.

At first there was no answer. A door behind me banged open. A Puerto Rican girl of ten bounced out and checked herself at the sight of me.

"Do the Todders live here?" I asked her.

She nodded and spun as if scared of me and raced down the stairs, no doubt on her way back to school after lunch. It was twelve-thirty, during my own lunchtime, the day after Cherry's husband had visited me at the office. I knocked again.

The door was opened by Frank Todder. He wore ruined pants and a torn undershirt that revealed his biceps and a thick curl of hair on his powerful chest.

He didn't seem glad to see me, though he should have been, considering I might be bringing a thousand dollars. He pulled the door half shut against his hip, blocking the rest of the opening with his body. "You bring the dough?"

"I'd like to see Cherry," I said.

"She's sick in bed. You can give me the dough."

I was in no mood for nonsense. "You don't have to ask me in. I'd as soon go back to work and forget about her."

The tip of his tongue appeared between his lips. He said, "Wait out here a minute," and stepped back quickly and shut the door in my face.

His mistake was in not locking the door. I didn't wait out there. I followed him in.

There was no foyer, no living room. You entered directly into a kitchen. Two inner doors opened out from that room; through one I could see a bedroom and through the other a bathroom. Hurriedly he was closing the bathroom door, but not before I had a glimpse of a bare arm and shoulder of somebody in the tub.

Frank Todder turned and saw me in the kitchen with him, and he worked up a smile of sorts. It was the strained, surly smile of an embarrassed kid, which was what he was.

"She's taking a bath," he said lamely.

"That's not what you told me in the hall."

He got that sullen look on his square face. "I figured you'd get the wrong idea if I said she was taking a bath. But that don't mean she ain't sick. The doc said hot baths are good for her."

Cherry's voice sang out, "Is somebody with you, Frankie?"

He opened the bathroom door just wide enough to sidle through. I turned away. The door banged behind him and I heard them whisper.

The kitchen equipment was lined up against one wall—a flaking sink without a drainboard, a rusty, dirt-encrusted gas burner on which a pot bubbled, a discolored refrigerator so old it had the motor on top. For the rest, there were three doors and one window and in between a scarred round table and some wooden chairs. Nothing else. Nowhere to relax except the unmade bed in what was a bedroom instead of a closet because there was a bed in it. This had been Cherry's journey over the years, from the shabbiest shack in Hessian Valley to a city slum where you had to do your living in the kitchen.

And not so very long ago she had had her hands on eighty thousand dollars.

Her husband came out of the bathroom. He strode head down into the bedroom and reappeared with a blue robe over his arm and sidled back into the bathroom without having said a word to me or even glanced at me.

I sat down at the table because there was nowhere else to sit. Dirty dishes were on the table, and a racing scratch sheet. I pulled the scratch sheet over to me. Three horses running that day at Hialeah were circled in pencil. A thousand dollars would cover a lot of bets.

This time the bathroom door opened all the way. They both came out, Cherry first, trying the cord of her robe.

Her feet were bare and her platinum hair was damp and her walk was firm. Her face, ruddy from the hot bath, was completely healed from the damage Trig's fists had done to it. Except for her eyes, which were always tired, she looked as healthy as I had ever seen her. Which by now was no surprise to me.

"Hello, Ray," she said.

I stood up and said hello and sat down.

She turned her head to her husband, who was pulling a crumpled pack of cigarettes out of his pants. "Frankie, honey, would you mind leaving us alone?"

He looked at her in that blue cotton robe clinging to her flesh. "Yeah," he said, "I mind."

"Just for ten minutes. Take a walk." She put a hand on his cheek. "Go on, honey."

He obeyed. He got his leather jacket from the bedroom and put it on directly over his underwear shirt. Cherry had told him to go out for a walk and he was going out for a walk. But there was this much to be said for him—he slammed the door angrily after he was through it.

"You can hardly blame him," I said when we were alone. "Especially after you'd made him believe we'd been lovers."

She gave me a bright smile. "We almost were. Twice."

"Almost doesn't count, I'm glad to say."

"Well, I had to tell him something to explain why I sent him to you, and I don't want even him to know all that really happened."

"Don't you trust him?"

"Frankie? He'd give his life for me. But that's now. How do I know the way things will stand tomorrow or next year? If I've learned nothing else in my life, I've learned that the way cops catch up to people is by somebody talking."

Her right hand went to her hair, fluffing it, and there on her finger was the diamond ring. She would always have it, I thought, no matter what.

"You're looking very well," I said pointedly.

That seemed to amuse her. "Frankie got kind of stuck with his story about me being sick, didn't he? When you showed up, he wanted to put on an act—carry me out of the bathroom to my bed while I pretended I was half dead."

"Not his story," I said. "Yours. The one you sent him to tell me."

"All right, mine. I told him in the bathroom you'd probably caught on already, so what was the use?" She moved to the gas range, where she turned down the light under the pot. "Want a drink?"

"Too early."

"Well, it isn't for me."

She took down a bottle from the cabinet over the sink and brought it and a glass to the table and sat down opposite me. She poured out a couple of ounces of the cheap whisky and killed it in two gulps. Then she scowled at me. "You crumb!" she said. "You've no right being jealous."

"Is that what you think I am?"

"Why wouldn't you give Frankie a job?"

"You set your sights too high for him. I don't know a thing about him, but he doesn't strike me as rating anything like a hundred a week."

"He can drive. What's there to being a driver?"

"A lot."

"He would've taken something else. At less pay. He said you sounded like you had something for him and then you changed your mind. You just don't want him working for you."

She was right there, but for the wrong reason. I said, "It's a big city. There are other jobs around."

Cherry twisted the ring on her finger. It was a habit of hers—anyway, whenever she was with me.

"There aren't," she said. "Go and look for one and you'll see. And it's tougher for Frankie. He has a record."

"Prison?"

"His first stretch was reformatory. When they let him out, he never had a chance. All he did was roll a drunk for a few lousy bucks and they sent him to the state pen. Eighteen months for that! The poor boy has been in more than out ever since he was a kid."

"When did he stop being a kid?" I said.

"All right, so he's a little young. What's the difference? He's all man. Built like a Greek god. And handsome. A lot better-looking than you."

"I'm sure."

"He's good to me. All the time. Every minute. I never knew a man could be so kind and considerate. And devoted. Never mean and nasty like you."

"Why bring me into it?"

She didn't answer that. She poured herself another drink. As she bent her head, I could see that her hair was turning dark at the roots, back to the original brown.

"There aren't any decent jobs waiting around for a man with a record," she said, holding the glass below her little upturned chin. "All he gets is part-time work, a few days at a time, and he hasn't even had that the last couple of weeks. I figured you would give him a break."

"You have a valuable ring."

"No. That's my insurance."

"For what?"

"Maybe for a time when things get even worse than they are now. Maybe because a girl wants to own one good thing, even when she has to live in a dump like this. I don't know. I told Frankie it's a fake stone."

She drank, this time in three gulps, and she shuddered when it was down.

I said, "Isn't it pretty early in the day to be hitting the bottle so hard?"

"I'm not asking you. You don't give a damn what happens to me." She put down the glass with a thump and suddenly she smiled. "But you want to do something for me, don't you, Ray? You've changed your mind and are going to give him a good job, huh?"

"No."

"Then you brought the dough?"

"All I had in mind was to pay your doctor bills."

"Let me explain about that," she said. "I thought you'd be quicker to find a good job for Frankie if I was sick."

"Or if not a job, give him money."

"You'd promised me a grand, didn't you?"

"I gave it to you. Remember?"

"The Barber got it," she said, pouting at my unreasonableness. "You can afford to lose it better than I can. And we need it so badly. Honest, we're down to our last cent."

"I've heard of wives working."

"My God, I didn't get married so I'd have to stand all day behind a counter."

"Why did you get married?"

"You're asking! You left me flat in that hospital. I'm feeling all right now, but I didn't for weeks after they discharged me. And I was broke and alone and I met Frankie and nobody's ever been so sweet and kind to me. He's a lot better man than you ever were. You have no right to sneer at him."

"I guess I haven't. At least he never killed anybody. Or did he?"

"What a son-of-a-bitch you are!"

I thought that maybe I was. The racing scratch sheet was under my hand. Once or twice I had been about to ask her if they needed the money so they could bet on the horses, but I was glad now I hadn't. I placed small bets now and then, and in what way did that make me better except that I could afford it?

"So I'm a son-of-a-bitch," I said, "and that's that." I stood up. "Glad I found you in good health."

"Sure you are, because it saved you a few bucks. You with your fine home and paying business and snooty wife and everything! It was easy for you to give up eighty grand. But what about me? Look at me!"

She twisted around on her chair with a sudden violent movement, and her robe fell open and her hair straggled over one eye and her cheeks were slack with whisky and her small mouth quivered with rage and self-pity.

"Look at me in this dump!" she said. "You pushed me into it."

"You didn't need to be pushed," I told her quietly.

But I wasn't sure. It was all mixed up, how much I had done to her and how much she had done and was doing to herself. At the door I said, "Goodbye, Cherry."

She didn't answer. She sat at the table with her back to me, and her hand with the ring on it reached for the bottle.

In the hall Frank Todder was leaning against the wall. He hadn't gone for a walk; he'd been out here all along, probably listening at the door. I said goodbye to him.

Cigarette smoke drifted up from the corner of his mouth across his deep-set, sullen eyes, and he didn't answer me either.

4

March passed and it was April, and the stories about the blonde bandit began to appear in the news. The holdups were very small stuff by big-city standards of crime. They occurred in scattered parts of the city, every other night or so, and were limited to isolated grocery stores and filling stations that were open late. Those two would come out of the night wearing red bandanna handkerchiefs tied below their eyes, and they had only one gun between them. Quickly and efficiently they took what there was to take and faded into dark streets. The loot was never much and nobody got hurt, so the holdups would have been lost among all the minor crimes committed nightly in the five boroughs. Except for one remarkable thing.

One of the two was a girl.

She was the one that held the gun and gave the orders while the husky young man who worked with her emptied cash drawers and pockets. Most important, she was a beautiful blonde, according to her victims. They couldn't agree on the color of her eyes or on her height or weight, but they agreed that her hair was platinum and her figure on the slender side. So she was made to order for the more sensational papers. After the first holdup, they gave her a name, the blonde bandit; after the third, they practically adopted her. She began to crowd the Communist menace and the current Hollywood divorce for space, and even the *Times* mentioned her on the bottom of the front page.

I began to wonder.

I told myself that there were eight million people in New York and millions more living in the outskirts, and that I could go out on any busy street and find a slender blonde girl and a husky young man. But deep down I must have known.

I knew, but I didn't want to know. Later I realized that I must have been pushing the knowledge or feeling or hunch or whatever it was out of my conscious mind. For when, on a Friday morning two or three weeks after the first holdup, I saw Frank Todder's picture in a newspaper, I wasn't at all surprised.

On the way to work, I always stopped at the same newsstand for the *Times*. As I fished out a nickel, a headline jumped up at me from the top of a pile of tabloids:

BLONDE FLEES
AS ACCOMPLICE
IS CAPTURED

So I bought that paper as well as the *Times*. Under the headline was the photo of a man—or a kid—being carried on a stretcher. He had flung an arm across his face to hide it from the camera, but it didn't cover his wavy hair and beetling brows and wide shoulders. The caption under the photo said he had been wounded in a gun fight with a detective.

Frank Todder was once again in the hands of the police. And once again Cherry had managed to elude them.

Standing beside the newsstand, I turned to page three and read about it.

At five minutes to nine the night before, a grocer in Far Rockaway had been getting ready to close his store. The door opened. He turned from the dairy counter to see a man and a woman wearing bandanna handkerchiefs over their noses and mouths and chins. The girl lifted her hand and there was a gun in it. She said almost gently, "We don't want to hurt you," and the young man moved down the length of the store toward the grocer.

This was their seventh holdup, and all over the city cops were waiting for them in stores and filling stations that customarily stayed open evenings. A detective stepped out from the back room and he had his gun out and he ordered the blonde bandit to drop her gun. The masked man, who was unarmed and within a few feet of the detective, hurled himself at him. The detective shot him in the hip. All that took time, the two or three seconds the blonde bandit needed to get out of the store. She vanished in the dark, deserted streets of Far Rockaway.

The wounded man wasn't so badly hurt that he couldn't talk. But he refused to talk. Not a word about himself, not even his name. And, of course, nothing about the girl. "You got me," he was reported as sneering at the police, "but you'll never get her."

And so Frank Todder, too, I thought as I folded the paper. He had joined the growing list of men destroyed by her in one way or another—destroyed because they had either fought her or loved her. Only I had somehow managed to survive.

I resumed walking to my office.

At nine o'clock that morning and again at ten I turned on the little radio beside my desk and listened to the news. The second time I heard Frank Todder mentioned by name. The police had been bound to identify him because of his reformatory and prison records. It wouldn't be much longer, I knew, before they found out where he lived and to whom he was married, and then they would have a line on Cherry. But at least he had given her time.

Where was she now?

I didn't want to know or think about it. This time I was surely out of it. This time I hadn't even a remote responsibility.

I kept the radio off the rest of the day, and when I went out for lunch I didn't buy an afternoon paper.

5

I was out of it, and I might have kept out of it if Florence's older sister, Gertrude, who lived in Philadelphia, hadn't started to have labor pains that Friday afternoon.

Gertrude had two small children, a girl of five and a boy of three, and Florence had promised to go out to Philadelphia and take care of them while Gertrude was in the hospital with her third. It hadn't been due for another three weeks, but the labor pains started and her frantic husband phoned Florence and Florence phoned me at the office. I was to come right home and take her out to dinner and drive her to Penn Station.

It was forty minutes to quitting time, but I knocked off work and took a cab home. She was dressed and waiting. I got the car out of the garage and we drove to Chinatown, which was on the way. In a cellar restaurant we ate wanton soup and shrimp in lobster sauce and spareribs. I was munching on a kumquat for dessert when a man at the next table lifted a spread newspaper and I was confronted with three words in large type: "BLONDE BANDIT IDENTIFIED."

You could keep yourself from buying newspapers and turning on news broadcasts, but you couldn't dig a hole to hide your head in.

". . . the night a truck broke down and you had to take a wheel out to New Jersey," Florence was saying.

I turned my head to her. "What?"

"You didn't hear a word I said. I was reminding you of the one night we didn't sleep together since we were married."

"I remember," I said.

"And now we'll be apart a week or so, until Gertrude leaves the hospital. The first time really apart." She looked very exciting sitting opposite me, and I said, "I miss you already," and we touched hands across the table.

We drove across town and then uptown to Penn Station and I went down to the train with her and we kissed on the platform. She reminded me about the cold roast beef in the refrigerator and I reminded her to phone me as soon as the baby was born and we kissed again. I watched the train pull out, and then it was gone and she was gone and I walked up the steps alone.

"Blonde Bandit Identified." It was there on the newsstand on either side of me as I entered the main rotunda of the station. I walked on, but what was I running away from? If I was out of it, why was I hiding from it? At the other end of the rotunda I bought a copy of the *Courier-Express* and read the story.

As I had expected, Frank Todder's silence had given her time, but nothing else. Once the police had found out who he was, the rest had followed—locating where he lived, learning from the neighbors that his wife was a slim, attractive platinum blonde, lifting from that slum flat plenty of fingerprints that were no doubt hers. As far as the police could tell, she hadn't been back there at all since her flight from the grocery store last night.

My car was parked on Seventh Avenue. When I reached it, I didn't get in. I stood beside it, recalling that night when Bradford Smith had left her and I was on the way out of her apartment and how she had said in near hysteria, "I can't stand being alone."

Nobody had ever been more alone than she was now.

Leaving the car where it was, I walked eight blocks uptown to the vast splash of light funneling out of the Seventh Avenue canyon at Times Square. I became one with the pleasure-bent crowd. I maneuvered my way up one side of jammed Broadway and down the other, and I ended up in a movie theatre because I had to go somewhere.

When I came out, the morning papers were piled high on every corner, and covering most of the front page of one, a tabloid, was her picture.

The police must have found the photo in her flat. It was a sleek studio portrait of her head and bare shoulders. Her hair was blonde, so it must have been taken since she had changed from a redhead, probably during the period when Bradford Smith had been her lover and she had owned mink and had been able to afford an expensive photographer. I stood against a store window, at the edge of the flowing stream of people, and I looked at that pretty, childlike face, that button nose and upturned little chin.

All this fuss over a girl who had stolen only a few dollars. But there was an ironical fairness to it, justice making up for other and more serious crimes. The newspapers, of course, didn't know; they merely had something small they had blown up. In a way the blonde bandit was their creation as much as hers, and she hadn't let them down. She had escaped dramatically and romantically through the self-sacrifice of her husband, and here in this picture she looked exactly as they would have wanted her to look—the stuff of which the front pages of tabloids were constantly made.

All night the presses would roll, and by morning millions of people would have the image of her impressed on their minds.

I walked to my car and drove home to the empty apartment and got into the empty double bed.

Pounding rain woke me. I listened to it shaking the windows and I wondered if Cherry was out in it, unprotected and unsheltered. Where could she go? Now that her husband was wounded and in the hands of the police, whom did she have?

"Ray, I need you."

That was like a cry out of the storm, the remembered words she had said over and over in the New Jersey hospital where I had left her last November. "Ray, I need you.... Ray, don't leave me.... Ray, I can't stand being alone." I turned over on my side, and the driving storm was like a haunting cry of appeal.

It was a long time before I fell asleep again.

The phone woke me. My eyes were only half open to the gray, rainy morning as I stumbled out to the living room.

"Darling," Florence said over the wire, "did I wake you?"

"Uh-huh. What time is it?"

"After ten. Were you out late last night?"

"Not very. I went to the movies."

"The children got me out of bed at six. They've kept me busy every minute since."

"Any news?"

"Gertrude is in the hospital, but nothing has happened yet. Ted's been there all night with her. I hope she doesn't have a hard time.

Her first two came so quickly."

"How are the kids?"

"Adorable. They—" Over the phone I heard a far-off howl. "That sounds like Kathy in some kind of trouble," she said. "I must say goodbye now. I love you."

I said I loved her too and hung up and ran my hand over my face. Then I turned on the radio. The ten-o'clock news was half over. If the blonde bandit was mentioned at all, it must have been at the beginning of the fifteen-minute program. I turned off the radio and went into the kitchen to boil water for coffee.

The morning crawled by. I wished this were a weekday so I could go to work. I wished Florence were home. I wished I had something to do except sit around.

At noon the rain stopped. I shaved and dressed and went out for lunch. Through dispersing clouds the sun broke bright and warm and the air had that washed, bland, after-rain smell.

Cherry's face was on the corner newsstand, looking up at me from the morning tabloid. The afternoon papers were out. I bought the *Courier-Express* and took it into the lunchroom next door and sat at the counter. There was nothing on the front page, but there was a whole column and that picture on the third page.

Hour by hour the police were digging up more information about her, closing in on her past. They had learned that her maiden name was Drew, that she used to live in Hessian Valley, that her father had been the town drunk, that her mother now lived in New Rochelle. During the night the police had visited Mrs. Drew. She said she hadn't heard from her daughter in months. "I can't imagine how Cherry could get into this kind of trouble," she was quoted as saying. "She was always a good girl. There must be some mistake." Mrs. Drew's address was given.

I had two Western sandwiches and two cups of coffee and lit a cigarette and stared at the mirror behind the counter.

"Anything else, sir?" the counter girl asked me.

I said no and paid her and got off the stool. Halfway out of the lunchroom, I stopped and went back for my newspaper, which I had left on the counter. I hadn't wanted it anymore, but suddenly I did. I wanted Mrs. Drew's address.

6

An old man watched me come up the broken concrete walk. He sat on a shabby open porch of a shabby little boxlike house on a shabby New Rochelle street. I went up the rickety steps and asked him if Mrs. Drew was in.

He removed a corncob pipe from his mouth and rubbed the stem against a sagging jowl. "You another cop?" he said after a while.

"No, sir. I used to know Mrs. Drew in Hessian Valley." Curtains stirred in a window. I was being given the once-over by somebody in the house.

The old man was in no hurry. He sucked his pipe, considering something or other, and then he said, "If it's anything about that girl, we don't want to hear it."

The door banged open. "Why, I believe it's the Whitehead boy," Cherry's mother said.

Her hair had turned completely gray, though she couldn't have been much over fifty. Otherwise she had hardly changed from the thin, neat, exhausted woman who had done once-a-week housework for my mother.

"How are you, Mrs. Drew?" I said.

"You heard about Cherry?" She stared at me, and her eyes were much like her daughter's, the same harassed tiredness in them. "It's on account of Cherry you're here."

Another woman had come out of the house—older than Mrs. Drew, but not nearly so old as the man. She paused at the door, and all three waited for my answer.

"I saw your address in the paper," I said. "I happened to be on the way upstate, so I thought I'd drop in and say hello."

"Now, that's real nice of you," Mrs. Drew said. "I'd like you to meet my sister and brother-in-law, Mr. and Mrs. Gregory—Mr. Whitehead."

I nodded to the woman and shook the man's gnarled hand. Then there was an uneasy silence before Mrs. Gregory said, "Come in the house, Joe. I guess they have things to talk over."

"If it's about Cherry—" Mr. Gregory growled.

"Come in the house, Joe."

He jammed his pipe into his mouth and followed his wife through the door.

There were two frayed canvas chairs on the porch. Mrs. Drew sat on one and I sat on the other. She put her toil-worn hands on her lap and asked how my folks were. I told her they were all well, that we were living in Brooklyn now, that my brother was going to NYU, that I was married.

"My husband is dead," she said.

"So I heard. I'm sorry."

"He was no good," she said. "I don't have to tell you. I work just as hard now, in a factory here in town, but at least there's nobody drinks up my pay. I have a nice home here with my sister." She paused. "Where did you hear my husband was dead? From Cherry?"

"Well . . ."

Mrs. Drew nodded. "Why should a young man come to say hello to me? Did Cherry send you?"

"No. I haven't seen her or heard from her."

"Were you seeing much of her?"

"We ran across each other in the city now and then. I read about the trouble she's in and I wondered if there was anything I could do."

"What can anybody do for her? I tried to bring her up right. It was hard, living in a place that wasn't fit for pigs and me out working all day and her father a drunk. A fine way to raise a girl! A wonderful example he set for her!" Her hands stirred on her lap. "But at least he was never a thief. He never did a dishonest thing in his life. Where did she get it? A thief. Holding up stores with a gun. My daughter!"

"Has she been in touch with you, Mrs. Drew?"

"She never came to see me. Not once since I've been living here in New Rochelle, and it's so close to New York. She sent a card, a few words, every few months, that was all. It's a wonder she bothered to write when she got married. But she never brought her husband to meet me. Ashamed of him, I guess." She drew in her breath, sniffling. "He made her do it. Made her steal. Deep down she's a good girl, but that man made her go wrong."

I had nothing to say to that.

"But in the end, when she needed her mother, when the police—" Mrs. Drew broke off and looked away from me, her worn hands twisting on her lap.

I said softly, "So she was here?"

"Why are you trying to find out?"

"I told you. We've known each other since we were children and

I'm sorry for her and would like to help in any way I can."

"Yes, she was here," Mrs. Drew said, and she was sitting perfectly still in that canvas chair. "She came yesterday afternoon."

I looked past her at the two windows fronting the porch. Somebody was standing at the curtains of one—probably the old man.

Mrs. Drew turned her head to the window. "It's all right," she told me. "They know. She was here with them when I came home from work yesterday. If you can't trust your own family, you can't trust anybody. She wanted money. All that robbing, those holdups, and she didn't have any money."

"Seems you don't get rich that way."

"People like us, we don't get rich in any way." She sighed. "I knew why she had to have money. On the bus home I'd seen it in the paper, how this blonde bandit they'd been writing about for weeks was my own daughter, Cherry. I was half crazy when I got home, and she was there. Being it was Friday, I had my pay envelope. I gave her most of my pay. Then she sent me out to the drugstore to buy some hair dye."

"Black, I suppose. The opposite of blonde."

"Yes, black. She dyed her hair and she kept fiddling with the radio, listening to news on the New York stations. Then late at night, after twelve and starting to rain, she said she had to leave. She said sooner or later the police would look for her here. She was right. She wasn't gone an hour and we were all in bed when the police came. Then they came again this morning, and there were men from the newspapers with them." She glanced around at the window where somebody was standing. "Blood is thicker than water. My sister and her husband, they said the same thing I did—we hadn't seen Cherry, she hadn't been here, we didn't know anything about her." She sniffled again. "What will become of her?"

I said, "Did she give you any idea where she was going?"

"I've no joy from my family. My husband a drunk and my daughter a thief, and God only knows what else she's done." Mrs. Drew lifted her head. "When she was leaving last night, I asked her did she have anywhere to go. Her answer was crazy. I guess she was just making fun of her poor mother, who was worried sick over her."

"What did she say?"

"It was crazy. She said she was going to take a ride on a roller coaster."

7

There was not much doing in Coney Island that Saturday afternoon in April. Most of Surf Avenue was still closed down, but a few of the rides had opened for the weekend. Including that roller coaster.

From in front of the boarded-up shooting gallery next door, where nine months ago I had snatched up a rifle and shot and wounded Trig Wacko, I watched a rumbling car hurtle down the highest incline of the roller coaster and listened to the shrill, long-drawn shrieks of girls. I thought of how Cherry had moaned, "How I hate these things!"

No, she wouldn't be here, and she wasn't.

I didn't expect her to be anywhere in Coney Island. Then why had I come? Partly because it was a place to go. Mostly, I supposed, because sooner or later a man had to return to the scene of his crime.

I walked to the boardwalk.

The sunny weather following the storm of the night and morning had brought strollers to the boardwalk, but they were trickling off with the afternoon almost gone and a chill wind sweeping in from the ocean. The beach, wide with the outgoing tide, was bleakly empty. I bought a hot dog and munched it as I walked. A sign said Bay 20.

My heart started to thump as I neared Bay 19. I was coming back to the beginning, to where I had met a girl in a yellow bathing suit, and I felt a kind of panic that was beyond reason. I felt an impulse to turn back, away from what was past and yet not done with. But of course I walked on, close to the rail, finishing the hot dog, and suddenly the beach was no longer empty.

For me it was completely filled by one person across that stretch of sand—by a girl standing beside a jetty. At that distance I couldn't recognize her. I didn't have to.

I went down the steps. The sand, still somewhat moist from the morning rain, got into my shoes. I plodded toward her.

Her back was to me. She stood so close to the water that the foamy breakers curled almost to her feet. With her hands plunged into the pockets of a tan coat, she looked out at the far and unattainable horizon. The breeze lifted her hair, and now I was close enough to see the blackness of it.

Cherry turned when I was a short distance from her. Her eyes went wide and her mouth opened, but she didn't speak and she didn't move. She faced me with her hair flying and her lightweight coat whipping about her thighs. And when I reached her, she said, "I had a feeling I'd meet you here, where we met last summer. It's like fate."

"I don't know about fate," I said. "I was in New Rochelle a few hours ago and saw your mother. She said you told her you were going for a ride on a roller coaster. So I came out."

"Did I, Ray? I don't remember. I must've had Coney Island in mind when I said that. Just a wisecrack." She smiled a weary smile. "But why did I think of a roller coaster? It wasn't fun the time we went on one together, was it?"

"Nothing has been fun since that day."

"It could've been. If you . . ." She let the rest of that hang in the air and drew her coat together. "You went looking for me, Ray," she said softly. "First at my mother's and then here."

I growled, "Don't make anything of that."

"Why shouldn't I? You looked for me." She snorted. "Oh, sure, your conscience. You know if you'd given Frankie a job I wouldn't be in this mess. It would've been such a little thing for you to do."

"Was I supposed to be your husband's keeper too?"

"Please, Ray, let's not fight for once, huh? I'm too worn out. I can't take anything." Her right hand appeared from her pocket and what was left of the sun caught the diamond. She came close to me and put that hand on my arm. "I'm at the end of my rope. The cops after me and my picture in the papers. I've changed the color of my hair, but I can't change my face. Every time somebody looks at me I die."

"Then why are you out here in the open?"

"It's safer than anywhere else. Nobody comes on the beach and they can't see my face from the boardwalk. My best bet is to get to Mexico, where I have friends."

"I heard about them last November," I said dryly.

"They're still there. But how do I get to them? Yesterday, before my picture was in the papers, I could still move around. Then when I came back from New Rochelle late last night I saw the morning papers and my picture. I've been half crazy ever since. I don't dare take a train or a plane or a bus. Even in the subway I had the jitters. I've got to hole up right here in the city till people stop remembering what I look like. But I don't know where."

I knew where. Florence would be in Philadelphia for about a week. But I didn't tell her.

I said, "At this time of the year Coney Island hasn't a crowd to lose yourself in."

"You're telling me! But why do you think I'm here?"

"To take a ride on a roller coaster."

"Seriously, Ray. I need a stake. My mother had only a few lousy bucks to give me—anyway, that's what she claimed. I'm here in Coney because its near you. I couldn't go straight to your place; your wife would see me and yell for the cops. Twice this afternoon I phoned your number to ask you to meet me. If she'd answered, I would've hung up. But nobody answered. Then suddenly you were here." Standing close to me, she put her head back, and through black hair streaming across her childlike face her soft lips twitched in that weary half-smile. "I still say it's fate."

Maybe it was, I thought—a remorseless fate that never let up on either of us. And the wind swept up cold with the coming of evening and knifed into me.

"Let's get off the beach," I said.

Cherry clung to my arm as we plodded across the sand. When we had covered half the distance to the boardwalk, she said, "Have you heard anything on the radio today about how Frankie is?"

"I listened on the way back from New Rochelle. He's off the critical list."

"The poor boy! They'll send him up for a long stretch."

"Do you love him very much?"

She gave me a sidelong glance. "What's that to you?"

"Not a thing. He sacrificed himself for you."

"He was a good kid," she said, kicking sand as we walked.

Was? She spoke of him in the past tense, as if he were dead and buried. In a way he was.

We sat on the steps leading up to the boardwalk and took off our shoes and shook out the sand. Then I lit two cigarettes and gave her one and we continued to sit there with our backs to the people on the boardwalk.

After a while I said, "With the bank closed till Monday, it will be tough for me to raise cash."

"It's not money I need right now. It's a hole."

"Isn't there anybody in the city who will help you?"

"One person. You."

I flipped away my cigarette and watched it smolder in the sand. At the horizon the sky was darkening, merging with the ocean. Soon it would be night, and what could I do with her?

There was only one thing I could do. I told her that Florence was away and that she could stay in my apartment for a few days.

She gripped my arm, the curled fingers digging in. "I knew I could count on you, honey."

She waited under the boardwalk while I brought my car from where it was parked a few blocks away. I pulled up to where the street turned to sand and honked the horn. She appeared from under the boardwalk, striding rapidly with her head down.

At my building, I left her in the car and went in alone, for here I had to be cautious on my own account. I didn't want any neighbors who knew me to see me taking a woman up to my apartment while my wife was away.

Cherry was a couple of minutes behind me. She threw off her coat and said, "God, I need a drink!"

I fetched a half-full fifth of bourbon from the bottom of the buffet. She stood beside me as I poured and reached for the glass before I could hand it to her. When she had it, she managed to restrain herself, waiting for me.

"Let's drink to Frankie," she said.

"A noble thought," I said. "To Frankie, who loved not wisely but too well."

She poured the bourbon down her throat and then frowned at me. "Was that supposed to be another one of your nasty cracks?"

"I'm not sure."

She refilled her glass and carried it to the tweed sofa. Her green dress had a wide white collar and a low bodice and a tight belt. She kicked off her shoes and pulled her legs up under her.

"Could be you're right about Frankie," she said broodingly against the edge of the glass. "I brought him my rotten luck."

"Didn't you know you couldn't get away with those holdups forever?"

"Sure we knew. We were bucking the percentages all the time, and for what? For peanuts. But . . ." She drank. "Frankie got a tip on a horse."

"I might've guessed," I said.

"This guy was no tout. He was really in the know and he was letting Frankie in on a sure thing running at Jamaica next day. A long shot, paying close to twenty to one. The kind of chance you dream of. But what good was it to us when we couldn't afford even a five-dollar ticket? We went out to pull just one job. Something small, so it wouldn't be dangerous. Just one job to get a stake. It was easy. We took around seventy bucks from a filling station. Next day we put it all on the long shot."

"I've read that script," I said. "The horse ran last."

"No. We went out to Jamaica to see. He led practically all the way, but he was caught by a head at the wire. My luck was riding him. My goddamn lousy luck!"

"I can go on from there," I said. "You needed more stakes for more bets."

"It wasn't that. The first job had been so easy and we were broke again. A couple of nights later we went out on the second one. If we'd been able to make one good haul, we would've stopped. But the take was never much—the most was a hundred and thirty bucks, and once only seventeen bucks."

"Seems crime doesn't pay."

"That kind doesn't for sure. But when you have nothing, anything is a lot. It didn't all go to the bookies. Some of it, and our luck stayed bad. Most of it went to paying up back rent and eating good for a change and having a little fun, and we bought clothes, especially for Frankie, who'd never had a decent suit in his life. Anyway, the money got spent right after each job and we'd go out for just one more. The Thursday night job in Far Rockaway, we said definitely that would be the last." She drank down what was left in her glass and shivered. "It turned out to be the last, all right. You know what life is, Ray?"

"It's different things for different people."

"It's one great big sucker trap, that's what it is," she said, and put her head back on the sofa and closed her eyes.

Night had seeped into the room, turning us into shadows. I switched on a light.

"Are you hungry, Cherry?"

"I could eat something."

I went into the kitchen and made coffee and sliced the roast beef Florence had told me not to forget was in the refrigerator and made sandwiches. When I called her to the table, she brought her glass with her. It was again full.

Her head drooped as she ate. She had trouble keeping her eyes open.

"I don't suppose you've had much sleep the last two nights," I said.

"None to speak of."

"I'll make up the bed for you."

Her mouth curved. "Where?"

"There's a spare room."

Slowly she stirred her coffee.

I finished my coffee before she had started hers and got the spare bed ready for her. When I came out, she was in the living room pouring herself a drink.

"I left a nightgown and a housecoat on the bed for you," I told her.

"Your wife's?"

"Of course."

She smiled in a way that annoyed me. "Aren't you afraid I'll contaminate them?"

"What have you got against her?"

"She's your wife, that's what I have against her." She had filled two glasses. "But seeing we drank to my husband, we'll drink this one to her. Here."

I took the glass from her and held it a moment and then put it down on the table. "I don't feel like any just now."

"What's the matter?" she taunted. "Afraid the same thing will happen as the last time you got drunk with me?"

"It didn't happen."

"It would've if Brad hadn't barged in." Laughing, she raised her glass. "So I'll drink a toast alone. To my favorite Boy Scout."

She gulped it down and shuddered and put a hand to her face, tottering on her stocking feet.

"Go to bed," I said.

"Yeah, I'm dead. Good night, Boy Scout."

She moved as far as the hall and then came back for the drink I hadn't drunk. She took it with her.

After a while I had a drink, right out of the bottle—a big one, but only one. My hands were sweating. I rubbed them on my thighs and turned on the TV, keeping the sound low so as not to disturb her. I looked at programs I'd never seen before because I'd never before been so desperate to kill time.

At around nine-thirty the phone rang. Florence, I thought, and I hated having to talk to her, having to lie to her that I was home alone. It turned out to be Ma. She asked me if Gertrude had had her baby yet and I said I guessed not because I hadn't heard from Florence. Then she invited me over for Sunday dinner tomorrow. I got out of that by saying I'd made other plans.

Not until after I'd hung up did it strike me there was no reason why I shouldn't have accepted Ma's invitation. I wasn't committed to keeping Cherry company—merely to giving her a hideout.

I spent another restless hour and a half looking at TV and then went to bed.

My bedroom was on one side of the hall and the spare room was on the other. She had left her door open; the hall light reached in to her as she lay on her side, showing her hair black against the pillow and her upper arm and shoulder bare. I closed the door of my own room.

8

What must have awakened me was the opening of the door and the hall light shining on my face. Florence, coming from the hall, paused just inside our bedroom, standing there in one of her misty nightgowns and with her black hair flowing to her bare shoulders. I squeezed my eyes together and opened them and she hadn't moved.

"Come to bed," I muttered, more asleep than awake.

The door closed and there was no longer light against my eyelids. I turned toward her side of the bed, waiting for her to get in with me and snuggle the way she always did—and then I remembered.

She wore Florence's pink nightgown and she had black hair like Florence, but she wasn't Florence.

I sat up, groping for the reading lamp on the headboard. One side of the bed gave as she sat down on it. I found the chain and pulled it and light poured over Cherry as she drew back the blanket.

"What the hell's the idea?" I said.

Cherry was bent toward me, her breasts spilling out of the negligible bodice, and she smiled. It was a lopsided smile, a kind of idiot smile, as if something had weakened the muscles that controlled it.

"You invited me," she giggled.

"I was half asleep. I thought you were my wife."

"I have everything she has and some things better." She pulled the blanket all the way back and put her knees up on the bed. "Honey, I couldn't stand being alone when you were right here in the next room."

"Get out!"

The smile was gone, but her mouth remained slackly lopsided. "Don't be mean to me, honey. You want me here. I know you do."

I was sweating under my pajamas. I pushed my shoulders hard

against the headboard, and I had a sense of cowering, not so much afraid of her as of myself.

"You're drunk," I said.

"Not so very. I know what I'm doing. What I want. This, honey."

She leaned to me, pressing soft and voluptuous against me, her femininity imposing itself on me, urging me. I slapped her face.

The blow twisted her torso. She recovered her balance and stared at me, her mouth hanging open, and there seemed to be no muscles in her face. The hand with the ring on it came up slowly to her cheek. The sight of that ring just made me almost want to kill her.

"Get out, you drunken tramp!"

Cherry gasped, flinching as if I had slapped her again. Then she jumped off the bed and ran out of the room. She left the door open; I saw her turn into the living room and I heard her sob loudly.

I wiped my sweating face with my sleeve. I was jumping inside. My hands opened and closed, and what frightened me most was knowing that I had come close to grabbing her by the throat.

She was running in the living room. I heard the patter of her bare feet and I heard her gasping sobs. Suddenly she was back in the bedroom, and upraised in her hand was the carving knife with which earlier I had sliced the roast beef.

Her voice rose in a keening, demented wail and her face contorted with hate as she hurled herself at me on the bed.

I had had time to get myself set for the attack. I threw myself away from the plunging knife. The razor-sharp edge brushed my shoulder and slashed glancingly along the upper part of my arm. Then I had her wrist.

She thrashed half on and half off the bed. Her nightgown pulled down at the top and up at the bottom. "I'll kill you!" she sobbed as her free hand reached out to claw at my eyes.

I protected my face by pushing it against the back of her neck. I twisted her wrist and she cried out and the knife came away in my other hand. I hurled it across the room and let go of her.

She slid to the floor and slumped there with her head on the edge of the bed. I could hear her pant for breath; I could hear myself pant, too. I looked at my right arm and saw blood staining the sleeve. Drained emotionally, I sagged against the headboard.

"No matter what I do for you," I said, pushing my voice up exhaustedly, "it's never enough."

She rose, averting her face from me as she did so, and shuffled listlessly out of the room. She crossed the hall and entered the spare room and closed the door behind her.

Blood trickled down my arm. I got out of bed and stripped off the pajama top. An inch of skin hung away from my arm like a hinge, but it was only a flesh wound.

I washed my arm with cold water in the bathroom and dabbed peroxide on the wound until the bleeding stopped. I stuck three plastic bandages side by side over the flap of skin. Stripped to the waist, I went into the living room and took a drink of bourbon. There wasn't enough left in the bottle to fill a pony glass to the top. I slumped down into the armchair and closed my eyes. After a while my insides stopped jumping.

"Are you hurt bad?" her voice asked.

Cherry had come into the living room. She still wore only that pink nightgown, sheer and transparent and low-cut, like all of Florence's.

I said, "I left a housecoat in your room. Put it on."

"Last summer in Coney you saw me in nothing at all. You didn't mind then. And a couple of months later in my apartment—"

"Don't start that again," I said tiredly.

Her face was no longer out of control, no longer slack or contorted with fury. It was merely peevish, the face of a little girl who had come out of bed in her nightgown to ask a grownup for a drink of water.

Except that the drink she was after wasn't water. She picked up the bottle from the table and peered at it. "Have you anymore?"

"You've had too much."

"I need one more."

It didn't matter, I thought. I wasn't the one to protect her from herself. Nobody was. I told her there was some in the bottom of the buffet.

She brought out a fresh bottle of rye and broke the seal and poured some into the glass I had drunk from a few minutes before. She gulped it down and then stood fingering the empty glass, and the light made the nightgown a pink transparency.

"I asked you, Ray, are you hurt?"

"It's only a scratch. The knife is in the bedroom, if you want to try again."

"Oh, God, Ray!" Cherry dropped down on the floor at my feet and put her cheek against my knee. "Why do we always want to hurt each other?"

"Tonight we wanted to kill each other."

Wide-eyed and solemn she looked up at me. "Do you know why you slapped me and called me that name?"

"So you'd let me alone."

"Because you wanted me. That's why you slapped me."

"No."

"You were afraid in another minute you'd let me stay with you."

The luscious softness of her was against my knee. I didn't push her away and I didn't slap her. I felt nothing for her. Maybe she was right, maybe a little while ago in bed I had been tempted. If I had been, there wasn't anything left of it. I felt nothing now but a pervading coldness.

I said, "You've been without your husband three nights. Must you have a man that badly?"

"Ray!" She screamed my name up at. me. "Are you trying to make me want to kill you again?"

"It's the truth, isn't it?"

"Goddamn you to hell and back! Can't you understand?"

I didn't want to understand. I slumped lower in the chair, all the way down to my spine, and I said dully, "Let me alone."

She went away from me then. She headed straight for the bottle and tilted it to her mouth.

What little there was to the top of the nightgown was more off her than on her and her black hair straggled over one cheek and her throat worked as she gulped the whisky. All at once she disgusted me.

I said, "Like your father."

She dragged the bottle from her mouth. "What did you say?"

"You're getting to be like your father. Another drunken sot."

"No! That's a lie!" The bottle dangled from her swaying hand and there was a wildness in her face. "I never used to drink so much. Only the last few months. I'll never be like him. Never." She pushed disheveled hair from her cheek. "You're lying, you bastard!" she shrieked, and threw the bottle at me.

It didn't come close, landing beside the chair. Whisky gurgled. I snatched up the bottle from the expensive rug. As I straightened, a door slammed. Cherry was back in the spare room.

After I had sponged up the spilled whisky, I dropped back into the chair. I felt as if I'd never want to move again. My eyes closed and I had terrible dreams I couldn't remember when I woke up. My arm was bleeding through the bandages. I put more peroxide on and fresh bandages and crawled into my bed.

9

Cherry was up and about before me. Lying in bed, I heard the shower going, and after a while I heard her bustle about in the kitchen.

It was after ten. The sun shone warmly and the piece of sky visible from where I lay was very blue. But this was no day I especially wanted to get up for. I pulled the cover over my head.

There was a rapping on my door; she was being quite formal this morning. I grunted, "What do you want?" and she sang out, "Breakfast will be ready in a few minutes."

When I entered the dinette in robe and slippers, I found the table set rather elaborately for a mere breakfast. She was humming a tune in the kitchen. I looked in. She stood at the stove turning flapjacks. Coffee dripped in the drip pot and on the worktable there was a pitcher full of frozen orange juice.

"Good morning," she greeted me with a cheerfulness that rubbed me the wrong way. "How's the arm?"

"I expect to survive."

She was wearing Florence's flowered housecoat over Florence's pink nightgown. Her hair was brushed and her face had a brand-new coat of paint. If she had a hangover from all she'd drunk last night, you couldn't tell. Neither could you tell that we'd wanted to kill each other a few hours ago or that an entire city was hunting her. She looked as fresh and bright as the morning. In her own peculiar way, I had to admit, she was quite a girl.

"Take the juice and coffee out to the table, honey," she said.

That was exactly what Florence would have told me to do and she would have said it in the same way, except that Florence would have called me darling.

She followed me out to the dinette with a heaping plate of flapjacks and sat opposite me, in the chair near the kitchen doorway that Florence always occupied. This looked like any Sunday morning domestic scene in any of thousands of other apartments.

"Like the flapjacks?" she asked.

"Not bad."

"The secret is making them thin enough. I'm really a good cook. Wait till you eat the dinners I'm going to make you."

I put down my knife and fork. "You're leaving today, Cherry."

"You said she'll be away all week."

"But you're leaving today."

Her mouth got sulky. "Because of last night?"

"Partly."

"Please, honey, don't hold a grudge. Remember all I've been through. I wasn't myself last night."

"You're always yourself," I said. "That's the trouble."

"It was as much your fault as mine, the way you treated me."

"I agree. It was as much my fault as yours. I asked for it by bringing you here."

"My God, if you make me go you'll practically be handing me over to the cops."

"You have a knack for avoiding them."

"But the money. The banks are closed today. You can't send me out broke."

"I'll raise the money," I said.

My appetite was gone. I left half the flapjacks on my plate and poured a second cup of coffee from the pot on the table.

"Ray, please! I'll promise to be good. Only let me stay. I'll cook and clean house for you and won't bother you. Just let me stay these few days. That's all I ask you to do for me."

"It's never all you ask. There's always more."

"Honest, I promise—"

"You're getting off my back, and this time you're staying off."

"Then the hell with you!"

"Fine," I said. "The hell with both of us."

I put down the cup and went to shave and dress.

As I was getting into a shirt, she appeared in the bedroom doorway. Smoke curled over her small-featured face from the cigarette dangling on her lower lip.

"I know why you want to get rid of me," she said. "You're scared to spend another night in the same apartment with me."

"Uh-huh. I don't care for being slashed with knives and having bottles thrown at me."

"Don't give me that. You're worried you can't keep yourself from crawling into my bed."

I muttered, "Have it your way," and took my tweed sport jacket from the closet and put it on.

She didn't budge to let me through the door. She looked at me defiantly, as if daring me to put my hands on her. I kept my hands at my sides, pushing past her without using my shoulder as hard as I had an urge to.

"I'm not leaving!" she yelled, following me into the living room. "What d'you think of that?"

I strode on as far as the foyer before I turned. "I'll be back in a few hours with enough money to get you to Mexico."

"I'm staying. Try and put me out. Go on, raise a fuss. Let all the neighbors hear it and call the cops. See if I care."

I felt a little sick to my stomach, looking at her standing there with her eyes blazing and her mouth twisted and shrieking at me like a fishwife.

"You'll go," I said. "I don't know how I'll make you, but I'll make you."

"Like hell you will!"

I stepped into the foyer and paused again. Florence hadn't phoned since yesterday morning, though it was almost two days since Gertrude had started to have labor pains. There should be news any minute.

"I expect a phone call," I told Cherry through the doorway. "Be sure not to answer."

"Yeah! You don't want your fine friends to know you got a woman here."

"For your own protection," I said quietly, and left.

The rest of the morning and a good part of the afternoon I spent calling on friends and stripping them of cash in exchange for my personal checks. It took that long because everybody had plenty of time on Sunday and in each house or apartment I had to linger to shoot the breeze. At Bob Stern's I got a steak dinner as well as an even hundred dollars. They were about to sit down at the table, and when Emily Stern heard that Florence was away she insisted I eat with them. That visit alone killed two hours.

Not that there was any reason for me to hurry back. I couldn't put Cherry out until darkness would give her some protection; meanwhile, I'd just as soon not be there with her. So my last stop was my parents' house, where I intended to visit until evening. By then I had accumulated around six hundred dollars.

Pa was polishing his car in the driveway. He counted the money in his wallet and decided he could let me have fifty. Handing it to me, he said, "Are you on the way to the station to pick up Florence?"

"Don't you ever know what's going on in the family, Pa? She'll be away till the end of next week."

"Then I've news for you. She's coming home today."

"What do you mean?"

"She called up here when she couldn't get you at home. Your mother spoke to her."

I found Ma in the dining room, where she was poring over the department store ads in the Sunday paper spread out on the table. I kissed her and asked her what Florence had said.

"All Gertrude had were false labor pains. Early this morning they sent her home from the hospital. I had the same thing with Lanny. It's only the baby settling down in the womb, but it feels exactly like—"

"Ma, what did Florence say about coming home?"

"She tried to get you on the phone to tell you she was starting back. It can be weeks before Gertrude gives birth. She's not due, anyway, before the beginning of next month. I remember with Lanny I—"

"Ma, what time did you speak to her?"

"It was before twelve. Perhaps eleven-thirty. She thought you might be here."

There was no use phoning Cherry to tell her to leave the apartment in a hurry. She wouldn't answer the phone now any more than she had when Florence had called earlier.

I asked, "Did she say what train she was making?"

"She said she was packed and ready to leave and waiting for Ted to drive her to the station."

And now it was ten minutes to four—four hours since she'd spoken to Ma. The train ride took around two hours; add to that a twenty-minute ride to the station at the Philadelphia end and at the New York end a half-hour taxi ride to Brooklyn. That still left me an hour short. I could only hope that she'd taken a long time saying goodbye to Gertrude and the children and that she'd had a long wait for the train.

I said a hurried goodbye to Ma and ran out to my car. I was too late. As I unlocked the door, I heard voices in the apartment. I entered the foyer and the voices stopped.

They were in the living room, both on their feet, facing each other.

Their heads turned to me, and for the worst moment in my life nobody said anything.

I couldn't have been more than a very few minutes behind Florence. She still wore her hat and still held her handbag and her suitcase was beside her on the floor. She looked quite a lot taller than Cherry because she wore dress shoes and Cherry was barefooted. Cherry hadn't yet, this late in the afternoon, changed out of the nightgown and housecoat.

I had never seen Florence so pale.

"Listen," I said, moving toward her.

Florence ran from me. She ran across the room and across the hall and into our bedroom.

Shrugging, Cherry stood twisting the ring on her finger.

10

Not many minutes later Cherry came out of the spare room fully dressed and freshly painted. She stopped at the table on which the bottle of whisky stood; during the hours I'd been away she'd taken it out of the buffet where I'd put it last night after she'd thrown it at me. There didn't seem to be much left.

"One for the road," she said wryly, and put the bottle to her red mouth. Then she uttered a strained laugh. "Well, this makes us even. Brad caught me with you and she caught you with me."

I sat on the sofa, holding a lighted and forgotten cigarette in numb fingers, and I didn't trust myself to speak, even if I'd had anything to say to her. There was no sound from the bedroom, no movement or weeping or anything. I couldn't go to Florence until Cherry was out of the place.

"Do you think she'll yell copper?" Cherry asked, staring at me with those eyes so much older than the rest of her face.

"No."

"She better not, or you'll be in plenty of hot water yourself." Cherry put down the bottle. "Though probably now the bitch doesn't give a damn what happens to you either. That's why I'm not hanging around."

"Then for God's sake, go!"

"Don't rush me. Where's my coat?"

I brought it from the foyer closet and held it for her. After she had it on, I gave her the cash I had accumulated. She didn't ask how much it was, didn't count it. She stuffed it apathetically into her handbag and pulled her coat together and stood there for a moment. I didn't want anything further from her. I turned my back, and behind me her heels clicked on the bare foyer floor and she was gone without any goodbyes.

I went into the bedroom, where Florence was lying face down on the unmade bed. She had kicked her shoes off. I sat down on the bed and put my hand on her hip. She didn't stir.

"It's not what you think," I said. "It's not as bad, and at the same time it's worse."

Her cheek turned on the pillow. Her eyes were dry; it would have been better if she had been weeping.

"I was so anxious to get back home to you," she said hollowly. "I took the first train I could." She shrank from my hand as if only now she'd become aware it was on her. "Don't touch me!"

I got up from the bed and sat down on the hassock half a dozen feet from her.

"I'm going to do a lot of talking," I said. "It's a long story. I've already told you what happened the day after you broke our engagement last summer, how I went to Coney Island and ran across her on the beach and later gave her the ring. That was only the beginning. Though you couldn't know it, you had a lot to do with all that followed."

I told Florence every bit of it.

She remained face down and motionless, without visible reaction, when I told how I'd gone up to the hotel room with Cherry and had consented to go off with her and she had undressed in front of me. But when I reached the part where she had killed the gangster named Shorty with the switchblade knife, she turned on her side, facing me, and horror appeared on her face and stayed there as she listened to me tell how Cherry had been part of a gang that had held up an armored truck and had had the eighty thousand dollars in loot right there and I had saved her and myself by shooting down a man on Surf Avenue.

I drove myself on, not sparing Florence or myself any of it. Once I hesitated, tempted to skip that night last September when Bradford Smith and the detective had broken in on us. But I gave her that, too, all the details about Cherry and me on the divan. She closed her eyes then, and they remained closed for a long time as I talked on and on. I told her the real reason I'd left her to go to New Jersey in the middle of the night last November and what I'd had to do there; and I told her about Cherry's marrying Frank Todder and becoming the blonde bandit, which may or may not have been my fault, as she claimed, but deep down I must have thought so when I went looking for her and brought her here; and I told her everything that had taken place between Cherry and me last night and this morning.

"That's it," I said at last with my voice hoarse and my mouth dry.

Her eyes were again open, looking at me with a fixed, unfathomable gaze I could not meet. I sat slumped on the hassock, waiting in that overbearing silence, and I told myself that whatever happened now, the one good thing was not to be lying to her anymore.

After a while I stood up and thrust my fists into the pockets of my pants. "All right, I'm through covering up for her and myself. I'll give her time to get to Mexico, then I'll go to the police."

"You'll do no such thing!" Florence sat up on the bed, and she looked and sounded angry. "You've made enough atonement. You've punished yourself enough. I won't let you punish me too."

"You?" I said softly.

"I'm your wife," she said angrily. "I married you because I love you." Suddenly she smiled tremulously. "I think it's easier for me to forgive you than for you to forgive yourself."

I dropped down on the bed, but I didn't touch her. I was afraid to. "You understand," I murmured.

"Isn't it a wife's place to understand?" She sat on her legs, looking at me with solemn dark eyes. "You know something, darling? Part of your story made me sick at heart, but most of it made me proud of you. Oh, my poor darling!"

And now she started to weep and I took her in my arms.

A little later, as we lay stretched out together on the bed, holding each other, just holding each other, Florence said, "She must love you very much."

"Her kind of love!" I snorted.

"It's the same as any other woman's love. In many ways she got to know you better than I do."

"Forget about her."

"Do you think I ever can?"

"I love you. I never gave a damn for her."

"That's not what I meant," she said.

I knew what she meant. But we didn't talk about it anymore. We lay on the bed until long after night had come into the room.

Part Five: The Wife

1

That summer we did the same as everybody in the city who was able to—we got out.

We rented a little place in the Catskill Mountains, a green-shingled bungalow in a colony of thirty or so strung on the side of a hill overlooking a crisp, clear lake. It was well over three hours from Brooklyn, much too far for me to come out every night. Instead of my regular two-week vacation, I took long weekends, driving out Thursday evenings and starting back at dawn Monday mornings. That left only three nights a week Florence had to spend alone.

At around eight o'clock one Thursday evening in July my car climbed the narrow oiled road to the bungalow colony. Below on my right the lake lay wet and inviting; after a scorching day in the city and a long, clammy ride, I was anxious to get out of my clothes and into the water. I topped a rise and heard my name shouted and stepped on the brake.

Florence came running from the Hickerson bungalow, which was on the way to ours. Her richly sun-tanned skin made a delightful contrast with her brief white shorts and white mannish shirt rolled up to just under her breasts. Four days had been a long time, and my hands were very anxious for her.

"I've been watching for you," she said when she reached the car. "Both Mrs. Hickerson's children have a fever and she's not well herself and I've been giving her a hand."

By then she was inside the car. But we were out in the open and after an avid kiss I had to let go of her. As we drove on, she sat close, hugging my arm, and asked me if I'd had dinner.

"I stopped off for a bite on the way," I said.

"That's good, because I ate with Mrs. Hickerson. Let's take a swim together before it gets dark."

"You bet."

Our bungalow sat against the hill. It was compact but adequate. Most of it consisted of an airy living room, to which a kitchen was connected by a wide, doorless opening. The only bedroom was a cubbyhole, all we needed. We seldom had overnight company, and when we did they had to make do on the day bed in the living room.

I pulled up in the dirt driveway. With arms about each other, we crossed the small lawn and went up the three steps to the open porch and through the screen door into the living room.

"Hi," Cherry said.

She sat in the armchair. The top two buttons of her gauzy blouse were open and her cotton skirt was high above her crossed knees and her shoes were off. A glass was in her hand. She seemed quite at home.

Florence dropped her arm from my waist and I dropped my arm from hers. We were silent; she had no more to say than I had. I was crushed by a sense of having been dropped into the midst of a recurring nightmare that was destined to haunt me all the days of my life. There was no escape.

"My God, you two look like you walked in on a funeral," Cherry said, smiling redly. "I got here around an hour ago. Had to walk all the way from the highway. A kid told me this was your place."

Florence spoke stiffly, asking the question I had so often asked Cherry in the past. "What do you want?"

"Me, I'm just dropping in on old friends," Cherry said amiably. And she drank.

A fifth of Canadian rye stood at her elbow on the end table. She had found it in the kitchen cabinet and helped herself.

Florence said, "You're not getting any more money. I won't let Ray give it to you."

"You won't let him! Say, listen, if you knew half of what—"

Florence cut her short. "I know everything." Her voice was controlled; her rage was all in her dark, snapping eyes. "I'll make you let him alone."

"Yeah?" Cherry rolled the glass against her little chin. "Don't you mind if your husband goes to jail? He will, all right."

Beside me Florence flinched. She glanced sidelong at me, and it was past time for me to say my piece in this recital.

I said, "There's the phone on the table, Cherry. Go ahead and call the police."

"You're bluffing."

"I don't think so," I said. "But I know you are. I've a chance with the police. You have none. I'm driving you down to the railroad station right now. If you don't like it, there's the phone. All you have to do is tell the operator you want the police."

Cherry didn't even look at me. She remained sunk low in the chair, and her eyes were a beaten, exhausted old woman's eyes in a child's painted face.

And she no longer had the diamond ring. It wasn't on any of the fingers of her right hand, curled around the glass, and it wasn't on her left hand, dangling down along the chair.

To both of us the ring had become a kind of mystic link holding us to each other since I had given it to her almost exactly a year ago, in a Coney Island beer joint. It was gone now, the chain was broken, but here she was back. Nothing was changed, nothing settled, nothing ended.

"Who wants your filthy money?" Cherry was saying petulantly. "I'm sick. I've nowhere to go. I need a nice cool place in the mountains to stay for a few days until I feel better."

"What trouble are you in this time?" I said.

"The old heat is still on me. The blonde-bandit thing. I can hardly go anywhere. And I'm sick, I tell you." She reached for the bottle.

Florence strode to her and snatched the bottle from her hand. "If you're sick, this is what's making you sick. Do your drinking somewhere else," She carried the bottle into the kitchen.

Cherry looked after her. "The bitch!" she muttered, and dipped her head limply.

I could see where her black hair was turning back to its original mouse brown at the roots. Her face was crumpled, boneless; she looked at the end of her rope. But I could no longer pity her. She had pressed my compassion too hard, and I had to fight myself from grabbing her and throwing her out bodily.

I said, "I'll drive you down to the village. There's a train leaves for New York in twenty minutes."

"I can't go to New York. The cops are looking for me there."

"I don't give a damn where you go," I said.

Florence had come back from the kitchen. Cherry looked at her and at me and her child's face puckered. She was well on the way to being drunk. She'd had as much as an hour with that bottle, and if I knew her, that wasn't the first she'd had to drink today.

"You can't chase me out in the middle of the night," she whined. "At least let me get some sleep. I'm so tired. I feel so rotten. A night's sleep and I'll be all right in the morning. You wouldn't put a dog out like this at night with nowhere to go. Let me stay just tonight? Huh? Please!"

Always before she had had an inner indomitable strength and a certain amount of dignity. Now she was merely pathetic.

From the kitchen doorway Florence said crisply, "Very well, you may have our bedroom tonight. But you'll take the first train in the morning."

I sighed. I didn't like it at all, but Florence was right. We couldn't be completely heartless.

2

We didn't take that swim after all. Cherry had spoiled it for us, along with everything else that evening.

Florence drifted out of the bungalow and started to putter in the flower bed—an excuse, I thought, not to be there with Cherry. I went into the bedroom and took off my city clothes and put on shorts and a T-shirt. When I passed through the living room, Cherry hadn't stirred from the armchair. Her eyes followed me, but she didn't say anything. Outside Florence was down on her hands and knees with a trowel; she didn't say anything to me either. I got the lawn mower from under the bungalow and pushed it back and forth.

The insects became pretty bad as night approached, but we stayed outside because Cherry was inside.

After a while Florence rose and brushed off her knees and dusted her hands. "I promised Mrs. Hickerson I'd stop in again to see how her children are."

I nodded and slapped at a mosquito on my bare leg and resumed pushing the mower.

Florence was hardly gone when Cherry came out. She was eating a sandwich.

"Will your wife raise a fuss if she catches me taking something to eat?" she said sarcastically.

"Isn't there any pleasing you? She's letting you spend the night."

"Yeah, I ought to get down on my knees and kiss her hand."

I walked on behind the mower. She sat down on the porch steps.

"It's a wonder she left you alone with me," she said after a minute. "You know, Ray, I had half an idea you two had split up."

I stopped and leaned on the mower. "Is that why you came—to help split us up if you could?"

"Well, she didn't seem too happy when she walked in on me in your apartment." Cherry bit into the sandwich and chewed. "Did you really tell her the whole story?"

"Yes."

"I mean everything—about the eighty grand and the killings and all?"

"Yes."

"That wasn't smart of you, Ray."

"It was smart for me."

"Why—just because she kissed and made up? She's jealous of me, Ray. I'd never trust a jealous woman with anything that can make trouble."

I didn't argue. There was no use trying to make her understand a woman like Florence. I said, "I read in the paper where Frank got ten years."

"Yeah," she said. "A rotten shame. He was a sweet boy."

"Isn't it dangerous for you to be so close to New York?"

"This is the closest I've been."

"Didn't you like it in Mexico?"

"I never got there."

"Let me guess," I said. "You met a guy on the way."

She shrugged. "Matter of fact, after I left your place I ran into somebody who was driving down to Florida. I went with him and after a while he went back to New York and I've been moving around here and there. A couple of days ago I was in Baltimore. I was in a gin mill and pretty high, I guess, and suddenly I got an idea and phoned you. There was no answer and I phoned your mother."

"No doubt to find out if Florence and I had split up."

She brought up her red smile. "Why not? It was a thought. I didn't tell your old lady who I was, of course. Just a friend of Florence's, I said. She gave me this address where you two lovebirds were spending the summer."

"You must have stayed drunk if you thought you'd be welcome here."

"Listen, Ray, I couldn't—I can't . . ." Her voice faded. She huddled on the porch steps, slowly chewing the last mouthful of sandwich.

The lawn was pretty well cut by now, but I kept pushing the mower to keep myself in movement. And twilight deepened and she turned into a shadow on the porch step, and presently she spoke again, saying in a tired murmur, "I haven't got your ring."

"So I noticed. What did you sell it for—whisky?"

"It's all right for you to talk. You're not running from anybody. You're not alone and afraid all the time. You can sleep nights." She paused. "Yeah, one day I met a man gave me four hundred bucks for it. It was worth a lot more, wasn't it?"

"I paid twelve hundred."

"Well, you never get anywhere near what you pay for diamonds. And I didn't give a damn. I needed dough and what the hell did I want a ring for? Four hundred bucks is four hundred bucks."

And whisky is whisky, I thought, when you're running and alone and can't sleep nights.

She stood up. "Ray, speaking of drinks, how about letting me have one?"

"I don't know where Florence put the bottle."

"She hid it. My God, she begrudges me even a drink. Haven't you another bottle?"

"It's bad enough having you on our hands tonight without having you roaring drunk in the bargain."

"I'm trying to stop. But you can't all at once. I'm trying to taper off." She leaned against the porch post, and her voice was suddenly so weary that she seemed hardly able to push it past her throat. "I know I've got to stop. I don't want to become like my old man."

Become? She already was. But I didn't tell her that. I kept on mowing the lawn that no longer needed any mowing at all.

"But just one more tonight," she wheedled. "So I can sleep. I won't be able to sleep without it."

"No."

"You're scared of your wife, that's why. You're scared stiff to do anything for me because of her. Not even let me stay a few days. All you did to me, and when I ask for one little favor—"

"Oh, shut up!" I said. "Go to bed and let me alone!"

She said, "You—" and stared past me and without another word went inside.

I turned around. Florence was coming back from the Hickerson bungalow.

When, a few minutes later, we went in, Cherry was in the bedroom. She had left the door open, and as I passed on the way to the bathroom I had a glimpse of her lying face down on the bed in all her clothes. Softly I closed the door, not only so we wouldn't disturb her, but also to shut her away from us.

For the next couple of hours Florence and I played Scrabble on the kitchen table. A great orange moon appeared at the rim of the lake below. I watched the shimmering track it made on the water more than I watched the game.

Once Cherry cried out. We both became very still at the table, listening. The cry wasn't repeated.

"She must be having a bad dream," Florence said.

"Who's more entitled to bad dreams?"

Florence picked up two letters from her rack, and as she changed the word "rack" to "racket" she said, "All the same, I pity her."

"You needn't. She hates you."

"I expect she does. Do you know why she came here?"

"You heard her reasons, for what they're worth."

"She didn't give the real one. I think she simply can't stay away from you." Florence caught her lower lip between her teeth. "Darling, I'm afraid of her."

"You just said you pitied her."

"I pity her and I despise her and I'm afraid of her."

"What do you mean, afraid? You haven't got a crazy notion I care anything for her?"

"No. If you ever did, you can't anymore."

"Then what?"

"I don't know," she said, and we both studied the board.

The game dragged on. We were both glad when it ended and it was eleven o'clock and not too early for bed. I opened the day bed in the living room while she slipped into the bedroom and brought out my pajamas and her robe and nightgown.

Florence fell asleep the way she usually did, within the circle of my right arm, her cheek on my chest and her right leg flung across my thighs. She was beautiful in the moonlight flowing in through the windows and the screen door. I kissed her brow and closed my eyes. But I couldn't sleep.

There was a stirring. Cherry, I thought drowsily, moving to or from the bathroom. Suddenly I roused all the way, listening to something scrape and something squeak. I raised my head.

From where I lay I could see through the wide opening into the kitchen, and moonlight fully revealed Cherry, still with all her clothes on, standing on a chair. She was searching the top shelf of the wall cabinet where we kept the dishes.

I had no doubt what she was after. I watched her climb down from the chair and look about. She approached the sink, stood for a long moment as if trying to remember where she had looked earlier, then stooped and tore open the twin doors of the cabinet under the sink. She uttered a half-stifled cry of triumph and came up with the whisky. It must have been behind the boxes of soap powder and stuff.

I dropped my head back on the pillow.

Let her, I told myself. I didn't intend to get out of bed and try to take it away from her. I had no stomach for her cursing and wheedling. Let her take it to bed with her for the only comfort she had left.

But now that she had it, she didn't hurry back to the bedroom with it. Past Florence's cheek I saw Cherry stand stock-still in the middle of the kitchen, holding the bottle cradled to her breast like a cherished infant, and she was staring at us lying together in bed. Her black hair straggled wildly over her cheeks, and maybe her eyes were wild, too, though I couldn't see them clearly. But I could feel the malice of her gaze.

Instinctively my arm tightened about my wife.

After a second or a minute, Cherry flitted on stocking feet out of the kitchen and across the corner of the living room and into the bedroom.

My arm was being cramped by Florence's weight. I slipped it out from under her and she turned on her side, reaching for me in sleep.

I dozed in restless snatches, and after a long time a voice startled me. It was a curiously incoherent mumbling voice, and for a moment I thought Florence was talking in her sleep. But she lay curled quietly at my side, and past her I saw that Cherry had again come out of the bedroom.

She stood at the table only a few feet from the day bed. Since the last time I had seen her, which could have been several hours ago, she had undressed, taking off every stitch, and that was the way she had come into the living room.

I raised myself on my elbow. She was digging into a large straw handbag on the table. It wasn't Florence's, so it had to be hers. She turned the handbag upside down, frantically shaking out its contents, and her mumbling turned into distinct sobbing words.

"Where is it? What happened to it?"

Abruptly Florence sat up. Startled and dazed, she swung her head from side to side before she saw Cherry. "Better get something on her," I told her quietly. "She seems to be drunk."

Florence leaped out of bed and snatched up her robe from the armchair. "Here, put this on."

Cherry looked at her, holding the robe spread open for her, then she looked at me in the bed, then she looked down at her nakedness.

"I . . ." she said hoarsely, and her voice cracked. "I want my . . . my . . ." With a sweep of her arm she brushed aside the robe. "My ring!" she shrieked. "You stole my ring!"

Florence glanced at me. "I noticed she wasn't wearing it."

"Give me my ring," Cherry sobbed, swaying. "It's mine, not yours. Ray gave it to me fair and square."

I said, "Don't you remember, Cherry? You sold it."

"Make her give me my ring back!"

"You sold it to a man for four hundred dollars, Cherry."

"Did I?" Cherry ran her hands over her crumpled face. "I—I forgot. Yeah, the guy, he had the cash in his pocket and I took the ring off my finger. I didn't know what I was doing. I didn't mean to . . ." She started to sniffle noisily.

Florence draped the robe on Cherry's shoulders. Cherry let it stay, and she let Florence lead her by the arm. The robe slipped off before she had taken two steps. Florence paused as if to pick it up from the floor and realized there was no point to it. They moved on toward the bedroom, the two black-haired women, Florence in her pale-green nightgown and Cherry in nothing at all. I sank back on the pillow.

I heard them speak low and indistinctly in the bedroom. Then Florence's voice rose in anger. "I see it was a mistake letting you spend even the night."

"Go to hell," Cherry said thickly.

Florence came out with the bottle of whisky. She carried it into the kitchen. There wasn't much left, but what there was she spilled into the sink.

As she was getting back into bed, she said in a small, musing tone, "The ring, it must have meant very much to her." Then she pulled up the cover and put her head on my chest.

3

I watched dawn seep into the bungalow. At my side Florence slept soundly. I envied her; for a good part of the night I'd been awake in fits and starts. I pushed my face into the pillow, but it was no good, and after a while I got out of bed. I put on my shorts and shoes and went outside.

Mist lay over the lake like a white cloud. I walked down the footpath to the community dock and sat on a wooden bench. The sun rose and burned away the mist and the water sparkled cool and tempting. My shorts would do for bathing trunks. I took off my shoes and dived in.

The lake was well over half a mile wide. I swam across to the other side and without pausing to rest I swam back. When I climbed out of the water, my skin tingled and the cobwebs were out of my head. I stretched out on the dock in the pleasant warmth of the sun, and before I knew it the sleep I hadn't been able to get during the night overwhelmed me.

I awoke with a start, my heart pounding. I hadn't my watch, so I didn't know how long I'd slept, but the sun was a lot higher. At least a couple of hours higher.

And all that time I'd left Florence alone with Cherry, who hated her—Cherry, whom I'd seen stab one man to death and shoot the head off another man, and who had once in drunken rage tried to kill me with a carving knife.

I ran up the hill to the bungalow.

On the way to the porch steps I passed close to one of the two bedroom windows, and through it I heard Cherry call, "Florence, can I see you?"

I looked through the window. Cherry was standing with her back against the chest of drawers. She had on her skirt and blouse; her hair was brushed and her face was sleekly made up. She looked all set to be driven to the station.

"What is it?" Florence said in another part of the bungalow.

"Will you come here for a minute?"

I started to go on and hesitated and turned back for another look at Cherry.

Something was not right about the way she stood there, so curiously immobile with her hands behind her back. She seemed to be holding her breath as she watched the door, and her profile was as static as painted wax. Somehow she made my spine prickle.

Florence entered the bedroom wearing a housecoat.

"I see you're ready," she said. "I imagine Ray went down for a swim. We'll have breakfast as soon as he comes back and then he'll drive you to the station."

"Breakfast," Cherry said tonelessly, and no part of her stirred. "Like you throw a bone to a dog."

"I've nothing to discuss with you," Florence told her coldly. "Why did you call me in here?"

"Because—" Cherry said, and stopped talking as if she had completed a thought. She moved sideways toward the door, sidling past Florence, who watched her, keeping her hands behind her back, then turned and stood again like something carved.

Even her lips remained almost lifeless when she spoke. Her voice pushed out flat and toneless, saying, "You took everything that meant anything to me. I would've had Ray, the only guy I ever gave a damn for, if it hadn't been for you. Yeah, and I would've had eighty grand. I know he gave the money up because of you. Oh, you bitch, in bed with him every night while I—"

A sob shook her, and her right hand came out from behind her back, and in it was the hatchet that I used to chop kindling for the outdoor grill.

I was away from that window before Florence cried out.

I dashed up the steps and across the porch, racing toward those scalp-lifting whimpers that were all Florence's constricted throat could manage after one shrill scream. And then the open bedroom door was before me and I saw that in those very few seconds since I'd left the window Florence had backed against the wall and was cowering there, trapped, her arms raised in front of her face in a desperate and futile gesture to protect herself, while Cherry, her back to me, advanced as slowly and stiffly as an automaton with the hatchet raised high.

"Ray!"

Facing the doorway, Florence saw me before I was quite inside the room, before I could reach Cherry and grab her arm. She cried my name in a tone of deliverance, and Cherry whirled around to me.

I checked myself. I watched the hatchet waver above her head, and I was poised to throw myself back through the door out of the way if she struck.

She didn't strike. Her face fell apart. Her eyes dulled. I said, "Put it down, Cherry."

Her arm went limp, sinking to her side. The hatchet dropped from lax fingers. It thudded to the floor.

I kicked the hatchet under the bed and brushed by her. Florence and I reached for each other at the same time. She clung to me as if she would never let go.

"It's all right now, sweetheart," I said, stroking her head. "She's not going to do any more harm to us."

Behind me Cherry whispered thinly, "Ray . . ."

I turned my head to her. "Get out! If you ever show up again, I'll turn you over to the police. By God, I will!"

With empty eyes and empty face she looked at me holding my wife. Then she shuffled out.

4

Some fifteen minutes later Florence tried to get into the bathroom and couldn't. I was in the living room, picking up my pack of cigarettes from the table, when I heard her call, "Cherry, are you in there?"

She rattled the door.

"What's the matter?" I asked, joining her.

She frowned. "The door seems to be locked from the inside. Did you see Cherry leave?"

"All I remember is she went out of the bedroom. I took it for granted she kept going."

"Then she must be in there. Why doesn't she answer?" We looked at each other, and Florence's face turned gray under her sun tan.

I said, "Stand back," and drove my shoulder against the door.

The lock was a simple hook and eye; the eye tore out and the door flew open. Cherry lay fully clothed in the bathtub.

Blood flowing from her right arm soaked her skirt, and blood formed a red pool on the tile floor from her left arm, dangling over the side. I bent over her.

Florence pressed against the doorjamb, uttering quivering sounds in her throat and then finding her voice and saying, "Is she dead?"

I nodded. "She cut open both her wrists with one of my razor blades. It must have been like falling asleep."

Florence moved back out of the bathroom and I followed her and put my hand on the doorknob. I paused to look back.

Cherry might have been asleep if you looked only at her face. It was relaxed now and quiet, like the face of a child who had found peace.

I closed the door.

THE END